Other Covenants
Alternate Histories of the Jewish People

Edited by Andrea D. Lobel
and Mark Shainblum

Ben Yehuda Press
Teaneck, New Jersey

Owing to limitations of space, permission acknowledgments can be found on page 351, which constitutes an extension of this copyright page.

Published by Ben Yehuda Press
122 Ayers Court #1B
Teaneck, NJ 07666

http://www.BenYehudaPress.com

To subscribe to our monthly book club and support independent Jewish publishing, visit https://www.patreon.com/BenYehudaPress

ISBN13 978-1-953829-40-5 pb, 978-1-953829-80-1 hc, 978-1-953829-81-8 ebook

Cover design by Isaac Brynjegard-Bialik

22 23 24 / 10 9 8 7 6 5 4 3 2 1   20221206

For Maya, light of our lives, who loves alternate histories.

Contents

Acknowledgements

This anthology has been a labor of love spanning more than fifteen years. We're delighted that it has finally come to life in this way, with the right publisher, at the right time.

Our thanks to the late David G. Hartwell, a real *mensch* and a gentleman, to whom we originally pitched *Other Covenants* a few years prior to his tragic death. He loved the idea, and encouraged us to develop it further and get back in touch with him. May his memory be for a blessing always. We'd like to think that he'd be delighted to know that the anthology has finally come to fruition.

Sincere gratitude to Claude Lalumière, Seymour Mayne, Lavie Tidhar, and Allan Weiss for their invaluable editorial help and in our quest to find a publisher. And thanks as well to all our friends and colleagues in the science fiction community who helped spread the word about the project.

Our child, Maya, is a teenager now, and has grown up hearing us talk about this project since she was very young. She has attended science fiction conventions with us over the years, and has met many interesting, creative people. But mostly, she watched and waited as we worked on *Other Covenants*, read through the submissions, experienced upheaval beyond our control with our previous publisher, and witnessed us as we did our best to keep the project alive through the pandemic while searching for a new publisher. Thank you, sweetie, for being the patient, kind, and compassionate person you are!

Mark would like to thank Andrea for co-conceiving this project and steering it through the good times, the bad times, and the weird times. This has been a true collaboration. In turn, Andrea thanks Mark for his support throughout, for conversations—spanning twenty years so far—about science fiction and the SFF world, and for his optimistic, uncanny intuition that *Other Covenants* would work out. Somehow.

It says a great deal about commitment to a project when all thirty contributors stick with it even during a lengthy period of transition. Heartfelt thanks to every one of you!

Deep gratitude to Bogi Takács for suggesting the editorial *shidduch* with Larry Yudelson, who had been considering a project like this one, and who immediately offered to publish *Other Covenants* when he heard that it was available. We can't imagine a more fitting publisher for this project than Ben Yehuda Press. From the bottom of these shmaltzy editors' hearts—*todah rabbah*!

And of course, our acknowledgements would not be complete without thanking the 392 Kickstarter backers of the crowdfunding campaign that helped this book see the light of day.

Mazal tov to all of us!

Foreword

Historian Thomas Cahill, author of *The Gifts of the Jews* (Knopf, 1999) suggested that it was the Jewish people who invented the very concept of history as we know it. That we were the first civilization to perceive time not as an endless circle of life, death and rebirth, but as the flight of an arrow, on a linear path *to* somewhere *from* somewhere.

In more recent years, Cahill's characterization has been dismissed by some academics as a gross oversimplification, and that may be so, but I think it's still useful as a metaphor.

Because a single arrow implies a quiver of arrows, a *volley* of arrows, doesn't it? What if there are other timelines, other histories, other Jews? Would they still have a covenant with the one God?

I have explored these types of ideas before, most notably in *Arrowdreams: An Anthology of Alternate Canadas* (Nuage, 1998), which I co-edited with my friend John Dupuis. *Arrowdreams* was the first anthology of Canadian alternate history fiction, and I see it almost as a bookend of this collection, the first anthology of Jewish alternate history.* Both sides of my identity, Canadian and Jewish.

I suppose it's natural that I would be attracted to alternate histories, to the roads not travelled. Without being maudlin about it, I am the child of a Holocaust survivor, my mother, Eva Shainblum. She and her family were deported from Transylvania to Auschwitz on the second day of Shavuot in 1944. There she lost her parents, Bela and Esther, and her brothers Paul and David. She and her sister, Ella, somehow survived for almost a year in the worst place on Earth, and upon liberation in 1945 were forced to *walk* home from Poland to Romania. Almost immediately upon arrival, Ella became ill and died, leaving my mother alone in the world.

With this as my family history, is it any wonder that I crave escape *sideways* to other worlds? To other timelines? To the hope that, in the seething, quantum foam of the multiverse, somewhere, somewhen, Bela and Esther, Paul and David and Ella lived. And were happy.

But it can't all be about the Holocaust, and suffering and misery. I reject the idea that Jewish history can be entirely summed up by "They tried to kill us, they failed, let's eat!" And how better to explore that notion than by exploring other worlds, other times and the other Jews that inhabit them?

As Andrea describes in greater detail in her Afterword, this book originated with a conversation in a car on a driveway. A conversation about the Jewish people, about historical trajectories, about things both good and bad, the horrible and the sublime.

This book is an exploration of paths we might have taken, a warning about paths we shouldn't take, and a celebration of the here and now, which may not be quite so bad after all, given the alternatives.

This book is a love letter to our people, the Jewish people. In all the universes we may find ourselves in.

Mark Shainblum
Ottawa, Ontario, Canada
September, 2022

*A shoutout here to Gavriel Rosenfeld's *The What Ifs of Jewish History* (Cambridge, 2016), a truly great collection of academic counterfactuals; similar to alternate history, but with a non-fiction approach.

OTHER COVENANTS

To the Promised Land

Robert Silverberg

They came for me at high noon, the hour of Apollo, when only a crazy man would want to go out into the desert. I was hard at work and in no mood to be kidnapped. But to get them to listen to reason was like trying to get the River Nilus to flow south. They weren't reasonable men. Their eyes had a wild metallic sheen and they held their jaws and mouths clamped in that special constipated way that fanatics like to affect. As they swaggered about in my little cluttered study, poking at the tottering stacks of books and pawing through the manuscript of my nearly finished history of the collapse of the Empire, they were like two immense irresistible forces, as remote and terrifying as gods of old Aegyptus come to life. I felt helpless before them.

The older and taller one called himself Eleazar. To me he was Horus, because of his great hawk nose. He looked like an Aegyptian and he was wearing the white linen robe of an Aegyptian. The other, squat and heavily muscled, with a baboon face worthy of Thoth, told me he was Leonardo di Filippo, which is of course a Roman name, and he had an oily Roman look about him. But I knew he was no more Roman than I am. Nor the other, Aegyptian. Both of them spoke in Hebrew, and with an ease that no outsider could ever attain. These were two Israelites, men of my own obscure tribe. Perhaps di Filippo had been born to a father not of the faith, or perhaps he simply liked to pretend that he was one of the world's masters and not one of God's forgotten people. I will never know.

Eleazar stared at me, at the photograph of me on the jacket of my account of the Wars of the Reunification, and at me again, as though trying to satisfy himself that I really was Nathan ben-Simeon. The picture was fifteen years old. My beard had been black then. He tapped the book and pointed questioningly to me and I nodded. "Good," he said. He told me to pack a suitcase, fast, as though I were going down to Alexandria for a weekend holiday. "Moshe sent us to get you," he said. "Moshe wants you. Moshe needs you. He has important work for you."

"Moshe?"

"The Leader," Eleazar said, in tones that you would ordinarily reserve for Pharaoh, or perhaps the First Consul. "You don't know anything about him yet, but you will. All of Aegyptus will know him soon. The whole world."

"What does your Moshe want with me?"

"You're going to write an account of the Exodus for him," said di Filippo.

"Ancient history isn't my field," I told him.

"We're not talking about ancient history."

"The Exodus was three thousand years ago, and what can you say about it at this late date except that it's a damned shame that it didn't work out?"

Di Filippo looked blank for a moment. Then he said, "We're not talking about that one. The Exodus is now. It's about to happen, the new one, the real one. That other one long ago was a mistake, a false try."

"And this new Moshe of yours wants to do it all over again? Why? Can't he be satisfied with the first fiasco? Do we need another? Where could we possibly go that would be any better than Aegyptus?"

"You'll see. What Moshe is doing will be the biggest news since the burning bush."

"Enough," Eleazar said. "We ought to be hitting the road. Get your things together, Dr. Ben-Simeon."

So they really meant to take me away. I felt fear and disbelief. Was this actually happening? Could I resist them? I would not let it happen. Time for some show of firmness, I thought. The scholar standing on his authority. Surely they wouldn't attempt force. Whatever else they might be, they were Hebrews. They would respect a scholar. Brusque, crisp, fatherly, the *melamed*, the man of learning. I shook my head. "I'm afraid not. It's simply not possible."

Eleazar made a small gesture with one hand. Di Filippo moved ominously close to me and his stocky body seemed to expand in a frightening way. "Come on," he said quietly. "We've got a car waiting right outside. It's a four-hour drive, and Moshe said to get you there before sundown."

My sense of helplessness came sweeping back. "Please. I have work to do, and—"

"Screw your work, professor. Start packing, or we'll take you just as you are."

✡

The street was silent and empty, with that forlorn midday look that makes Menfe seem like an abandoned city when the sun is at its height. I walked between them, a prisoner, trying to remain calm. When I glanced back at the battered old gray façades of the Hebrew Quarter where I had lived all my life, I wondered if I would ever see them again, what would happen to my books, who would preserve my papers. It was like a dream.

A sharp dusty wind was blowing out of the west, reddening the sky so that it seemed that the whole Delta must be aflame, and the noontime heat was enough to kosher a pig. The air smelled of cooking oil, of orange blossoms, of camel dung, of smoke. They had parked on the far side of Amenhotep Plaza just behind the vast ruined statue of Pharaoh, probably in hope of catching the shadows, but at this hour there were no shadows and the car was like an oven. Di Filippo drove, Eleazar sat in back with me. I kept myself completely still, hardly even breathing, as though I could construct a sphere of invulnerability around me by remaining motionless. But when Eleazar offered me a cigarette I snatched it from him with such sudden ferocity that he looked at me in amazement.

We circled the Hippodrome and the Great Basilica where the judges of the Republic hold court, and joined the sparse flow of traffic that was entering the Sacred Way. So our route lay eastward out of the city, across the river and into the desert. I asked no questions. I was frightened, numbed, angry, and—I suppose—to some degree curious. It was a paralyzing combination of emotions. So I sat quietly, praying only that these men and their Leader would be done with me in short order and return me to my home and my studies.

"This filthy city," Eleazar muttered. "This Menfe. How I despise it!"

In fact it had always seemed grand and beautiful to me: a measure of my assimilation, some might say, though inwardly I feel very much the Israelite, not in the least Aegyptian. Even a Hebrew must concede that Menfe is one of the world's great cities. It is the most majestic city this side of Roma, so everyone says, and so I am willing to believe, though I have never been beyond the borders of the province of Aegyptus in my life.

The splendid old temples of the Sacred Way went by on both sides, the Temple of Isis and the Temple of Sarapis and the Temple of Jupiter Ammon and all the rest, fifty or a hundred of them on that great boulevard whose pavements are lined with sphinxes and bulls: Dagon's temple, Mithras's and Cybele's, Baal's, Marduk's, Zoroaster's, a temple for every god and goddess anyone had ever imagined, except, of course, the One True God, whom we few Hebrews prefer to worship in our private way behind the walls of our own Quarter. The gods of all the Earth have washed up here in Menfe like so much Nilus mud. Of course hardly anyone takes them very seriously these days, even the supposed faithful. It would be folly to pretend that this is a religious age. Mithras's shrine still gets some worshipers, and of course that of Jupiter Ammon. People go to those to do business, to see their friends, maybe to ask favors on high. The rest of the temples might as well be museums. No one goes into them except Roman and Nipponese tourists.

Yet here they still stand, many of them thousands of years old. Nothing is ever thrown away in the land of Misr.

"Look at them," Eleazar said scornfully, as we passed the huge half-ruined Sarapion. "I hate the sight of them. The foolishness! The waste! And all of them built with our forefathers' sweat."

In fact there was little truth in that. Perhaps in the time of the first Moshe we did indeed labor to build the Great Pyramids for Pharaoh, as it says in Scripture. But there could never have been enough of us to add up to much of a work force. Even now, after a sojourn along the Nilus that has lasted some four thousand years, there are only about twenty thousand of us. Lost in a sea of ten million Aegyptians, we are, and the Aegyptians themselves are lost in an ocean of Romans and imitation Romans, so we are a minority within a minority, an ethnographic curiosity, a drop in the vast ocean of humanity, an odd and trivial sect, insignificant except to ourselves.

The temple district dropped away behind us and we moved out across the long slim shining arch of the Augustus Caesar Bridge, and into the teeming suburb of Hikuptah on the eastern bank of the river, with its leather and gold bazaars, its myriad coffeehouses, its tangle of medieval alleys. Then Hikuptah dissolved into a wilderness of fig trees and canebrake, and we entered a transitional zone of olive orchards and date palms; and then abruptly we came to the place where the land changes from black to red and nothing grows. At once the awful barrenness and solitude of the place struck me like a tangible force. It was a fearful land, stark and empty, a dead place full of terrible ghosts. The sun was a scourge above us. I thought we would bake; and when the car's engine once or twice began to cough and sputter, I knew from the grim look on Eleazar's face that we would surely perish if we suffered a breakdown. Di Filippo drove in a hunched, intense way, saying nothing, gripping the steering stick with an unbending rigidity that spoke of great uneasiness. Eleazar too was quiet. Neither of them had said much since our departure from Menfe, nor I, but now in that hot harsh land they fell utterly silent, and the three of us neither spoke nor moved, as though the car had become our tomb. We labored onward, slowly, uncertain of engine, with windborne sand whistling all about us out of the west. In the great heat every breath was a struggle. My clothing clung to my skin. The road was fine for a while, broad and straight and well paved, but then it narrowed, and finally it was nothing more than a potholed white ribbon half covered with drifts. They were better at highway maintenance in the days of Imperial Roma. But that was long ago. This is the era of the Consuls, and things go to hell in the hinterlands and no one cares.

"Do you know what route we're taking, doctor?" Eleazar asked, breaking the taut silence at last when we were an hour or so into that bleak and miserable desert.

My throat was dry as strips of leather that have been hanging in the sun a thousand years, and I had trouble getting words out. "I think we're heading east," I said finally.

"East, yes. It happens that we're traveling the same route that the first Moshe took when he tried to lead our people out of bondage. Toward the Bitter Lakes, and the Red Sea. Where Pharaoh's army caught up with us and ten thousand innocent people drowned."

There was crackling fury in his voice, as though that were something that had happened just the other day, as though he had learned of it not from the Book of Aaron but from this morning's newspaper. And he gave me a fiery glance, as if I had had some complicity in our people's long captivity among the Aegyptians and some responsibility for the ghastly failure of that ancient attempt to escape. I flinched before that fierce gaze of his and looked away.

"Do you care, Dr. Ben-Simeon? That they followed us and drove us into the sea? That half our nation, or more, perished in a single day in horrible fear and panic? That young mothers with babies in their arms were crushed beneath the wheels of Pharaoh's chariots?"

"It was all so long ago," I said lamely.

As the words left my lips I knew how foolish they were. It had not been my intent to minimize the debacle of the Exodus. I had meant only that the great disaster to our people was sealed over by thousands of years of healing, that although crushed and dispirited and horribly reduced in numbers we had somehow gone on from that point, we had survived, we had endured, the survivors of the catastrophe had made new lives for themselves along the Nilus under the rule of Pharaoh and under the Greeks who had conquered Pharaoh and the Romans who had conquered the Greeks. We still survived, did we not, here in the long sleepy decadence of the Imperium, the Pax Romana, when even the everlasting Empire had crumbled and the absurd and pathetic Second Republic ruled the world?

But to Eleazar it was as if I had spat upon the scrolls of the Law. *"It was all so long ago,"* he repeated, savagely mocking me.

"And therefore we should forget? Shall we forget the Patriarchs too? Shall we forget the Covenant? Is Aegyptus the land that the Lord meant us to inhabit? Were we chosen by Him to be set above all the peoples of the Earth, or were we meant to be the slaves of Pharaoh forever?"

"I was trying only to say—"

What I had been trying to say didn't interest him. His eyes were shining, his face was flushed, a vein stood out astonishingly on his broad forehead. "We were meant for greatness. The Lord God gave His blessing to Abraham, and said that He would multiply Abraham's seed as the stars of the heaven, and as the sand which is upon the seashore. And the seed of Abraham shall possess the gate of his enemies. And in his seed shall all the nations of the earth be blessed. Have you ever heard those words before, Dr. Ben-Simeon? And do you think they signified anything, or were they only the boasting of noisy little desert chieftains? No, I tell you we were meant for greatness, we were meant to shake the world: and we have been too long in recovering from the catastrophe at the Red Sea. An hour, two hours later and all of history would have been different. We would have crossed into Sinai and the fertile lands beyond; we would have built our kingdom there as the Covenant decreed; we would have made the world listen to the thunder of our God's voice; and today the entire world would look up to us as it has looked to the Romans these past twenty centuries. But it is not too late, even now. A new Moshe is in the land and he will succeed where the first one failed. And we *will* come forth from Aegyptus, Dr. Ben-Simeon, and we *will* have what is rightfully ours. At last, Dr. Ben-Simeon. At long last."

He sat back, sweating, trembling, ashen, seemingly exhausted by his own eloquence. I didn't attempt to reply. Against such force of conviction there is no victory; and what could I possibly have gained, in any case, by contesting his vision of Israel triumphant? Let him have his faith; let him have his new Moshe; let him have his dream of Israel triumphant. I myself had a different vision, less romantic, more cynical. I could easily imagine, yes, the children of Israel escaping from their bondage under Pharaoh long ago and crossing into Sinai, and going on beyond it into sweet and fertile Palaestina. But what then? Global dominion? What was there in our history, in our character, our national temperament, that would lead us on to that? Preaching Jehovah to the Gentiles? Yes, but would they listen, would they understand? No. No. We would always have been a special people, I suspected, a small and stubborn tribe, clinging to our knowledge of the One God amidst the hordes who needed to believe in many. We might have conquered Palaestina, we might have taken Syria too, even spread out a little further around the perimeter of the Great Sea; but still there would have been the Assyrians to contend with, and the Babylonians, and the Persians, and Alexander's Greeks, and the Romans, especially the stolid dull invincible Romans, whose destiny it was to engulf every corner of the planet and carve it into Roman provinces full of Roman highways and Roman bridges and Roman whorehouses. Instead of living in Aegyptus under the modern Pharaoh, who is the puppet of the First Consul who has replaced the Emperor of Roma, we would be living in Palaestina under the rule of some minor procurator or proconsul or prefect, and we would speak some sort of Greek or Latin to our masters instead of Aegyptian, and everything else would be the same. But I said none of this to Eleazar. He and I were different sorts of men. His soul and his vision were greater and grander than mine. Also his strength was superior and his temper was shorter. I might take issue with his theories of history, and he might hit me in his rage; and which of us then would be the wiser?

✡

The sun slipped away behind us and the wind shifted, hurling sand now against our front windows instead of the rear. I saw the dark shadows of mountains to the south and ahead of us, far across the strait that separates Aegyptus from the Sinai wilderness. It was late afternoon, almost evening. Suddenly there was a village ahead of us, springing up out of nowhere in the nothingness.

It was more a camp, really, than a village. I saw a few dozen lopsided tin huts and some buildings that were even more modest, strung together of reed latticework. Carbide lamps glowed here and there. There were three or four dilapidated trucks and a handful of battered old cars scattered haphazardly about. A well had been driven in the center of things and a crazy network of aboveground conduits ran off in all directions. In back of the central area I saw one building much larger than the others, a big tin-roofed shed or lean-to with other trucks parked in front of it.

I had arrived at the secret headquarters of some underground movement, yet no attempt had been made to disguise or defend it. Situating it in this forlorn zone was defense enough: no one in his right mind would come out here without good reason. The patrols of the Pharaonic police did not extend beyond the cities, and the civic officers of the Republic certainly had no cause to go sniffing around in these remote and distasteful parts. We live in a decadent era, but at least it is a placid and trusting one.

Eleazar, jumping out of the car, beckoned to me, and I hobbled after him.

OTHER COVENANTS

After hours without a break in the close quarters of the car I was creaky and wilted. The reek of gasoline fumes had left me nauseated. My clothes were acrid and stiff from my own dried sweat. The evening coolness had not yet descended on the desert and the air was hot and close. To my nostrils it had a strange vacant quality, the myriad stinks of the city being absent. There was something almost frightening about that. It was like the sort of air the Moon might have, if the Moon had air.

"This place is called Beth Israel," Eleazar said. "It is the capital of our nation."

Not only was I among fanatics; I had fallen in with madmen who suffered the delusion of grandeur. Or does one quality go automatically with the other?

A woman wearing man's clothing came trotting up to us. She was young and very tall, with broad shoulders and a great mass of dark thick hair tumbling to her shoulders and eyes as bright as Eleazar's. She had Eleazar's hawk's nose, too, but somehow it made her look all the more striking.

"My sister Miriam," he said. "She'll see that you get settled. In the morning I'll show you around and explain your duties to you."

And he walked away, leaving me with her.

She was formidable. I would have carried my bag, but she insisted, and set out at such a brisk pace toward the perimeter of the settlement that I was hard put to keep up with her. A hut all my own was ready for me, somewhat apart from everything else. It had a cot, a desk and typewriter, a washbasin, and a single dangling lamp. There was a cupboard for my things. Miriam unpacked for me, setting my little stock of fresh clothing on the shelves and putting the few books I had brought with me beside the cot. Then she filled the basin with water and told me to get undressed. I stared at her, astounded. "You can't wear what you've got on now," she said. "While you're having a bath I'll take your things to be washed." She might have waited outside, but no. She stood there, arms folded, looking impatient. I shrugged and gave her my shirt, but she wanted everything else, too. This was new to me, her straightforwardness, her absolute indifference to modesty. There have been few women in my life and none since the death of my wife; how could I strip myself before this one, who was young enough to be my daughter? But she insisted. In the end I gave her every stitch—my nakedness did not seem to matter to her at all—and while she was gone I sponged myself clean and hastily put on fresh clothing, so she would not see me naked again. But she was gone a long time. When she returned, she brought with her a tray, my dinner, a bowl of porridge, some stewed lamb, a little flask of pale red wine. Then I was left alone. Night had fallen now, desert night, awesomely black with the stars burning like beacons. When I had eaten I stepped outside my hut and stood in the darkness. It scarcely seemed real to me, that I had been snatched away like this, that I was in this alien place rather than in my familiar cluttered little flat in the Hebrew Quarter of Menfe. But it was peaceful here. Lights glimmered in the distance. I heard laughter, the pleasant sound of a kithara, someone singing an old Hebrew song in a deep, rich voice. Even in my bewildering captivity I felt a strange tranquility descending on me. I knew that I was in the presence of a true community, albeit one dedicated to some bizarre goal beyond my comprehension. If I had dared, I would have gone out among them and made myself known to them; but I was a stranger, and afraid. For a long while I stood in the darkness, listening, wondering. When the night grew cold I went inside. I lay awake until dawn, or so it seemed, gripped by that icy clarity that will not admit sleep; and yet I must have slept at least a little while, for there were fragments of dreams drifting in my mind in the morning, images of horsemen and chariots, of men with spears, of a great black-bearded angry Moshe holding aloft the tablets of the Law.

✡

A small girl shyly brought me breakfast. Afterwards Eleazar came to me. In the confusion of yesterday I had not taken note of how overwhelming his physical presence was: he had seemed merely big, but now I realized that he was a giant, taller than I by a span or more, and probably sixty minas heavier. His features were ruddy and a vast tangle of dark thick curls spilled down to his shoulders. He had put aside his Aegyptian robes this morning and was dressed Roman style, an open-throated white shirt, a pair of khaki trousers.

"You know," he said, "we don't have any doubt at all that you're the right man for this job. Moshe and I have discussed your books many times. We agree that no one has a firmer grasp of the logic of history, of the inevitability of the processes that flow from the nature of human beings."

To this I offered no response.

"I know how annoyed you must be at being grabbed like this. But you are essential to us; and we knew you'd never have come of your own free will."

"Essential?"

"Great movements need great chroniclers."

"And the nature of your movement—"

"Come," he said.

He led me through the village. But it was a remarkably uninformative walk. His manner was mechanical and aloof, as if he were following a prepro-grammed route, and whenever I asked a direct question he was vague or even evasive. The big tin-roofed building in the center of things was the factory where the work of the Exodus was being carried out, he said, but my request for further explanation went unanswered. He showed me the house of Moshe, a crude shack like all the others. Of Moshe himself, though, I saw nothing. "You will meet him at a later time," Eleazar said. He pointed out another shack that was the synagogue, another that was the library, another that housed the electrical generator. When I asked to visit the library he merely shrugged and kept walking. On the far side of it I saw a second group of crude houses on the lower slope of a fair-sized hill that I had not noticed the night before.

"We have a population of five hundred," Eleazar told me.

More than I had imagined.

"All Hebrews?" I asked.

"What do you think?"

It surprised me that so many of us could have migrated to this desert settlement without my hearing about it. Of course, I have led a secluded scholarly life, but still, five hundred Israelites is one out of every forty of us. That is a major movement of population, for us. And not one of them someone of my acquaintance, or even a friend of a friend? Apparently not. Well, perhaps most of the settlers of Beth Israel had come from the Hebrew community in Alexandria, which has relatively little contact with those of us who live in Menfe. Certainly I recognized no one as I walked through the village.

From time to time Eleazar made veiled references to the Exodus that was soon to come, but there was no real information in anything he said; it was as if the Exodus were merely some bright toy that he enjoyed cupping in his hands, and I was allowed from time to time to see its gleam but not its form. There was no use in questioning him. He simply walked along, looming high above me, telling me only what he wished to tell. There was an unstated grandiosity to the whole mysterious project that puzzled and irritated me. If they wanted to leave Aegyptus, why not simply leave? The borders weren't guarded. We had ceased to be the slaves of Pharaoh two thousand years ago. Eleazar and his friends could settle in Palaestina or Syria or anyplace else they liked, even Gallia, even Hispania, even Nova Roma far across the ocean, where they could try to convert the redskinned men to Israel. The Republic wouldn't care where a few wild-eyed Hebrews chose to go. So why all this pomp and mystery, why such an air of conspiratorial secrecy? Were these people up to something truly extraordinary? Or, I wondered, were they simply crazy?

✡

That afternoon Miriam brought back my clothes, washed and ironed, and offered to introduce me to some of her friends. We went down into the village, which was quiet. Almost everyone is at work, Miriam explained. But there were a few young men and women on the porch of one of the buildings: this is Deborah, she said, and this is Ruth, and Reuben, and Isaac, and Joseph, and Saul. They greeted me with great respect, even reverence, but almost immediately went back to their animated conversation as if they had forgotten I was there. Joseph, who was dark and sleek and slim, treated Miriam with an ease bordering on intimacy, finishing her sentences for her, once or twice touching her lightly on the arm to underscore some point he was making. I found that unexpectedly disturbing. Was he her husband? Her lover? Why did it matter to me? They were both young enough to be my children. Great God, why did it matter?

✡

Unexpectedly and with amazing swiftness my attitude toward my captors began to change. Certainly I had had a troublesome introduction to them—the lofty pomposity of Eleazar, the brutal directness of di Filippo, the ruthless way I had been seized and taken to this place—but as I met others I found them generally charming, graceful, courteous, appealing. Prisoner though I might be, I felt myself quickly being drawn into sympathy with them.

In the first two days I was allowed to discover nothing except that these were busy, determined folk, most of them young and evidently all of them intelligent, working with tremendous zeal on some colossal undertaking that they were convinced would shake the world. They were passionate in the way that I imagined the Hebrews of that first and ill-starred Exodus had been: contemptuous of the sterile and alien society within which they were confined, striving toward freedom and the light, struggling to bring a new world into being. But how? By what means? I was sure that they would tell me more in their own good time; and I knew also that that time had not yet come. They were watching me, testing me, making certain I could be trusted with their secret.

Whatever it was, that immense surprise which they meant to spring upon the Republic, I hoped there was substance to it, and I wished them well with it. I am old and perhaps timid but far from conservative: change is the way of growth, and the Empire, with which I include the Republic that ostensibly has replaced it, is the enemy of change. For twenty centuries Roma has strangled mankind in its benign grip. The civilization that it has constructed is hollow, the life that most of us lead is a meaningless trek that had neither values nor purpose. By its shrewd acceptance and absorption of the alien gods and alien ways of the peoples it had conquered, the Empire had flattened everything into shapelessness. The grand and useless temples of the Sacred Way, where all gods were equal and equally insignificant, were the best symbol of that. By worshipping everyone indiscriminately, the rulers of the Imperium had turned the sacred into a mere instrument of governance. And ultimately their cynicism had come to pervade everything: the relationship between man and the Divine was destroyed, so that we had nothing left to venerate except the status quo itself, the holy stability of the world government. I had felt for years that the time was long overdue for some great revolution, in which all fixed, fast-frozen relationships, with their train of ancient and venerable prejudices and opinions, would be swept away—a time when all that is solid melts into air, all that is holy is profaned, and man is at last compelled to face with sober senses his real conditions of life. Was that what the Exodus somehow would bring? Profoundly did I hope so. For the Empire was defunct and didn't know it. Like some immense dead beast it lay upon the soul of humanity, smothering it beneath itself: a beast so huge that its limbs hadn't yet heard the news of its own death.

OTHER COVENANTS

✡

On the third day di Filippo knocked on my door and said, "The Leader will see you now."

The interior of Moshe's dwelling was not very different from mine: a simple cot, one stark lamp, a basin, a cupboard. But he had shelf upon shelf overflowing with books. Moshe himself was smaller than I expected, a short, compact man who nevertheless radiated tremendous, even invincible, force. I hardly needed to be told that he was Eleazar's older brother. He had Eleazar's wild mop of curly hair and his ferocious eyes and his savage beak of a nose; but because he was so much shorter than Eleazar his power was more tightly compressed, and seemed to be in peril of immediate eruption. He seemed poised, controlled, an austere and frightening figure.

But he greeted me warmly and apologized for the rudeness of my capture. Then he indicated a well-worn row of my books on his shelves. "You understand the Republic better than anyone, Dr. Ben-Simeon," he said. "How corrupt and weak it is behind its façade of universal love and brotherhood. How deleterious its influence has been. How feeble its power. The world is waiting now for something completely new: but what will it be? Is that not the question, Dr. Ben-Simeon? *What will it be?*"

It was a pat, obviously preconceived speech, which no doubt he had carefully constructed for the sake of impressing me and enlisting me in his cause, whatever that cause might be. Yet he did impress me with his passion and his conviction. He spoke for some time, rehearsing themes and arguments that were long familiar to me. He saw the Roman Imperium, as I did, as something dead and beyond revival, though still moving with eerie momentum. Call it an Empire, call it a Republic, it was still a world state, and that was an unsustainable concept in the modern era. The revival of local nationalisms that had been thought extinct for thousands of years was impossible to ignore. Roman tolerance for local customs, religions, languages, and rulers had been a shrewd policy for centuries, but it carried with it the seeds of destruction for the Imperium. Too much of the world now had only the barest knowledge of the two official languages of Latin and Greek, and transacted its business in a hodgepodge of other tongues. In the old Imperial heartland itself Latin had been allowed to break down into regional dialects that were in fact separate languages—Gallian, Hispanian, Lusitanian, and all the rest. Even the Romans at Roma no longer spoke true Latin, Moshe pointed out, but rather the simple, melodic, lazy thing called Roman, which might be suitable for singing opera but lacked the precision that was needed for government. As for the religious diversity that the Romans in their easy way had encouraged, it had led not to the perpetuation of faiths but to the erosion of them. Scarcely anyone except the most primitive peoples and a few unimportant encapsulated minorities like us believed anything at all; nearly everyone gave lip-service instead to the local version of the official Roman pantheon and any other gods that struck their fancy, but a society that tolerates all gods really has no faith in any. And a society without faith is one without a rudder: without even a course.

These things Moshe saw, as I did, not as signs of vitality and diversity but as confirmation of the imminence of the end. This time there would be no Reunification. When the Empire had fallen, conservative forces had been able to erect the Republic in its place, but that was a trick that could be managed only once. Now a period of flames unmatched in history was surely coming as the sundered segments of the old Imperium warred against one another.

"And this Exodus of yours?" I said finally, when I dared to break his flow. "What is that, and what does it have to do with what we've been talking about?"

"The end is near," Moshe said. "We must not allow ourselves to be destroyed in the chaos that will follow the fall of the Republic, for we are the instruments of God's great plan, and it is essential that we survive. Come: let me show you something."

We stepped outside. Immediately an antiquated and unreliable-looking car pulled up, with the dark slender boy Joseph at the stick. Moshe indicated that I should get in, and we set out on a rough track that skirted the village and entered the open desert just behind the hill that cut the settlement in half. For perhaps ten minutes we drove north through a district of low rocky dunes. Then we circled another steep hill and on its farther side, where the land flattened out into a broad plain, I was astonished to see a weird tubular thing of gleaming silvery metal rising on half a dozen frail spidery legs to a height of some thirty cubits in the midst of a hubbub of machinery, wires, and busy workers.

My first thought was that it was an idol of some sort, a Moloch, a Baal, and I had a sudden vision of the people of Beth Israel coating their bodies in pigs' grease and dancing naked around it to the sound of drums and tambourines. But that was foolishness.

"What is it?" I asked. "A sculpture of some sort?"

Moshe looked disgusted. "Is that what you think? It is a vessel, a holy ark."

I stared at him.

"It is the prototype for our starship," Moshe said, and his voice took on an intensity that cut me like a blade. "Into the heavens is where we will go, in ships like these—toward God, toward His brightness—and there we will settle, in the new Eden that awaits us on another world, until it is time for us to return to Earth."

"The new Eden—on another world—" My voice was faint with disbelief. A ship to sail between the stars, as the Roman skyships travel between continents? Was such a thing possible? Hadn't the Romans themselves, those most able of engineers, discussed the question of space travel years ago and concluded that there was no practical way of achieving it and nothing to gain from it even if there was? Space was inhospitable and unattainable: everyone knew that. I shook my head. "What other world? Where?"

Grandly he ignored my question. "Our finest minds have been at work for five years on what you see here. Now the time to test it has come. First a short journey, only to the moon and back—and then deeper into the heavens, to the new world that the Lord has pledged to reveal to me, so that the pioneers may plant the settlement. And after that—ship after ship, one shining ark after another, until every Israelite in the land of Aegyptus has crossed over into the promised land—" His eyes were glowing. "Here is our Exodus at last! What do you think, Dr. Ben-Simeon? What do you think?"

✡

I thought it was madness of the most terrifying kind, and Moshe a lunatic who was leading his people—and mine—into cataclysmic disaster. It was a dream, a wild feverish fantasy. I would have preferred it if he had said they were going to worship this thing with incense and cymbals, than that they were going to ride it into the darkness of space. But Moshe stood before me so hot with blazing fervor that to say anything like that to him was unthinkable. He took me by the arm and led me, virtually dragged me, down the slope into the work area. Close up, the starship seemed huge and yet at the same time painfully flimsy. He slapped its flank and I heard a hollow ring. Thick gray cables ran everywhere, and subordinate machines of a nature that I could not even begin to comprehend. Fierce-eyed young men and women raced to and fro, carrying pieces of equipment and shouting instructions to one another as if striving to outdo one another in their dedication to their tasks. Moshe scrambled up a narrow ladder, gesturing for me to follow him. We entered a kind of cabin at the starship's narrow tip; in that cramped and all but airless room I saw screens, dials, more cables, things beyond my understanding. Below the cabin a spiral staircase led to a chamber where the crew could sleep, and below that, said Moshe, were the rockets that would send the ark of the Exodus into the heavens.

"And will it work?" I managed finally to ask.

"There is no doubt of it," Moshe said. "Our finest minds have produced what you see here."

He introduced me to some of them. The oldest appeared to be about twenty-five. Curiously, none of them had Moshe's radiant look of fanatic zeal; they were calm, even businesslike, imbued with a deep and quiet confidence. Three or four of them took turns explaining the theory of the vessel to me, its means of propulsion, its scheme of guidance, its method of escaping the pull of the Earth's inner force. My head began to ache. But yet I was swept under by the power of their conviction. They spoke of "combustion," of "acceleration," of "neutralizing the planet-force." They talked of "mass" and "thrust" and "freedom velocity." I barely understood a tenth of what they were saying, or a hundredth; but I formed the image of a giant bursting his bonds and leaping triumphantly from the ground to soar joyously into unknown realms. Why not? Why not? All it took was the right fuel and a controlled explosion, they said. Kick the Earth hard enough and you must go upward with equal force. Yes. Why not? Within minutes I began to think that this insane starship might well be able to rise on a burst of flame and fly off into the darkness of the heavens. By the time Moshe ushered me out of the ship, nearly an hour later, I did not question that at all.

Joseph drove me back to the settlement alone. The last I saw of Moshe he was standing at the hatch of his starship, peering impatiently toward the fierce midday sky. My task, I already knew, but which Eleazar told me again later that dazzling and bewildering day, was to write a chronicle of all that had been accomplished thus far in this hidden outpost of Israel and all that would be achieved in the apocalyptic days to come. I protested mildly that they would be better off finding some journalist, preferably with a background in science; but no, they didn't want a journalist, Eleazar said, they wanted someone with a deep understanding of the long currents of history. What they wanted from me, I realized, was a work that was not merely journalism and not merely history, but one that had the profundity and eternal power of Scripture. What they wanted from me was the Book of the Exodus, that is, the Book of the Second Moshe.

✡

They gave me a little office in their library building and opened their archive to me. I was shown Moshe's early visionary essays, his letters to intimate friends, his sketches and manifestos insisting on the need for an Exodus far more ambitious than anything his ancient namesake could have imagined. I saw how he had assembled—secretly and with some uneasiness, for he knew that what he was doing was profoundly subversive and would bring the fullest wrath of the Republic down on him if he should be discovered—his cadre of young revolutionary scientists. I read furious memoranda from Eleazar, taking issue with his older brother's fantastic scheme; and then I saw Eleazar gradually converting himself to the cause in letter after letter until he became more of a zealot than Moshe himself. I studied technical papers until my eyes grew bleary, not only those of Moshe and his associates but some by Romans nearly a century old, and even one by a Teuton, arguing for the historical necessity of space exploration and for its technical feasibility. I learned something more of the theory of the starship's design and functioning.

My guide to all these documents was Miriam. We worked side by side, together in one small room. Her youth, her beauty, the dark glint of her eyes, made me tremble. Often I longed to reach toward her, to touch her arm, her shoulder, her cheek. But I was too timid. I feared that she would react with laughter, with anger, with disdain, even with revulsion. Certainly it was an aging man's fear of rejection that inspired such caution. But also I reminded myself that she was the sister of those two fiery prophets, and that the blood that flowed in her veins must be as hot as theirs. What I feared was being scalded by her touch.

The day Moshe chose for the starship's flight was the 23rd of Tishri, the joyful holiday of Simchat Torah in the year 5730 by our calendar, that is, 2723 of the Roman reckoning. It was a brilliant early autumn day, very dry, the sky cloudless, the sun still in its fullest blaze of heat. For three days preparations had been going on around the clock at the launch site and it had been closed to all but the inner circle of scientists; but now, at dawn, the whole village went out by truck and car and some even on foot to attend the great event.

The cables and support machinery had been cleared away. The starship stood by itself, solitary and somehow vulnerable-looking, in the center of the sandy clearing, a shining upright needle, slender, fragile. The area was roped off; we would watch from a distance, so that the searing flames of the engines would not harm us.

A crew of three men and two women had been selected: Judith, who was one of the rocket scientists, and Leonardo di Filippo, and Miriam's friend Joseph, and a woman named Sarah whom I had never seen before. The fifth, of course, was Moshe. This was his chariot; this was his adventure, his dream; he must surely be the one to ride at the helm as the *Exodus* made its first leap toward the stars.

One by one they emerged from the blockhouse that was the control center for the flight. Moshe was the last. We watched in total silence, not a murmur, barely daring to draw breath. The five of them wore uniforms of white satin, blindingly bright in the morning sun, and curious glass helmets like diver's bowls over their faces. They walked toward the ship, mounted the ladder, turned one by one to look back at us, and went up inside. Moshe hesitated for a moment before entering, as if in prayer, or perhaps simply to savor the fullness of his joy.

Then there was a long wait, interminable, unendurable. It might have been twenty minutes; it might have been an hour. No doubt there was some last-minute checking to do, or perhaps even some technical hitch. Still we maintained our silence. We could have been statues. After a time I saw Eleazar turn worriedly toward Miriam, and they conferred in whispers. Then he trotted across to the blockhouse and went inside. Five minutes went by, ten; then he emerged, smiling, nodding, and returned to Miriam's side. Still nothing happened. We continued to wait.

Suddenly there was a sound like a thundercrack and a noise like the roaring of a thousand great bulls, and black smoke billowed from the ground around the ship, and there were flashes of dazzling red flame. The *Exodus* rose a few feet from the ground. There it hovered as though magically suspended, for what seemed to be forever.

And then it rose, jerkily at first, more smoothly then, and soared on a stunningly swift ascent toward the dazzling blue vault of the sky. I gasped; I grunted as though I had been struck; and I began to cheer. Tears of wonder and excitement flowed freely along my cheeks. All about me people were cheering also, and weeping, and waving their arms, and the rocket, roaring, rose and rose, so high now that we could scarcely see it against the brilliance of the sky.

We were still cheering when a white flare of unbearable light, like a second sun more brilliant than the first, burst into the air high above us and struck us with overmastering force, making us drop to our knees in pain and terror, crying out, covering our faces with our hands.

When I dared look again, finally, that terrible point of ferocious illumination was gone, and in its place was a ghastly streak of black smoke that smeared halfway across the sky, trickling away in a dying trail somewhere to the north. I could not see the rocket. I could not hear the rocket.

"It's gone!" someone cried.

"Moshe! Moshe!"

"It blew up! I saw it!"

"Moshe!"

"Judith—" said a quieter voice behind me.

I was too stunned to cry out. But all around me there was a steadily rising sound of horror and despair, which began as a low choking wail and mounted until it was a shriek of the greatest

intensity coming from hundreds of throats at once. There was fearful panic, universal hysteria. People were running about as if they had gone mad. Some were rolling on the ground, some were beating their hands against the sand. "Moshe!" they were screaming. "Moshe! Moshe! Moshe!"

I turned toward Eleazar. He was white-faced and his eyes seemed wild. Yet even as I looked at him I saw him draw in his breath, raise his hands, step forward to call for attention. Immediately all eyes were on him. He swelled until he appeared to be five cubits high.

"Where's the ship?" someone cried. "Where's Moshe?"

And Eleazar said, in a voice like the trumpet of the Lord, "He was the Son of God, and God has called him home."

Screams. Wails. Hysterical shrieks.

"Dead!" came the cry. "Moshe is dead!"

"He will live forever," Eleazar boomed.

"The Son of God!" came the cry, from three voices, five, a dozen. "The Son of God!"

I was aware of Miriam at my side, warm, pressing close, her arm through mine, her soft breast against my ribs, her lips at my ear. "You must write the book," she whispered, and her voice held a terrible urgency. "*His* book, you must write. So that this day will never be forgotten. So that he will live forever."

"Yes," I heard myself saying. "Yes."

✡

In that moment of frenzy and terror I felt myself sway like a tree of the shore that has been assailed by the flooding of the Nilus; and I was uprooted and swept away. The fireball of the *Exodus* blazed in my soul like a second sun indeed, with a brightness that could never fade. And I knew that I was engulfed, that I was conquered, that I would remain here to write and preach, that I would forge the gospel of the new Moshe in the smithy of my soul and send the word to all the lands. Out of these five today would come rebirth; and to the peoples of the Republic we would bring the message for which they had waited so long in their barrenness and their confusion, and when it came they would throw off the shackles of their masters; and out of the death of the Imperium would come a new order of things. Were there other worlds, and could we dwell upon them? Who could say? But there was a new truth that we could teach, which was the truth of the second Moshe who had given his life so that we might go to the stars, and I would not let that new truth die. I would write, and others of my people would go forth and carry the word that I had written to all the lands, and the lands would be changed.

Perhaps I am wrong that the Republic is doomed. What is more likely true, I suspect, is that this world was meant to be Roma's; so it has been for thousands of years, and evidently it always will be, even unto eternity. Very well. Let them have it. We will not challenge Roma's eternal destiny. We will simply remove ourselves from its grasp. We have a destiny of our own. Some day, who knew how soon, we would build a new ship, and another, and another, and they will carry us from this world of woe. God has sent His Son, and God has called Him home, and one day we will all leave the iron rule of this eternal Roma behind and follow Him on wings of flame, up from the land of bondage into the heavens where He dwells eternally.

Nights at the Crimea

Jessica Reisman

Kabbalah Nine II was playing at the Crimea and Micah had seen it three times so far. But Shay Ballentyne said yes when he asked her out, so he took her to the seven o'clock show. Shay had a way of fingering the tiny gold cross that hung on a slender chain around her neck while giving Micah a sizing-up look with her gray eyes that made his hands sweat and produced a sweet ache in his circumcised Jew-boy heart.

They sat in the balcony, center-front, and it was only them in the alchemical dark. The brass balcony rail glimmered dully in the flicker of the previews, antediluvian stream of story above them moted and radiant. *A Hasid Demon Tale*, *The Legend of Judah Aryeh*, and a Scandinavian film that looked to be all snow and obscure discussion. The Crimea's mural painted arch-and-groin ceiling and the alcoves with winged beings peering from them were sketched out of the dim in the projection stream's brighter currents. The Crimea, originally a pre-war opera house, now screened *Zohar* films and other cult movie phenomena, foreign films, black and white classics, and general art house fare. Micah had written articles on everything from Kurosawa to Marilyn Monroe's performance in John Huston's *The Misfits*, but the *Zohar* movies hit him somewhere beneath, or beyond, any analytical function. They made him long for things he couldn't name.

The drums of *Kabbalah Nine's* opening sequence thrummed through the theater's bones. Micah thought the meeting of the nine heroes in the ruins of a temple one of the most beautiful opening scenes ever filmed. Though he'd seen the movie three times, and Shay Ballentyne was the apotheosis of a wet dream, he forgot her for a moment. Through the rolling of the drums, in the rich, spurling images, he reached for a time that had never really existed, of power and possibility—and passionate kick-ass battles for righteous causes.

And for none of that, for something that slipped from words like wind through fingers.

When the old donkey driver, who was a master of wisdom in disguise, said the incantation, the Ayin—the Nothingness Stone—held in the circle between the nine heroes, Micah mouthed the words with him.

"Nine from one, glasses filled with light, vessels of the *sefirot*. From *Ayin*, as *Ayin* from All: *Hohkmah*—Wisdom; *Binah*—Understanding; *Hesed*—Love; *Gevurah*—Power; *Tiferet*—Compassion; *Netsah*—Eternity; *Hod*—Splendor; *Yesod*—Foundation; *Shekhinah*—Secret of the Possible."

Shay settled lower in her seat, eating her popcorn one piece at a time, eyes on the screen whenever Micah glanced at her. He slid down and leaned his head near hers.

"Wow," she said when Darda, one of the nine, whipped her pike into a deadly whirl, leaping and flipping as she dispatched materialized *dybbukim*, just banished from the bodies of the villagers by Mozel the *lamdan*. When the wandering rabbi told his story to the gathered heroes, illustrating with his beard, Shay laughed, a soft sound that slid like a warm hand over Micah's skin. When Darda knocked the wineshop keeper out with a swift blow from her pike, Shay's fingers touched Micah's arm.

"Why did she do that?" she whispered.

"See how the body of the slain man is bleeding from the mouth?" Micah whispered back. "It's because his murderer came close to him: the wineshop keeper."

"Wow," Shay said, and her hand stayed on his arm.

During the valley of demons scene, Micah excused himself for a bathroom break.

Down from the balcony steps to the small mezzanine, past the deco wall mural; the Crimea's restrooms were oases of sea green tile and white porcelain. Alone in the men's room, Micah thought about Shay, who was a little like a silvery Marilyn Monroe, but with a tough-girl quirk to her lips completely at odds with her sober high forehead and clear, soft features.

As he left the restroom, he heard a sound: a gentle, wordless singing. It wasn't the soundtrack of the movie, which Micah knew intimately. He couldn't tell where it was coming from. Passing through the tattered anteroom, he lost track of it and then it was gone. He pushed through the heavy swinging door and caught a clean, cool scent: rain and wind, lightning-charged.

A woman stood by the mezzanine balustrade, leaning forward to look over the lobby. The dim lights in the mezzanine made her little more than a silhouette.

Micah thought of Shay and started back to join her on the balcony. Then the woman turned. For a moment, less—a compressed flake of experience which didn't partake of time—Micah felt like he was waking up. That was the feeling. Like waking up.

In the dim, what he could see of the woman was dark, wavy hair, an impression of long eyes, a nose and cheekbones like whetted swords. She wore jeans and a white tee-shirt that showed strength in a tall, slender body. She met Micah's gaze. A shimmer of light flashed through her eyes.

Thunder crashed outside, so close it shook the old theater. Lightning broke through the night with a citrine splash against the glass doors at the front end of the Crimea's lobby.

"*Shekhinah*," the woman said.

"The secret of the possible," Micah responded without thought. A shiver nettled along his arms and back.

She nodded. "Do you think heroes and demons ever miss the familiar things—the," she peered into the space between them, searching, "the safe world? The coveted, sweet moments of everyday life?" A wistful, quiet sadness was in her face, in the words. "They might, don't you think?"

Micah watched her, puzzled. But it was a film discussion, more or less.

Known territory that he couldn't resist. "How do you know they lose them?"

She met his gaze and the shiver prickled through him. "They have to be willing to let them go. For that which they seek: the power, the Possible."

Micah took a step back, finding the need to resist after all. "Well," he said, lamely, "I guess they might." He nodded, more a duck of the head really, and escaped to return to the balcony. Back to Shay.

✡

By the time the movie let out, the thunderstorm had passed. The last of a long summer evening lit the sky a drunken purple and orange. Saturated light cast every old building into potential-filled relief. Even the trash in alleys, deeply shadowed and etched in late gold, was full of possibility; everything was potential. Micah took Shay's hand as they walked.

"And I really liked when Ruth used her sash as a weapon," Shay said, "unfurling it through the air like that—it was so unexpected and really so cool, you know?"

"Yeah. The director, Izzy Mermell, he does these really gorgeous visuals. In *Gehenna's Rain*, there's this scene set in the ruins of some underground caverns that were supposedly carved by good *shedim* in the service of Solomon, and there's a sacred spring. A caravan of merchants is camped there, and under a full moon, while they all sleep, two of the movie's heroes, Amnon and Zinah, who don't yet know they're both on the same side, have this battle that's really half a romance, a dance—they fall in love later on." Micah gestured with his free hand. "The whole fight is nearly silent and Zinah uses the trader's bolts of silk and brocade, sending them streaming through the air, while Amnon uses reeds and wild flowers from the spring, and silk tassels—"

"Tassels? Like on pasties?"

Micah felt himself flush from cock to crown. "Um—yeah; or, well, pillows, maybe."

Shay laughed and squeezed his hand. "Micah," she said softly, just saying his name.

Micah couldn't believe his fortune. Holding his hand was the young man's dream-come-true, a sweet, sexy angel of a girl. He really hoped he didn't fuck it up.

A little wind frisked through the street, shushing through the heavy summer foliage on the trees. The wind carried the scent of recent rain. Micah thought briefly of the woman on the mezzanine. *Shekhinah*, she'd said, the secret of the possible, like a challenge. A shiver—not altogether pleasant or unpleasant—chased the flush from his body.

✡

OTHER COVENANTS

"You went out with a girl whose name is Ballentyne?" His aunt Muriel, who had married his father ten years ago when Micah's mother—Muriel's sister—died, a tradition dragged over from the old country, threw up her plump, age-spotted hands and made the noise: a kind of whining, croaking exclamation unlike any sound Micah had ever heard another human make. She sat on a stool by the stove, snapping beans and tossing them into a pot. The warm, sweet smell of a kugel rose from the oven. "This is not a Jewish name."

"I know that."

"Is she pretty?" His father, Elias Saunderstein, sat on a stool and leaned at the kitchen counter, reading the newspaper.

"Yes, and sweet. And fun. She's…" Micah gestured, unwilling to say more.

"So leave him alone," his father said to his wife-in-law—which was how Micah had come to think of his father's sister-in-law turned wife, Micah's own aunt turned mother. "She's a person, Muriel, not a religion." Elias waved one hand in the air and imitated the noise, the whole thing delivered without raising his eyes from the article he was reading.

"These," snap, snap, like little green bones, "*cult* movies. They mock and make a mish-mash of our sacred texts and history. At least you could go with a Jewish girl. A goy." Snap. "Named Ballentyne." The noise was made again.

"They don't mock," Micah said. "And her name is Shay. Anyway, the films draw more on folklore than anything else. Well, and the Kabbalah." His aunt made the sound again. "They're good, Aunt Muriel. There's nothing wrong with them. They're about good and evil and fighting for what you believe." He leaned back against the counter by the refrigerator, arms folded. His aunt wore the blue and red apron she'd worn every day, except Saturday, since she came to live with them. Micah's two older sisters had moved out several years ago, one after another. Except for his sisters' absences, their positions in the kitchen were the ones they had occupied for every discussion and argument he could remember. He couldn't remember where they'd had discussions before his mother died.

"Anyway, I think they make Judaism a little more accessible to some people."

"Accessible?" Muriel shook her head.

"A little accessibility, maybe it would have been a good thing at certain points in our history," his father said. "Though God knows, it's the basis of the *goyim*'s religion, so you'd think, in a sensible world." He shrugged and waved one hand dismissively. "Everything's movies now, Muriel."

She sniffed and said nothing further; she snapped beans fiercely and ignored them.

"So, Micah, you going out with this girl again? Shay, right?"

"We're going to that premiere at the Crimea, and the after-party."

"A premiere no less. They going to have celebrities, red carpets?"

"Depends what you mean by celebrities; some actors from the movie, a couple of directors. Not what the mainstream calls celebrities. But it'll be cool. Definitely no red carpets."

Elias finished his article and folded the paper. "You looked over those things from the graduate programs yet?"

Micah nodded. "Yeah."

His father dipped his head. He wore thick bifocal lenses with dark tortoise shell frames, still had a full head of hair, mixed waves of white and black. His eyebrows bushed over the frames like wet sheepdogs, and he seemed to get a new mole every year. He smiled like an old wolf at Micah, and Micah grinned back.

"So, Muriel, that kugel smells beautiful," he said.

✡

Shay held his arm, her skin silky and warm. She looked amazing, in a lilac-brown dress that embraced her to mid-calf, little gold rhinestones on its straps that were a shade darker than her mint-gold hair. The low sandals she wore brought her almost up to Micah's five foot eight.

The premiere of *Black Sages* was being held as a benefit for the local film society, made possible by Yiches Studios, a small studio that put out relatively successful action and sortilege tales, though years ago they'd put out D-class flicks like *Blood Mohels* and *Dybbuk Woman's Revenge*. Yiches was local, while most of the other studios making *Zohar* films were in New York and Vancouver since the industry had fled Israel's growing militancy. The studio head was Jacob Schacter, who was an old friend of Izzy Mermell, the director of *Black Sages*.

Because Micah wrote reviews and did interviews for *Golem Film Magazine*, the main print 'zine for the *Zohars* industry, he'd gotten passes to the film and the after-party.

Inside, the Crimea's house lights and chandelier showed the theater's ceiling mural and the winged creatures peering from the alcoves. Micah and Shay sat in the middle floor section, just behind the rows reserved for VIPs and their entourages, which were being guarded by a film society volunteer. The VIP rows remained empty until just before the lights went down, when the two stars in attendance sailed in. The older star, Samuel Cohen, had his wife with him; Micah recognized her from photos, a stately older woman with a somewhat overstretched face. The younger, Matt Ziporsky, had four young women with him, all wearing small dresses that showed off muscular thighs. The director, Izzy Mermell, came in with a beautiful young man at his side, in the company of a dark-haired woman and a short, stocky, olive-skinned man with a cherub's face and villain's foxlike beard: Jacob Schacter. The woman, Micah saw just before the lights went down, was the woman from the mezzanine. Long, dark wavy hair down the back of something silvery; sharp elbows, lean muscles.

Micah shuddered slightly and looked for remedy to Shay's delicate, liquid-soft profile in the sudden dusk.

Yet he found his gaze wandering during the film, trying to find one head among many in the flickering dark.

✡

The party was at a club called the Soulcake, a few blocks from the Crimea. The Klezmantras played, nimble, velvety music soaking through the club's Hindi-inspired, space-age decor and smoky air.

Circulating slowly, they made it to the crowded dance floor and got sweaty with the jazz-shot mix of clarinet, saxophone, balalaika bass, and violin. Micah got them two bottles of dark beer at the bar. Then he caught sight of Clara Chen and led Shay through the press of sweaty people flesh.

Clara waved. She had a shy, nebbishy face, a silver nose ring, and short hair rucked up into several spiky dandelions atop her head. She perched cross-legged on a big speaker, near the industrial-sized fan aiding the club's air-conditioning.

She greeted Micah with a light clink of her beer bottle to his. Shay leaned her head back in the breeze from the fan and groaned.

"Clara Chen, I'd like you to meet Shay Ballentyne." He bowed slightly between them. "Shay, this is Clara; she's a projectionist at the Crimea."

"Really? Did you show the movie tonight?"

Clara nodded, smiling shyly. "Did you like it?"

"Yeah! I think I liked *Kabbalah Nine* better, though; this one had such a downer ending."

"I liked that about it, but I'm morbid, I guess." Clara sipped her beer. "The final scene was awesome."

"I liked the scene in the desert—it was really hallucinogenic," Shay said.

"Micah, what'd you think, eh?"

Clara had a way of saying "eh" that made him think of old Italian men out walking their dogs, arguing politics. They'd spent many hours together, watching movies, and then more hours over beer and sushi picking them apart and defending their opinions. "I liked it; especially the editing. Really nice rhythm." He threw back the last few swallows of his beer, still cold. The fan blew through his sweaty clothes. He lowered the empty bottle to find Shay watching him and blushed.

Micah, she mouthed, without sound, put her own bottle to her lips, tipped it up and finished it off in several swallows. Clara's eyes widened slightly; Micah grinned.

"Another?" He took Shay's empty, touching her fingers lightly.

"Yeah, thanks."

He looked at Clara and she shook her head, then gestured over her shoulder. "There's another bar out back, less traffic."

"So," Shay turned to Clara, "how long have you been a projectionist?" She sounded like an interviewer doing a story.

A corridor, half-hidden by a six-panel folding screen with lilac-skinned gopis frolicking across it, led outside, past two bathrooms each with a Krishna and a Rada on its door. A few people loitered by the doors, under dim wall sconces. The Soulcake's back courtyard lay beyond. Warm, furzy air breathed over Micah, fuzzed the edges of strung white lights and colored lanterns. A few people at tables, relatively dry under the trees, braved the muggy night. Micah ordered two more beers from a bored bartender.

Snatches of low conversation at a nearby table reached him.

"If we include the witches of Ashkelon section we're screwed on the budget, Jacob."

"Why didn't you bring this up earlier, Lili? The way we've shot so far, the Ashkelon string is essential to the story."

"You hadn't insisted on Gittle Rachmann earlier. I thought you were going to go with Lise. She's much less of a bitch."

"I know, I know, but Gittle—well, she's Gittle. Even the *goyim* love her."

Micah looked to see the speakers. It was Jacob Schacter, the squat man with the villain-bearded cherub's face. And the dark-haired woman of the mezzanine. Schacter nodded, hands clasped around a glass. The woman's back was to Micah; she leaned over the table on her sharp elbows, arms crossed, hands gripping biceps. She had the kind of very pale olive skin that sometimes looked dusky, sometimes ivory. Lean muscles showed in her arms.

Micah paid for the beers, raised his face to the mist for a moment, and turned to head in.

The woman stood in his path. Her eyes were an unexpected blue. And she was taller than him. Micah glanced down; she wore flat sandals, her feet slender, toenails unpainted and pretty. When he looked back up, she was watching him.

A streak of lightning flashed quite clearly through her eyes. Micah blinked. "Hello again."

"Hello." He actually stuttered on the word.

"Micah Saunderstein, right? You write for *Golem*?"

"Uh—yes." He cleared his throat. "I do."

"We're looking forward to your visit; very pleased *Golem* is doing a story on Yiches." A glint of laughter and of something he couldn't name coursed beneath the surface of her words.

"What? I'm not—there's no story scheduled."

"Oh, really? My mistake, then." A wind skittered through the trees. She tilted her head. Then she said, "If you want to know the secret of the possible, you have to untie the knots that bind your soul."

Micah found he had to look away from her. He drew a deep lungful of rain-and-lightning-scented air. His heart beat light and quick.

When he looked back, she was gone. The air was muggy and warm-smelling. Jacob Schacter sat at the table alone.

Micah felt so awake, he thought his hair must be standing on end.

✡

Shay had an apartment near the university. It was in one of the new, medium-sized, gated complexes. They passed a pool, glowing blue, reflections from its underwater lights flickering on the trees above; the smell of chlorine rose through the air. Shay stumbled, and Micah after her, suppressing giggles in the quiet.

Biting her lower lip in concentration, Shay slid her key in the lock and opened the door; they both fell in and ended up rolling together on the carpeting.

Her mouth tasted like beer, lipstick, and mints; under that, of heat and saliva. Under the dress, her pretty, tough girl charm remained, her breasts high and small, waist slender and strong; she was champagne gold between her thighs. She seemed to think he was okay, too.

✡

He got home later the next day, after coffee and a shower with Shay. As he was changing out of his smoky, sweat-creased clothes, he found a card in the back pocket of his pants. *Yiches Studios, 3133 Southeast 10th.*

When he checked his messages, there was one from the editor at the magazine. "Micah, I'll need the Yiches story in two weeks. You're on top of it, right? Right." Well, Micah thought, stranger things had happened than his editor not communicating with him. He must have missed a message, or an editorial meeting, or something.

If you want to know the secret of the possible, you have to untie the knots that bind your soul. That was from Kabbalah interpretation. It had parallels in most every religious mystical system: the world is illusion, shadow-play. Happiness isn't found in material or worldly definitions of it; free the mind—untie the knots—from such definitions, from constrictions of thought, desire, expectation, and it becomes possible to know the boundless. The boundless, beyond imagining. It, too, had a million names, and none of them, supposedly, touched the truth of what they described.

What had she said, the woman with lightning in her eyes? Such seeking, such unbinding, also meant loss. Of the familiar—creature comforts, security—*the coveted sweet moments of everyday life,* which had magic of their own.

So, did he really want to know the secret of the possible?

The answer rose within him, from a place beneath thought, unfolding like a rose, vivid and alive.

✡

Yiches Studios occupied a set of old warehouse buildings on the southeast side of the city, in a forgotten pocket of neighborhood moated off by highway bypass and overpass. A few decrepit old shack houses, a turn of the century cemetery filled with trees and stained, leaning grave markers, and the studio.

Micah circled the area three times before he found the only turn-in that actually accessed it. He parked his car, checked his mini-recorder, and mentally reviewed his questions.

From the outside, the warehouse buildings were neat, the grounds around them well-kept, all very unassuming. A small, hand-painted sign affixed to the corrugated sheet metal on the outside of the smallest building read *Yiches Studios.*

The building proved to be the office, from which he was led by a friendly guy wearing a *Blood Mohels* tee-shirt out the back and to a bigger building interconnected with several others. They went in through a human-sized door next to the closed, hangar-sized ones. The friendly assistant left him there after getting the attention of another assistant, this one carrying a clipboard and wearing a headset.

"Sarah Shapiro," she shook his hand. "We're about to shoot. I'll take you to Jacob, but you'll have to just watch quietly for a bit, okay?"

"Sure." He followed her to where the cherub with the villain beard sat on a tall stool with armrests, near a camera on a boom. He was speaking intently to three people, with lots of arm motions and hand gestures, but his voice was low and intimate and Micah couldn't hear him over the general murmurous clamor.

"Now," Sarah Shapiro said, "if you need anything later, stills, archive access, press kits, facts, figures, correct spellings, you let me know, okay? Sarah." She left him and disappeared into the chaos. Micah turned his attention to the scene about to be filmed.

A craggy bit of mountainous landscape had been built, with a cave and a detailed section of a mountain palace made to look as it were hewn from the mountain itself. Scrim was behind that, which Micah knew would be filled in later digitally, along with the other digital manipulations that would enhance fight scenes, supernatural phenomena, and the appearance of such things as *shedim, dybbukim,* babuks, devils, and the dead.

There was a crane off to one side, and high above the hot lights he could just see the wires and steel frameworks that supported them. Off to another side, an actor was being fitted with a wing framework; he wore embroidered red and orange robes and carried a long sword. He would be digitally enhanced later; Micah edged closer to Jacob Schacter and got a look at the slate. *Desert Song: Scene 15: Benaiah Fights Ashmodai.* Ashmodai, king of the demons. Micah wondered if they were actually sticking to the story in which Benaiah and Ashmodai traditionally appeared together. It had been told already in a number of different interpretations, so he doubted it.

Ashmodai and the actor playing Benaiah, whom Micah recognized from other Yiches films, were harnessed and attached to their wires and took a few test flights, swooping past and around each other, landing on the craggy ground, then flipping up, or flying to a higher point. There were shouts back and forth to the wire operators, and then everything got quiet suddenly, very quiet, for the fifty-plus people that were at work. Micah realized a fair number of people were wearing headsets.

"Rolling," someone yelled. An assistant slated the scene. "Okay," Jacob said quietly into his headset, "action." Micah thumbed down record on his recorder.

They shot the scene four times with two cameras, one moving in and out, through and over the action. Then they began to go through the blocking slowly, stopping for reaction shots. The noise level slowly resumed its former clamor. After the first take, Micah had thumbed off the recorder.

Jacob spoke to his camerawoman briefly as they started the close-ups, then turned to Micah and gestured him over.

"So, Micah, right?" He held out his hand and pumped Micah's. "What did you think?"

"Looked great." He held up the recorder and Jacob nodded. "This film, *Desert Song*, is it a traditional storyline or a neo-traditional?"

"Oh, neo, very. The idea is that this is not Solomon's Benaiah, but his descendant, and he's fighting Ashmodai to free the she-demon of the desert from her curse, which she got for drinking the water of immortality, which, of course, a mortal just shouldn't drink."

"Can you talk a little about what you feel *Zohars* are about—what it is that's so compelling about them?"

"Sure, sure." He folded his hands together and thought a moment. "The folk legends of a people, they're a record, a kind of mirror of the very complicated historical and cultural experiences of that people, yes? Darkness and superstition; well, you know, somewhere it says, 'evil must be encountered, not evaded.' So, the films we make, they're about what?" He gestured. "Life—in metaphor, right? Our ancestors, history, blood, roots, family. And wonder, of course, the experiences that inspire us to be the best we can be." He ran one hand over his beard and looked into Micah's eyes, his slightly bloodshot brown eyes sincere. "Also, a lot of the films, they're fun as well as serious, and laughter: laughter is sacred."

Micah nodded. "What do you look for in a story or a script—what makes a story a great film?"

"For me, a good script is about two things, within the action and the story, the characters and the various *shedim*. The first thing is that it has to be about what the heart wants, on one level, the worldly, purely existence-defined level, the second thing is what the heart, the man or woman or *shed*, yearns for on another level." He pronounced "yearns" emphatically, underlining with a hand gesture.

"Do you work with an in-house writer, or do you look at scripts? That's something our readers always want to know."

"Well, *Desert Song* is in-house, but we're really open to anything good."

They talked for another ten minutes, then one of the crew gave a high sign.

"So," the director said, shaking Micah's hand with both of his, "Micah, thank you. If you need anything else, information, stills, talk to Sarah, yes?"

"Yes, thank you, Mr. Schacter."

"Jacob," he waved his hand.

Micah wandered around loose for a while, searching for the elusive Sarah. He passed two crew members in a divided-off area, going over several carts of smaller props and racks of costumes.

"Have you seen the Ineffable Name for the *golem* scene?"

"I think—ummm" one of them bent, looking through a box. "Yeah, here it is," she waved a rolled piece of parchment and held up the box. "Whole bunch of them."

He glimpsed Sarah, then, disappearing through an inner door—into another of the connected warehouses, he guessed. He followed, came around a stack of flats, and ran into someone. The someone steadied him, hands held firmly to his shoulders. He smelled rain, storm-scent. Flowers.

Today her hair was in braids and she wore black. She let him go. "Micah." Her eyes smiled. "Did you get a good interview?"

"Yes." He felt the imprint from her fingers and thumbs on his shoulders and each one tingled, a shiver of bells under his skin. "How did you—"

"I'm Lili, by the way. Lili Hamim." She studied him. The sad, wistful look touched her face again. "It was yes, wasn't it?"

Micah blinked.

Then, as if she hadn't asked him anything at all, she smiled and said, "It's fun here. Enjoy yourself. Sarah went that way." She left him.

✡

That night, as he pulled off his shirt, he heard a shimmer of sound. His shoulders tingled. It felt like ten small insects hummed beneath his skin.

Looking in the mirror, he found ten small marks across his shoulders, five on each. They were the Hebrew for the ten *sefirot* of the kabbalah. *Keter*, which was also *Ayin, Hokhmah, Binah, Hesed, Gevurah, Tif'eret, Netsah, Hod, Yesod, Shekhinah*. They were right where Lili's fingers and thumbs had gripped him.

He found that he wasn't breathing and did so, chest burning.

It was a yes, wasn't it?

His hands shook, mouth dry. He could see the pulse beating fast in his neck. He met his own eyes in the mirror. Hot saliva suddenly filled his mouth, his stomach convulsing. He ran to the bathroom and retched into the toilet until he was heaving only air.

✡

The next day he was eating breakfast with his father and aunt when Lili knocked on the glass doors that let off the kitchen to the patio. She had a small stack of files under one arm. Micah looked at her in alarm, a spoon of cereal halfway to his mouth; for a moment he looked around for a place to hide. Then there was a tight, contracting pain somewhere inside him. Knots being pulled tight, picked at, loosened, then pulled tight again.

"Micah?" His father looked at him curiously, sheepdog brows raised.

"She, um." He gave up and went to let her in, feeling his father's eyes, and his aunt's, from her perch by the stove where she was making crepes for blintzes in a little pan.

"Here you go," Lili said as he slid the glass door open. She handed him the files. "Sarah asked me to bring these to you."

"Oh." Micah frowned. He tried to see into her eyes. "Look, we need to—"

"Hello," his father interrupted. "I'm Elias, Micah's father."

"Lili Hamim."

Micah swallowed what he'd been about to say, lowered his gaze, and set the files on the counter. "And this is my aunt, Muriel Saunderstein."

"Hello," Lili said softly, almost gently.

Muriel sniffed and smiled experimentally. "Lili? Is that short for—"

"Just Lili." She looked at Micah. "Would you like to go out to our location shoot tonight?" She smiled. "You never know. We might attract some real demons. It's out in the woods near the lake. I'll come by the Crimea tonight, around eight-thirty. If you want to go." She nodded to his father and aunt. "Good to meet you." She waved and left.

His aunt muttered something under her breath, then sighed and scooped two spoons of sweet cheese gloop into a crepe and folded it over. "At least she's Jewish," she said then, philosophically.

"I'm not going out with her, aunt Muriel."

"I think you may be safer with the little *goy*," his father commented, and snapped his paper open.

This was exactly what Micah thought. And there was Shay; and the marks on his shoulders. And the fact that he was terrified of her, of Lili.

And yet.

With her—he might really see *shedim*. And wonders.

✡

Late that afternoon he went by to see Clara at the Crimea. He found her in the balcony, near the booth, where they had watched hours of *Zohars* and other movies together. Her sneakers propped on the seat before her, eyes shining blackly in the reflections of screen light, she gave him a lift of the chin. He sat with her through the last third of *Shining Soul*. As the action built to climax in the final battle, Clara went back to the booth. Micah watched alone through the credits and the reedy, soaring music.

The lights came up softly, and Clara flicked the system over to a CD of a local band. He joined her in the booth where she was rethreading the thirty-five projector from the middle platter onto the upper one for the next showing. He sat in the metal folding chair by the sixteen millimeter build-up table, watching her without really seeing her.

She finished threading the projector, checked the time, and leaned against the build-up table. "What's up?"

He rubbed a hand over one shoulder, shook his head.

Clara pushed blunt black hair behind her ears and scratched her nose for a moment.

Then Micah said, "In *Rachel's Ghost*, which demon won the last fight?" This was an old argument, now refrain and joke between them.

"The demon of the sea."

Micah shook his head. "She-demon of the desert."

"Sea."

"Desert."

Clara glanced at her watch again and went to check the threading. "Sea," she muttered.

Micah laughed, then sobered and asked her another. "If a demon gives you a choice between the familiar safety and the unknown possibility, which do you choose?"

Clara snorted. "The unknown."

"Yeah," Micah said.

✡

Clara started the next movie. Micah ate some take-out potstickers with her, watched a little of the movie, then went downstairs. He stood at the Crimea's glass doors, looking out at the darkening sky. He found himself trying to imagine what Lili's mouth would taste like. He thought of lightning, deep mineral waters, the taste of time and starlight.

An old convertible with rust spots, no make or model Micah recognized, pulled up in front of the theater. Lili sat at the wheel. Slowly, Micah pushed open the glass door and went to the car. A breeze pushed against him, smelling of rain. His hands trembled, palms sweaty. He was terrified. Lili turned to him. "You coming?"

He opened the car door with a creak, got in. Something eased slightly, a knot loosening within him.

Lili rested her head back and stared up at the sky. She held one hand out over her head and put her thumb and forefinger together as if she were pinching the light of a distant star. A tiny, luminous glow appeared between her fingers; she let it go and it shot straight into the sky.

The Mall: A Providential Tale

Jack Dann

"John Hancock Fleischer, get out of that window this very minute!"

John, who was nine and a half and slightly overweight, ignored his mother and leaned even farther out of the open clerestory window just below the ceiling. How he had managed to climb up onto the rather narrow window sill seemed beyond her comprehension, even though the door to the stepped armoire was cracked open.

"There's nothing to see from there," Myna Fleischer said as she brushed a flyaway wisp of blond hair away from her forehead. Thanks to plastic surgery, she was the living, breathing image of Botticelli's golden Aphrodite as depicted in his most famous painting.

"There's *lots* to see up here," John said, scratching his bottom with one hand while he held onto the side casing of the window with the other. He was wearing a black-striped American flag teeshirt and aquamarine shorts.

"It's a mall, for Chrissakes," Myna said. "There's nothing to see but ... the mall."

"I can see the slaves marching around in the park on the Johnson Street side," John said. He could see black-uniformed security soldiers herding people toward somewhere beyond his sightline, as if they were cowboys herding cattle ... but without any horses, of course. "Near where Daddy's probably disappeared."

"Daddy hasn't disappeared! How many damn times do I have to tell you? He's away on a business trip. And now I'm going to have to call the super to get you down from there. Before you break your damn neck." She lit a cigarette, which she held out at an odd angle. But instead of calling the apartment building's blackshirt security volunteer, she snapped her fingers for Carrie, her maid. The fan-shaped Tiffany wall lamps blinked on and off in response. "And there aren't any damn slaves over there, either," his mother continued. "It's not a concentration camp. It's just a damn mall with factories and offices and warehouse outlets."

John heard a muffled cracking noise. Even though he couldn't see anything over at the mall now, he was sure it was gunfire. "Did you hear that, Mommy? I bet one of the slaves probably just got shot in the head. It probably exploded like a—"

"That's quite enough of that, young man," Carrie said as she stepped out of the penthouse elevator into the palatial, Louis IV-inspired living room. She nodded to Myna, as if, indeed, she was the person in charge and Myna the employee. Then she ordered John to close—and lock!—the window and get his fat little kike ass down from there this very minute.

"And if I don't?" John said in a whiney voice.

Carrie didn't answer him. She just stood where she was, her legs apart, her starched black uniform creaking as she breathed, until he finally said,

"Aw, okay," and made the dangerous and acrobatic descent using the armoire's shelving as rungs.

"Don't do that ever again," Myna said, "unless you really want to give me a heart attack."

John smiled at his mother, as if that would be a fine intention, until Carrie slapped him hard in the face and said, "And never speak such hooey and nonsense about the mall ever again. Next time I'll report you, and that's a promise. Now go to your room and stay there until you have permission to leave." Then she turned to Myna, who extinguished her cigarette in a huge opalescent Lalique glass ashtray and gazed up at the closed clerestory window as if nothing whatsoever had happened ... or would ever happen.

✡

It was a beautiful summer morning in Johnson City, New York. The cicadas were already buzzing, and the sky was soft and blue. You could just see the palest crescent of a silvery moon as the park's sprinklers went *phft*, *phft*, *phft* like little steam engines pumping rainbow showers into the pellucid air.

"Well, you really can't see anything from *here*," John's friend Ken Wentworth Lewiston said as they skirted around the vined fencing that separated Recreation Park from the vast property that was once known as the Oakdale Mall. "But I was talking to Mickey Levit, and *he*—"

"Who?" John asked.

"Mickey Levit, like I said. He's one of the Jews whose father—and mother, I think—is in the mall. He's the one with the nose and big lips. He transferred over from the conversion school. Don't you remember him from American Ethos class with Mrs. Sheinhold?" He parodied his teacher by twisting his lips into a moue, clicking his heels, and putting his hand over his heart as if he was going to recite the Pledge of Allegiance.

"Yeah, now I think I remember," John said.

"He's a Jew just like you," Ken said, grinning; and he pointed out an old man and woman strolling in the park: both wore yellow Star of David patches on their chests: yellow badges of shame. Then he pulled a plastic gun candy dispenser out of his side pocket and shot a sour watermelon pellet into his mouth.

"I'm *not* a Jew," John said, his face flushing with anger. "And if I was, you wouldn't be hanging out with me, would you?"

"Maybe, maybe not," Ken said. He shot another pellet into his mouth and offered one to John.

John refused.

"Sorry, but my Dad says—"

"Well, your Dad is wrong. We're as God fearing as you or anybody else."

After a beat, Ken said, "Yeah, yeah, I know, I'm sorry. It's just your last name, is all."

"How many times I got to tell you: it's *German*. Like Keitel. Or Katzmann.

Or Goebbels."

"Yeah, I know, but my father says—"

"So what's all this about Mickey Levit?" John asked, changing the subject before he said something about Ken's father that he'd regret: Ken was too strong to fight—he was almost a foot taller than John—and, anyway, wasn't self-control supposed to be a sign of true manhood: what Christian heroes called "hardness"?

"Oh, yeah, so Mickey said that he heard that somebody found a place where the wires and hedges were cut straight through over by Johnson's Fruit Market. Mickey said his friend actually got *into* the mall. But that was bullshit. I searched all around the fence, and the barb wire was all rolled over and over same as it is here." They both gazed at the high blackthorn hedges and barbed wire fencing: the demarcation between public land and protected mall.

"Maybe you just couldn't find the right place," John said. "Or maybe one of the greens saw it and called it in."

"There ain't any greens in the park anymore," Ken said. It's all secpo's now."

"Since when?"

"Since this week. My father told me."

John nodded with grudging admiration and jealousy: Ken's father was a big shot in the secpo's. "Really? Security police?"

"And junior military guards, too, for support."

"Wow," John said, impressed. "Maybe we should forget about the mall."

"Yeah, maybe you're right," Ken said. "But it would've been great to actually get in there and see stuff, you know what I mean?"

John nodded, thinking that if his father really was in there, maybe he could figure out a way of getting him out … of getting *anybody* he wanted out. But he knew that was all hooey and nonsense, as Carey would say. Just like she told him he couldn't tell shit from Shinola, whatever the hell Shinola was.

"You want to go check out the carousel instead?" Ken asked "They repainted the pavilion and all the horses, too. And they replaced the old steam engine so now it works all the time."

But John wasn't quite ready yet to let go of the idea of getting into the mall. "Did you check behind the dumpsters?"

Ken shook his head. "No, how could I? They're blocked off. You'd have to go through the ass-end of the fruit market to get to them."

"What if we just snuck into their side storage sheds? They all have back doors. We should be able to get into one of them."

Ken smiled nervously. "Yah … might be worth a try." He pulled out his candy dispenser; and this time John accepted a sour watermelon pellet, which Ken shot right into his mouth.

✡

Seeing a gang of junior guards standing in front of the side sheds and cat-calling young women, John and Ken decided their best chance was to try going straight through Kearns' Market.

"And for all we know, the sheds might be locked up, anyway," John said, feeling an adrenal rush in response to anticipated danger.

Ken nodded, but his face had gone pale when he saw the guards. He looked unsure of himself, so John took the lead and walked right into the market, big as day. He snaffled a rather soft, bruised apple—the best on the fruit display stand—and then pretended to look in the synthetic meat section, which flanked two ceiling-high swinging doors that led into the back of the market: the hamburger patties and striated steaks looked as red as candied apples.

When Ken finally caught up with him, John whispered: "Glad you could make it. Are you ready?"

Ken gave him a dirty look and nodded.

"Okay, I'll go first," John said.

"Hell if you will," Ken said angrily and almost collided with a floor clerk pushing a cart of lettuce through the swinging doors.

John was about to say, "That was dumb"—the doors could have been security alarmed—but Ken had already slipped through. John was about to follow when one of his mother's friends called to him.

"Hi, Boo Boo!"

"Hello, Mrs. Dockerty," John said, flinching, then scowling. He hated that nickname, which he had acquired when he was a baby and couldn't talk properly. Even his mother had stopped using it ... and that was *ages* ago.

"Well, I didn't know that *you* were the little shopper in the family." Mrs. Dockerty's hair was the exact same color as John's mother's and was combed back into a French twist. "Are you taking over for your maid?" She seemed to enjoy her own joke.

John made small talk with her about school and church and how his family was doing financially until she saw someone she knew and skirted away, but not before tousling his hair. He hated that, just as he hated having to wear it in a pageboy because his mother had read it was the absolute latest on her favorite Junior Style family lifestyle blog. Then, looking around to make sure he wouldn't be noticed, John waited for another clerk to come through the doors so he could slip through just before they closed. He didn't have to wait long: he slipped past an ancient old woman of about forty who was carrying a bunch of food registration benefit protectors.

The storeroom was huge. It was pleasantly cool inside ... and rather dim, except for thick shafts of sunlight that cut through the dust-roiling air from a row of skylights way above. There were bins and drums and crates of various sizes everywhere, and forklifts and telehandlers were moving quietly around the room as if they were programmed just to float around like clouds. John looked around for Ken. He must have already reached the back door that looked out onto the fence.

"So where the hell *are* you, Ken?" John whispered as he ducked behind one row of stacked crates and then another, carefully making his way toward the back door without disturbing the machines moving this way and that. And then he froze. He felt like something hot had just been pressed onto his face; and he also felt a chill, as if ice-cold water was leaking out of his solar plexus, leaking all over his insides, right down into his crotch.

Someone had just shouted, "Hey, you, what the hell are you doing over there? Yeah, I mean *you!*"

"Oh, shit!" John whispered, realizing that he had peed right there in his brown corduroy pants.

"Get your skinny ass out where I can see you!"

It was then that John saw the junior guard, who stepped out from behind a row of Blue Bliss soda containers. But this junior guard didn't look very junior: he was old enough to have gray hair in his sideburns, a thick, full beard, and a pot-belly. He wore a belted black and gray service jumpsuit, but no helmet; and he was aiming a nasty-looking LSAT machine gun in the direction of the back door.

Thank God it's not me ... it's not me...

John stood frozen. He felt the dampness in his crotch and legs.

How will I explain this to Momma ... and to Carrie...? If I can ever get home. I just want to get home. Somehow ... somehow. He held his breath, which he finally let out in a thin stream, his mouth pursed as if he was whistling.

Ken stepped into the central aisle and stood under the skylight, which made him look like a ghost or something, or so John thought. Ken raised his arms.

"Put your arms down, you idiot," the guard said. He had a gravelly voice and a northern drawl. Ken did as he was told and now held his arms stiffly at his sides, as if he were trying to stand at attention. "What the hell are you doing sneaking around in here, anyway? Don't try to bullshit me, or I'll make sure you never see your mommy and daddy again. And you can start by telling me your name."

"It's Ken Lewiston, sir. Ken Wentworth Lewiston."

"Are you Winston Lewiston's boy?" the guard asked.

"Yessir, he's my father."

The guard lowered his rifle and said, "Okay, so what's a boy like you doing sneaking around in a place like this?"

But instead of admitting to trying to steal a bottle of beer or an off-the-list can of tunafish, Ken told the guard the truth.

The guard laughed. "You were trying to get *into* the mall?"

"Yessir."

"And who told you about a cut in the wire?"

"It was Mickey Levit."

"Mickey Levit, huh. And how did *he* happen to know about it?"

"I dunno, sir, but he's a Jew just like John Fleischer. This whole thing was John Fleischer's idea. It's him you should be arresting, and he's *supposed* to be right in here somewhere, unless he chickened out or something."

John had indeed chickened out after hearing that; and as he made his way quickly and quietly toward the double doors that led back into the market, he heard the guard say, "Don't worry, wherever Levit and Fleischer are, we can find them. Seems the Jews are dying to get into the mall." He chuckled. "Now I'm not going to report *you*, but—"

John made it through the doors and ran as fast as he could out of the market, and he kept running until he reached a little alcove in the southwest corner of Recreation Park where he would be safe.

And he stayed right there even after the blotchy stains on his pants dried.

He imagined that those stains were piss-yellow six pointed stars as he waited in the damp, autumnal space behind the hedges that were as tall as Franklin's Guest Motel on Academy Street. He waited as dusk turned the air a shadowy blue before giving way to urban darkness. Above him, the lights came on in the form of the crescent moon and a pinpoint that was Venus. John was hungry and thirsty. He wanted to see his mother and his father.

He even wanted to be called Boo Boo.

Yet there he sat.

He tried to picture his father on a business trip, sitting around a big desk with a bunch of people all wearing ties, and then he wondered if his father was wearing a star like the old people in the park and being marched around the mall.

Or probably he was already dead.

Just then, John heard a deep voice inside his head. It sounded echoey, sort of like his own voice did when he popped his ears and made the Ohm sound … or when his father sang oom-pah songs in the shower.

"You can't save your father. He's dead. And you can't go back home either 'cause an army of secpo's are there right now. Waiting for you. So you'll just have to sit right here forever on your fat little kike ass.

"Forever and ever and ever."

As he listened to his stomach groaning—as he imagined that something ugly and hungry was gnawing inside him—he heard the distant zing-zip of an automatic rifle.

He waited for another burst, but that was all there was.

His father was surely dead now … or still on his business trip.

And there was nothing left but the trilling and chirping of a thousand field crickets. An army of crickets carrying teeny-tiny automatic rifles. And so John Hancock Fleischer waited in the murmuring darkness and pretended that his mother was calling to him. He whispered his name as a swirl of fireflies appeared, blinking on and off around him like glowing semaphores.

"Boo Boo…

"Boo Boo…

"Boo Boo…"

The Golden Horde
Jane Yolen

If they had not stopped
at the foot of Vienna,
but wandered further,
in between the umlauts,
what gracious families
we might have spawned,
who accepted Jews
amongst the strangers,
held great Valse parties,
sprinkled with pastry and challah,
noodles, and a dash of white wine.
The toasts would have been
as endless as a seder,
with less talk, and more *gemutlichkeit.*
My German less guttural,
more palatable, like my heart.

Psalm for the First Day of Space Travel
Jane Yolen

The Lord is my pilot, I shall not fear
the treacherous heavens, nor the cold stars.

If we make it to green waters, a habitable land,
it is He/She who will have held the wheel, steering us there.

These are but a slipstream between the valleys of death,
no more frightening than the storms of our home planet,
but without the true evil of unrighteous Nazis.
Therefore we are not to fear.
Death is part of life, and we Jews manage
to go through worse travels and travails.
So, be comforted.

Surely there will be tables full of honey and challah at journey's end.
Surely we will build small houses between green hills.
Once again our cups will run over
We will both give and take mercy and
teach our new planet-mates about the Word.
Surely we will live in the House of the Lord forever.

The Green Men Learn to Read

Jane Yolen

They weren't exactly green,
more gray, like stone.
But at certain times of the long day
the planet's air filters the twin suns oddly.

All of us knew about the green men,
passed along in our morning prayers:
Treat the Green Man fairly.
Though this wasn't Mars, merely metaphor.

We tried to teach them to speak like us.
Only Hebrew sort of worked.
The rest, filtered through
their mossy teeth, was gibberish.

Then the chief rabbi spoke, saying,
"They must become a people of the Book."
It puzzled some who listened without metaphor.
I knew he meant we must teach them to read.

But first we had to show them a book.
They held it strangely, dangling from
those watercourse hands, the webbings taut,
passing it around, one to the other.

Being the Linguistics Guy, I pointed
to the succession of Hebrew characters.
They pointed as well, but no lights lit.
Then I remembered stories the old rabbis told.

Teaching the yeshiva boys to read,
they spread honey on a slate,
The boys licked up alef and bet,
Learning to read became a sweet task.

Despite our captain's single No vote,
I unrolled one of our precious tubes of honey,
Spread it on a page of text—not Torah but a manual.
I mimed licking the letters. The light lit.
They scrambled each for his/her own page.

Then they ate the paper, asked for more.

All Zion weeps.

Why the Bridgemasters of York Don't Pay Taxes

Gillian Polack

Manuscript note: This manuscript is unique and is held in the library of the Bridge at York. The hand is a very fine Bastard *Anglicana* from the middle decades of the fifteenth century. The work echoes the much earlier Dialogue of the Exchequer in its didactic form, and is one of the core texts for the Order of the Penitents of the Bridge, which was dissolved under the Suppression of Religious Houses Act 1535. This is the first time it has been translated into English.

✡

Lord Abbot, you ask me if I am ready to take my oath, but I do not understand why we are here.

Our warm limestone walls comfort us and protect us from both the cold winds of the north and the people who hate us. We have green and verdant leisure gardens as well as gardens that supply our food.

Why do we not live in the cold hills, as the Cistercians do?

Why do we not wander the roads as must the Franciscans?

Why do we not follow the Dominicans and preach?

Why does our monastery have an exit for each bridge?

Why do we learn these strange languages and copy books in such odd scripts? Why do we speak in the language of God and not in Latin?

Why is our prayer atonement for the sins of many? Why do we not spend our lives as monks seeking the redemption of our own souls?

When I first came, you said you would explain why we pay women wages and read the Passover service as the Jews have since ancient times, and I find my understanding still lacking. We are so different from other monastic foundations that I fear we are but a mockery.

I cannot take my oath until I know that we meet God's needs on this earth. I cannot take my oath until I understand why we have a garrison and three scriptoria as well as much land.

I shall tell you what you need to know. When you understand, you will be ready to take your oath. Ask me your questions.

✡

We are the Order of the Penitents of the Bridge. What is this bridge? Is it the main bridge that leads to York, glorious in its stone arches, with its fortified gatehouse benevolently overlooking the road? Is it a metaphor for the path of our worship? I do not understand.

To understand, you first need to learn about the bridges of the Devil. Our plight was greater than that in any other place and yet we did not seek sin. We do not possess anything given by any demon, much less by the Devil himself. Ask me about the Devil's bridges and then you will begin to understand our bridge.

✿

What are the Devil's bridges?
They are stone bridges that were built by the Devil in times past, when the inhabitants of certain places found no succor elsewhere. Our river is not the only one that flows fast and dangerous, nor the only one that is hard to cross.

Our town is greater and more beautiful than others and our walls are splendid. The rivers are both its greatest protection and its most difficult citizens. They overflow their banks too often and, for many years, one river refused to accept a bridge at all. When the wooden bridge was built, it was swept away, over and over again. It had no time to develop lichen or rot: it was completed only twice and within a day of its completion on both occasions, the clean new wood floated down the river like debris. When a stone bridge was finally attempted—an elegant bridge with three arches and the most beautiful cream stone the town could find, bought with the money of both the duke, Edmund, and the town—it killed three people and would not stand. Many people were hurt by this, for the stonemasons could find no work, and the town had no money, and the duke would not speak of it. Yet still the bridge failed.

The stone from that collapse remains in the river to this day. Look from the window above your bed and you will see the ripple it creates, for all the dormitories overlook that section of the river. This is left there to remind us that the townsfolk thought to seek help from the Devil, and it reminds us that they stood steadfast and accepted poverty rather than sin and that we, too, must be steadfast.

At first, no one knew the reason for the collapse of our bridges. It was when the great abbot, Michael, examined the history of Devil's bridges that the matter became clear and the problem was solved. It was then that the popes were petitioned to change our foundation's nature.

Michael was the greatest of our abbots. He traveled across England and Wales and France and as far as Rome in an attempt to discover why the bridge in York would not stand. This was prior to the first stone bridge. He braved war and plague and horrors. He did not return to York until after the Great Death. The people of his childhood were buried and the places he knew were bereft of life when he re-entered our gates, but he had an answer to his question: he understood why no bridge would stand in York. At first his advice was ignored, but when the stone bridge fell, the duke and the town and the archbishop listened.

Michael was a great man. When he was not allowed to act on one matter, he acted on another, for his long life contained not a year when he did not act. He established the little chapel in memory of all the people who were dead due to the bridge, so that their souls would be guided after their untimely deaths. This is one of the three chapels in our monastery that are dedicated solely to prayers for Christians.

When you take your oath, you will be responsible for prayer in the other chapels and in the community. Prayer in these other places is far more difficult. Remember Father Michael, for he made your novitiate simpler, by giving you Christian prayers for Christians. After your oath is taken, your life will not be so easy.

We seldom pray for Christians.

Father Michael discovered that bridges in other places were replaced by the Devil in return for human souls. One of the bridges Father Michael examined is near Aberystwyth, one crosses the Verdus in Languedoc, and there are two in Cumbria. One of these latter crosses the River Lune, and leads to a wicked place. Each and every one of these bridges involved a bargain. Thus the bridges remain standing forever, but also thus souls are damned forever.

I myself have been to the bridge in Ceredigion and they say that no soul was lost there, for an old lady fooled the Devil. I saw there a bridge that crosses a high and narrow ravine, and the path underfoot is smooth and even as the path to Hell. The water is deep and far below and the bridge is small.

The old lady said to the Devil "I bet you that you can't build a bridge by dawn." She took stones out at one end, so the last stone that completed the crossing of the gorge was only discovered missing after the sun had risen. The Devil lost his bet. I do not believe their claim, for how can an old lady trick the Devil?

Some say that these are old bridges and that the Devil did not build them, but these people do not know the history of our own bridge and do not wish to. Wilful ignorance is dangerous.

✡

Why do some call our bridge the Bridge of Penitents? Why is our monastery called The Order of Penitents of the Bridge? Am I here because I am giving penitence for the evils that the bridgemasters do?

We are the penitents. We are witnesses of the history of this place. We testify to the horror of York's past and keep the memory alive so that it will not happen again. It is because of our penitence that we can maintain a bridge here, where no bridge should be. The bridgemasters claim that their prayers save the town from flooding, but we do not give penitence for that. We atone for the people of York and their past deeds.

We pray for the bridgemasters, too, for they need our prayer. They sacrificed their salvation in order to maintain our bridge. We pray for them, and this is what you must do, every day and night of your life.

Our other task is to guard the bridgemasters and their families from evil-doers. Many are those that wish them harm, and they are forbidden to defend themselves. We are monks militant, even though the Holy Land has not been Christian for generations. Our soldiers work alongside us and some take our oath.

✡

What evil-doers are these?

These are the wicked ones who burned the cousins and the ancestors of our bridgemasters alive in the castle tower. The tower is rebuilt, but those who took refuge there refuse to visit and the mayor and town and its lords respect their wishes. When the bridgemasters need a place of refuge, they enter the gatehouse on the south, next to the chapel for travelers who use the bridge. From there, they can enter the monastery, if they must. Neither the bridgemasters nor their family will ever enter the castle.

The Tower of the Jews will be finished soon, and then they will have their own fortification and the money from our lands will pay for its maintenance and they will be safe. They will not need to sully our holiness when they are in danger, for we can protect them within their own tower. We keep them safe with our prayers and our tower will keep them safe with its thick walls and our garrison. The city will have atoned for its deeds and there will be only us to keep the memory of the burning and the massacre alive.

✡

This is why you wish to teach me? To record what was, in this time of change?

The pope in Avignon says "Do not forget" and the pope in Rome says "Do not forget." This is the only matter on which they are agreed, so we are compelled to write these things down and to ensure that the memory continues. We are also asked to ensure that all monks understand fully before taking their oath, and thus we record your questions and my answers.

✡

Why is this?

Father Michael's successor sought the bridgemasters from families that had been expelled from France and had gone to Spain. Their ancestors may have been English, but these people had wandered for generations. They were sent from England in 1290, then from France not once but three times: it took much persuasion by the good father to persuade them to return to England to take care of our bridge.

Since they have come, however, we have had safe and clear access to and from York on both Ouse and Foss, so the effort was not in vain. We must record the story, and to remember that these people did not arrive here unannounced: they were asked, nay, persuaded, and at first they were reluctant.

If you will remember, my son, last year they threatened to leave.

A crack developed on the stone bridge. A second crack. The bridge over the Foss lost planks and teetered dangerously. The townsfolk blamed a storm, but the problem was how the townsfolk treated the bridgemasters. They had thrown stones and vile names had been shouted across the street.

We were in danger of losing our bridges and so it became important to reassure the bridgemasters that we remembered and that we were working to keep them safe so that they could keep the bridge safe.

✡

What caused these cracks, when the bridge had been stable for so many years?

The first crack came the day that the Jewish woman Elizabeth was murdered. There was a rumour that a passing lord had admired her beauty, for her hair was gold as a fairy's and her eyes were blue and her cheeks were pink, but that she had refused him. She was modest for one of her kind, and told me nothing of this. She brought us the work of her hand and the hands of her sisters, to sell in the market and the only converse I had with her concerned the quality and nature of the cloth she wove. She was cousin to the Bridgemaster-General.

News of the murder of the woman Elizabeth was brought by our archbishop to the Papacy.

The pope sent a messenger to say that the cracks were due to our dereliction. First, we had neglected to remind the townsfolk that Jews should not be murdered. Second, we had failed to maintain our own memory of why our foundation was different.

Our oaths had lost their meaning.

✡

Why did he send this news? Surely a murder is a local matter? Surely our oaths and how we keep them are our own business?

When the bridge was rebuilt in 1400, permission for the Jews was given by the popes. Christendom was in an uproar that Avignon and Rome were agreed on this matter when they could not agree on the cure of Christian souls.

It was winter. The matters between Edward and Richard were unresolved, so there was no appeal to the king. York was cut off, for the river was high and the floods were unexpected and the small bridges were unsafe. The popes said "You may call in the Jewish bridgebuilders from the Continent."

✡

It was not that simple, surely?

No, it was not. The matter had been broached many times earlier.

The history of the bridge prior to 1400 is full of tale and wonder, but it almost killed the prosperity of York and its people, time after time. The stonecutters could cut the stone and the builders here could build the bridge, but it never remained standing.

It fell first in 1174. Another wooden bridge was constructed. This was swept away in 1190, when the river rose in mourning for the murdered Jews. From 1190, bridges were built and fell. In 1290, when the Jews were expelled from England, all the bridges of York crumbled. From 1290, it did not matter how we built, our bridges fell.

It was the Abbess of St. Mary's who first said "Our sins manifest. We must atone."

St. Mary's founded a chapel on the new bridge, but it was not sufficient. They appealed to the pope for a foundation to atone for what was done to the Jews and this scriptorium in which we sit is part of that foundation. We copy the Hebrew and the Aramaic and we repair the old rolls and we preserve that which no-one wants. We save the Jewish manuscripts and we tell the Jewish stories, but we do not imperil our Christian souls. Scholars visit from other Holy Orders and they press us to watch and maintain guard against any such lapse. This room is musty from the worked vellum and parchment and sharp from the smell of the inks and glues, but it is always guarded by one who knows when souls might stray.

Even with our monastery and its prayers and vigil and learning, the bridge did not hold. Father Michael discovered the reason and refused to permit a Devil's bargain. The archbishop and the lords and the mayor appealed to the king.

The king said "My ancestor expelled the Jews. I will not ask them to return."

The archbishop said in reply "Your ancestor permitted a small number of Jews to return, one of whom was his physician. This is all we ask."

"I will not be master of Jewish men. I will not permit a synagogue."

"Be master of Jewish women, then, for I do not ask for a synagogue."

This is why our bridgemasters are women. This is why there is no synagogue and no prayers, for without ten Jewish men, there can be no prayers and no synagogue.

The leader of these men is a woman, who cannot lead at prayer. The current leader of the Jews is Bridgemaster-General Rachel. Their first leader was Benedicta, and she was the one who built the current bridge. It stood for twenty-seven years, without a crack, without a flaw until the hatred of Jews welled up. The Bridgemaster-General has promised to repair the cracks in the stone and the holes in the wood the day the tower is finished.

✡

But the king allowed Jewish men into England? I have met Jewish men.

No. The king allowed Jewish women into England. If Jewish men happen to accompany them they do not appear on any record. There is no synagogue and no Jewish court of law, so the work of Jewish men is not recorded.

✡

Yet I have met Jewish men. Why are they here? Our oath is an oath of chastity, why do we not demand the same of these Jewish women?

These women are not good Christian women. Their religion does not demand chastity. You will notice that they do not cover their hair as carefully as our women do. They use their own religious rules for their food and require their own butcher. They have their own teachers and do not observe our Sabbath. They do not enter our churches.

They do not distinguish between man and woman as we do. When you walk down the street and encounter one, she will look you in the eye and shake your hand and do business with you as if you were her equal. Only a few of our women do this, and even those will cover their hair fully outside the home and will look down demurely when they meet a superior.

Their customs are strange and yet we may not condemn them. It is no sin for Jewish women to sleep with a man before marriage and any child born from this is not illegitimate. We are horrified and we are bewildered, but we may not force change upon them. Their souls are lost. Their ways are not our ways. We may talk with them, but we may not force these women to behave decorously, for that would undermine our atonement and the atonement of this town which is why they are here. They are here for us: they must live as they choose.

When I was appointed abbot I petitioned the pope, as did my predecessors and as will my successors, for permission to do what others do and force the Jews to attend our services and to convert them and to save their souls. The pope refused me, as the pope always refuses. The only souls we are permitted to save are Christian souls.

Our monastery is here to keep the Jews from harm and to permit them to live and to be testament to Christ, as Augustine demands. The Jews are damned, and yet we must protect them.

This is why you must ask your questions and consider your answers carefully, for in taking your oath, you not only swear to a life of God as other monks do, but you swear to a life where you may not convert those who will be lost without conversion, and you must save them from harm and prevent their words from being forgotten. We are one of only three monasteries in the whole of Christendom that follow this path.

It is not easy. Ours is a lonely order.

Augustine's reasons give us our truth: Jews must live to witness. Our lives are, however, colored by the ordinary. If we had demanded chastity of these

OTHER COVENANTS

women, they would not have come and saved our city. If we had demanded chastity of these women, then they would not have borne children. Without children, there would be no-one to repair and maintain the bridge. The position of Bridgemaster-General would return to the town and the Mayor would serve a term or two, early in his career and we would be forced to return to the town its gifts of land and income. Also, the bridges would fall.

✿

The town did not give us the land and income so that we could pray for them and live in purity?

The original foundation was made to atone for what was done to the Jews. One hundred and fifty Jews died in the massacre and the fire. One hundred and fifty innocents died for attending a wedding in this city. Five of those who were guilty wished to secure their souls. This part of our foundation is permanent and it is ancient.

The Rule was different then. We prayed for the souls of those who died in the flames of the castle tower, and we prayed for the souls of those who caused those deaths. This part of our foundation consists of the chapel, the old dormitory, the old wooden kitchen, the small scriptorium and the refectory. Even the cloisters, my quarters and the kitchen gardens were built from the town's money and are conditional on our management of the bridgemasters.

✿

Who manages Jewish business?

The townsfolk will sell goods to the Jews directly, but the Jews may not own land or building or farm, for the king does not recognize them and neither do the courts. If a matter involving a Jew goes to court, then a Christian must speak for them.

These are but examples of why our work is essential for all, why we are not the same as other monasteries, and why we depend on the Jews as much as they depend upon us. We are their protectors and their lawyers and their merchants and their landowners. We are not their lords and masters, nor are our oaths to them. Our oath is to God.

You must consider these matters before you take your oath, for you may be put to work as a lawyer for the Jews or as a manager of the property that gives them food and drink.

✿

Do these men (who do not exist) pay taxes?

All taxes are paid by the hearth, and the head of each Jewish hearth in York is a woman. If they were to pay taxes, then, it would be the women who paid.

However, they do not pay taxes, or tithes, or any impost. They do not even pay the heriot. We pay for them. We pay for them, just as we pay their wages.

✡

Why do we pay them wages?

Legally, there are no Jews in England still, and if there are no Jews, then they cannot hold land. Edward III said that Jews could not hold land, and that law has not been changed. We hold the land and provide them with all they need for their upkeep.

This covers more than wages or taxes. Last year we made a single copy of the Talmud for the lady Rachel, for she required it for the teaching of her children.

Others burn the books that five of our scribes spend a year copying, thus we must protect the lady and her children, and we must protect the books. Thus their demands: for sustenance and for learning always march alongside the oaths we gave when we entered this foundation.

We maintain the memory of the Jews and the books of the Jews and now we also pay them for their labors.

✡

If it were not for the Jews, we would not need to employ soldiers.

It is true we employ soldiers to defend our Jews, but the townsfolk use the bridge and accept the Bridgemaster-General and her people as their own. It is not a burden on the community for us to operate a garrison, and it makes York's defences stronger. We are the true capital of the north and our strength could change history.

✡

If it were not for our sins, then, York might fall?

This is false logic and glorifies the sinner. If it were not for the atonement of our sins, York would still have no bridge. If it were not for our sins, many Jews would have lived out their natural lives in peace, in our walls. It may be that the Jews would have been allowed to remain in England from 1290 and our bridges would have been built earlier.

✡

Some say that it is right these Jews of olden times went to judgement early.

It is for God to judge, not us. If you think this, you should not take your oath. You are not fit for orders.

Now go and contemplate my answers.

Yossel the Gunslinger

Max Sparber

There are many miracle stories of the Old West. The Rebbe, God rest his soul, used to tell them around the table. He would break bread, and, as was our custom, we would rush his holy table, wrestling each other for scraps of the Rebbe's meal. Then we would sway and pound on the table and all would sing a *niggun*, wordlessly crying up to heaven. And the Rebbe would gather us close, and he would tell his tales, such tales! And we would know he was elevating our souls.

He had been West when it was young. He was there as a boy, a little *yidele*, just when the Western territories opened. He described it like the great flood in *parashat Noach*, the story of Hashem pouring forth the waters over all the places of the Earth. The Rebbe described it like a sea of humanity swept over the lands. But, as we know, the sea retreated, and all that was left in the West were Jews.

Sometimes the younger ones would ask, why the Jews? Why were the mountain men, the cowboys, the ranch hands, the Rangers, the barkeeps, why all of them Jewish? And the Rebbe would laugh and gently correct the child. "Nu," he would say, "not all Jews. Mostly Jews." And mostly Jews, he would say, "because Jews know how to make a community!"

He would lean close to the children and whisper, and they would crane forward to hear. "It is a very great *mitzvah* to make a community," he said.

That's when we knew we were going to hear the story of Yossel the Gunslinger. And we would dance in place and some among the Hasidim would turn somersaults, because the story was so beloved.

I can still hear the Rebbe's words today, as though he were still speaking and I was still pressed up against his table, drinking in his words. He would tell the story in this way:

Yossel, Yossel, oy, what to say of Yossel? He was a boy, just a *pisher*, you know, a *pisher*?

(Here everyone would laugh. *Pisher* is used to mean a young boy in Yiddish, but it literally describes someone who urinates.)

But what a *pisher*! He had such an opinion of himself! Oh ho! He dressed in black, like a Hasid should, but not like a Hasid! No! He wore a black shirt, and a black leather vest, and black pants, and a black hat, and a black gunbelt around his waist with two black pistols. Were it not for the white fringes he let hang out from under his shirt, and his sidelocks hanging from underneath his hat, you might not have known he was a Jew at all!

(Here, a child would inevitably interrupt to ask what sorts of guns he had. The Rebbe, having grown up on the frontier, had no trouble answering this.)

His guns? Oy, such beauties. They were Paterson Colt revolvers, with a reloading lever and capping window, a folding trigger, and such exquisite curlicues carved into the cylinder and stock. *Azoy!* Such craftsmanship is a blessing, even on such a wicked item.

But if Yossel's guns were wicked, his bullets, *gevalt!* His bullets were cursed.

This is the story of how it happened, Hashem protect me from *lashon hara*, the wicked tongue. But it was the story Yossel told himself.

I was a boy when I met Yossel. He came to my little town in the West, little Odessa, and he came to the West a hunted man. My father, the Alter Rebbe, may his memory be a blessing, my father took him in, even though we knew he brought *tsuris*, and such trouble. What could we do? It is a *mitzvah* to welcome the stranger, and how much more of a *mitzvah* to welcome the stranger that nobody else will welcome!

So we sit down to eat with this stranger, this gunslinger, and he tells us that he will soon move on. He tells us that he had sought work in the north, in Canada, near the border with Alaska. And who should come riding over the border, but Cossacks! They came from a place called Arkhangela Mikhaila, and they raided Canada, stealing from woodsmen and trappers. And, as is their way, if they saw a Jew, they killed a Jew.

Yossel says he shot in self-defense, but the Tsar said otherwise and put a bounty on his head, saying that no Jew should ever take the life of a Russian. And so Yossel fled south, with Cossack bounty hunters behind him the entire way, until he found his way to Odessa.

My father, the Alter Rebbe, looked at Yossel for a long time. Then he spoke, and when he spoke, he told him of Odessa. Not of this Odessa, but the original, in Ukraine, where the Alter Rebbe had been a boy.

He told of a place of great beauty, where generations of Rebbes had built great synagogues and centers of learning. But it was also a place of great terror. Odessa is a city on a sea, the Black Sea, and the city was always filled with Greek sailors. Sometimes the sailors would get it into their heads to kill the Jews, usually on some Christian holiday or another, Hashem preserve us from such horrors! And the people of Odessa would do nothing, they would stand back and watch the Jewish places burn.

The Alter Rebbe wept as he told this story.

(And, indeed, as our Rebbe told of his father weeping, he too would weep. He would dab his tears with linen napkins, and then those napkins would be given to Hasids with grave health problems, as the Rebbe's tears were said to cure all illness. But the Rebbe continued):

My father, the Alter Rebbe, told of how the Hasids of Odessa feared for their lives, and so moved west, and continued west. And here they found themselves, in a little plot of Earth near a desert, where they farmed and raised cattle for milk. Hashem had been good here.

But the Alter Rebbe knew that the West was a place of great peril. He had heard of communities wiped off the map by bandits, or burned down by a careless fire, or abandoned when fields suddenly failed to produce crops and cows grew sick and died. All the world is a very narrow bridge, Rabbi

Nachman said. And it was so everywhere, but especially in the West, where the slightest thing could bring catastrophe.

The slightest thing, the Alter Rebbe said to Yossel. This includes Cossacks, who would not think twice about killing every single Jew in this new Odessa of the West.

Yossel took the Alter Rebbe's words very seriously, and went out after supper to meditate on what he should do. And I followed, because I was a boy and had never seen a man like this before, a man with such guns, with Paterson Colt revolvers.

(Here the Rebbe would pause. He would then turn to the children, making a grand gesture with his arms, and they would cry out in terror, to everyone's amusement.)

I saw a devil!

A devil came to Yossel in the form of a rattlesnake. Yossel knew it was a devil, and, from my hiding place, I knew too, because what rattlesnake sings as it glides across the sand? What rattlesnake sings a Ukrainian folk song, moving its head back and forth in time, its eyes like two burning coals?

Yossel, the devil said.

Yes, Yossel said.

And the devil made a bargain. The devil would give Yossel five bullets.

Four of the bullets shall be yours, the devil said.

The devil told him that those four bullets would hit whatever Yossel desired.

The fifth bullet will be mine, the devil said.

The devil told Yossel that when he fired the fifth bullet, the devil would choose its target, and it would not miss.

Yossel agreed to the bargain, and the next day the Cossacks came.

There were five, dressed in high fur hats and burka overcoats, each riding a black horse. They rode to the center of Odessa and drew their guns.

(What sorts of guns, a child would inevitably ask, and here he would be shushed.)

The leader of the Cossacks, a man with a scarred face and large beard, named Ilovaiski, called out for Yossel. The Jews of Odessa scattered, knowing violence was to follow. They ran into buildings, closing doors, shuttering windows, and saying the *Shema Yisroel*, which Jews say if they think they are to die.

Yossel met them in the street. He was no longer dressed in his black gunslinger clothes, but instead in the garments of a humble peasant. To look at him, you would think he was any peasant, but for the single pistol he carried, a Paterson Colt revolver with a reloading lever and capping window, a folding trigger, and such exquisite curlicues carved into the cylinder and stock.

Yossel stood before Ilovaiski, unafraid. And he spoke to him.

(Here the Rebbe would rise on tiptoes, as though speaking to a man atop a horse.)

"I am Yossel," Yossel said, "and if you leave now, I will not kill you."

Ilovaiski stared at Yossel, a smile creeping across his scarred face, and then he spoke.

(Here the Rebbe leaned down, as though speaking to somebody below him.)

"You are Yossel? I heard you were a gunslinger, but you look like a peasant to me."

And Yossel, who was, after all, just a boy, just a *pisher*, looked very small next to these Cossacks on their horses.

Yossel spoke to Ilovaiski, asking him: "Nu, what does a gunslinger need?"

"A gun," said Ilovaiski.

"I have a gun," said Yossel, showing him the Paterson. Then he spoke again.

"What else does a gunfighter need?" Yossel asked.

"Bullets," roared Ilovaiski.

"I have five," said Yossel. He opened his other hand, palm forward, showing Ilovaiski the bullets, and then loaded them into his gun.

(Here the Rebbe mimed loading the gun, and all the Hasids watched, every one of them silent.)

"We have more guns," Ilovaiski said, confused. "We have more bullets."

"Not like me," Yossel said, and fired his gun.

(Now the Rebbe would stop. He would be still a while, and then he would dance slightly, speaking in a singsong.)

I was a boy. I was a boy, and I did not know to be afraid. I watched it all, standing in the street. And I saw the devil. I saw the devil! He watched too, and he hissed with pleasure, his eyes now a conflagration, his tail rattling wildly.

"Yes," the devil hissed.

With each shot, the devil said yes. One shot, one Cossack died. Yes! Two shots, two Cossacks died. Yes! Yes! Three shots, three Cossacks. Yes! Yes! Yes! Four, four, and yes, yes, yes, yes.

And the devil said, Yossel, fire the final shot. The shot will be mine, and will go where I want. And the devil looked at me, and I knew he had decided it would go to me.

(Now the Rebbe would dance wildly, his voice rising.)

But did I die! No I did not! And how! How did I survive!

Yossel did not fire the final shot. The fifth bullet remained in the gun. And Yossel lowered his pistol, his Paterson Colt revolver.

Ilovaiski stared at Yossel, and then spoke.

"Why do you not shoot?" Ilovaiski asked.

"Because I would kill you," Yossel said, even though he knew this was a lie.

"So kill me," Ilovaiski said.

"But who would go back," Yossel asked. "Who would go back to Arkhangela Mikhaila, to give my message?"

No, said the devil. No, no, no!

"What message?" Ilovaiski asked.

"That I will kill any man who comes after me," Yossel said. "Do you believe that?"

Ilovaiski nodded, dropping his gun.

"Go back to Alaska," Yossel told Ilovaiski. And the Cossack turned and rode away.

And the devil cried "no" one final time, and then consumed himself in a rage, starting with his rattle and chewing until he was entirely gone.

(Now the Rebbe would stop, looking satisfied. But he knew the children would not be happy with this. "But what happened?" they would ask. "What happened to Yossel?")

You know what happened to Yossel.

(Here the Rebbe would point to a very old Hasid, sitting by himself across the room, blind and almost entirely deaf, but smiling to himself.)

Yossel the gunslinger became Yossel the dairyman. You eat his cheese every day!

Now the children would rush to Yossel the dairyman, besieging him with questions. What they wanted to know most was where was the gun, the Paterson? Where was the bullet, the final one from the devil?

But Yossel could not hear, and would instead mumble blessings and hand the children coins, and they had to be satisfied with that.

The Holy Bible of the Free People of Hasmonea

Esther Alter

Book of Creation

In the beginning, El ruled the cosmos, and all was chaos.
With every inhale, he created. With every exhale, he destroyed.
And the cosmos were without permanent form.
Then Asherah arose from the deeps of the ocean in wind and darkness and
  challenged El.
For six years they battled. On the first day of the seventh year, Asherah slew El.
Holy Asherah declared the cosmos and all within them to be Hers, saying:
  "Thus will I bring about order and beauty."
She then subdued the seraphim who were once servants of El and bid them
  to rebuild the world in Her name.
The seraphim did as She commanded.
Yet some still carried evil in their hearts, and they are known as the Elohim.

In the name of Asherah, blessed be She, the seraphim lifted the continents
  from the waters.
They fixed the stars in the sky, and the sun, and the moon.
Trees took root. Animals were born, lived, and died.
Thus was the First Creation completed, and Asherah deemed the world worthy
  of a still greater creation.
She breathed into the ocean waters, and from them arose Lilith, the first
  woman.

Lilith lived in the forests of Adomea and learned great wisdom from the trees
  and beasts there.
Yet she was lonely, and begged Asherah for a companion. Asherah heard her
  pleas.
While Lilith was sleeping beneath a cedar tree, Asherah gathered the dust of
  the earth and created a second woman, Naamah.
And Lilith was bewildered when she awoke. She shouted as if a screech owl,
  but Naamah quieted her, and held her hand.
And Lilith laid with Naamah. Then they praised Asherah, and named that
  place Eretz Nashim.

Then Lilith and Naamah left the cedar forests of Adomea and roamed the
  young world.
They delighted in all aspects of Creation and worked to improve the world,
  and their own lives.

To better understand each other, they created the first language.
To keep themselves warm at night, they learned to start their own fire.

Twelve years passed, and Asherah saw the love between Lilith and Naamah
and was pleased.
She decided that they were ready to bring about the Second Creation, and
complete the world.
Yet Asherah knew that more women were needed for the task, and so She
sent three consort-seraphim.
Thus would the earth be populated by innumerable humans, working together
for a better future.

Lilith and Naamah met the consort-seraph Resh on the wild plains of Terea
as he tracked the great beast Erkhis.
He saw Lilith and Naamah from the hilltop, and bowed before them in
humble servitude.
Lilith grasped his spear and declared: "You will teach me how to hunt so that
I might slay this beast."
And Resh did as he was bidden. Thus did women learn the art of the hunt.

Then Lilith took his spear, and Naamah took his bow and quiver.
They pursued the great beast Erkhis for three days before encountering it.
Naamah wounded it with her bow, and Lilith then slew it.
Resh butchered the beast with his knife and they feasted on its flesh for six
nights and six days.
Thereafter, Resh was a companion to Lilith and Naamah.

Lilith and Naamah met the consort-seraph Koth in the deserts of Kadesh.
Tormented by the hot sun, the women sought refuge in a cave.
To their amazement, the cave was dank, and full of edible greenery, arranged
in rows.
Lilith praised Asherah, saying: "Thank you, my God, who has given us the
gift of edible plants."
Thus Koth heard Lilith, and approached the women from the shadows of
the cave.

Koth welcomed his guests and superiors, and begged that he may teach them
how to grow plants as he did.
Lilith and Naamah agreed. They stayed in Koth's cave for sixty nights and
sixty days.
Thus did women learn the art of farming.
Thereafter, Koth was a companion to Lilith and Naamah.

Lilith and Naamah were at first content to stay in the comfort of Koth's cave, but Asherah placed restlessness into their hearts.

They took Resh and Koth and traveled to distant Turia, to the land of Onamir.

There, they came upon a mighty construction of piled stones.

Then the consort-seraph Akhat, mightiest of all, emerged from the structure.

And Akhat spoke, saying, "I built this temple in reverence for Holy Asherah, blessed be She.

Follow me, and I will teach you how to manifest this miracle."

Lilith and Naamah followed Akhat into the temple, and Akhat taught them to bake bricks and stack them.

Thus did women learn the art of construction.

Then Lilith commanded that Resh, Koth, and Akhat build a second temple alongside the first.

For six years, the women worked alongside the consort-seraphs.

When it was done, it was even mightier than the first.

Resh caught a mighty elk, and sacrificed it at the temple's altar in praise of Asherah.

These were the Five Progenitors:

The two women: Lilith and Naamah.

The three consort-seraphs: Koth, Akhat, and Resh.

Together, they journeyed throughout the world.

Lilith and Naamah laid with the consort-seraphs, and each gave birth to sixty children.

The Five Progenitors raised the children and taught them of the Second Creation.

When they reached adulthood, the children left to the far corners of the world to bring about order and progress.

Lilith and Naamah lived for six hundred years, and at last grew weary of the world.

And Asherah rose from the sea and invited them to abide in Her holy Queendom with Her.

Lilith and Naamah each took a hand of Asherah, and together they descended into the depths.

And Resh, Koth, and Akhat followed them.

✡

Book of Strife

The children of Lilith and Naamah grew and multiplied. They traveled to every corner of the world.

They planted crops, tamed animals, and founded mighty cities.

These were the first cities: Haraseth, Akhalon, and Deben.

And there was harmony in the world, as all labor bent towards the improvement of the lives of all.

Now Kheron was the mightiest of the seraphim, and an old favorite of El.

He is deemed one of the Elohim, and his heart was as of steel.

Kheron looked upon the Earth with jealousy and saw the humans working.

Kheron spoke to himself, saying, "Has my Queen become lazy? Now she allows beasts to do the work of seraphim!"

Kheron went to Deben, which is in Maheyal. He went down to the port of that city.

There he met Tzalaam, a man who sailed ships to carry grain to distant lands in need of sustenance.

Kheron spoke to Tzalaam: "All the corners of the Earth desire your grain. Should you not demand recompense?"

Thus did Tzalaam become the first merchant, charging others for his grain. And Kheron was his advisor.

In time, the other mariners followed Tzalaam's example, demanding more for their work.

They no longer gave willingly, but demanded repayment.

Some cities could meet the new prices. Some chose not to.

Thus, the first conflicts began, and there was strife throughout the world.

And Kheron rallied the Elohim, and they joined him on Earth.

The Elohim spread throughout the cities and made themselves kings.

They taught the men how to forge weapons, and make women their property.

They led the men into battle to butcher each other.

In those days, all of humanity nearly perished.

Then Lilith the Lady of the Sea heard the prayers of the innocent, and begged Asherah to save them.

Asherah then saw the foul treachery of Kheron that had poisoned Her holy work.

She gathered her loyal seraphim and rose from the depths.

Kheron's army of men and Elohim met Asherah's divine force on the plains of Aron.

There, Asherah battled Kheron for six nights and six days. At last, she was victorious.

And Asherah slew Kheron, and the surviving Elohim scattered like dust.

Yet the wounds inflicted by Kheron have still not healed.

Greed, violence, and sin persist to this very day.

Only at the completion of the Second Creation will they be extinguished.

✡

Book of Heroes

After the war against the Elohim, the strong few still subjugated the impover-
ished many.

In those days, kings and queens ruled all of Hasmonea, and they did as they
saw fit.

And Asherah raised heroes in every land to deliver Hasmonea.

Yeviah was the mightiest man in of all of Adomea, and was cruel to its people.

Mod, the strongest seraph, saw the plight of the victims.

By the will of Asherah, Mod went to Yeviah's household in the city of Tirs,
in Adomea.

"I challenge you to a wrestle," Mod announced.

"Who are you to dare to challenge me, the greatest wrestler of Adomea?"
asked Yeviah.

"I have no name, but should I win this contest, you will harm your neighbor
no more," Mod said.

"You have no name, but I admire your physique. Let it be so," said Yeviah.

They stripped bare and wrestled.

Now Yeviah was a mighty warrior, and nearly won, but Mod prayed to Asherah, and at last pinned Yeviah to the ground.

So impressed was Yeviah with Mod's prowess that he took Mod as a friend
and lover.

Together, Yeviah and Mod traversed the extents of Adomea.

And Yeviah repented his ways, and sought to undo the cruelties he had inflicted.

They slew brigands, relaxed taxes, and opened safe passage between towns.

They adjudicated disputes, and brought justice to the people.

They built storehouses for grain, and temples for worship.

When Yeviah died, Mod died of grief as well.

The people of Adomea mourned the loss of Yeviah and Mod, and swore to
uphold their legacy.

The queen of Adomea, knowing her authority was no longer needed, abdicated,
and Adomea was free.

Ohad was a shepherd in the land of Hadinea, which was ruled by a wicked
king named Elimelekh.

Asherah spoke to Ohad, saying: "In My holy name, you will deliver Hadinea from Elimelekh."

Ohad hid a sword on his left thigh, as he was left-handed.

Ohad went to the palace of Elimelekh as an entertainer. The guards did not see his sword.

That night, Ohad danced before the king and seduced him.

The king led him into his bedchamber and laid with him.

Ohad waited until the palace was asleep.

Then, taking his sword, Ohad slew the king, and his family, and his guards, and the rest of the court.

And there was peace in Hadinea for two generations.

Shimshas was the greatest warrior in his day.

The king of Issalon sent Shimshas to oversee construction of a temple to El.

Shimshas journeyed to the port-city of Yaffa.

There, Shimshas saw the overseers of Bashan throwing the people out of their houses and beating them when they resisted.

"What is the meaning of this?" asked Shimshas.

An overseer answered him: "The king of Issalon has demanded that we build a temple to El."

Thus, we must evict this rabble from their homes."

"How can you say that this is justice?" asked Shimshas.

"The king wills it, and so it is just," answered the overseer.

Enraged, Shimshas struck the overseer, killing him on the spot. And then Shimshas fled into the desert.

Shimshas gathered the dispossessed around him, and together they waged war against the king of Issalon.

Now the king of Issalon saw that he could not contain the rebellion.

And he called forth Ezravel, his most handsome servant.

"I bid you," the king of Issalon said, "to enter the camp of Shimshas as if you were one of his followers. There, you must discover the secret of his strength."

And Ezravel journeyed to the camp of Shimshas.

He offered much food and drink to Shimshas, and the two laid together that night.

The next morning, Ezravel spoke to Shimshas, saying: "I beg of you a favor."

Shimshas replied: "Anything for so mighty a bed-fellow."

Ezravel said: "Only that you teach me the source of your strength."

Shimshas said: "This is a great favor to ask, but I will tell you. My chest hair is the source of my strength. If shorn, I will be powerless."

That night, Ezravel got Shimshas drunk, and then took a razor to his chest, and shaved his chest.

He then bound Shimshas and fled with him in the night.

He delivered him to the king of Issalon saying, "Thus lies your foe, now weakened."

And Shimshas was imprisoned by the king.

Yet the rebellion continued, for its strength lay not in the chest hair of Shimshas, but in the will of the people.

Two years passed before they stormed the palace of Issalon.

They slew the royal family and its palace.

Two righteous warriors found Shimshas in the prison, and released him.

The victorious people nursed Shimshas back to health. His chest hair re-grew.

Then Shimshas traveled to Yaffa, and with a single strike utterly destroyed
the temple to El.

He helped the people re-build their houses.

The people ruled Issalon in those days, and there was peace throughout the
land.

✡

Book of Naomi

In the time of the heroes, there was famine throughout the queendom of Terea.

In that land, there lived a woman named Naomi.

Now Naomi heard of food in the land of Bashan, and resolved to journey there.

She ventured to the farms on the outskirts of the city of Mahan.

There she met Ruti, who was tending to barley in the fields.

When Ruti saw Naomi, she begged Naomi to work the farm with her.

"I cannot join you," said Naomi. "For what is yours is yours, and what is mine
is mine."

But Ruti clung to her, saying, "Do not urge me to cast you away. Where you
will work, I will work. Your people will be my people."

Thus did Naomi joined the household of Ruti.

Naomi worked alongside Ruti throughout the harvest season.

One day, when Ruti was winnowing barley on the thresher floor, Naomi put
on perfume and her best clothes.

When Ruti lay down, Naomi approached quietly, uncovered the feet of Ruti,
and laid down with her.

Ruti awoke in the night, and saw Naomi lying next to her.

"I am yours, and you are mine," said Ruti.

And Ruti and Naomi knew one another as Lilith knew Naamah.

Now there were two men named Boaz and Asheramisherat who worked an
adjacent field.

When they saw the great bounty of Ruti and Naomi's field, they grew jealous,
for their yield was poor in comparison.

They took up weapons, and prepared to seize Ruti and Naomi's fields by force.

Ruti saw the men approach, and bade them to halt.

"These fields are yours, and all fields are ours," said Ruti.
"Yet you have kept your harvest, while our harvest is meager," said Boaz.
"Let our harvest be yours, then," Naomi said. "There is enough barley for everyone."
And Boaz and Asheramisherat shared their harvest with Ruti and Naomi, and both couples were prosperous.

Then more neighbors saw the good fortune of the barley farm, and asked to join.
In time, they became well-fed and strong, such that the soldiers of the king of Bashan would not dare approach them.
The king then fled the land to distant Kerosea.
Then the soldiers cast their weapons aside, and joined the people in the fields.

✡

Book of Sarai

In the time of the heroes, the monarchs of Hasmonea were all cast down.
Then the whole of the land of Hasmonea toiled to fulfill the Second Creation of Asherah, Blessed be She.
And yet, wicked self-appointed task masters stalked the fields. They beat those who fell from exhaustion, or failed to meet quotas.
The taskmasters slaughtered the fallen and baked their blood into the clay bricks.
Thus it was that for every tower palace raised, the Second Creation was spoiled.

Sarai was a Hasmonean smelter. Life was bitter, and filled with hardship.
One day, she gathered all of the smelters in her factory to her.
Sarai spoke to the people, saying, "There can be no Second Creation when the people suffer!"
Then the workers cast their hammers to their feet, and would work no more.

The lead taskmaster, Azekhel, learned of the deeds of the workers.
And Azekhel sent forth his warriors to kill one-tenth of all of the workers in Sarai's factory.
When they arrived at the town, they found that all of the workers, in every factory, had cast aside their tools.
"We cannot fight so many, for surely we will be killed in the press," said the warriors.
And the warriors withdrew to the camp of Azekhel.

Azekhel was enraged by the timidity of his warriors, and all of his officers and one-sixth of his soldiers.

He then marched on Sarai's town with one thousand of his finest troops.

When he arrived, he found that the workers had constructed towering barricades.

And Azekhel said: "Let the leader of this rebellion step forth."

And Sarai appeared atop the battlements.

Sarai said: "I am not the leader of the rebellion, but I will speak as its voice."

Then Azekhel said: "How dare the people of Hasmonea refuse to work! Your idleness is profane to Asherah, blessed be She!"

Then Sarai said: "It is a sin to work the people to exhaustion and death. It is you who have profaned the Second Creation."

Azekhel said: "Do you not see my army before you? We will burn your town to the ground and rebuild it in the name of Holy God."

Sarai said: "If this is the will of Asherah, then I despise you, being but dust and ashes."

Then out of the depths of the ocean came Lilith and Naamah, first of women.

Lilith and Naamah rose from the depths, advanced across the Valley of Bashan, and entered the town.

And Lilith spoke: "Who are you, Sarai, to make such demands of Asherah?

Gird your loins like a woman, and answer me:

Were you there when Asherah laid the foundations of the Earth?

Were you there when Holy God laid out the plans for the Second Creation?

Were you there when we, first of women, were sent forth to seek the consort-seraphs?

Can you know the fate of this world, and what is to come after?

Can you slay El, cursed be the name, and bring order to chaos?

Would you discredit Her justice? Or will you take up the labor that She demands?"

Sarai answered, saying: "Yet there must be peace as well, and time for contemplation, and study.

And until Asherah, blessed be She, relents, we will lift our hammers no more."

Then Naamah spoke to Sarai, saying: "Then let this be the will of Asherah:

The workers of Hasmonea will rest on the seventh day of the week, and there will be peace in the land.

And on the six other days of the week, they will work to repair this broken world."

"These terms are fair, and we will accept them," said the workers.

Then Lilith spoke to Azekhel and his soldiers, and said: "Go now from these lands, and trouble its people no more."
Azekhel begged for forgiveness, and then left with his army.

Naamah then spoke to Sarai, saying: "Yet the Second Creation is not yet complete.
The suffering of Azekhel will heal in time, but only with the labor of the people."
And Naamah and Lilith kissed Sarai, and returned to the ocean depths.

Then the people tore down their barricades and returned to their labors.
For six days, they tended to those who had been harmed by the soldiers of Azekhel, and removed all statues and icons of him.
And the people of Hasmonea rested on the seventh day.

This is why a Hasmonean will welcome the Sabbath Brides on the seventh day of every week, and rest on that day.

✡

Book of Lilith

All of Hasmonea mourned as one:
How crushed are the people, once so full of vigor!
How like mourners of children they are, once favored among all workers.
Once free, now subjects of imperial whim.
The warriors of Hasmonea have been slain. The wooden poles have been burned.
After proud labor in the name of Holy God, Hasmonea serves a base master.
The roads once distributed material to the needy, so all may have enough.
Now the roads channel the best of this land to fatten the rich.

We remember that bitter day, the ninth of Av,
When the Pharostines appeared in their tall ships.
They disembarked in every port city, and massacred the carpenters and dock-workers.
The harbors turned the color of blood, and a wail went up from the people.
The Hasmoneans were powerless to resist.

And the filthy Pharostines broke the temples of Hasmonea and burned the holy texts.
They forced the people of Hasmonea to worship their Elohim.
They forced the children into their own schools, and the children forgot the language and song.

The Pharostines deemed themselves holy.
False! For no one is holy who oppresses the people.

Look, O Queen, and consider, for I am despised.
See, Queen, how distressed I am! I am in torment within, and in my heart
I demand justice.
The children of the Elohim have heard my distress, and rejoice at my de-
struction.
This is why I weep and my eyes overflow with tears.
My people are desiccated and the enemy of all hope has prevailed.
The Queen is righteous, yet I must rebel and end my suffering.
May you bring the day of redemption swiftly. Let me take up the Second
Creation once more.

And Asherah spoke: "I will send Lilith, first of all women to you. Find her
in the town of Arekhem.
In my name, she will deliver you from the whip of the Pharostine Empire."
The people journeyed to Arekhem, and: Behold! There stood Lilith, first of
all women.

And Lilith spoke to the Hasmoneans:
"I am Lilith, first of all women, redeemer of Hasmonea. In the name of
Asherah, I declare:
I will guide you with an outstretched hand, and deliver you from the Phar-
ostine Empire.
Each of you will be my Hammer, with which I will smite the imperialists.
Go now, and bring justice and peace to the people!"

✡

Book Of Hasmonea

Thus it was that we waged our war against the Pharostine occupiers.
For Lilith raised hundreds of righteous Hammers to smite the Pharostine bat-
talions.
Wherever the Pharostines went, we ambushed and killed them.
Then we left the factories and refused to work until ownership of the land was
returned to us.

Yet Lilith proved to be faithless, as all messiahs must be.
For Lilith, seeking personal advantage, signed a truce with the wicked Phar-
ostines.
The Pharostine Empire appointed Lilith as queen of Hasmonea.
The land remained a dominion of the Empire, and Lilith was its queen and tyrant.

Thus it was that we cried out in anger, saying:

"Hasmonea needs no queens or masters! Let Hasmonea be ruled by the people."

Then the majority of the Hammers proved to be faithless to Asherah, and followed the orders of Queen Lilith.

But a small group of Hammers resisted. They became known as the Hammers of Asherah, and they were righteous in the eyes of Asherah.

And there was bitter war in Hasmonea between the faithful Hammers of Asherah and the Hammers of the False Lilith.

The Hammers of Asherah journeyed throughout the land of Hasmonea, from Maheyal to Rabath.

They spoke to us of a better future, without queens or masters, where no messiah was allowed.

And we desired this future, and believed it possible.

Thereafter, passage was denied to the Hammers of the False Lilith.

We refused to give them food or shelter.

The Hammers of the False Lilith then sought to take these things by force.

They burned our farms and killed our children in the name of a false peace.

Outraged, we at last joined together as one.

We did not need Lilith-the-false-messiah.

We never needed Lilith-the-false-messiah.

For the Second Creation could only be completed in a world of peace, ruled by the people.

And we could not have a single guiding person.

We had to act together without hierarchy or perish in the attempt.

The Hammers of Asherah multiplied in number.

For every life lost by those who fought for Asherah, another two took their place.

Gradually, the reach of Lilith was diminished until she controlled only the city of Haraseth.

And the Hammers of Asherah surrounded Haraseth and demanded that Lilith step down as queen.

And yet even then, Asherah hardened the heart of Lilith, who resolved to flee and call for Pharostine reinforcements.

Then six brave Hasmoneans infiltrated the city of Haraseth. And their names were: Ori, Dvora, Rakhel, Esther, Yezevel, and Asaf.

They found Lilith sitting on her throne. They slew her guards. And Ori cut off the head of Lilith.

Then all of the remaining Hammers of the False Lilith laid down their arms.

They opened the gates of Haraseth and invited in the righteous.

We cast down the statues and icons of the wicked Pharostines, and of the false Lilith.

And the Pharostines, seeing the strength of the people, sued for peace.

And thereafter, we have ruled our land together, in peace, harmony, and toward the repairing of the broken world.

The Premiere

Hunter C. Eden

> *"We only kill each other."*
> —Benjamin "Bugsy" Siegel

I was the best shot in the whole goddamn division, no kidding. Even the farm boys from the Midwest couldn't outshoot me. My old man ran a dry goods store in Brooklyn; I didn't know from shooting. But they put that M1 carbine in my hands, and magic happened. At Eisenborn Ridge, I put a round clean through the eye of an SS piece of shit. Two hundred-fifty yards out, and I shot a hole in the bastard's face like he was standing ten feet away. I'm not saying I never missed. Everybody misses. But I never missed when it really counted. Except Bugsy.

1947, two years after I got out of the service. They offered me $10,000 if I could pull it off. I don't know why they wanted it done and I didn't ask. Story I heard was he helped himself to money the Commission gave him to build hotels in Vegas. Meyer didn't want him killed, but boyhood friendships don't feed the bottom line. So I went out to Beverly Hills at midnight. I could see him in his living room from where I crouched in the bushes. I had an M1 carbine, exactly what I used in Europe, but a kid with a pellet gun could have hit him. I missed. That made 1956 possible.

We all stood on that beach, under the palm trees. A leaky little yacht—the *Granma*, they called it, like your *bubbe*—lurched across the water. Bugsy stood next to me, dressed in pinstripe like he was going to a Hollywood party. "Look at this! It's fucking *Sands of Iwo Jima*! You ever see *Sands of Iwo Jima*, Katzie?" I told him I didn't watch movies. Maybe he knew it was me nine-and-a-half-years before and maybe he didn't, but he made amends with the Commission and business went on. You forgive a lot in this line of work. It's too expensive not to.

I think there were about forty of us with Thompsons and grease guns and a couple boxes of grenades, a chilly night wind tousling the palm trees. We smelled the diesel, watched them clinging like ants as the yacht tilted back and forth like maybe it would flip. Eighty-one guys on a twelve-man boat; give the Reds credit for *chutzpah* at least. The yacht hit a sandbar and they climbed off and started wading towards the beach, rifles held up over their heads. Bugsy clapped me on the back. "Show these commies how you did it in Germany." We opened up.

There wasn't enough left of that Castro fella to take back, but the other one, I'll never forget. Greasy asshole in a beret, lousy beard and hair probably hadn't been washed in a couple weeks. I had the barrel of my M1911A1 to the back of his head, and he started babbling in Spanish. Bugsy turned to the soldier they sent to "supervise" us, an old Cuban in a pressed green uniform.

"What's he saying?"

The Cube smiled. "He says, 'Do not shoot! I am Che Guevara and I am worth more to you alive than dead!'"

"He thinks we're CIA," I said.

Bugsy laughed. "Just contractors, Che. Just fucking contractors." He lit a cigar, nodded to me. Turns out you can end a revolution in fifteen minutes.

That was December 2nd. The fourth night of Hanukkah, '56. The menorah my *zeyde* brought with him from White Russia sat cold in my drink cabinet in Brooklyn, but we lit enough fires to make up for it.

✡

1971, Havana. Now it all comes back around. I'm out front of José Marti International Airport, all the way on the opposite end of the island from that beach. The city's changed in some ways: the skyline's got more light in it, for one, and you can finally get a decent corned beef on rye. In others, not so much. We got a different Batista, but one tinpot island asshole is as good as another, so long as the climate stays business-friendly and Red-free. And it will. That was the deal, and everybody wins except eighty-one assholes in four feet of water. Stars, execs, producers, heiresses, Kennedys, President Nixon with his winter villa . . . everybody comes to Havana, all the way down to the schmoes standing around me on the sidewalk, laughing and backslapping, champing at the bit to blow their quarterly bonuses on roulette and bring a case of the clap home to wifey.

I finish my cigarette as the car pulls up—nice, new Cadillac—and an oily-haired kid steps out. Probably a gigolo when he's not driving for Bugsy. I think he's Cuban, but he could be Italian or Jewish or all three. "Señor Black," he says. "Welcome." He takes my suitcase and I sit down in the passenger seat. We're going to Calle 23 in Vedado. That's where the premiere happens.

He pulls out into traffic, aiming deep into Havana, a tangle of skyscrapers, Spanish villas, and palm trees barely hiding the barrios where the actual Cubes live, kids in ratty shorts and t-shirts begging for a few pesos so they can eat, widowed mothers selling themselves on filthy sidewalks, homeless men passed out in alleys. There's more of that Cuba than Calle 23. You think Che and Fidel would have changed that? Don't bet on it.

The kid offers me another cigarette. "Your first time here, Señor Black?"

"Not hardly," I say, lighting it. "I probably been coming here since before you were born."

"You more Cuban than me, maybe," he says. He's right. Without us, what would this city even look like? If they'd left things in Batista Senior's hands, we'd have the hammer and sickle a hundred miles from Miami. Instead, this island's so kosher you could eat it for Passover. Israel is for the prophets and pioneers, the reformers and rabbis. Our kind of yid, we remade Havana in our own image. It's Scumbag Jerusalem.

You don't get a lot of second chances in life—especially when it comes to guns. I can thank Meyer for this one. We met in Cohen's Deli in Miami at a little table in the back. You'd think he was just another *alte kacker*, sitting all alone eating his matzah ball soup. This is how he wants it done:

The Shtarker premieres at the Harry Cohn Theater, next to the Playboy Club Havana. I'm going to sit up in the box with Bugs and watch the picture, have a few drinks, make sure he's at ease. The credits roll, I'll down another quick drink, pull that same M1911A1 out of its shoulder holster, and empty the clip in Bugsy. By sunrise I'm in Miami.

"Why now?" I asked.

He cut a matzah ball in half with his spoon. "I didn't think this *Shtarker* picture would go anywhere. I figured nothing would come out of it except he'd waste a bunch of dough, which is why I told him he had to use his own. I turn around, and the picture's going to be released in a week."

Time was, Meyer would have been on top of that and I would have been to Havana and back months ago. He's old now. They're all old. Alex Birns is on parole; spends more time on the racquetball court than running Cleveland. Abe Bernstein's done shit since the end of the Purple Gang. Mickey Cohen's rotting in the Atlanta pen. Fuck Mickey anyway, palling around with Billy Graham, pretending to be Christian.

Meyer took a sip of Dr. Brown's celery soda and looked into his soup. "I'm sick of this, Katzie. I been friends with this schmuck since we were running whiskey, but always with the limelighting. Thinks he's a goddamn movie star. And he cast a bunch of Italians. He couldn't have at least hired Jews?"

It's funny that *The Shtarker's* what pushed Meyer to end things. Bugsy does nothing but limelight.

He tried to get Batista Two to name him Mayor of Havana in '64. A couple years later, he called the Pentagon and offered to send a bunch of us to Vietnam to kill more commies. Just last year, he tried to become the U.S. ambassador to Israel.

Straws and dead camels, I guess.

"I don't pay attention to the movies," I said. Not when I can help it.

"Well you know who does? Every other fucking person in the free world. We've got a delicate thing going on in Cuba. The deals they made with us, the moment we start advertising is the moment it all falls apart, and Bugsy knows it. So the asshole decides he's going to make a gangster flick. Last thing any of us need is a picture like this coming out. Don't miss this time."

"Forty-seven was a fluke."

He looks at me, half the matzah ball quivering in his spoon. "Yeah, well, no more flukes. Now go get yourself some brisket or something."

✡

We hit Calle 23 and the last thing I want to do is go to this premiere. If it were up to me I'd take care of Bugsy and head right back to the airport. You don't think of guys in my line of work not wanting to go into the office, but there you have it. I don't want to have to watch the damn thing is all. You either believe in the pictures or you don't, and I don't.

The Calle feels like a giant pinball table. You bounce around, hitting all the targets in a neon daze until you find a hole somewhere to collapse in. It's five times the size of Vegas with a hundred times as many ways to go broke. You'll probably lose most of your savings by the time you've been through the blackjack tables at Solomon's Palace, Ezekiel's Wheel, and the Maccabee. If you've still got money left over, you won't after a few hours at the tracks and a few lap dances at Burning Bushes. Then it's back home to explain to the kids why they're not getting birthday presents. That's the story of Havana. Infinite variations but the same old tired plot. Like the movies.

I drop my bags at the Havana Rivera and head over to the Harry Cohn. Everyone's waiting around to catch glimpses of the stars as they pull up. I don't know why people care. It's all fake anyway. A bunch of putzes from the Anti-Defamation League chant and wave signs: *We won't stand by for public image genocide!" "MORE than gangsters!" "Schande fur die goyim!" "We're better than Bugsy!"* Dumb kids with shaggy hair and ugly moustaches, looking like *faygeles.* Someone's yelling about the movie being in "kosherface" because it's got more Italians than Jews in it; the director's some guy named Coppola and they gave the leads to this Al Pacino and this Marlon Brando. Everybody's all worked up over that. It's just a movie. I push through the crowd and head to the side door like Bugsy said. Up a set of stairs to Box #5, open the door and there he is.

Used to be people mistook Bugsy for a movie star. Good-looking guy, dressed sharp, always joking and laughing and throwing money around. And of course, he hung out with movie stars. Used to be friends with George Raft—you know, *Scarface.* Of course, when Raft stopped being big in Hollywood, Bugsy stopped giving a shit. Not giving a shit is probably the reaction you want from Bugsy anyway.

I remember once this asshole producer from L.A. came up to Bugsy when he was hanging around in Vegas. I can't remember who all was there. Elizabeth Taylor, maybe? They had a thing for a while. Those actors are all the same to me anyhow. Anyway, this producer makes a big show of greeting everyone except Bugsy. I'm sitting at the bar drinking a scotch and he turns to him and says, "I'm sorry, I don't recall seeing you in anything." Bugs says, "I direct." And this dumb fuck still doesn't know he's smoking dynamite, so he says, "What do you direct, Mr.—?" "Siegel," says Bugs. "And the answer is everything."

I used to box amateur. I was no Barney Ross, but I did okay. The worst part of boxing was waiting for the bell to ring on the first round, because you know you're going to take the kind of hit that rearranges your entire world.

This fucking producer stepped in with George Frazier and didn't even see the ropes. "Oh yes, *Bugsy*." You never, never call him that to his face.

I'm no rabbi, God knows. I've smacked around some assholes who deserved it and some who didn't, but you do it until the message registers and you walk away. Bugsy never walked away. He put that poor stupid bastard in a wheelchair for life.

That was Bugsy back when. Today he looks wilted. The hair he's got left is white, and his face is so loose and wrinkled it looks like it hangs off his skull. But his eyes—predatory blue, sharp as the neon cage he and Meyer built around this city. Eagle eyes in the face of a vulture.

"Katzie!" One spotted claw crawls up onto my shoulder, and the other steadies him on a cane. He waves to some Spanish starlet with a nice rack behind him. "Raquel, this is Katzie Black, from New York."

"Nice to meet you," I say, shaking her hand and trying to keep my eyes out of her cleavage. Bugsy gives her a hundred-dollar bill and a pat on her fine, round ass and tells her to go get a drink downstairs.

The box is something. Like a big balcony. There are armchairs to watch the show, a wet bar with plates of cold cuts and fresh fruit, and a full liquor cabinet. Bugsy put autographed photos all over the walls: Humphrey Bogart, Lauren Bacall, Jean Harlow, and a bunch of others I don't know. Bugs hands me a Montecristo #2 and points at the bar top. "Matches and the cutter over there. Fix yourself a drink."

I mix a mojito, light the Montecristo, and we exchange bullshit about how things are in the States. Meyer's fine, Carlo's fine, everybody's fucking fine. Then he cuts all that off and says, "Screw what those ADL *pishers* say, Katzie. This picture's going to change everything for us."

"How do you figure?"

He sits back in his armchair. "It's a true story." I think about how old Bugsy is, all the things he's done, and I'm not surprised he's crazy. Hell, he was always crazy. It's why people call him Bugsy to begin with. I start to wonder if this movie is some kind of life story. I hope I'm not important enough to be in it.

"There's no such thing as a true story in a movie. Even if it's based off somebody's life they change up so much that it's a lie in the end."

He looks out over the theater, all the stars gathering in their seats and up in the boxes. "No, all the best movies are true. But there are two kinds of truth. There's what happens, and there's what people want to believe happens. You maybe call that a lie, but that's the kind of truth our whole world is based on. Take '56. The papers just said it was "forces under the command of President Batista." People want to believe that. They don't want to realize the Feds came to me and Meyer. They want it to have happened a different way, so it might as well have, and that might as well be the truth. That's the kind of truth this movie is. About us."

I help myself to a slice of mango from the bar.

"Why tell any kind of story? Why bring the attention?"

Bugsy ashes his cigar.

"You watch it, and then you tell me."

Which is exactly the part of this game I don't want to play. I haven't sat through a whole movie since *Casablanca*. Last thing I saw in a theater before I shipped out. When I returned from Germany, I knew I could never go back to working in my old man's dry goods store, so I kicked around, did day jobs. Some nights I woke up in a sweat thinking I was back on Eisenborn Ridge. The furnace would make a loud clunking noise, and my dreams turned it into shellfire. First time it happened, I took the subway to a late-night theater and tried to watch *Back to Bataan* with John Wayne, that draft-dodging cocksucker. I left the movie after fifteen minutes. Like I said, you either believe in the pictures or you don't, and I couldn't. Not war movies, not comedies, not gangster flicks. They aren't real. I used to love that about movies. Not anymore.

I drank a lot, got into fights. Meyer heard about me after two Irishmen in Hell's Kitchen wanted to know what a kike was doing at their bar and ended up picking broken glass out of their faces. He liked the fact that I served, that I had fought the Nazis, that I was such a good shot. He asked me if I had a steady job.

Bugsy points me to one of the big armchairs and the lights go down. The Coppola guy gets up and talks about what a fight it was to get *The Shtarker* made. Paramount didn't want Pacino, Paramount didn't want Brando, but thank God Mr. Ben Siegel was willing to front the money and pull strings, because what we're about to see is like no other film ever made. Everybody goes crazy clapping and Bugsy stands up and waves from the box. This movie runs three whole hours. I get up and mix another mojito. Strong.

The Shtarker starts at a wedding in New York City, back in 1945. We see a *huppah* and a klezmer band and a bunch of people dancing the *hora*, but the scene is all about this fat, bulldog-faced guy sitting at a desk upstairs. That's this Marlon Brando, except in the movie he's called Vigdor Kornblum, and he's the Shtarker. He sees all these peddlers and shopkeepers and everything and they all fucking love him. He's their king, holding court.

The Shtarker has three sons: Max, who's just back from fighting the Nazis and has some *shikse* girlfriend; Sol, who's a hothead, banging some chick he met at the wedding; and Felix, who's a whiny little *nebbish*. Now there's a pushcart peddler talking about how much he believes in America and how he fled the Czar and all this Old Country shtick, but now some *goyim* raped his daughter after he did everything right and played by all the rules. Vigdor's going to take care of it because he's the Shtarker.

That's small, though. The Shtarker's big problem right now is that some Hollywood producer doesn't want to cast this singer (I guess he's supposed to be Eddie Fisher or something) because he fucked some broad the producer wanted. He's got to protect his investment, so what's the Shtarker going to do? "*Oy*, I'm going to make him an *onbot* he can't refuse." He gives the producer a warning—sends some *goy* henchmen to cut the head off a pig and leave it in his bed. The producer wakes up screaming. He sees all the blood and thinks he's been shot, but then he gets the message when he sees the pig head, staring back from between his feet. The singer gets the part.

The whole picture's full of that message stuff. Like this big bastard Lewis Brodsky, who's the Shtarker's muscle, gets clipped by one of Vigdor's enemies and instead of just making him disappear, they send a packet of lox wrapped in a bulletproof vest. The Shtarker's lieutenant, Kleiman, explains that back in Odessa, that meant that Lewis Brodsky sleeps with the fishes. We don't do things all cute like that and Bugsy knows it better than anybody. It's a lot of trouble, that symbolic shit, when a .40 caliber barrel to the temple takes two seconds to get the same result. It's got style, though, I'll give it that. The lines stick with me: "Someday—and that day may never come—I will call upon you for a *toivah*." "Revenge is a nosh best-served cold." "Leave the gun, take the knish." I wish we talked that way.

The Shtarker's son Max (that's Pacino and he's my favorite—went to the War like me) has to flee the country after he kills a bent mick cop in a restaurant, so he goes and spends some time in Israel. They shot it on location in Tel Aviv. I never went to Israel, but I feel like I'm seeing the best parts of it, even if it's an Italian showing me. Max marries a beautiful Israeli girl and it looks like maybe he'll never go back to New York, except she gets killed. I usually hate that sentimental tragic bullshit, but it makes me a little sad, I have to admit. Sometimes you can't catch a break. Believe me, I know.

The Shtarker dies and hothead Sol gets gunned down (that's James Caan) and Max takes over. The first thing he does is have all his rivals whacked. It's a hell of a scene. He's at his baby son's *bris*, and all that time there are these assholes who tried to screw him over getting strangled and shot and knifed. The last scene is him sitting in Vigdor's office, doing business while the door closes on his *shikse* fiancée. The new Shtarker.

It doesn't feel like three hours.

Bugsy pats me on the arm. "What'd you think?" I light a cigarette, sip my drink. I'm on straight rum now: Havana Club. I let the warmth run through me, wait for it to calm me down. You're always a little nervous, no matter how many times you do this. It'll be one-hundred and three once I'm done with Bugsy.

"I think it's a lot of bullshit, Ben."

"But it's good bullshit," he says, and he smiles.

"Yeah," I say, taking a drag. "It is. That Coppola, he's got some style."

Bugsy shakes the ice around in his drink, smile deepening. "It's based off a book. Guy named Philip Roth wrote it. He's pretty famous now."

"I don't care about famous, but I liked it." I can't believe it, but I did. Down below the audience is filing out to the afterparty at Solomon's Palace.

"Everybody's on about James Caan being the only Jew in a big role, but you know we used to play the Italians in the old gangster flicks?" Bugs chuckles, pulls another cigar out of his breast pocket. "Ed Robinson—you know, 'Mother of Mercy, is this the end of Rico?'—he was a yid. Now the Italians play us. That's what you call progress." He lights his cigar and stands up. "Now how about you finish your drink and do what you came here to do." I look up at him, and he smiles that smile that used to have all the broads in Hollywood at his feet. "'Forty-seven all over again." He pats his chest, right over his heart.

"What do you mean?" I stand up, but I don't draw, not yet. He laughs, puffs the cigar and focuses his eyes on me, blue and sharp and broken as a smashed glass.

"This ain't a Western. I'm not going to quickdraw you. But we both know why you're here. Hell, I asked for you. Just like I wanted you on that beach in '56."

He wouldn't bother with a setup. If he wanted me dead, I would've been dead. I pull the M1911A1 and aim it at his forehead. He can look down the suppressor, but he doesn't flinch—just sits smoking his cigar like I'm the firing squad.

"Go on. Pull the trigger."

He sees the question in my face and sighs. "You want to know why? Here." He pulls down his right eyelid to show an angry red knot of meat. "Stage Five. It spread to my liver, and from my liver wherever it wants."

"How long you got?" I lower the gun just slightly.

"The doctors say six months. But you and I know it'll be any second now."

I raise the barrel again, point it right at the center of his chest. In this line of work you get used to the idea that the Angel of Death rides on a twitch of your finger, but you also know that in the big picture, most of those deaths don't mean anything. The degenerate gambler who skipped on paying was always going to be a degenerate gambler who skipped on paying. The rat was going to rat out someone, somewhere anyway. You outlive your purpose, well, anyone who signs on with guys like Meyer and Bugsy knows that day's coming, that the guy you're drinking scotch with today will pat the dirt over you tomorrow. Our lives are as interchangeable as car parts: some cost more to fix than others, but we're all replaceable.

But sometimes there's something more. Sometimes you feel like maybe you aren't just deciding life or death—you're deciding something bigger, redirecting the little trickle of water that becomes a river. In '47, I felt it. Maybe that's why I missed. In '56, I felt it again, looking Che in the eyes as he begged. And now?

I don't feel it at all. Bugsy's damage is done. He's circled right back around from a no-account asshole to a king to a no-account asshole again, just with money and fame this time. This is waste management, nothing more. But I still hesitate, because he's grinning. Ear to ear. You never saw someone about to get clipped so happy.

"What the fuck are you so giddy about?"

He shakes his head, wheeze-cough-laughs out a spicy cloud of smoke.

"You know what makes the movies so great?"

"I hate the fucking movies."

"But you liked *The Shtarker*."

"That's one movie."

He drops the cigar in the ashtray, closes his eyes, spreads his arms like he's going to fly. "My parents were out of Letychiv. It's in the Ukraine now. Five of us in a one-room flat, barely enough money to put food on plates. You know the story. Bet you lived some version of it."

"We all did." I never hesitated before. You may miss, but you don't think about whether or not you should shoot, not when you've already drawn. It's when, not if. Do I fire now? In thirty seconds? Five minutes? Twenty years? When. Not if. But here I'm hesitating. Bugsy opens his eyes, like he's coming out of a dream.

"My kid brother's a doctor in L.A. I'm real proud of him. So were my parents. They were proud of me too. They knew maybe I broke some laws, but they saw a successful son, somebody important. Anything bad was just background, dust under the rug.

"You liked *The Shtarker* because it's realer than real. We ain't Meyer Lansky and Ben Siegel and Katzie Black, not as soon as those lights go out and the projector starts rolling. People see the way it *should* have been. Vigdor and Max and Sol. Men of honor. Tough guys. We're a little notorious, a little dangerous, but we're heroes. They'll want to be us, and then the way it *should* have been becomes the way everybody wants it to be, and that's as good as true. Che and Fidel understood that. How do you think they got eighty-one schlubs to pile onto a boat that couldn't fit twenty? They sold the legend. Everything was swept away."

Bugsy holds his hands up like he's framing a headline. "Hollywood mogul and gangland figure Benjamin Siegel assassinated by notorious hit man 'Katzie' Black. People will hear about you and I, and they'll flock to see the movie. It's great publicity. But it's more: they won't see the bloodstains, they won't know about the cancer. They'll just know the legend, and *The Shtarker* fills in the rest. We live forever. You want a World to Come? That's your World to Come."

Publicity. This was Meyer's idea. Bugs never thought like that. He had the vision but never the strategy. "Why do they have to know it was me?" I ask, but we both know the answer. '47. This isn't exactly revenge, but when the company gets downsized, the ones who pissed off the boss go first. Somebody shuffles outside the door, metal clicks on metal. I'm leaving this room under a sheet. As a legend.

"Do it."

I never liked Bugsy. A lot of guys did. He threw money around, bought drinks, always had beautiful women with him . . . it *was* like hanging out with a movie star. You know what I think about the movies, but that wasn't why I didn't like him. In our line of work, you're bound to be a piece of shit, and we deal with it in all kinds of ways. Lots of drugs, lots of booze, lots of women. Lots of excuses: families to support; it's the Jews against the world; we're kike Robin Hoods; it's just the way things are; in our day you either worked under gangsters or you became a gangster, and on and on. I always told myself that it all balanced out. I killed Nazis. If I killed a few more schmucks back home, well, you look at the camp photos and tell me I didn't redeem myself. I'm a soldier, that's all. Not everyone agrees with every war. Just differences of opinion.

But Bugsy—Bugs does this shit because he flat-out fucking loves it. The pain, the double-crosses, all of it. A shark in bloody water. A shark who can make you think the beach is safe because you can't see his fin. A shark who wants me to tell everyone else to never mind and keep swimming while I'm carrying the bodies off the sand. I'm not part of the legend. I'm just its janitor.

He picks up his cigar again, looks like a producer at a board meeting.

"You and I'll be in the sequel. Cast Robert Redford as me. Open on the beach, waiting for the *Granma* to land. Show us as patriots. Coppola'll get somebody good to play you, don't worry. End in this room, you and I. Cut."

The nerves leave me, and I feel a sudden peace. I don't want to believe this story he's telling. I know the truth.

"You know what?"

He looks like I just woke him up by screaming in his ear. "Know what? Know fucking nothing, Katzie. Conversation's over. Do it."

I loosen my finger on the trigger, drop the pistol on the armchair.

"Fuck you, Bugsy."

His eyes narrow, two coals of blue fire sinking into a sea of wrinkles.

"What did you just say to me?"

"I called you Bugsy," I said. "And I told you to take this legend and go fuck yourself."

I turn and walk towards the hallway with ten footsteps left on this earth. The business will go on. Cuba will be a neon jewel with a rotting belly until either the people or the CIA get sick of us. They'll get somebody else, probably, but as far as I know, Bugsy will die in a hospital bed, wasted and numb with morphine, too proud for suicide as Catholic priests sniff around like vultures. That's the story I want to believe. That's the truth I take out of this world.

This isn't the first time I walked out of a theater mid-show.

Roll credits.

If the Righteous Wished, They Could Create a World

Jack Nicholls

"In the name of God, wake up."

Then a grinding crash, followed by a series of mechanical clicks.

He had been rising to consciousness slowly, turning gentle somersaults in the workshop and letting the varied voices of Metatron filter through the background noise of the station. But it was that crash that pulled him fully awake.

"Perfect timing, Rabbi Oberman, Oberman," said Metatron. "Nicely done, done."

He was still wearing his spacesuit. The voice of Metatron crackled from the station's speakers and from his helmet's radio. There should have been no time lag, but they were out of sync, giving him the feeling that there were other people in the station. Voices overlapping.

He muted the module's speakers and strained to hear something else. Fans whirred and the coolant pipes rattled. Then a series of distant clangs towards Zenith. Sound where there should be no sound.

His headset crackled again: "It is 10:16 Jerusalem time, and we are looking good on ISA composition five-six-four, three-two, one-one."

He kicked off clumsily, his limbs sluggish, and rose from the workshop towards the *sukkah* module. Passing through a connective corridor choked in cabling and freeze-dried food, he braced himself in the doorway and halted his rise to survey the room.

The *sukkah* was marked by the dried palm fronds strapped to the wall. High-powered fluorescents chased away any shadow—there was nowhere to hide. He counted one fold-out table. One bedroll velcroed opposite the palm leaves. One unlit menorah safely in its combustion chamber. Two pictures held in place by magnets: a faded family snapshot from Gordon Beach, and a black-and-white photograph of President Einstein with his inauguration quote, "Let us remember our past, but turn to our future."

One red marker pen drifted loose over the table, the only object out of place.

He returned the pen to its sheath on the wall.

Had he heard something? Solitude bred odd fears, but he couldn't help but remember the Talmud's warning that space was hostile to God, and home to monsters.

Beyond the *sukkah* module was a cheap plastic curtain that shielded the toilet cubicle. There was room for someone in there.

He reached out his glove and twitched aside the curtain.

Empty. The suction tube was crusty with old urine in the depths of the nozzle. He should clean that. Hygiene was important, though not his priority.

He was still alone. Of course he was. He let the curtain fall.

"Are you secure, Rabbi Oberman?" asked Metatron.

He nodded to the camera.

There was a long pause, during which he let himself drift, meditating on the whir of the fan. Then Metatron spoke again.

"We'll begin the sculpting."

He had work to do. He gripped the edges of the doorway to launch himself, and swam back up to the workroom at Nadir.

Aboard the *Maharal*, every movement could be interpreted as a rise or a fall, but he liked to think of himself as always ascending. He spun as he rose to the cupola, so that the hexagram of viewing windows rotated above him. The windows looked out onto 2100 Ra-Shalom, a C-Class asteroid gripped tight in the *Maharal*'s robotic pincers. Blasted out of its parent body, the asteroid was only thirty meters across, but it filled most of the view.

Beyond Ra-Shalom and currently drenched in sunlight—the Earth. What would it have looked like from up here, during the Creation? Shifting colors against the darkness as the waters gave way to land, and the land bore fruit.

He could just barely make out Israel, a narrow strip of green between the desert and the sea. A nation forced to launch its Shavit rockets west, against the rotation of the Earth, for fear of provoking its neighbors. It was a tiny, fragile place that could be wiped out in an instant.

The station reflected the homeland in that way.

He felt protective, but there was nothing he could do for the community down there except pray. His work was up here with Ra-Shalom, and the fifty-three creatures built from it.

They were barely visible, black on black, the asteroid devouring itself. In total silence, the crawling golems scraped at the regolith. The mining eroded their hands faster than it did the rock, but the golems could work down to their elbow nubs, and were an endlessly replenishable resource. Silicates, iron and nickel were kicked up into the dust canopy, from where they could be filtered into the *Maharal*.

His little children. Were they content? He thought they probably were. They were doing exactly what they were made to do—something few enough of God's creatures could boast. And through their labor the children of Israel would dominate the Heavens as they had never been able to dominate the Earth.

"Recording on, we are launching ISA ritual one-two-two, three-one, seven-two: testing remote prayer with *in situ* assembly," declared Metatron. "Simulating total isolation. Is our maker pure and undefiled?"

"Purity...check," confirmed another of the voices.

"Okay, Oberman, it looks good. Proceeding."

The rock and dust from Ra-Shalom was loaded into exterior chutes from where it was crushed, sieved, and deposited into an internally accessible drawer. He pumped some air in to break the vacuum seal, then pulled open the bin of regolith.

Unformed substance, leftover from Creation. Primarily clay and silicate rock, with a smattering of iron and nickel. Much weaker than terrestrial kaolinite, and in a gravity field it could never be made to hold its own weight. Here in the Heavens, however, it would do.

He took a water pack from among the fifty-one strapped to the workroom walls. It was stamped with an ideogram of Mt. Hermon, marking it as sourced from the mountain's snow, launched by Shavit rocket and transferred to the *Maharal* by golem, without ever touching human hands. Pure.

He tilted the pack over the bin of regolith and squeezed gently. A drop of water appeared at the nozzle and swelled until it was the size of his fist and quivered with tension. He cupped the water in his gloves and eased it free, then guided the ball of water towards the bin of powdered rock. He had to press it down carefully, wetting the surface so he could mix the water and earth without sending a cloud of debris up into the module.

Once he had kneaded the snowmelt and regolith into a gritty paste, he began to rub it back and forth between his gloves. The mud rose in a tube from his hands, swaying back and forth in front of his face. He tried a forty-degree bend, and hairline cracks spread at the curve—more water needed.

The cylinder grew and twined around him in the weightless cabin. When he had fifteen handspans he tore off a good chunk from the top and swam to the worktable where he could lock his boots into two grips on the floor. Braced in place, he slapped the mud against the tabletop.

He kneaded the shapes quickly, joyfully. It wasn't easy sculpting with insulated gloves, but the long tapering fingers had been designed with craftwork in mind. He formed, weighed, and created, while sunset flared briefly across the planet and they rotated into night. Ra-Shalom fell dark.

Metatron was silent, except to mark the time.

"Ten minutes."

"Twenty minutes."

At thirty minutes he had made the shape of a man, about a meter high. Its legs were proportionally short, its head sunken into the torso, its mouth gaping open to receive the Word. Clay fingers were too fragile for manual work, so the hands were just a paddle with an opposable thumb.

It was as practical as he could manage without breaking the outline of the human form. A golem's material didn't matter—any inorganic would do—but the form was everything. God created man in his own image, and something in that initial Act had set the laws governing creation forever after.

Satisfied, he poked two eyeholes into the clay and released his little man to drift up to the cupola, limbs splayed. That was the easy part.

"We have first stage completion, Rabbi. Well done! We'll begin composition now."

He glanced at the laptop clipped beneath the window. The letters of the previous composition still glowed on its screen, *VavYud-BeitSamekh-PeiKaf* (Thinking-Working, Wisdom-Sleep, Dominion-Life). Now they flashed and rearranged as new instructions arrived.

The workroom printer chattered, and from its slot he pulled a square of tissue-thin paper printed with Hebrew letters. Two hundred and thirty-one pairs, arranged in thirty-three rows of seven columns.

Five millennia of rabbinical experimentation had uncovered only a few working rituals. The Sweeper. The Echo. The Guardian of Rabbi Loew. In the pre-modern era, a composition like this would have taken a master rabbi a day of painstaking work, and a single misshapen stroke would have rendered it unusable. Today, the ISA's computers could spit out a perfect recipe in seconds, and their software was faster than any scholar at identifying successful patterns.

He studied the Word. Today's composition was only a slight variation on Tzadok's 1867 formula for industrial work. The familiar string of *MemGimel-MemYud-YudDaleth* (Earth-Wealth, Earth-Working, Working-Fertility) held the key position in the seventeenth row, modified by Kushner's 1981 *AlephZayin* (Air-Walk) for zero-gravity. Together, that cluster formed the lynchpin of Israel's offworld mining technology.

After memorizing the formula, he painstakingly rolled the composition into a tight cigar and pushed it into the slick mouth of the unfinished golem. Once it was securely lodged inside, he pinched the lips closed.

"Things are looking good in there," said Metatron approvingly.

The cameras watched his every move. Even if the composition were successful, it could be tricky to replicate. Every sound and gesture would need to be studied by the ISA's future rabbis.

There was a click on the radio, and then a new, expressionless voice. A recording of a solemn male voice, his pronunciation perfect.

"*Aleph-Shin... Lamed-Kaf...*"

Creation was the chokepoint. At best, a traditional craftsman could compose two golems in a day, barely keeping pace with the loss rate. But if the compositions could be automated and the golems sourced from local material, then a single artisan could found a colony.

He closed his eyes, and began to rotate himself clockwise.

He spun in a vessel which spun around a planet which spun around its star. The universe was always spinning, and God was the tether. He reflected on this, as the computerized chant wove together the energies of creation.

"*Aleph-Ayin...*"

Aleph was the beginning and end, the sum of life.

"*Hey-Zayin...*"

$E=mc^2$. Mass is a form of energy. The First President had used those Latin letters to describe Creation, but only Hebrew had the power to channel it.

"*Reish-Yud... Vav-Tav...*"

There were twenty-two letters, from *aleph* to *tav*. Through them, God formed all beings which are in existence, and all those which will be formed in all time to come.

"*Chet-Tav... Pei-Tav...*"

Picture the twenty-two letters arranged on a sphere. There are 231 lines that can be drawn between the letters, linking each to each. These combinations of pairs are the gates of knowledge. All 231 gates must be spoken, and their sequence defined the capacity of the golem.

"*Samekh-Beit...*"

Two hundred and thirty-one gates could be combined in more ways than there were grains of sand in the universe, and only one in ten thousand compositions had any discernible effect at all. For millennia, the best a scholar might hope for was to discover one successful composition in his lifetime. But then came the digital age. Coding advances and biogenetics had sparked new techniques for deciphering the letters of creation, and vice versa.

There was no end to learning.

"*Reish-Nun...*"

The gates had been spoken, the recorded voice fell silent. He became aware again of the whirring and clanking of the *Maharal*. Metatron came back on the radio, speaking reverently. "The patterning is complete. Awakening."

He wrapped an arm around the golem's back and pulled it close. The clay was hardening quickly in the dry air, but with his free hand he scored the final inviolate word into the golem's forehead. The first, middle, and last letters of the alphabet. *Aleph Mem Tav: EMET.*

Truth.

Where did truth come from, he wondered? Was our knowledge passed to us in the letters of the books, the letters of genetics, or the letters of God? Were the golems imprinted by their makers' personalities, or humans by God? Did God feel fear, anxiety and wonder? Could you feel wonder at your own creation?

The golem stirred and opened eyes still wet with snowmelt, and he decided that yes, yes you could.

The room filled with applause. "Congratulations Rabbi! Life has begat life!"

Another successful composition, another step towards perfection, but he felt blank. It didn't feel like a world-changing moment to him.

But the personnel down at Metatron were celebrating, not listening to him. "This opens up everything! A full cradle-to-grave assembly station..."

Cocooned in cheers, he watched the squat, awakened golem test its limbs, making little star jumps that sent it cartwheeling harmlessly into the viewing window. It took new ones a while to find their feet.

His gaze shifted from the golem diligently pumping its legs in a circle, to the darkness beyond the windows. There was a figure in a spacesuit, standing on the asteroid. A man.

It stood still, ignored by the golems at its feet, seeming more real with every passing moment. He became horribly aware of how clearly the thing could see him—framed in the hexagram, lit up brightly against the darkness of the void. He swam for the controls and switched off the fluorescents.

The station fell dark, leaving only a few LEDs to outline the bulkheads and console in green half-light. The cheers on the radio died away. A long pause, then: "Are you alright, Rabbi? What's happened to the lights?"

Ignoring them for the moment, he pressed himself back to the viewing window. The figure was gone.

An old story came to his mind. In the age of Rabbi Akiva ben Joseph, four righteous men had descended into the realm of darkness. One went mad, one died, one became a heretic, and only Rabbi Akiva returned safely home. He said that he had met himself.

Something touched him from behind. He jolted away, but then in the phosphorescent light, he saw it was only his new golem, still drifting loose across the workshop.

"Rabbi, what's happening in there?" asked Metatron again.

He was sure he had seen it. A man in a spacesuit, full height. But the *Maharal* held only one person. There were no other missions, and the last Shavit capsule had arrived two weeks ago. Nobody could have got out there.

Unless something had been there the whole time. Nahmanides wrote in his commentaries that spirits lived in cold and desolate wastes, and what was more desolate than an asteroid? What if something had lain spreadeagled against the rock for billions of years, until the agency had hauled it into low-Earth-orbit. A clinging spirit, which had stolen the form of a man.

A dybbuk.

"Oberman?"

He hesitated. The Israeli Space Agency was a rabbinical organization, but he still didn't want to report a dybbuk without evidence. This could even be some kind of stress test they had devised, to measure his psychological soundness.

He couldn't launch an EVA without authorization, but he needed to know what was going on outside. He turned back to his golem.

The clay man floated patiently while he gouged out enough of a hole in its chest that he could press a torch into it. Then he strapped a wrist-camera to its head, secured like *tefillin*. He linked the feed to a monitor built into the arm of his suit, and tugged the golem down with him to the airlock.

With a little push, the golem drifted slowly into the airlock, feebly waving its arms and legs. He slammed the hatch on it with a bang, and tapped the controls to begin the slow process of depressurization. The hatch bolts clicked into place and the hiss of escaping air filled the module.

Like all the golems, its instincts for its environment were sound. Once the airlock was in full vacuum it opened the outer hatch itself and climbed out onto the external trusses. He watched its camera feed on his arm-monitor. The lights of Earth hung upside down beneath it.

The golem pulled itself arm over arm down the spine of the *Maharal*, past the darkened solar sails where its brothers floated up and down, weaving a web of silicon to extend their reach and glory. He could hear its progress as well—little tap tap taps through the thin walls—and he drifted in sympathy with it, following its progress along the station.

Where was it? The golem was panning the camera across the surface of the asteroid, but its narrow torch beam picked out no sign of an intruder.

"Oberman, are you getting this?" asked Metatron. "We've lost visual."

The golem resumed its examination of the trusses. Illuminated in the circle of its torch was an ISA tether, clipped securely to the *Maharal's* rail.

It turned around, and the dybbuk filled the frame, clinging to the side of the *Maharal*. He glimpsed a faceplate, smooth and black like a mirror, then it launched itself with a hand outstretched. The visual-feed spun madly, he couldn't understand what was happening. He rose to the cupola, and in the light of the stars he saw the dybbuk wrestling silently with the little golem, the pair of them tangled in the tether only a few meters from the window.

Metatron was shouting, a senseless cacophony of overlapping voices. It was impossible to issue commands from inside the module, but golems had the instinct to defend their territory. It unclipped the dybbuk's tether at its belt, so that the struggling figures began to drift free from the cord. The dybbuk tried to snatch it back, but now the golem had wrapped itself around its face and was hammering away at its head.

The dybbuk gave up on the tether and seized the golem, tearing its leg away at the hip. Weakened, the golem was helpless to stop its further dismemberment, and then the dybbuk flung its broken little body out into space. It waved its last arm in farewell as it fell toward the darkened Earth, its chest torch shrinking to a pinprick.

The recoil from the throw had pushed the dybbuk into a spin, and the distance between it and the *Maharal* was growing. But it fired a series of short nitrogen busts from its backpack to right itself, and managed to get close enough to Ra-Shalom to snatch hold of the dust canopy.

It crawled upside down until it could rotate and settle onto the regolith, its boots kicking up puffs of dust. The golems at its feet went busily about their tasks, ignoring it.

The radio crackled again, and now Metatron sounded more panicked than he had ever heard. "Rabbi, you have to act, it's endangering the station."

They had seen it too, then. His hand strayed to the servo-controls. If he decoupled the *Maharal* from Ra-Shalom, he could send the creature back into the void. But only at the cost of disrupting the entire Israeli off-world mining project—and abandoning his children.

It was too late. The dybbuk launched itself silently from Ra-Shalom, glided across the gap, and disappeared out of sight of the cupola. A second later the *Maharal* resounded with a clang as it crashed into one of the trusses above.

Clank. Clank. It was scuttling around the outside of the ship, looking for a way in.

He pushed off the cold windowpane and glided silently backward into darkness. His priority was to defend the *Maharal* from anything that could threaten Israel's military secrets, whether it be natural or supernatural.

One clang, two clangs—heading towards Zenith. Then everything fell silent. He hung watchful in the dark.

The whirr of the fans picked up as they started pumping more air through the station. The creature was repressurizing the airlock. It was going to come inside.

He cast about for a weapon, but the *Maharal* had been designed with safety in mind. And if it was a dybbuk coming inside, what weapon could stop it?

Rabbi Eleazar had driven out spirits with the words of Solomon and a basin of pure water. He didn't have a basin, but there were still fifty packets of ritual-grade water in the workroom. He tossed a dozen down the length of the station and swam after them, gathering them up outside the airlock at Zenith. Through the porthole on the airlock door he could see a shadow shift in the darkness.

Metatron was chattering still, but he had stopped listening. He aimed the first pack down at the door and squeezed it hard, so that a ropey tube of water spurted out and splattered against the door. He tried again more gently. The water formed a hovering ball between him and the airlock.

The dybbuk was watching him through the porthole, and the barometer had climbed to 60 percent. He snatched water packs and pushed their nozzles into the growing ball of water, squeezing out their contents so that the quivering sphere swelled larger and larger. Its surface shimmered with pinpoint reflections of the station's emergency lights.

The wheel began to turn in sixty-degree arcs. Finally, the hatch bolts released loudly, and the dybbuk sprang.

Through the distorting lens of the blessed water, he saw a spaceman without a face, rising up from the darkness. His perceptions tumbled as he shrank back, and now he cowered in the depths of a deep well. The demon was falling towards him, its hands outstretched and gesticulating.

The dybbuk dove into the water without hesitation, and for a moment it hung frozen inside the fragile sphere. Then it burst through the surface, sending droplets spraying in every direction. The blessed water had failed. He had missed his moment.

He spread his legs to brace himself against the corridor and pushed back to collide with the dybbuk in the *sukkah* module. The world spun and they crashed together into the miniature Torah ark.

"Oberman, be careful, careful!" Metatron was shouting, the voices echoing from every direction.

They wrestled in the murky green light, pawing at each other as they careered through modules strewn with empty water packs. His gloves left streaks of clay on the dybbuk's shiny spacesuit. The demon was trying to undo the catches of its helmet, but he didn't want to see its face. He had to protect the work, it was endangering the work.

"It's run amok! Shut it down Oberman, Oberman!"

They fell together through the darkness, helmets knocking together. He glimpsed piercing eyes, a dark beard. He locked his legs around the dybbuk's torso and had raised his fists to bring down onto its faceplate, when he was transfixed by seven shafts of light.

Sunrise, through the star window of the cupola. *The Maharal* had crested another dawn.

Now he could clearly see that the dybbuk wore an ISA regulation space-suit, the same as his. Its tinted faceplate shone gold in the glare, and reflected his own identical helmet. Except, written in red marker above his own visor, he saw the mirrored word EMET.

He loosened his hold, and the dybbuk lashed out at his face, knocking his tinted visor up. He looked into his reflection and saw... nothing. His helmet was empty.

The form of a man. A hollow man.

He released his hold and flexed his empty gloves. "Wait," he tried to say, but he could not speak.

The other figure passed its hand across his helmet and drew back a thumb stained red. It had smeared away the letter *aleph*, so that his Word now read *MET.* Death.

His arms and legs went rigid. The intruder drifted back, unclipped its helmet, and revealed a narrow face framed by two floating, sweat-slick ringlets.

"Congratulations, Rabbi, Rabbi." said the voice of Metatron, echoing from both suits' headsets.

His mind was a fading echo. All matter is part of God's creation. And all matter returns gladly to God. He had done what he was made for, he realized, as he crumpled inwards. Israel was safe, and the balance tipped towards merit.

White Roses In Their Eyes

Matthew Kressel

They come into my house, stinking of weed, of prostitutes, of sweat. They stare at the indentations in the sheets where my family once slept. They weep. They pray. They curse G-d, beg his forgiveness, then curse him again. The floorboards are rotten from all their tears.

Sometimes I hold their hands. They feel me, but pretend it's their imagination. Sometimes I whisper in their ears. They hear me, but pretend it's their own troubled thoughts. (*Is this what we are? Are we all such monsters?*) Sometimes babies look up at me and point, and their mothers pretend not to see.

I touch them all, every last soul who walks through my house, even the ones full of doubt and hate. I reach for them so that I might leave a fragment of myself behind. So that I might linger in their thoughts like a troubling dream. So that tomorrow they might choose a different path. But how many will remember me in a day, a year?

Father used to say, "Don't curse the darkness, light a candle!" And I never understood that. Not until I heard you sing.

You heard my cries, Jeff, and turned them into music.

✡

Saturday, March 2, 2019

Dearest Mimi,

I awoke today to such wonderful news! I am beyond ecstatic to hear you will be receiving a Sholem Aleichem Award for Excellence in Yiddish Literature! Readers in the English-speaking world know you for your translations of the vast body of European Yiddish works. But I have always felt, as I'm sure you have too, that your translation work has overshadowed your own fiction. My heart soared like a gull when I learned that you are finally receiving recognition for your great contribution to world literature. Mazel tov!

So let me gush and flatter you to death, again for the umpteenth time, as you know I must. Oh, Mimi, this is not just because we are good friends. I truly believe *Ale Shtern in Himl* ranks among the best novels I've read in any language, and I am fluent in a dozen!

I visited Czernowitz in 1967 to receive my award, and the International Yiddish Conference was celebrating its 59th year. That number seemed large to me then. Is this year really its 111th? "To 120 years" indeed! How is this possible, Mimi? I merely blinked, and the Earth spun around the sun fifty-two more times.

I admit, I was severely tempted by your invitation to join you as your guest, but I'm afraid travel has become too difficult for me. And besides, this event is to honor *you*. You should not have to babysit this doddering old woman. No, go alone and enjoy the lavish attention and praise to be heaped upon you, which is most deserved.

I am also very happy to hear that Eve has at last received tenure. Besides you, Mimi, she is the smartest woman I know, and I'm sure the Germanic Languages department will be in good hands for decades to come. I do miss all of you dearly, and think about those days often. (But not the grading! I shiver to think of it!)

As for speaking to your class on the Haskalah, I assume this was asked in jest. You do know my age, yes? But if you were indeed serious, Mimi, even if I could travel all the way up north to see you, I haven't taught a class in years! What interests me now is not what interested me then. I would bore your students with long tangents on the differences in the early translations of Shakespeare into Yiddish. Or worse, I might forget what I was saying in the middle of a sentence. Yes, Mimi, I worry I may have (*kaynehoreh*) the beginnings of dementia.

I forget things sometimes, but these occasional senior moments are not what trouble me. I've been having horrible nightmares. I find myself back in Amsterdam, where I lived until I was twenty-five. But oddly I am not in our apartment on Merwedeplein. No, Mimi, I find myself on the top floor of Father's office, his Opekta building on Prinsingracht. There I float around like a disembodied ghost, while sad, moping people linger about, examining the furniture and walls as if this is a museum. I never lived in this space, Mimi, yet in these dreams it feels as if I've lived there for an eternity.

In these dreams there is so much sadness I feel the whole world might break and come crashing down upon us all. And then I awake, crying and afraid, and it takes me many minutes to remember who and where I am.

I know I am not this disembodied girl, that this is merely a delusion brought on by a slowly degrading mind. But these dreams feel so *real*, Mimi. I feel as if I am this girl and she is me, and if but for the flip of a coin we might share each other's fate.

I've dreamt of her every night for weeks. And in a strange way, I have grown quite fond of her. I know this sounds crazy, but I hope to learn all about this strange girl before I depart this earth. Because I believe she is trying to tell me something.

With Love,
Anne

✡

She was only a little older than me when she came into my house with her parents. It was 1998, long before smartphones and iPods. She had her headphones on, and her eyes were far away. And as she turned into the sun, the little spinning disc on her hip sent rainbows dancing across the wall.

I thought she was hiding. Sometimes they close themselves off to hide from the truth any way they can. And it is my deepest wish to make them see. To make them *feel*.

I leaned in to say discomfiting things in her ear. To stir her to wakefulness. But this was my mistake.

She was already awake.

I heard a voice sing about a girl, born in 1929, launched to life on a bottle rocket, her wings drenched in milk and holy water.

You never said my name, Jeff, but I knew of whom you sang.

The girl with the music wasn't hiding. She was drowning. In me.

As were you.

I never found out her name. I never got to thank her for her gift.

✡

Saturday, March 9, 2019

Dearest Edie,

The babies! *Kaynehoreh*, they are as beautiful as sun through parting clouds! And two of them to boot! I love the photos dearly! I have stuck them on my bedroom mirror so that I may gaze upon their faces as I lay down to sleep and as I rise up each day to remind myself of the beauty of this world. I treasure them more than you know.

Little Petele does indeed resemble his namesake, don't you think? I am humbled and grateful that you chose to name him after his great-grandfather. I am sure Peter, may his memory be a blessing, would be deeply honored to know that his name lives on.

And Susan! What a lovely little bean! The joy in her eyes is infectious, and I smile and laugh each time I gaze upon her cherubic face. What a wonderful way to commemorate David's mother. Please, *please*, keep sending pictures! The children are so very beautiful.

I must confess, Edie, it baffles me how I have become a great-grandmother. In my mind, I am still that same little girl playing in the streets of Amsterdam. But my body daily tells me otherwise. Make sure you never get old!

I am delighted by your invitation to come and visit you and the family in Budapest for Pesach, but with tearful regret, I must decline. By some cosmic mixup, I'll be ninety this June—a great impossibility. And yet the woman who stares back at me in the mirror reveals the hard truth: I am old. I'm afraid such a long flight would be too much for this fragile body. I am sorry, Edie, that I will never get to meet my great-grandchildren. This saddens me more than you know.

As for what's new here in Miami, not too much. I take slow walks on the boardwalk and feed the gulls with stale bread. I play bridge with friends on Thursday nights. And sometimes, when the mood strikes, I go to shul. Mostly,

I read. A life of endless excitement, I know.

I just finished reading an excellent book called *Di Zumer Yorn* by Leah Ringelblum (the granddaughter of the famous historian Emanuel Ringelblum), about a Jewish family growing up in Alaska. Have you read it? I must admit all these Yiddish neologisms have me confused at times. I wish you could have seen Deborah's expression when I asked her what "butt-dialing" means.

Yiddish may be thriving in Europe, but here in the States, immigrants toss out their mother tongue like used bars of soap. Only *alte kockers* like me speak Yiddish, which is ironic because I only learned it as an adult! My first language was Dutch. Such is the twisted path of life we weave. Nevertheless, it's wonderful to write you in the Mother Tongue. I don't get to do that often enough.

It delights me to receive your letters in the mail, Edie. Please don't stop. While your father is insistent I use email, computers seem so impersonal, so cold. (I'm glad I retired before the university made email mandatory!) In handwriting you can really get to know a person.

My beloved Edie, may your beautiful children live to a hundred and twenty, in a world free of suffering and despair. Please let them know that I love them so very much.

Love,
Grandma Anne

P.S. What is this "Skype" thing?

✡

I listened, I listened, until the words flowed through me like honey. And I wondered, what made you think I'd never be afraid? I'm not afraid for myself. No, not anymore. After what I've been through, what could possibly frighten me?

No, I'm scared for all of you, Jeff. You make all sorts of vows, which you never keep.

All of you break your vows. You forget. You say, "Never again." And then you let it happen again and again and again and again and again...

✡

Monday, March 11, 2019

Dearest Joseph,

Thank you so much for the box of Jaffa Oranges in the mail! These days I have not been sleeping well, so their unexpected arrival has brightened these otherwise dreary and troubled mornings. Curiously, their vast number has declined to fewer than ten, as if by sleight-of-hand. And you should know it is with great willpower that I do not drop this pen and tear into another orange right now. Have you ever before tasted such deliciousness? Palestine is truly the land of Milk and Honey.

I am always delighted to hear about your success in forming another Integrated Kibbutz. I have thought long about this issue, and I agree wholeheartedly with you. The only way the Arabs will accept that Jews have an historic right to Palestine is if we, the Jewish people, accept that they have a right to live there as well. And so do the Christians. The firstborn of a household should not say to her siblings, "This house is mine," simply because she has lived in it for longer. No, siblings must share their ancestral home.

In the same way, simply because we Jews have a more ancient claim to the Holy Land does not mean it is the *only* claim. The solution is to share, and I believe your Integrated *Kibbutzim* are a profound way to express your ideals through action. That the product of your labors are fruits so delicious is testament to your cause.

While I know you and your mother had difficulties, that she was a firm believer that Palestine—Israel—should be a land ruled by Jews, I know for a fact Margot was proud of you and your work, even if she never expressed it.

On an unrelated note, I have a question you might be able to answer for me. I know you wrote your dissertation on 20th Century European Jewish History. In your readings, have you ever heard of a German man with the surname Hitler, somewhere in the late '20s to early '40s, just before the European Conflict and the Pan-Asian War? A man who might have figured in the history of that period?

I took a bus to the university library this week, but all I was able to discover after hours of research was an obscure reference to a young anti-Semitic radical with the surname Hitler being killed in a shootout in a Munich beer hall. I am wondering if you might shed some light on this. But please don't worry if you haven't heard of him. Don't go on one of your infamous knowledge quests. This man is not very important at all.

Fruits, on the other hand, are always welcome.

Love,

Aunt Anne

P.S. I'm serious about the fruit.

✡

Yemach shemo. May his name be erased.

✡

OTHER COVENANTS

Tuesday, March 12, 2019

Dear Madam or Sir,

I hope this letter finds you well. I am a former resident of 37 Merwedeplein, Amsterdam, having lived there from 1934 to 1954.

My father worked at the Opekta offices on 263 Prinsingracht for several decades, and I am writing to inquire if your office has any record of that building ever being used as a residence, possibly by multiple individuals, circa the early 1940s. I would be grateful if you might provide their names and contact information, even if it is out of date.

Get it together, Anne. You're losing your mind...

✡

You once asked, "Would everything make more sense to me if I knew the history of the world, or would I just lose my mind?" I'm sorry for your suffering, Jeff, but look at what you turned that suffering into.

You lit a candle for me. Do you understand what I'm trying to say? I never thought it possible, but you got me dancing again.

✡

Tuesday, March 12, 2019

Dearest Sanne,

Time passes like a dream. While writing this letter, I almost began the year with 19--. It seems our thoughts are like travelers in the woods, preferring well-worn paths. These days my thoughts return to Amsterdam, to our childhood there.

Do you miss the tulips? Here in Miami there are palm trees and giant succulents, and of course the beautiful Everglades. But I miss the spring flowers, the great bursts of color after a long darkness. Their blooms always brought a song to my heart, because it was a sign the long winter had at last ended. Mother used to put rows of them in our kitchen window, so I could spot our apartment a mile away by its colorful frame.

Do you remember the boys mock-proposing to us with them? How Ilse would fake a fit of uncontrollable sneezing if she didn't approve of the boy? Do you remember that school trip to the fields, when Nanny accidentally crushed that rare tulip? Do you remember the face of the poor horticulturist? To this day, when I think of it I smile.

Do you dream of those days? I have been dreaming of them often. Do you ever find yourself back there, as a girl, in a world just a little bit different from what you remember? I suppose it's inevitable at this juncture to turn back and look, to dream longingly of our salad days.

We had so much fun, didn't we, Sanne? These days, my life is as exciting as a loaf of bread. But I am happy. I no longer hunger for excitement, even while I despair at the awful feeling of the past slipping away. I often wonder, did those things happen to me, or did they happen to someone else, a girl of whom I merely share her memories? Identity is a strange thing, isn't it? It's strange to be anything at all.

I fear I am not making sense. I write to you, dearest Sanne, my oldest friend, in the hopes that you might understand and offer me a word of consolation. Or, if that fails, simply an ear.

I miss you and love you.

With eternal love,

Anne

✡

The tulips are in bloom. Such popping reds and yellows! My God, they're so beautiful. So fleeting.

You sing about places far away, where there is sun and green and spring eternal. I wonder if the place you imagined is like the fields outside my window. I dreamt of tulips when they took me to that awful place.

✡

Wednesday, March 13, 2019

Dearest Sonya,

Thank so much for your letter. Writing is such a solitary pursuit. We sit alone at a keyboard for thousands of hours to create a book. Then, with a little fanfare, our work is loosed upon the world. Perhaps we receive a review or two in a newspaper or magazine. Perhaps some leave their varied impressions on the Internet. But after a few weeks, the fanfare fades, like the dying embers of a fire, and we are left wondering if we have truly reached anyone, if our countless hours of labor ever touched another soul.

Your letter, and letters like it, convince me that I have. I am so very pleased you enjoyed *Di Shvester fun di Goldene Gasn*. You are right that I wrote the novel in English first. But since it concerned the life of two Dutch-speaking sisters in Amsterdam, the American publishers turned it down, believing it was not commercial enough.

It was heartbreaking, yet with writing, as in life, one must not despair for long. After a period of mourning, I decided to translate the book into Yiddish. That went rather quickly.

I sent it off to the Vilnusian publisher *Peretz Hoyz*, and they snatched it up for a modest advance. I was happy, and expected little: a few modest mentions in the European Yiddish papers. A typical scathing review from the American

Forverts. What I did not expect was how quickly the book exploded. A million copies sold in less than a year. And it received the Sholem Aleichem Award for Excellence in Yiddish Literature. That year, my husband Peter and I took a leave of absence from our teaching jobs, and he dutifully played the stolid husband while I gave readings and talks in fifty cities across Europe. A year before we were living a quiet life in New York's Catskill Mountains, now a half dozen universities offered me tenured positions and honorary degrees. It was surreal.

Not long into this adventure, those American publishers who had turned me down came knocking on my door. Now I was able to negotiate a *much* larger advance for the English version of *The Sisters from the Golden Streets*. The English version didn't do nearly as well as her Yiddish sister, though it managed to reach the *New York Times* Bestseller list for five consecutive weeks.

But this was 1967, an eon ago now, and none of my follow-up works received quite so much attention. But that is fine with me. The money I made from *Sisters* has allowed me to live a comfortable life, and I am so very grateful for it.

To answer your question, yes, I still write. Every day, in fact. But mostly that consists of letters to friends and family, and the occasional response to people like you. I cannot overstate how happy it makes me that *The Sisters from the Golden Streets* affected you to such a degree. I am a different person from the woman who wrote that book, but even after all these years it brings warmth to my heart knowing there are people out there still reading and enjoying it.

As for any advice I might give an aspiring writer such as yourself, I can only offer this: write to give, never to take. Once the words reach the page, they are no longer yours. Give them to the world as you would a gift and you will never despair.

With warmest gratitude,
Anne

✡

When the house is dark and quiet and everyone has gone home, I put on your record, Jeff, and I sing and dance and tap on the floor, and I make all the noise I couldn't make when I lived here, and it is grand and it is joyous, and it is impossibly beautiful, like a flower gone to seed.

✡

Wednesday, March 13, 2019

Dearest Howie,
Have you seen the babies yet? Don't you want to just eat them up, they are so adorable? How does it feel to be an uncle twice over again? Is the train ride from Hamburg to Budapest long? Even so, go see them as soon as possible

and give them each a big kiss for me.

And what great news in your last letter! I am delighted to hear that the Reformed Rabbinical Assembly of Germany has finally accepted your marriage to Jonathan. You must be so relieved. I know how hard you and he lobbied for change, and now thousands of others will be able to marry because of your hard work. May your lives together be long, blessed, and full of peace.

A question for you: last time you visited, I witnessed a little miracle. We were in a restaurant, waiting to be seated, when a song played from the speakers. Neither you nor Jonathan could remember the song's name, so you held up your cell phone to the sound and it identified the song for you. I didn't want to make too much of it, but I must say this seems more like magic than science to me.

Tell me, Howie, does this tool also work with humming? I have had these songs stuck in my head for weeks. They pervade my dreams each night, but when I awake, I only remember a few bars. And the lyrics hang on the tip of my tongue, just out of reach. I thought perhaps if I hummed these melodies into a cell phone, I might discover their origin. It would help solve a mystery that has been bugging me for some weeks now. Could you point me in the right direction?

With Love,
Grandma Anne

P.S. When are you and Jonathan coming to visit?

✡

You're right, Jeff. Time isn't linear. The world is an incredibly blurry, crazy dream we're all sort of stumbling through. I'm both alive and dead and you've already saved me a thousand million times, the number of times I've heard you sing.

Do you understand, yet? When I listen to you, I'm neither here nor there, and yesterday is the same as tomorrow. When I dance to your music I become eternal.

You granted your own wish. Your music is the time machine.

✡

Friday, March 15, 2019

Dearest Mimi,

There are divine miracles, like the parting of the Red Sea. And there are technological miracles. One of them is called Shazam. Have you heard of it? It's this computer program that runs on a cell phone and can identify songs just by hearing them.

I was at Starbucks this morning, when I struck up a conversation with Michael, the barista. I told him how for weeks I've had these songs stuck in my head, and yet I could not for the life of me remember where I had heard them before, or who sang them. (I dared not tell Michael that I've been hearing these songs only in my dreams.)

Michael was kind and let me borrow his cell phone, and there I sat, in the sunny corner by the window, this stooped old lady humming songs she'd heard in a dream. Needless to say, his phone couldn't find a match. Michael said it might be just that my songs were not in its catalog, but I know the truth now. These songs are entirely products of my imagination. My dream-self made them up.

When I got home, I started transcribing the melodies onto the piano. They are strange and beautiful, at times disharmonic, at times chaotic, but always plaintive, always grasping for something just out of reach. I wasn't certain before, but I know it now. These songs were composed for the girl in my dreams. They are sung for her.

I hope that you may visit one day soon and hear them.

With love,
Anne

✡

I will remember you too, Jeff, fifty, a hundred years later. I will sing you praises forever and ever, as you've sung holy praises for me. For me.

When you sing to me, Jeff, for a moment just for a moment I forget the past. What a precious gift life is. Do you know it while you live? Do you, right now, in this moment, know it?

Or this moment?

Or *this*?

Hold onto this feeling. That's the simple, holy secret.

✡

Sunday, March 17, 2019

Dearest Mimi,

A terrible morning. I awoke from another nightmare. And this time I remember it all. Everything, Mimi. Every horrible thing. The girl and her family were hiding in the attic at 263 Prinsengracht for nearly two years, because to show their face was to be sent away to their deaths. But someone told the authorities where they were, and soldiers stormed their hiding place. They took her and her family away, and they separated them and oh, Mimi, I can't begin to tell you what I saw.

Such incomprehensible horror! Millions of bodies, many frail and broken, but too many of them young, thrown into pits. And millions more, burned to ash. And most of them, so many of them, were Jews!

I know what you're thinking. The deterioration of my mind has been made manifest. I know you're already choosing hospices to lock me in and aides to make sure I take my pills.

I will have none of that, Mimi! I have seen the truth. This girl is me, an Anne from another world just a hairsbreadth from ours. A world where this inconceivable horror actually happened, but for some strange reason it didn't happen here. And when this girl died, her soul cried out to G-d, and it shook the world. And decades later, a man named Jeff felt the world still shaking from Anne's cries, and he wept with her. And from their tears he made music. And Anne's ghost heard his songs, and together they sang, and together they cried, and together they danced, and their songs, Mimi, their songs were holy prayers that parted the veils that separated our worlds like the divine curtain.

Don't you see, Mimi? She is trying to show me what a precious gift I have been given. I cry for her, for all of them, but I am no longer afraid. These aren't nightmares. They are wakeup calls.

I love you so very much,
Anne

✡

I once wondered what I could be if there were no other people in the world. In this busy house, where people come and go and stare at my face, but never see me, I have my answers daily.

But when I hear you sing, Jeff, it's like you're holding my hand through the worst, the most awful moments of them all.

When you sing, I am no longer alone.

I wanted to keep white roses in their eyes too. I wanted to run and dance and ride my bike down a hill. I wanted to sing at the top of my lungs and I wanted to make love. Can you make me a promise, Jeff?

Keep plucking your silly strings. Keep bending your notes for me.

On and on and on and on and on....

✡

Monday, March 18, 2019

Dearest Edie,

When you live for as long as I have, you notice inflection points in your life, moments at which everything changes. For me, they were first moving to Amsterdam, marrying Peter, moving to the United States, having my first child, the publication of *Di Shvester fun Di Goldene Gasn*; and now, this moment.

The morning sky outside my window is bright and orange. The sun, newly risen, sends scintillating beams across the Atlantic. I imagine that these beams are the bright rays of your family, of little Petele and Susan, streaming across the oceans to light my page. I know in my last letter to you I said I could not travel to Budapest, that it was too hard and too far. But the truth is that I was afraid. Afraid of realizing how much time has passed, of how old I really am. I see now that my fears were unfounded. My life may not be one that will be documented in history books. It was not a life of great adventure or peril. But it was a life fully lived. I have no regrets. But I do know that if I go to my grave without holding my great-grandchildren in my arms, I will.

So yes, Edie, I accept your invitation. I will fly to Budapest to see you and the family for Pesach. I will kiss my great-grandchildren. I will hold them in my arms. I owe it to them.

As I write this, Mimi is on her way down to visit me. She got a little spooked after a few of my recent letters, but she seems to have calmed after I told her I would speak to her class, that I would travel to Czernowitz with her this summer, where she will receive her Sholem Aleichem award, as I did there so many years ago. Mimi will help me with the logistics of travel, so don't you worry at all about that. I am in good hands with her. I am in good hands with you all. Oh, Edie, I wouldn't give any of you up for the world.

With warmest love,
Grandma Anne

✡

You're right, Jeff. It's so strange to be anything at all. But don't ever forget how wonderful life can be too.

Another Son

Seymour Mayne

Why does he call me Ishmael now
that I've been kicked out
of the family tent. First they wanted me
and then, got fed up caring. He took
me up the mountain and lucky
the angel and ram appeared
in the nick of time. I was favored then
and they called me Isaac, and she laughed
the whole Sabbath through and half the week.
But when their spirits fell
and they got tired
and wouldn't let me out with the shepherds
and their girls, they sent me off
to Hagar's tent and told me she would be
         my mother now.
I'm Isaac, I told the woman, Sarah's son.
"For me, you're Ishmael," she replied.

Ishmael, that's what he calls me
and in his aging fits, who knows,
he'll throw us both out into the desert
while he talks to himself about another son,
a perfect Isaac subservient to his dreams.

Covenant

Seymour Mayne

The rainbow we were supposed
to behold the next day
or the day after
never appeared.
Our eyes grew strained,
our necks stiff,
and the heavy ashen clouds
settled over the hills and streams.
The fish rose to the top

and rolled over
like silver bombers in maneuvers.

Who could believe it?
No rainbow, no
break of color, no
sign? Someone's forgotten,
we reasoned.
And we began to pray
for the cleansing rains again
and the waves rising
to wash our cities—
friend's and foe's alike—
with the green tow of return.

One

Seymour Mayne

And God said, Let there be—
. . . and hesitated. Wasn't
it slightly off-key? They would get it
wrong for centuries, perhaps even
longer. A great smile
widened over the deep. God
said, Let there be a profusion
of words on the tongues
that will speak. And God knew
it would be good. It had
to be. After they mistakenly call
me *He*—oh long after,
they will finally utter *She*.
She for another few millennia
before I become *One*
once again.

The Golem with a Thousand Faces
A Chronicle of the Second Global War

Claude Lalumière

1. Three Djinns and a Snake

As I step off the Flying Leonardo a gust of hot, harsh wind hits me like the angry slap of an unforgiving Yahweh. Even three hundred meters above sea level I can taste sand in my mouth. The city below, Yafo, is ringed by giant towers. In peacetime, there were always a number of ships tethered to these towers—Angels of Allah, Flying Leonardos, Sky Dragons, even the occasional Vahana. But now the towers look derelict. The United Emirates' entire fleet of Angels has been called to war. Against the Eternal Chinese Empire. Against the newfangled United States of Europe. Against the Antipodes. Against the High Aztec Empire.

Today, there is only this one airship tethered here, a diplomatic Flying Leonardo not outfitted for combat. We have just now returned from Firenze, from the penultimate round of negotiations outlining the alliance among the Mediterranean Communities, the United Emirates of Allah, and the city-states of Santa Roma and Jerusalem. Early in the process Free Iberia was also at the negotiating table as a potential member of this bloc, but it has since been reabsorbed by the United Emirates of Allah—the Emirates had long ago lost possession of it, during the First Global War. Should I rejoice at this tactical gain by the nation of my birth or be saddened at this further dissolution of the Treaty of Monaco, which had kept peace for more than a century? At this point, especially with the Second Global War exacerbating and complicating everything, I barely understand my own allegiances and loyalties.

We are now headed for Jerusalem, to formalize the Treaty of the Mediterranean Alliance. The Firenze government values the near-neutrality of the Mediterranean Communities, but once this treaty goes into effect all signatories will officially be at war with the United States of Europe and the Eternal Chinese Empire. So far, two years into the Second Global War and about a year since the formation of the USE, the Mediterranean Communities has maintained a tenuous peace with the fascist supernation with which it shares a long border—but escalation was inevitable.

The lift can take up to twenty people at a time, and, not counting the flight crew, the delegations total twenty-five. So we split into two groups. First, our guests on these shores, Foreign Minister Athena Tsirbas of the Mediterranean Communities and Cardinal Nero Infantino of Santa Roma, and their respective military and diplomatic entourages. Then, the rest of us follow: Ambassador of War Ibrahim al-Jazzar from the United Emirates of Allah and Secretary of Defense Aaron Jordan of Jerusalem, and their military and diplomatic staff—and me.

Officially, I'm an executive liaison posted at Qubbat al-Sakhrah—a Jerusalem institution created in the nineteenth century by that same Treaty of Monaco whose articles of peace are being torn to shreds the world over. Jerusalem is the only remnant of the former Kingdom of Judah, the only Jewish city in the world. Of course, there are Jews everywhere on the planet, especially in the United Emirates and the Mediterranean Communities, and not every one of the one million citizens of Jerusalem is Jewish, but the metropolis survives as a hybrid: it is both an independent Jewish city-state and a protectorate under the aegis of the United Emirates of Allah. Qubbat al-Sakhrah houses the governor representing the United Emirates, and it is the only secular government that serves the king of the otherwise Islamic United Emirates, as all residents of Jerusalem not registered as Jews answer to Qubbat al-Sakhrah. The systems of laws, taxation, and jurisdiction in Jerusalem are intricate webs that only the functionaries at Qubbat al-Sakhrah and the Knesset, the seat of the Jewish government, can pretend to understand. My background makes me one of those Jerusalemites who must answer to both Jerusalem governments.

As Qubbat al-Sakhrah is both within and apart from Jerusalem and tied to—yet outside—the United Emirates, it was judged that it should have a voice in the negotiations, albeit a minor one. It was decided that an official from Qubbat al-Sakhrah should sign the treaty, lest a loophole might allow it to operate outside of the agreement. I was chosen as that official, mostly due to my ties to several of the signatories: a Jewish resident of Jerusalem born in the UEA city of Istanbul, my father was an Italian Jew from Constantinople, across the bridge in the Mediterranean Communities, and my mother was a rabbi's daughter from Istanbul. At the time, their romance was complicated by the border, but the twin cities have since gained independence, reunified under the historical name of Byzantium.

At the base of the tower, three djinn cruisers await us. Only the Emirates, the Hindu Supremacy, the High Aztec Empire, and the Eternal Chinese Empire possess cruiser technology—officially. Operatives the world over are no doubt trying to wrest this secret from the scientific superpowers for their spymasters, if they haven't done so already. Indeed, only three days ago, I successfully handed over plans for the Emirates' newest cruisers to my handler at the Gabinetto Segreto, the secret service of the Mediterranean Communities. Compared to any current model, these new military-grade cruisers are faster, have a greater weight capacity, and can hover higher.

While the others negotiate how the assemblage will be divided, I discreetly send a snake slithering ahead of us to Jerusalem. Because of my position within the secret service of the United Emirates, the Mukhabarat, I legitimately have possession of the snake—a handy long-distance messenger device that powers itself on sand, travelling faster than any vehicle, technology well beyond the capabilities of any other nation. Am I breaking my own code of ethics by using it for the benefit of Emet, which the UEA considers a terrorist organization?

The MC delegation boards the first djinn, the Jerusalemites (save for me) and the Romans gather on the second, and I am invited to join the UEA delegation aboard the third. Among the Muslims is the physically and politically powerful Souad Haboba, from the Emirate of Ethiopia, whom I know to be a spymaster high in the ranks of the Mukhabarat, renowned for his fierce loyalty to the Muslim empire and notorious in some circles for the extreme debauchery of his private life, including keeping a sizeable retinue of barely pubescent sex slaves of all genders at his ancestral palace in the outskirts of Addis Ababa. A few minutes after our djinn starts floating toward Jerusalem, Haboba shocks me by outing me in front of the rest of the delegation: "So, Agent Gabriel Mazza, before we all gather at Qubbat al-Sakhrah, what have you to report regarding the Gabinetto Segreto and Firenze's plans?" I can only hope that there are no double agents among either the delegation or the crew. My position as a triple agent working officially for a fourth interest is tenuous and perilous enough as it is.

2. Spy Fictions

As a young man, I studied political science abroad, at the Università degli Studi di Firenze. I lived off-campus; my father was, and still is, a successful textile importer/exporter who could afford to rent me an apartment in the city centre of beautiful and vibrant Firenze, near a cornucopia of markets, restaurants, theaters, museums, and bustling piazzas. In early April of my final year, coming home after a full day of classes and lectures, I was struck by the acrid stench of cigarette smoke as soon as I opened my door.

In my living room, visible from the doorway, was the source of the smoke: a woman, perhaps five years older than I was, whom I had never seen before, rifling through my papers. Before I could muster a response to her presence, she said, "Don't worry. I'm not a thief. Well, not in this case."

I stammered, struggling to find the words, or even the reaction, appropriate to the situation.

With a hint of a Slavic accent—Russian? Ukrainian? Czech? or . . . ? I couldn't be sure yet—the woman continued: "It's interesting that you so idolize Valérie Lyon."

The mention of my thesis subject—the rogue agent who had only recently leaked state secrets and become the Utopia of France's most wanted criminal—focused my thoughts. Without hesitation, I said, "You're a spy."

"I knew you were a smart boy."

I prodded her with questions, but she ignored them. She stood up and walked to my bookshelf. "And you think being a spy is romantic. Exciting. Thrilling." Her green-tinted fingernails brushed against the spines of my paperbacks, my hundreds of novels, anthologies, and collections of espionage fiction. "All this fiction. Do you think it's like that in real life? Danger. Sex. Megalomaniacal villains. Daring escapes." She picked up a book—*The Golem with a Thousand Faces*, by Michael Barak—the first in a long series about a Jerusalem spy, an expert in disguises, codenamed the Golem. "You read in all these languages?" Her tone sounded approving. I nodded, but she wasn't looking at me. She scanned the multilingual spines of my books, spy fiction from around the world; I was fluent in Italian, Hebrew, Arabic, German, French, and Turkish, and my collection included books in all those languages. "So this obsession is why you write about the politics of espionage. Tell me: what do you believe in?"

"Are you asking me if I'm religious? Or if I'm a zealot nationalist of some stripe or other? Of course not. I love the chaotic bustle of my home city, Istanbul, but I would never convert to Islam. I'm intrigued by the mysteries of Judaism, although I'm not a theist, to my rabbi grandfather's eternal chagrin. I find Jewish traditions both beautiful and absurd. I love life here in Firenze. Cosmopolitan. Secular. But I will not stay here forever. I want to experience everything, everywhere. And I don't want my exploration of life's wonders mitigated by any belief system or arbitrary allegiance."

That came out more earnestly pompous than I'd intended, making me somewhat self-conscious, but it was sincere.

She made a throaty noise whose meaning eluded me, then abruptly changed the subject. "Let's go out. I know the perfect restaurant. It has no street sign, but it is one of Firenze's jewels." She led me by the hand, and I let her. Her body language commanded submission; spurred by curiosity, bemusement, and lust, I felt no need to resist. She exuded a powerful sexual aura that was not lost on me.

The meal was indeed delicious, in a basement establishment not ten minutes from my apartment. Was I really under her spell, or was I playing a game pretending to be, so as to satisfy the various appetites that were driving me? Perhaps there was no difference.

Afterward we went dancing—again at a clandestine venue, brimming with the countercultural elite of Firenze. I still did not know her name, or anything about her, but she prodded me ceaselessly about every detail of my life and thoughts. She outdrank me considerably, showing no sign of intoxication. We ended up in my bed, where I drunkenly fumbled along as she expertly navigated the needs of our bodies.

When I woke up, she was gone. The following day, I could barely concentrate in class, having no clue exactly what had really happened the night before, or why.

One week later, I returned home from the university to the familiar stench of her cigarette smoke. She was not alone. An older woman, unambiguously Italian, addressed me: "Halya recommends that we should recruit you."

Halya! So that was her name. A beautiful name. I was smitten, of course, fully aware that she would, probably sooner rather than later, mercilessly break my heart (which she did, the following summer).

I tried to dampen my enthusiasm, tried to appear confident, trustworthy, sophisticated. "You're from the Gabinetto Segreto."

And that is how the uncommonly cunning Ukrainian Halya Nazdratenko lured me into the world of espionage. I would soon learn that she was a triple agent, working for the Northern Reich, the Mediterranean Communities, and the Ukrainian Independence Underground. Did that influence the course of my own career? Within the next decade, I was also recruited by the Mukhabarat and by Emet—an independent group operating from Jerusalem but with no ties to any government. By some bizarre coincidence—perhaps it was no co-incidence (the world of espionage is like an overripe onion, with layers upon layers of unsavory truths and lies and machinations and alliances)—all three of my spymasters pulled strings to have me posted at Qubbat al-Sakhrah, the institution to which I officially answer. As to whom I truly serve, I long ago stopped asking myself that unanswerable question.

3. The Wrong Questions

Souad Haboba is asking me the wrong questions. Today, it is not the Gabinetto Segreto that should concern him. Rather, he should be worried about Emet—but perhaps my association with the clandestine organization has escaped the notice of the Mukhabarat. I have endeavoured to keep my work with Emet secret from every other interest I serve, although both the Gabinetto Segreto and the Mukhabarat believe I'm a double agent working for them from within the ranks of the other. For me these are not contradictory positions.

Very soon, if everything goes according to schedule, no one in the United Emirates of Allah will be able to ignore Emet. If he should ask the right questions I would reveal the truth to Haboba, but I will not betray Emet's plans unprompted. Few would understand or credit the ethics that govern how I manage my conflicting allegiances—I'm not sure I always do—but there is a method to my confusion.

I glance out the window, toward Jerusalem; already the cityscape is visible. I worry that perhaps things are not proceeding according to plan. Shouldn't they have emerged by now? Shouldn't they be protecting Jerusalem? Was my snake intercepted? Or did something change or go wrong in my absence?

Thirty minutes later we disembark the djinns at the border station of the western city wall with still no sign of the golems. Something has gone terribly wrong.

4. News from the Front

After I make sure that each delegation is properly housed in the diplomatic quarter, I make my way to Qubbat al-Sakhrah, where a young page accosts me as soon as I pass through the security desk. "Mister Mazza, Governor Gadot requests an immediate audience. Please follow me."

Rebecca must be eager to debrief me about the negotiations. I was tempted to try to contact Emet before returning to Qubbat al-Sakhrah, but I can't risk having my movements or my schedule questioned at this critical juncture. I wish I'd been allowed time to go to my office and see what had piled up in my absence and verify, also, if there were any coded messages awaiting me from any of the three covert organizations to which I belong. There are many ways to get information through to me at my office that would look innocuous to prying eyes.

Just before I step inside the governor's office, a thought runs through me like an ice pick: what if Qubbat al-Sakhrah has gotten wind of Emet's plans and, worse, of my role in those plans?

"Sit down, Gabriel." Something is troubling Rebecca. Having worked with her closely for four years, I know the telltale signs. The fidgeting fingers. The subtle twitch of her right eye. Despite these ticks, she remains an intimidating figure, with her perfectly smooth bald head, her strong nose, and her razor-sharp cheekbones. I prepare for the worst. I was not arrested upon arrival, however, so perhaps things are not as dire as I fear.

"Did the negotiations go as planned? Any detractors, any red flags, any changes?"

"We can run through the details, but it all went smoothly. Everyone involved wants this alliance to work."

"Good. I don't need to know more for now. I trust you."

I suppress a sigh of relief. But what is weighing on her, then?

She continues: "Two hours ago, we received intel from the Asian Front. Word is the Chinese have broken through into UEA territory and are headed toward Jerusalem. To capture it for Empress Lai Zhou. The Emirates' Ministry of War is suppressing the news, to avoid panic."

Why didn't Souad Haboba discuss this with me aboard the djinn? No, if this news is as fresh as Rebecca believes, he could not have known yet. If this is true, it could change everything. Or perhaps create an opportunity. For the fledgling Mediterranean Alliance or for Emet, depending on who moves quickest.

"How reliable is this intel? Could it be disinformation from the Chinese?"

"Truth is, I don't know. Can you look into this right away? No one at Qubbat al-Sakhrah has a better network of foreign contacts."

"I'll get started now. Anything else?"

She shakes her head and pushes a file folder toward me. "Here's everything we know, including about the source of the intel."

5. The Truth?

The guard at the gate of the diplomatic compound of the United Emirates examines my diplomatic credentials with exaggerated scrutiny. This precise officer has seen me dozens of times, and yet he still always goes through the motions of security theatre with passive-aggressive meticulousness.

Normally I would have to be circumspect when contacting a fellow agent of the Mukhabarat, but having been officially tasked with the investigation of this rumored Chinese breakthrough on the Asian Front gives me a perfectly aboveboard reason for calling on Souad Haboba.

The compound, situated at the foot of the Mount of Olives, doubles as an Islamic quarter for the wealthy and the influential—very different in character from the chaotic mess of Jerusalem's Muslim ghetto, with its throngs of feral children, its pungent aromas, its ceaseless din, its ubiquitous merchants selling wares of dubious quality and provenance, its religious zealots preaching unorthodox interpretations of the Quran without the threat of the legal consequences that would befall them within the United Emirates proper.

Here, in the high-security gated diplomatic compound, with the ostentatious faux-classical Mosque of al-Quds at its center, the sense of order is so extreme that the effect is macabre, as if the whole area were nothing more than an elaborate and sterile necropolis, especially at this time, after sundown.

The meeting with Haboba is swift. The rumors are true. He was informed immediately upon his arrival. He tells me that Ambassador al-Jazzar agrees that this development makes the ratification of the Mediterranean Alliance all the more urgent. Haboba suggests an emergency gathering of the delegations to speed the process.

"Yes. At Qubbat al-Sakhrah—our scheduled meeting room has already been arranged for the negations that were scheduled for tomorrow." I hurry away, to rally all the necessary dignitaries.

Within minutes of walking out of the compound, I run into Avram Shalev, which cannot be a coincidence. Avram is my contact within Emet—sometimes, I believe he is in fact the head of Emet. Emet may be the Hebrew word for truth, but Emet the organization is particularly adept at hiding the truth. As always, I am startled by Avram's appearance. We are both of us the perfect spies. Absolutely nondescript Semitic men in their thirties—we look as if we were cut from the same anonymous mold. We can blend in unnoticeably anywhere in the Emirates or in Jerusalem; there is nothing in our physical description to distinguish us from thousands of other Jewish, or even Arab, men.

We embrace. I whisper, "What went wrong? Did you not get my message?"

Avram stiffens momentarily but then continues, ignoring my question. "Follow me."

"Not now, Avram. I have no time. The situation has changed. The Chi—" I'm cut short. From behind me a rough linen hood is slipped over my head, a strong arm chokes me, my hands are quickly shackled, and I'm dragged on my feet. Within seconds, I sense that we have entered a building. I'm punched in the stomach and kicked to the floor.

The hood is pulled from my face. Avram towers overs me, grimacing. He spits at me. "Traitor."

"I have no idea what you're talking about."

"I've had enough of your lies. I always suspected you did not really believe in our cause, that you did not really care about expulsing the Emirates from

OTHER COVENANTS

Jerusalem. Perhaps that's where your loyalties truly lie, with the Emirates. Have you turned away from your heritage and converted to Islam?"

"I do not believe in God, whatever the version of that belief. I've never lied to you about that."

"No. Perhaps not about that. But about so much else. Your message said you were coming back alone—that the negotiations had failed and that none of the delegations were coming to Jerusalem; yet those foreign diplomats are here after all. You said that the timing was not right for deployment, that our plans had been compromised."

That is not what my message said. Is Avram lying? Or did someone intercept my snake? Who would gain from framing me? Does the Mukhabarat know about my association with Emet, despite all my precautions? Any denial would sound hollow.

Avram continues, now leafing through a file folder: "It's telling that you made no effort to contact us once you returned to Jerusalem. Then there's this: evidence that you also work for the Gabinetto Segreto. You never told us about that. How many competing organizations do you work for? Whom do you ultimately answer to?"

I open my mouth, as if to speak. But there's nothing I can say to make Avram believe that I never betrayed Emet. But I know that I might have, given the right circumstances. I can sense that Avram is perhaps glimpsing the real me for the first time, instead of seeing an asset to be exploited.

"I believe in Jerusalem." I didn't intend to say that, but the words tumbled out of me.

"But which Jerusalem? Ours? Or theirs?"

I repeat, "I believe in Jerusalem." Even I'm not sure what I mean. Yet I feel unexpectedly moved, almost to the point of tears. I've lived here for a decade. It's not as beautiful as Istanbul. It's not as exciting as Firenze. And yet this ancient place replete with mysteries and intrigue has become my home, my city. Yes, it's true. I identify more viscerally with it than any city I've ever set foot in. Its history and beauty have seeped into me, become part of me, and I've become part of Jerusalem. Aloud, I reiterate, "I do believe in Jerusalem." But in this moment—when my life is in peril and I should be more concerned with self-preservation—it's clearer to me than ever that I don't believe in Emet's vision.

Avram scoffs at me. "I don't care about your platitudes. I think I'll let Ben and Abner here—" He shakes his head toward the two alarmingly muscular men buffeting me "—soften you up a bit before I seriously interrogate you."

"Avram—there's no time for this. The Chinese have broken through the Asian Front. A fleet of Sky Dragons is heading toward Jerusalem right now. I need to gather Jerusalem's allies, put things in motion to protect us all, to protect the city we both love."

"And why should I believe these new lies?"

Out of the shadows three bullets hit my captors in the head, dispatching them with gory efficiency.

In Arabic a female voice I do not recognize says, "Because, effendi, they are true." Wielding a small pistol, a woman steps out of the shadows, swathed in a black uniform that covers every millimeter of her body, save for the eyes. I recognize the model of her gun—the Stinger 2.5, standard issue for Mukhabarat assassins. They are the quietest, fastest, lightest, and most reliable firearms in the world, the envy of weapons manufacturers and gun enthusiasts the world over. The technology has yet to be stolen or duplicated—these guns are designed to self-destruct if mishandled. Death by a poisoned Stinger bullet is one of the ways I've long suspected I was likely to die an early death. The assassin points the weapon toward me. "Your mission to gather the Mediterranean Alliance is irrelevant; the Chinese are at most a few hours away." She pulls the trigger.

The chain of my handcuffs shatters.

"You might have killed me!" Emboldened by the realization that she is here to rescue me, I can't strip the indignation from my tone. Inwardly, I chide myself for such a petty and unprofessional response.

"You're welcome. And, no, I'm too good a shot."

I collect myself. "Of course. Thank you."

"I presume you know how to activate the golems?"

"What makes you think Emet trusted me with that information?"

She raises the gun toward me.

I raise a hand in surrender. "Emet didn't trust me with that information, but that doesn't mean that I don't have it. How did the Mukhabarat find out about Emet's golems?"

"What makes you presume I'm an agent of the Mukhabarat?"

My mind spins trying to figure out which interests she's representing. And, if not those of the United Emirates, how she got ahold of a Stinger 2.5.

She laughs. "You're thinking so hard, the veins are popping out of your forehead. I'm just fucking with you. Of course I'm Mukhabarat. And so are you. I'm here to make sure you remember that. Now, lead me to the golem command centre."

6. Games of History and Espionage

I glance dispassionately at the fresh corpses of the two Emet guards. "You don't have to kill everyone we encounter en route. I work with Emet. I know the codes and the passwords."

"They were about to torture you when I stepped in. I think your security clearance has been revoked. Besides, the more of them I kill now, the fewer will have to stand trial for treason later."

The Mukhabarat assassin—she had proved her credentials earlier with the proper exchange of code phrases—has yet to reveal her face or her name. I suspect that, even if we both survive this incursion deep into the underground Emet stronghold, she plans to kill me at the resolution of this affair, regardless of the outcome or of my cooperation. I'll have to figure out a way out of that once and if we reach that point.

"You may have rescued me, but you put me in that position in the first place."

"You put yourself in that situation. By your lack of serious commitment to any one cause. And also by being naïve enough not to figure out that the Mukhabarat monitors all snake usage."

Regardless, for now, I find myself on her side, seriously engaged with the mission objective. I believe this is the only way to save Jerusalem, both in the long term and from the imminent threat of a Chinese invasion. Safeguarding Jerusalem strikes me as the most important and noble thing I can do.

The Kingdom of Judah was a casualty of the thirty-year First Global War. Magnanimous in its victory, the United Emirates of Allah conceded to the international community that Jerusalem should remain a predominantly Jewish independent city-state, as long as it was understood that the Emirates would retain a stake in the affairs of the former capital of Judah. Thus was born the peculiar dual government of the city—sitting at Qubbat al-Sakhrah and the Knesset—with its composition enshrined in the Treaty of Monaco, a document that secured slightly over a century of world peace. Although before the war of 1881–1911 Jerusalem had been a cosmopolitan city within the Jewish nation, home to many ethnic and religious groups, this new state of affairs did not sit well with some radical members of the Jewish population. Stinging from the loss of their country and the humiliation of their now diminished autonomy, these Jews formed a secret society called Emet, whose explicit (but covert) goal was to reclaim Jerusalem for the Jews and the Jews only, and eventually push back the borders so as to reinstate the Kingdom of Judah.

These were not impatient people. They knew this would have to be a slow-burning plan, one that would take many generations to bring to fruition. The United Emirates was perhaps the most technologically advanced nation in the world and one of the largest empires in history. So Emet sent its sons and daughters to Muslim universities to study science, mathematics, politics, and more.

In 2002, Emet's technology division, headed by robotics genius Mattityahu Ephron, came up with the idea to use golems in a scheme to finally achieve Emet's goals.

By then Emet had a vast underground compound forming a ring around the city-state of Jerusalem. But even that was not enough space for the Golem Project. It took a decade of hard labor by hundreds of Emet zealots to dig facilities large enough to begin the work of transforming Ephron's vision into reality. When the Second Global War broke out in 2016, the project schedule was accelerated. The golems are now ready.

However, faced with the potential realization of their generations-long dream, the leaders of Emet wanted to make sure not to fumble their only chance at reclaiming Jerusalem. How and when should the golems be deployed? Operatives at Qubbat al-Sakhrah, the Knesset, the police, and the city security forces must all be in place at the same time—and at the right time—to wrest power from those unsympathetic to a Jewish Jerusalem.

I don't believe in Emet's ideology, or its goals, save perhaps that of fully wresting the city-state from the Emirates. But now I question why I should even want that. At the moment, that goal seems more emotional than practical, or even truly desirable, a reflex position inculcated in all Jews. A century of this peculiar form of dual government and Jerusalem has thrived, become more populous, more learned, and more cosmopolitan than ever. I love the city exactly the way it is. Why risk ruining its current magnificence? Why did I join Emet?

Six years ago, I uncovered an Emet cell at the Knesset, while I was on the rise in the world of Jerusalem politics. Instead of reporting the infiltrators to the authorities, on a whim, sensing the potential for adventure, I volunteered. How could they refuse? So deeply enmeshed in Jerusalem governance, and with my background in espionage, I was an invaluable resource. Navigating so many layers of intrigue was such a thrilling game. In peacetime, the stakes were never that serious. But now, with the world at war, perhaps playing so many sides is no longer a game, if it ever was.

Several corpses later—this woman from the Mukhabarat is a most efficient killing machine—we are there: at the threshold of the golem command centre.

The assassin puts a gun—a standard 9-millimeter pistol—into my hand. "I'm still not sure if I can trust you, but I have no choice. I hope I can trust your attachment to the city. Either we succeed now, or Jerusalem falls to the Chinese."

7. The Milchamah Protocol

My gun is now out of ammunition. There's blood and gore everywhere. None of it is ours. Several of the Emet operatives staffing the command centre were... well, not quite friends. Like everyone else in the room (fifteen in all), they are now dead. At the hands of the assassin. And at my hands. In all the years I've played at being a spy I had never killed anyone. I familiarized myself with firearms as tools of my trade. I practiced shooting until I became an expert marksman. I always wondered how I would react if I ever had to kill.

In books and plays, first-time killers either vomit or develop a taste for murder. I feel neither. If anything, I feel dead myself, as if even the possibility of emotion had been bled out of me. Only one thing matters: the mission.

The assassin orders me: "Activate the Milchamah Protocol."

I nod. I'm no longer surprised that the Mukhabarat knows so much about the Golem Project. The golems can be activated into several modes, one of which is the Milchamah Protocol—combat mode. I key in the appropriate codes on the command console. "It's done."

I look up. The Mukhabarat assassin is pointing her Stinger at me. She says, "I was given discretion as to how to handle you. Bring you back into fold. Execute you. Take you prisoner. It's up to me."

"I've been in this game long enough. I guessed you were going to kill me. But at least Jerusalem might be saved now."

"Get out. Leave. Leave Jerusalem. Leave the Emirates. In twelve hours, you'll be branded a traitor, exposed as a triple agent. If you ever set foot in the Emirates again, you'll be shot on sight."

"Thank you."

"Stop wasting time, or I might change my mind. I never want to see you again."

Without another word, I make my way outside through the tunnels, exiting to east of the city. My career is finished. I'm useless to anyone. I have a safe house in Yafo, with fake passports. Time to assume a new identity. Perhaps I'll head to the New World—I've long dreamed of seeing Montreal. Eventually, I'll process everything that happened this night. But for now all that matters is the mission: survival.

Looking back toward Jerusalem, I see the golems rise from the ground—twelve gigantic robots, sixty meters high, forming a defensive ring around the city-state, armed with the most high-tech weaponry Emet was able to steal from the United Emirates. Although I'm too far away to make out such precise detail, I know that on each of their brows is etched the name of one of the twelve tribes of Israel: Asher, Benjamin, Dan, Ephraim, Gad, Issachar, Judah, Manasseh, Naphtali, Reuben, Simeon, Zebulun.

Suddenly emotion wells up in me. I'm heartbroken that I will probably never set foot in any of the cities I have loved. Byzantium. Firenze. Jerusalem. I'm devastated at being severed from Jerusalem. Yet I was never much of a Jew; it was only one of my many faces, though I was good at playing the role when it suited me, as in my dealings with Emet. But I did become a Jerusalemite, a true Jerusalemite, more so even than if I'd been born there.

Farther in the distance, in the dawn light, a fleet of Chinese Sky Dragons approaches from the northeast.

The golems are ready for war, ready to protect Jerusalem.

The Sea of Salt

Elana Gomel

Kirsten is dead. Or perhaps she had never been born.

I met her when I came to campus for preliminary registration, still feeling awkward in civilian clothes. I literally bumped into her as I was backing out of the registration office, leafing through the hefty package of meaningless forms. She made a polite sound of protest: a sure indication that she was foreign. She looked foreign too, which accounted for my attraction. She was not pretty. Her peaky face was dominated by bulging eyes. Her large mouth looked squashed rather than sensuous. Her only truly attractive—or truly abhorrent—feature, depending on your taste, was her milky-white skin, so uncompromisingly Aryan that the Mediterranean sunlight seemed to slide off her in defeat.

We sat on the grass while long-legged ibises stepped gingerly around us, and went through the booklet of instructions together. I wish I could say that by this point we were at ease with each other but it would be a lie. We were never at ease with each other.

But we did have coffee together, and eventually I got invited into her room in the dorms. She worked so hard at being uninhibited that I felt more like a medical specimen than a lover. She told me she was going to study the history of the Jewish people. I felt I was demeaning myself in her eyes when I confessed my goal was business administration.

When we went out she would wear tight-fitting black dresses and a golden six-pointed star around her neck. She insisted I call her Avital, and told me she wanted to convert. I laughed the first time I heard it. But she was impervious to hints or veiled insults. She took everything at face value. The stare of those pale eyes froze absurdities into horrible truths. Later, my grandmother taught me the expression *tierischer Ernst*: the bestial seriousness of the Germans.

After a while, we moved in together. She paid the rent with her family money.

It was at this time that she started telling me about her grandfather. She told me his name on one of the few occasions our sex was truly passionate, whispered it like a love confession. It meant nothing to me. All I had gotten from the history lessons in school were cartoon images of waving flags and goose-stepping soldiers. And my grandparents never talked.

Now, of course, I know a lot about him, having read all I could lay my hands on. Some of those stories are stuck in my memory like bits of gristle between the teeth. He distributed sweets to the Gypsy children and they called him "Uncle." He would take his favorites for a ride in his car and sometimes drop them by the gas chamber. Once he gave his prisoner assistant—he called them "colleagues" and was invariably polite to them,

OTHER COVENANTS

especially to women—a box to prepare for delivery. She opened it: it was filled with human eyes.

The first semester was ending, and we began to make plans for the winter break. I wanted to go to Germany with her, but she was reluctant. We quarreled, and I even accused her of being ashamed of me. I expected vehement denials, but she was silent. I stormed out; she called me ten minutes later and offered, as a gesture of reconciliation, to finance a long weekend at the Dead Sea.

James Joyce called the Dead Sea "the cunt of the world." Set inside the ring of ancient crumbling rocks, so old they have become soft and wistful, edging into mineral senility, the heavy-water lake called the Sea of Salt in Hebrew defies time. It is alive with a frightening concentrated vitality like the flow of a woman's juices: a doorway into the womb of the past.

We went spiraling down the new highway into the oldest place on Earth. The scanty vegetation was disappearing to reveal the baroquely shaped bones of the earth: pink, and scarlet, and dull bronze; elaborately folded and pleated; surrounded by aprons of scree. I felt loose, as if the cord that bound me to everyday life was unraveling. I glanced at Kirsten; she looked inscrutable, gilded by the sunset.

On the shore, the viscous water glistened beyond the wide stretch of salt flats. Ragged birds swooped over our heads. I still remember the tranquility of that moment.

We checked into the Nirvana Hotel. Kirsten went straight to the spa. I walked down to the pebbly beach and touched the oily swell. Under the surface, I could see white convoluted shapes like corals. They were salt crystals, growing in the sterile water in a perfect imitation of life. I heard the crunch of footsteps and turned around. Kirsten stood behind me, her white top luminescent in the dusk.

"I thought you were at the spa," I said.

"I like it better here."

We stood together in companionable silence.

"Is this where Lot's wife … ?" she asked.

"Somewhere around," I shrugged. "A guided tour would show you the exact pillar of salt supposed to be her. Each tour has a different one."

We went back to the hotel, had a lavish dinner, and made love on the king-size bed. When I woke up in the middle of the night and found myself alone, I thought she had simply moved over to the other side. Kirsten was never one for cuddling. But a quick glance told me she was not in bed. A longer investigation assured me she was not in the suite.

I was annoyed rather than concerned. Unable to fall asleep, I turned on the TV and watched a soft-porn film on the hotel's channel. Just as the moans of assorted male and female actors rose to a crescendo (they appeared to speak Turkish on the rare occasions they spoke at all), the door creaked and she walked in.

The Sea of Salt

She was stark naked. In the ghostly TV light her skinny body glistened from head to toe, her hair lanky and wet. I stared. Had she gone swimming in the Dead Sea in the middle of the night?

"Turn this filth off!" she yelled. And then she started sobbing.

She was covered in dirt mixed with oily water into a sort of paste. I took her to the bathroom and turned on the shower. The water swirling down the drain had a reddish tint.

Wrapped up in one of the hotel's huge towels, she swallowed a drink I thrust into her hand, pulling a bottle at random from the mini-bar. I was seized by panic, wondering whether she had gone off her head. Kirsten had always appeared to me insufferably self-possessed, and such people have the capacity for sudden and spectacular breakdowns. Finally she started talking.

"It wasn't like that at all," she said. "It was not supposed to be that way."

"What wasn't?" I asked.

"The place. I thought it would be cold. But it was hot, stifling. Summer, I thought. But there was no vegetation, nothing, just a field of ashes. Like the volcanic ash, but heavier. Wasn't it supposed to be among the fields? I read about neighboring villages gathering their harvest just a couple of kilometers away. But there wasn't a spot of green I could see."

"There is no green here," I said stupidly.

"And the smell," she went on. "I knew there would be a smell, but not like this. I thought it would smell like … like roast, like a joint in the oven."

Kirsten was a strict vegetarian; the cause of many a squabble when we ate out.

"But it wasn't. It was bitter, chemical, like toilet cleanser, only stronger. Disinfectant. What do they do with the bodies to make them smell like this?"

This was getting to be too much for a holiday weekend.

"What the fuck are you talking about?" I yelled. "Where have you been? What happened?"

I think my presence fully registered only then. She looked at me and smiled, almost tenderly.

"Poor Gilad," she said. *"Mein Süße."*

I felt like slapping her face but then I saw something that made me gulp in horror. There was a dark spreading patch on the white terrycloth around her chest.

"You're bleeding," I said.

She looked down and lifted the towel. There was no wound. The blood was oozing from her nipples, pooling in the crease of her stomach. She made a face and swabbed it with the stained towel.

"I thought these puddles were sewage," she said.

I rushed into the bathroom and threw up. When I came back, Kirsten was in bed, asleep.

✡

I had dozed off on the couch and woke up, groggy, with the sound of the shower. When Kirsten came out, she seemed her usual self. I postponed serious talk until after breakfast. Then, fortified with black coffee, I told her we should go back immediately to seek medical help (I was careful not to say "psychiatric"). She smiled and shook her head. Despite the dark circles of fatigue under her eyes, she seemed elated.

"No," she said. "You go back if you want. I'm staying here. Perhaps I'll look for cheaper accommodations. I don't know how long it'll take."

"How long will what take?" I shouted.

"I'm going to find him," she said.

✡

The Dead Sea and its environs are crawling with Mediterranean history. There are Sodom and Masada; there are remnants of Roman fortifications; there are abandoned bunkers of the Jordanian army. If the past were to invade the present here, why should it be that alien European past, the graveyard stench of Poland, the war madness of Germany?

But she did go somewhere. I saw it myself. I saw her walk into the heavy water that parted before her like some colossal amoeba, the smooth flanks of the sea drawing in upon themselves as she stood on the oily shingles. It was as if she covered an immense distance with each step, visibly shrinking, becoming the size of a child, a toddler, a doll. There was a silver flash as she vanished into somewhere else and the roiling water resumed its normal appearance.

She swore to me there was no magic formula. All she had to do was visualize the tunnel of light. At the time I did not know what she was talking about. Since then, I have read books on out-of-body experiences: people who float up a heavenly rabbit hole to meet their dear departed, or have a chat with Jesus. It's easy if you know how.

But wherever she went, it was not to heaven. She was convinced—at least, at the beginning—that she had found a door to the past. I quickly realized it was not. But I did not know what brave new world she had discovered in the depth of her guilt. That world reached out and devoured her; that much was certain. But was it merely her own nightmare? Was I just a bystander, innocently caught in the turbulence of her family history? I pretended to believe it then; I don't pretend now.

Perhaps the pretense was thin even then, for the fact is, I did not run away. We moved into a bungalow in a holiday village: cheaper and more private. We developed a daily routine that was almost cozy in its insanity. The horror only came back occasionally. One morning, looking down into the pink wadi, I saw a herd of gazelles pass by so close I could touch them. They walked in single file, and as they passed the fenced overhang where I stood, each of them stopped and looked at me.

After breakfast we would drive down to the sea, seeking a secluded place.

It was not easy because the shore is as flat as a pancake. There are no bays or coves. But we counted on indifference. If a passing driver got a glimpse of Kirsten's white buttocks, so what? There is no law saying you cannot go skinny-dipping in the Dead Sea. She insisted on going in naked because this is how it had worked for her the first time. But since the time of the day was not affected by her passage, she did not want to go at night. She needed daylight: to see, to observe, to witness.

But witnessing was tricky, because it changed every time she went there. The basic outline was the same: a field of ashes; a sullen sky that ran the gamut from fire-gray to crimson; and the watchtowers on the horizon. Those spidery black silhouettes, she was convinced, marked the camp where he was waiting for her. On the first visits she did not manage to come close enough to make out the gates because assorted obstacles barred her way. It was the variety of these obstacles that made me realize she could not simply journey into the past. Sometimes the wasteland would be cut by trenches, filled with skeletons in tattered uniforms like World War I soldiers felled by a cloud of gas. Sometimes she encountered a maze of ravines threaded with foul-smelling streams that built up dams of human excrement. And once the plain was alive with tiny lemming-like rodents that scrambled and fought, rising tiny plumes of ash.

The length of her visits also varied; occasionally she would come out in twenty minutes, faint with hunger, and claim to have spent a whole day there. Other times I had to wait until the moonrise to hear the crunch of her footsteps on salt crystals. I fed her and tried to do something about the stigmata of her journey, mostly with no success. And then I would debrief her. This is what I called it to myself, as if I was still in Lebanon. I tried to record her, but she refused. So I bought a notepad in the holiday village's souvenir shop and wrote it all down in longhand.

On her fourth journey, she said, she saw a line of prisoners weaving among the hillocks of cinders and stretches of black porous stone that comprised the landscape around the camp. She hid behind the rusty ruin of some agricultural machinery; or perhaps it was a military truck. She was vague about such details. She was very precise about the prisoners and their guards, however.

The prisoners, she said, were both men and women. There were no children. They were horribly emaciated, the striped rags of their uniforms barely covering the skeletal bodies, but even this scanty covering was almost too much for the stifling heat of that place, the boiling air reeking with sulfur and acid fumes. Some of them, even women, pulled off the shirts, baring their torsos in a vain attempt to escape the heat. The guards did not interfere because the most important part of the outfit was impossible to remove. The yellow patches stuck to the prisoners' bare skin; mostly on the chest, but sometimes on the forearm, the upper thigh, the shaven head, or even covering most of the face. The patches stood out in relief, as thick as a man's hand: not merely a swatch of cloth, but a plump padded thing. The patches seemed to her to twitch and change shape. She wanted to come closer but was afraid of the guards.

"They were not human," she said.

"Sure," I said sarcastically, "make them into monsters so we don't have to accept that we are all capable of cruelty."

"I don't mean metaphorically," she said impatiently. "I mean they were something else."

They wore immaculate black uniforms. But unlike in the familiar movies, they also had shiny black helmets that covered the entire face.

"Like medieval knights?" I asked dubiously.

"Yeah, only medieval helmets are very elaborate, with moving parts. These were completely featureless—a sort of hemisphere with a thick curving edge that sat on the shoulders."

"How did they breathe?"

"I don't know."

But what made her believe the guards were not quite human was the way they moved, slinking with a boneless grace around the stumbling column of prisoners. And then there was the way they killed.

"She stumbled and fell, this woman. I think she was young, but ages were difficult to tell. She tried to get up, but a guard approached, flipped her over with the tip of his boot, and ground his foot into her chest. She wailed and thrashed, but he kept on and his foot actually sank into her body as if it were made of rotting cheese. Blood jetted out, but I think—I could not be sure—that it slid off his uniform like water off a duck's back. A couple of other guards joined him, and one of them bent and tore off the woman's arm—just tore it off, with no visible effort, twirled it in the air and threw it away. It landed not very far from me and it was … it was a *real* arm, real flesh and blood, because when he did this I thought, it can't be, these people are not real, they are puppets or simulations, nobody can pull a human body apart like a paper doll. But they did. And the rest of the prisoners watched."

✡

Several times, I wanted to call a doctor. I could not be responsible for what was happening to her. And I admit, I was squeamish.

But in the end, I did not. I gave in. I became her assistant, chronicler, witness, and nurse. I obeyed her orders. She had this effect on me. Without love, without gratitude, commitment, or obligation, she bound me to herself more securely than any other woman before or since.

Her nipples did not bleed after the first time. But when she crawled out of the sea for the second time and stood shivering as I threw a robe around her, I noticed angry red stripes on her back. The skin was puffy, as if she had been lashed with a belt.

"What is this?" I asked.

She shrugged.

"Does it hurt?"

"A little," she said reluctantly. I put some aloe gel on her back and tried to pretend it was the effect of the seawater. But the third time she came back with half her hair torn out by the roots, the bare patches on her scalp raw and bleeding. She cut off the remnant of her hair and shaved her head with my electric shaver. Were it not for the scabs, it might have even suited her.

I thought that perhaps she had been discovered. I imagined her naked figure crawling in the ashes. Had she been gang-raped? I was afraid to ask. But that night she pushed herself against me with a startling desperation and we made love like two castaways on some bleak shore. This was the last time; when she returned the next day she tried to hide her body from me, but I could see how her journey had marked her. More than mere mutilation, it was as if her flesh had melted in the passage and then cooled into a ragged new shape. After that, she came back every time with a new brand, like notches on a gun to mark the killings.

She did not mind; she was preoccupied with more practical concerns. She wanted to spy on the camp. She was upset because she had not managed to approach it any closer: her way had been blocked by a giant pile of discarded clothing, suitcases, shoes, toys, all mixed together and dumped in the midst of the wasteland. Rooting in it, she found a teenager's pants and a man's khaki shirt that fit her, dug a little hole and hid the clothes, marking the site with a rock. Next time she would snoop around properly dressed in dead people's hand-me-downs. I was struck by the gruesome irony of it, but she was not; rather, she was puzzled by the seeming senselessness of the dump.

She could not understand the economic logic of the camp, she said. I laughed when she first talked about it. But then I began to realize she was serious. She had to come to terms with the camp with by squeezing it into the procrustean bed of her rationality. She was not content to turn away in disgust from the meaninglessness of atrocity; she had to force atrocity to make sense, and then she could live with it. It made her abhorrent in my eyes; it made her admirable; and as distant as if we were denizens of different galaxies.

The prisoners were often marched around the camp, going nowhere. To me, it sounded familiar, almost mundane; there were the death marches after the camps had to be evacuated, and the purpose of these marches was killing, pure and simple. This camp, however, seemed in no danger of liberation, as there were no signs of war around it; no drone of warplanes or distant rumbling of the artillery. There were crematoria inside and they worked at full capacity. She saw the tall chimneys protruding into the yellow air, belching oily smoke and an occasional tongue of flame. Even the sickening stench of the burnt human flesh that she had missed on the first occasion was there, only masked by the piercing odor of unknown chemicals. So, she insisted, there was no point to those impromptu death marches.

"Perhaps the gas chambers and crematoria are overloaded," I suggested.

It was possible, she agreed reluctantly. There was a railway line that brought prisoners in: occasionally she could see a tiny train on the horizon. Still, there was something about the killings that puzzled her. When she came back after her fifth visit eager and excited, I knew she had solved the mystery.

"I know now!" she exclaimed.

She came across a heap of dead bodies, not very large, perhaps twenty people in all. Most seem to have died of sheer exhaustion; several were shot. The bodies were stacked together like firewood. Approaching them cautiously, trying not to breathe in the death-stink, she saw stirrings in the heap. She thought of rats; but the creature that wriggled out and plopped onto the cindery ground resembled a starfish. It was poisonous yellow, with a rough tegument and six radial arms that it proceeded to flex as it flopped around.

"Those patches," she explained, "are not sewed-on pieces of fabric but living organisms. They are parasites, feeding on the prisoners. I think that they need dead bodies for the incubators. This is why a certain percentage of prisoners are not burnt but killed outside the camp. I saw groups of inmates on the plain before, moving from one pile of bodies to another. I thought they were *Sondercommando*. But now I believe they were harvesting the stars."

I stared at her. There is a threshold in horror beyond which lies sheer numbness and a kind of detached curiosity. I was at this stage but she—she was somewhere else. Her cheeks were flushed.

"Where do you think these creatures come from?" I asked.

"I think they've been made in the camp," she replied. "I think ..." she hesitated slightly, "I think *he* made them."

Next time she came close enough to the gates to see the familiar inscription *Arbeit macht frei*. She was relieved; she had heard a prisoner scream something in a language she did not understand, and was concerned about the possibility of miscommunication. This was also the first time she saw the guard dogs. They were large sleek brutes with naked pink paws like rats and semi-human faces, pug-nosed and slit-eyed. She was convinced they talked to the prisoners.

She refused to let me tend to herself, but when she fell asleep I saw a pink growth, like a fleshy coral, on her thorax. I lay down on the couch, revolted, and hating myself for my revulsion.

How to get into the camp? That was the problem she pondered incessantly.

"Most inmates wonder how to get out," I said sarcastically. She just shrugged, but I began to consider whether this was true, whether there was, in fact, any place to get out to. It seemed to me that her stories of the camp world were growing more bizarre, more hellishly elaborate, as if that world was diverging further from our knowledge of the past. Perhaps by now there was no war, no opposition to the camp system, and no hope for the people who were used as hatcheries for monsters.

"There is a camp ecology I have to understand," she said. "The yellow stars I think are just larvae. Perhaps at the next stage they become the guard-dogs."

"What for?" I asked.

"I read his diaries," she said. "He really believed in what he was doing. He was a scientist, not a butcher. Perhaps here he has the chance to put his theories into practice. Perhaps in that world they are *true*."

"How do you know he even exists in that world?" I asked.

"Oh, I know," she said unhesitatingly. "He's there, I can feel him. This is why ..." she added after a while, in that contemplative tone that always gave me the chills, "this is why it all looks so familiar."

"Why don't you just walk to the gate, then, and say you have come for a family visit?" I asked.

She looked at me with those bulging eyes. Her face by now had the uncompromising look of a martyr.

"If I don't find any other way, I will do it," she said.

"I want to come with you," I said.

"No."

Of course, I could have argued. I could have followed her.

I did neither.

The last time, I waited for her for the entire day. The brief violet dusk came and went, and she was not back. I prowled the edge of the sea; the sounds of singing and laughter came from the new promenade.

Exhausted, I drove back to the bungalow. When I saw the light streaming from the windows I almost crashed the car.

Kirsten was inside, sitting on the bed, her head in her hands. She had put some clothes on but there was black water pooling at her feet.

"I've seen him," she said.

"How did you get here?" I yelled.

"I walked," she said vaguely. "Listen, I've seen him."

I don't believe she had walked up half a mile, naked and barefoot, from the shore to the bungalow. I suspect the worlds were bleeding into each other and she was the wound, the raw place where they rubbed. Her mutilations were signs of their contact; and the wider the zone of contact became, the more randomly was she tossed along the edge.

Apparently, she had taken my advice. She had simply walked to the camp entrance and announced herself. I imagine her standing at the bottom of the curving ramp, a tiny figure in the wasteland of ashes and poison, looking up at the towering ironwork of the gate.

Her description of the camp was rather vague but also surprisingly prosaic: prosaic, that is, in the sense that it was not all that different from the descriptions I have read since then in historical books. She talked about the barbed wire, the churned-up bare earth, rows of barracks, smell of excrement. Not too many inmates were around. Those she saw were shuffling Musselmen, living skeletons with extinguished eyes covered in filth and sores. They, however, were free of yellow stars, confirming her hunch that the creatures were parasites that needed relatively healthy hosts. The guards who escorted her did not speak, and seeing them from close up, she decided they could not. The helmets were actually their real heads, covered with a shining black carapace like a beetle-wing. She tried to figure out how they fed, and came to the conclusion that they had mouths in the palms of their hands. She was convinced now that the guard-dogs were their masters.

Brought to the medical barrack—she caught a glimpse of a room filled with small cots, a child in each—she was led into an office. There was a desk with a typewriter, a fringed Art Deco lamp, and a portrait on the wall. Not the familiar face with a tiny mustache. Not a human face at all.

She was left waiting in the company of a nurse, a youngish woman in a starched uniform. She refused to talk, but gave Kirsten a sugar cube. And then her grandfather walked in.

They talked. There were no spy-novel attempts at disguise; she did not pretend to be a special envoy from Berlin. She told him she was his descendant from the future; she said she had traveled back in time. He was familiar with the concept; being an educated man, he had read H.G. Wells. However—and this indicates to me he had realized there was something fishy about the situation—he did not ask her many questions about the future, though he did inquire about his family. Instead, he seemed to be only too pleased to talk about his work in the camp.

It was, as she had suspected, an attempt to create a total ecology of death, in which the energy released by torture and extermination would be used to promote the malleability of the living flesh.

"Think of it as a fountain of youth, like the legendary spring of Eldorado," he said enthusiastically. "There is no limit to improvements we can achieve. Total freedom from disease, physical perfection, mental acuity, all fertility problems solved once and for all."

The yellow starfish, the black-helmeted guards, and the talking guard-dogs were just experiments, she gathered (inside the camp, most personnel seemed ordinary enough, but on her way out she caught a glimpse of a creature like a giant dun-colored caterpillar crawling on two rows of human hands). The prisoners were vermin whose extermination was a necessary hygienic precaution; it was the greatest boon to science that this simple public-health measure also opened a window of opportunity for the human race.

What else had passed between them at this family reunion, I wonder. What else was said, perhaps not in words but in exchange of looks, in the body language? She had spent her entire life in his shadow, thinking and dreaming of him, hating him, but perhaps also admiring his courage in stepping outside the bounds of the merely human. All she had ever wanted, she told me, was to separate herself from him. But is it really possible? The more she looked into the past that should have been dead but wasn't, the more the past looked back at her. The past had reshaped her in its image even before she took off her clothes that evening. Her white skin was festooned with hanging sacs of skin filled with milky liquid, and there was a tiny dark core in each, a fetus-like form turning head over heels.

"I am going back tomorrow," she said. "I am going to kill him. You are a soldier; you will teach me how."

I took her with me, bundled in layers of my t-shirts, as we sped on the empty highway. It was pretty late to come knocking at the door, but the owner of the flat-roofed house in a small village owed me a favor. Arms are easy to come by in a country at war. The handgun could be hidden under her clothes. All she had to do was pull the trigger.

We were back at the Dead Sea just as the first rays of the sun broke over the Jordanian hills, turning the heavy water into a sheet of beaten gold. In that glorious light, Kirsten's wasted skull-like face looked frightful. And yet I felt something close to adoration as I looked at her. We both knew she was not coming back. Heroism is the opium of fools.

I tried to postpone the moment, offering her coffee, keeping up the feeble pretense of normality. She refused, and tucking the gun, carefully wrapped in a plastic bag, inside the waistband of her pants, walked to the sea edge. It occurred to me that it was the first time she was going to cross over while dressed.

I watched her as she paused with her feet planted in the viscid swell. I hoped she would look back at me. But she did not, and I realized, once again, how little I meant to her. It had been between him and her all along.

She started walking in and the sea parted as usual. But something was different; there was angry churning, and the water, normally so sluggish, rose in foamy billows that twisted as if whipped by a gale, even though the air was still. A piercing whistle assaulted my ears, rising to an unendurable pitch as the sea exploded into a harsh blaze. I fell down. Groveling on the ground, my eyes watering from the Hiroshima radiance that turned the flying foam into the hail of fire, I could still see Kirsten's dark silhouette.

She must have screamed, but her voice was drowned in the rage of the Dead Sea, offended at her presumption in carrying an instrument of death into its domain. I could see the metallic glitter of the sky through her body as the waves dissolved her flesh, eating holes in legs, buttocks, and thighs. An especially large wave broke over her and when it retreated, a pristine skeleton was standing in the sea, its arms still raised in supplication. But the sea was already giving it new flesh, covering the slender bones with the coat of interlocking crystals that grew into a structure of surpassing beauty, as lacy and delicate as the rime patterns on the windowpane. This new creation, however, endured for an even shorter time than Kirsten's own fragile body, for the salt statue broke up and fell into the hungry water that swallowed it up and buried it in its own salty depth.

✡

It has been ten years. I don't remember the days that followed, but eventually the routine won, as it always does. I called her parents and told them their daughter had left me, but I did not think she would be coming home soon. They were not surprised.

I make good money. I am married and have a three-year-old daughter. When she was born, I wanted to call her Kirsten. My wife was shocked by the idea. We called her Shirley.

Recently, I took a day off work and drove down to the Dead Sea. I walked on the promenade in the pale silvery light of the late afternoon. A boy was sitting on the parapet, reading a book, resting his feet on his huge backpack. He was blond and blue-eyed. As I approached, he lifted his head and smiled at me.

"U.S.?" I asked as I sat down beside him.

"Germany," he replied.

We chatted a little. His life was brand-new, untarnished by memory. He was highly complimentary about my command of Deutsch.

"History is a nightmare from which I am trying to awaken," said Joyce. But what if a nightmare becomes history? I imagine Kirsten and myself yoked together by elastic bonds that warp out of shape as they stretch back in time but never snap. Unless they are cut.

My wife kids me for working out so obsessively. But I have to be in top shape when I'm ready to cross the Sea of Salt and enter the undead past in order to put it to rest.

I will be ready soon.

The Bat Mitzvah Problem

Patrick A. Beaulier

"Gods damn it, Rita, the membership is just too high. I'm not ten thousand dollars Jewish. Hell, I'm barely five hundred dollars Jewish!"

Daniel Pearlstein sat as he always did, slumped back like a sloth at the kitchen table, wringing his hands in a neurotic ritual that should have torn his skin off by now. The glow of incandescent light always shone on his bald head, the few remaining hairs of his curly combover dancing like silver tinsel. Beads of sweat congregating on his face, a nervous leg bouncing on the floor like a broken blender, and the moans and groans of torture were like stress-induced performance art.

All this stress was for his daughter Caroline. Soon, Caroline would be *bat mitzvah*—a Jewish woman with all the rights and obligations of an adult, whatever those are. But until then, Daniel was crunching numbers, trying to figure out how to afford Hebrew school tuition, membership, the building fund, the priests' offering, and eventually, a party with all of Caroline's school friends, never mind having to fly the relatives in from all over the country.

It also didn't help that the family was planning a vacation to Cancun during the same winter as Caroline's hypothetical *bat mitzvah*, which left Daniel certain that a second mortgage on the house was the only viable option.

Daniel's wife Rita, for what it's worth, just wanted this done. Rita grew up a Christian, like everyone else in Indiana, and while she never believed that Bar Kokhba had been the messiah, and was never really religious, her cultural differences with Daniel were becoming more obvious the older their daughter got. In the beginning of their relationship, Daniel's Jewish identity was somewhat fun, mysterious, dangerous, like most mystery cults. But the allure after fifteen years just wasn't there anymore.

Rita figured the two religious upbringings would get along fine, but they didn't. Rita would remind Daniel that, at least according to her Sunday school teacher, non-Jews did offer sacrifices in the Temple, and after all, the "Son of the Star" was a Jew! But it never worked. "You just can't understand," Daniel would say. "You didn't grow up like I did. Knowing you were a Jew and knowing that made you different."

For Caroline, all of this was dumb. She spent all her time on a cell phone texting with friends. Like most kids of interfaith relationships, she grew up with both religions in the household. Christmas trees and presents for Christmas, milk-boiled lamb for the spring Passover. Neither mom nor dad was religious, and that was fine: one less thing to deal with in her eleven year old life.

Daniel had what some might call Jewish post-traumatic stress. While the family attended a large Orthodox Temple, with its shrines to Asherah, Baal, El Elyon, and the whole nine yards, at home the Pearlsteins were not exactly religious. Like every other kid, Daniel just wanted to play video games and meet girls. After his *bar mitzvah,* he moved on. No more Asherah. No more Baal, and certainly no more Yahweh.

But now they had to be good Jewish parents and get their kid *bat mitzvah*ed. She had to learn the magical rite of *sotah*, the Song of Balaam, all of it. How could Daniel, in good conscience, visit the graves of his grandparents with offering bowls knowing that his daughter, their great-grandchild, could not chant from the Book of Enoch or cast spells on other tribes? He could hear it now: Daniel married a non-Jew and was therefore personally responsible for destroying the Jewish people.

The whole thing was a mess, as Rita saw it. Daniel was not religious, so they moved to the suburbs for the schools. Not a lot of Jews there, but Daniel didn't care until one day he realized his daughter would soon be thirteen and he had his moral responsibility to bring her into Jewish womanhood.

As far as they could tell, their small suburban town offered two options: Reform and Chabad.

Without a mainstream Orthodox option, Chabad seemed like the closest thing to what Daniel had as a kid, and would be good for Caroline. The tuition was low, and since Daniel was a Jew it did not matter that Rita wasn't. Chabad didn't judge and Daniel liked that.

Caroline would learn a sort of stripped-down Orthodoxy: Chemosh, Baal and Dagon, CHaBaD. Easy enough. And they let you use the dining hall for free, and you could feel good that your kid did it right, the Orthodox way, but you didn't need to feel guilty about never showing up again. Plus, the priest was a nice guy, and his wife made good *kugel.* But in reality, Rita wouldn't be able to participate in the all-Hebrew services. Maybe that didn't matter, Daniel thought. But if he said that to Rita, he would be sleeping on the couch for a week.

Reform seemed like the reasonable option, and Rita's go-to. Temple El was almost exclusively attended by interfaith couples just like them. The Temple sisterhood, Bat Lilith, was a nice club whose members mostly played canasta and planned the canned food drives. They were fine with phonetic transliterations of the prayers, so even if she didn't really understand the Hebrew, Caroline could still participate. But as Daniel would complain, "it's just not tradition. They cut the service down to nothing. It's all in English and they use a red light bulb instead of the fire offering, Rita! What the hell is that? A fire offering is called a fire offering for a reason!"

So they were stuck. Chabad was too traditional. Reform was too liberal.

"What about Messianic?" Rita would sometimes ask. She explained it this way: if she needed some Bar Kokhba and Daniel needed a little El Elyon, why not meet in the middle? Caroline would be a *bat mitzvah,* Daniel would get his Hebrew and enough English that everyone could follow along, and it would be fine.

"Not a chance, Rita! Those people aren't Jews. Just because you have a name like Pinchas doesn't mean you're Jewish. That *brit hadash* thing is more ludicrous than those Talmudists you see walking around in robes offering people flowers and copies of the Torah at the airport."

At midnight, Rita and Daniel would lie in bed and ponder their daughter's future. Would she have a *bat mitzvah*? Would they plant a tree in Judea, with a red string tied around it? Would she make Jewish friends? Would she wear her small, golden calf necklace with pride?

And perhaps more importantly, would they make it to Cancun?

Of course they would. *A bat mitzvah* is nice, but the family deserved a vacation.

A Sky and a Heaven

Eric Choi

"There is a sky, and there is a heaven. The sky is a matter of height. Heaven is a matter of depth."
-Shimon Peres

✡

Bergen–Belsen
March 1944

Joachim Joseph was nine years old when the Germans invaded the Netherlands. He remembered his father looking out the window at the columns of Nazi armor outside their home. His father was crying.

They were sent to the death camp at Bergen-Belsen. Joseph was separated from his brother and his parents, each assigned to a different barrack. The poorly-constructed wooden buildings were dank and filthy. Alone and hungry, Joseph lay on the straw mattress, curled in a fetal position as if trying to squeeze warmth out of his thin prison garb.

"Hello, young man."

Joseph looked up and saw the gaunt, bearded and bespectacled face of Rabbi Simon Dasberg. One of his eyes was swollen, and there was dried blood around an ear. Joseph had heard that Rabbi Dasberg was often beaten for saying prayers outside the crematorium and refusing to shave his beard.

"What is your name?" Rabbi Dasberg asked.

"Joachim Joseph."

"And how old are you, Joachim?"

"Twelve."

"When is your birthday?"

"March 31st."

Rabbi Dasberg smiled. "I thought you looked bar mitzvah age." He lowered his voice conspiratorially. "Would you like a real bar mitzvah ceremony?"

As Joseph watched in amazement, Rabbi Dasberg opened a little box and unwrapped a cloth to reveal a four-inch Torah scroll. "I can teach you to read from this, if you are willing."

For the next few weeks, Rabbi Dasberg woke Joseph early every morning, and together they studied the text of the tiny scroll. From their bunks, some of the other men looked on. A few even smiled at the defiant little conspiracy that was taking place.

"Well, the time has come," Rabbi Dasberg said one morning, a few days before Joseph's thirteenth birthday.

The men peered outside, looking for the guards, and then covered the windows with blankets. Four candles were lit, their faint light flickering in the pre-dawn darkness. Rabbi Dasberg placed a small towel on a table, put down the Torah scroll, and unrolled it.

"Stand up, bar mitzvah boy," Rabbi Dasberg said softly.

With tears in his eyes, Joachim Joseph approached the table and took hold of the scroll. Rabbi Dasberg and the other men huddled around the boy. Joseph opened his mouth, and poised himself to read.

Someone knocked on the door.

✡

Near Baghdad, Iraq
June 7, 1981

Captain Ilan Ramon held the stick of his Israeli Air Force F-16 fighter jet with intense focus, his other hand resting on the throttles. The head-up display in front of him indicated an airspeed of 450 knots and accelerating, and an altitude of 102 feet above ground level. Outside his canopy, he could see the other seven fighters of the attack squadron in tight formation. Ramon was "flying the tail," the last plane of the group.

They had taken off from Etzion Airbase over an hour and a half ago, and were now just 12 miles from their target—the Osirak nuclear reactor southeast of Baghdad. Ramon selected full afterburner and pulled back on the stick, following the planes ahead in a climb up to 6,000 feet. They were now visible to Iraqi radar. At 6,000 feet, they pitched over into a dive, aimed at the containment dome of the reactor complex.

The planes ahead released their bombs in pairs at thirty second intervals. Ramon stood up the throttle and flicked the master arm switch. Smoke, explosions, and anti-aircraft fire were already obscuring the target. He pressed the weapon release button, feeling a kick in his seat as the bombs fell away.

Ramon pulled back on the stick and advanced the throttle, bringing his plane to a banking climb away from the smoldering reactor. He looked over his shoulder and, at the periphery of his vision, spotted the serpentine plumes of two surface-to-air missiles.

There was an explosion.

The control panel lit up. The engine flamed out. Stick and throttle no longer responded.

Ramon grasped the ejection handle and pulled. The canopy flew away with a bang, and then a small rocket motor blasted his seat clear of the disintegrating plane.

Ilan Ramon fell into the sky, and was thrown into darkness.

✡

Five-year-old Dean Issacharoff looked up at the sky in wonder.

Suspended from the ceiling, historic aircraft floated in silent majesty. Dean could see the bright orange Bell X-1 that broke the sound barrier, and the silvery gray *Spirit of St. Louis* flown from New York to Paris by the American aviation pioneer (and antisemite) Charles Lindbergh.

Jeremy Issacharoff, a political counselor at the Embassy of Israel in Washington, took his son's hand. "Hey Dean, let's see the space stuff over there."

They ambled past the Apollo 11 command module and the Skylab orbital workshop, and soon found themselves before a model of the Space Shuttle.

"Check it out."

"Cool!" Dean smiled as he surveyed the Shuttle model, the white-and-black orbiter straddling the large orange external tank, flanked by a pair of white solid rocket boosters.

"Look at this." Issacharoff gestured at a display. "Here are some of the astronauts who have flown on the Shuttle. They're from many countries." He pointed. "What's that flag there? The one with the red maple leaf?"

"Canada."

"That's right. Mr. Garneau is from Canada. And the blue, white and red flag? Where is Mr. Baudry from?"

"France."

"And this green flag with the sword. Do you know what country that is?"

The boy shook his head.

"It's Saudi Arabia. A prince from the Saudi royal family once flew on the Shuttle."

Dean furrowed his brow. "Papa," he said. "Why are there no astronauts from Israel?"

✡

Directorate for Defense Research and Development (Maf'at)
Israel Ministry of Defense, Tel Aviv
February 1996

"Is this Yael Dahan?" asked a gruff sounding voice on the phone.

"Yes," the research engineer replied. "Who is this?"

"I am Aby Har-Even. I am director general of the Israel Space Agency."

"Hello." Dahan gripped the phone tighter, a frisson of excitement sweeping over her.

"Let me get to the point. Would you like to be Israel's first astronaut?"

Her jaw dropped. She stammered something nonsensical.

"What is it?" Har-Even barked. *"Is there a problem?"*

"N-no, no problem."

"You did express an interest, did you not? You did submit an application, did you not?"

"Yes, of course." Dahan composed herself. "It's just that ...well, I'm a little bit surprised. What I mean is, I was expecting some kind of formal selection process, a competition—"

"Listen to me," Har-Even said. *"We do not have the time or money for an extended search. Peres and Clinton announced the astronaut opportunity last year, and now we need to put forward a candidate immediately to make the start of this year's NASA astronaut class for mission specialists."*

"I ... see."

"So, Yael Dahan," Aby Har-Even said. "Are you in?"

✡

Department of Geophysics and Planetary Sciences
Tel Aviv University
Summer 1996

Professor Joachim Joseph walked into the conference room for the weekly meeting of his research group. He sat down at the head of the table.

"Yoya, you are smiling," said the summer student Mustafa Asfur, calling Joseph by his nickname. "You have good news?"

"Yoya is always smiling," said Meir Moalem, a master's candidate.

"Indeed, I have good news," Joseph said. "Our MEIDEX payload has been selected to fly on the Space Shuttle mission with the Israeli astronaut." The objective of MEIDEX, the Mediterranean Israeli Dust Experiment, was to study how dust particles blown off the Sahara Desert affect climate and weather across North Africa, the Mediterranean and the Atlantic Ocean. "Launch is scheduled for early 2000."

"This is so exciting!" exclaimed Asfur.

Joseph's smile broadened. "Yes. This will be an amazing scientific adventure."

✡

Ramat Aviv Gimel, Israel
January 2002

"Thanks for the ride," Aby Har-Even said in the grumpy old man voice that Yael Dahan had grown to adore.

"No problem," said Dahan's husband, Omer Bitten. "We're glad you could join us for Shabbat dinner with Yoya."

"It's the least we can do," she added. "After all, I owe you for *my* ride."

Har-Even harrumphed. "Yes, well, you can be sure there will be discussions about that."

"Is there a problem?"

"It's these delays, Yael," Har-Even sighed. "You were supposed to have flown almost two years ago. Frankly, we are running out of money to keep you in the program. And if that wasn't enough, I get letters from Haredis who object to a woman representing the Jews in space."

"Well, they don't have to sit next to me on the Shuttle if they don't want to." Noa, her fifteen-year-old daughter, giggled.

When they arrived at the Joseph home, the professor and his wife Stella greeted them. They all went into the dining room.

Stella lit the Shabbat candles, covered her eyes, and recited. *"Baruch atah Adonai Eloheinu Melech haolam asher kideshanu bemitzvotav vetzivanu lehadlik ner shel Shabbat kodesh."*

As they ate, Dahan looked up and saw a little wooden ark sitting on a shelf. "Yoya, what is that?"

Joseph got up from the table and took the ark down from the shelf. He opened it, revealing a tiny four-inch Torah scroll inside.

"It's beautiful," Noa said.

Dahan looked at Joseph. "There must be a story."

✡

Bergen-Belsen
March 1944

Someone knocked on the door.

Everyone froze. Rabbi Dasberg went to the door and slowly opened it. Joseph's eyes widened.

"Eema!" he cried, throwing his arms around his mother's emaciated frame.

"It is dangerous for you to be here," Rabbi Dasberg said quietly. "Women are not allowed in the men's barracks."

The boy held his mother tight. Gently, she finally pushed him away and touched his cheek. "I will stand outside the window and listen."

Joseph nodded, wiping his eyes. Rabbi Dasberg led him back inside to continue the ceremony. *"Baruch atah ..."* he began, reciting the blessings and reading from the Torah. Rabbi Dasberg cupped his hands on Joseph's head and blessed him. The men rose from their bunks to congratulate the boy. One gave him a sliver of chocolate, barely larger than a thumbnail, wrapped in a small piece of paper.

Rabbi Dasberg took Joseph aside, and to the boy's surprise, pressed the little Torah into his hands. "I want you to take this."

Joseph gasped. "How can I take a Torah?"

"Listen to me," Rabbi Dasberg said. "You must take this, because I will not leave here alive. You must promise that when you get out, you will tell the story of what happened here. Do you promise?"

Joseph looked at Rabbi Dasberg. "I promise."

✡

Ramat Aviv Gimmel
January 2002

A solemn silence fell on the dinner table. Dahan's head was bowed, and the eyes of her daughter and husband were moist.

"Yoya," Dahan said at last, "I must tell you something. My mother and father were also 'graduates' of Bergen-Belsen. I am an only child. My parents waited quite late in life before having me. They were almost forty when I was born. I always got the sense they were hesitant to bring a child into the world, a world that seemed for so long to be without goodness and hope."

Dahan looked squarely at Har-Even. "I will be going back to Houston soon, to continue training for my flight. I look forward to operating the MEIDEX experiment and getting good science. But more than that, more than that ..." She turned to Joseph. "Yoya, I wish to ask you—may I please have the honor to bring your Torah with me to space?"

The man who was the boy at Bergen-Belsen said yes.

Dahan gazed at Har-Even. He closed his eyes, and nodded.

✡

Mission Control Houston
NASA Johnson Space Center, Building 30
January 16, 2003

Smiles, waves and the occasional call out of "hello" and "good morning" greeted Ilan Ramon as he entered Mission Control. He took his place at the Flight Director's console, resting his cane against a filing cabinet. This would be his eighth Space Shuttle mission and his first as the Lead Flight Director. The screen at the front of the room displayed a live feed from the Kennedy Space Center, showing the Shuttle *Columbia* sitting on the launch pad.

The countdown clock was stopped, holding at T-minus 9 minutes.

Ramon adjusted his headset and keyed the mike. "Good morning, STS-107 flight controllers. Please give me a go/no-go for launch."

"FDO?" "Go."

"EECOM?" "Go, Flight."

"INCO?" "We are go."

"CAPCOM?" "We're go, Flight."

After polling the rest of the flight controllers, Ramon switched to an external loop. "Launch Control, this is Houston. You are 'go' for launch."

✡

Kennedy Space Center, Florida
10:39am EST, January 16, 2003

Yael Dahan's family gathered with those of the other *Columbia* astronauts to watch the liftoff from the roof of the Launch Control Center. Beside Noa and Omer were Yael's parents Eitan and Michal, survivors of Bergen-Belsen who had endured the depths of hell and were now about to watch their daughter soar into the heavens. Noa saw her stepfather's parents, Moshe and Rivka, and his sister Neta, talking quietly to Stephanie Wilson, her mother's friend and fellow graduate from the NASA Astronaut Class of 1996.

"*T-minus 31 seconds, and we have a 'go' for auto sequence start,*" announced the voice from the loudspeaker. "*Columbia's on-board computers have primary control of all the vehicle's critical functions.*"

Holding Omer's hand, Noa walked closer to the railing.

"*T-minus ten … nine … eight… seven, we have a 'go' for main engine start …*"

From the distant launch pad, a bright flash appeared at the base of *Columbia*, obscured a fraction of a second later by a rising column of steam.

"*… three… two… one … we have booster ignition and liftoff of the Space Shuttle* Columbia *with a multitude of national and international space research experiments.*"

A second dawn lit the horizon. Cheers erupted from the crowd as *Columbia* roared off the launch pad and started rolling onto its back, angling upwards in a northeasterly direction over the Atlantic Ocean.

Noa squealed and jumped like a child, covering her mouth with her hands. "*L'hitraot, eema! Kol tuv, eema!*"

✡

NASA Johnson Space Center, Building 13
Houston, Texas
January 17, 2003

Engineers stared at a screen on the far wall, mesmerized by a grainy film that was being played in a repeating loop. Over and over, the film showed an object breaking away from *Columbia's* external tank and smashing into its left wing, bursting into a shower of particles.

Ilan Ramon recognized Rodney Rocha, the division chief for structural engineering, and approached him. "What do we have here?"

"Something, probably a piece of insulating foam, came off the external tank about 82 seconds after launch and hit the left wing of the vehicle," Rocha said.

"Is there a danger?" Ramon asked immediately.

"We don't know," Rocha replied. "It depends on the size of the foam, the speed and angle of impact, and where it hit. Based on this footage, our preliminary estimate for the foam size is between 21 to 27 inches long and 12 to 18 inches wide, with an estimated impact speed somewhere between 625 and 840 feet per second relative to the vehicle."

"And the impact location?" asked engineering manager Joyce Seriale-Grush.

Rocha picked up a model of the Shuttle and tapped his finger on the leading edge of the left wing. "Somewhere here, probably on the reinforced carbon-carbon panels, or maybe on the thermal protection tiles just below."

"That is a lot of uncertainties," Ramon said.

"The uncertainties are due to the slow frame rate and poor resolution of the camera," Rocha explained. "These views were taken by a film camera 17 miles away."

"What does your team need to resolve the uncertainties?" Ramon asked.

"Better images," Rocha said, without hesitation.

"Can the astronauts see that area, by looking out the windows?"

"No. The open payload bay door blocks the view."

"You know," Seriale-Grush said, "back in the early days of the Shuttle program, they sometimes got spy satellite images of the Shuttle in orbit to see if the thermal protection tiles were all right."

Rocha's eyes widened. "Can we do that? Can we petition for outside agency assistance?"

"Let me take an action to bring this up with the MMT," Ramon said, referring to the Mission Management Team.

✡

Payload Operations Control Center
NASA Goddard Space Flight Center
Greenbelt, Maryland
January 19, 2003

"Wonderful!"

With each new set of MEIDEX data coming down from *Columbia,* Joachim Joseph called out and pointed at the screen with delight. The instrument had captured images of dust plumes off the coasts of Nigeria, Mauritania and Mali. A color scale showed the dust concentration from green for thinnest to red for heaviest.

"Look at this, Yoya." Scott Janz, his NASA co-investigator, pointed at a grayscale contour plot. "I'd say we've captured ourselves some ELVES," he said, referring to electromagnetic perturbations in the upper atmosphere.

The new message flag appeared. Joseph opened the email and double-clicked on the attachment. A low-resolution video of Yael Dahan with Commander Ben Hernandez floating in the middeck of *Columbia* began to run.

"*Good morning, Yoya,*" Hernandez said. "*From the crew of* Columbia, *congratulations on the successful activation of MEIDEX. We hope you're getting good data. And we know you'll be heading back to Israel later today, so we'd like to offer this little poem.*"

Hernandez passed the microphone to Dahan, who began reading from a piece of paper:

"Yoya Joseph, our friend on the ground,
We send him our data as we go round and round,
His warm friendly eyes make us all realize,
What a wonderful friend we have found."

Dahan and Hernandez waved at the camera. "*Nesiyah tovah, Yoya! From the crew of* Columbia, *best wishes for a safe trip home.*"

✡

NASA Johnson Space Center, Building 13
January 19, 2003

Ilan Ramon hated PowerPoint.

Over the course of his twelve year career at JSC, he watched in dismay as the use of PowerPoint presentations instead of technical reports became endemic. PowerPoint was fine for marketing hucksters, but when complex engineering analyses were condensed to fit into bullets on standardized templates, crucial information was inevitably lost.

A young engineer was presenting the results of the impact analysis his team had performed using a computer model called Crater. On one slide, the vague words "significant" and "significantly" were used five times without quantification. The slide also had "cubic inches" written inconsistently: "3cu. In," "1920cu in" and "3 cu in". Such inconsistencies and lack of precision were antithetical to Ramon's military background, where a misplaced decimal or mistaken unit of measurement could have deadly consequences.

"We've seen these foam impacts on past missions, and it's never been a problem." The speaker was Peter Delaney, a senior engineer with thinning gray hair and Coke-bottle glasses who was regarded by management as an expert on the Shuttle's thermal protection system. "As the Crater analysis has confirmed, there is no threat to *Columbia*. We are dealing with a post-flight maintenance issue, not a safety-of-flight issue."

Ramon, Joyce Seriale-Grush and Rodney Rocha looked at each other.

"Wasn't there a slide that said Crater predicted damage exceeding the thickness of the thermal tile?" Seriale-Grush asked, her voice a mixture of confusion and alarm.

"The Crater model is very conservative," Delaney explained. "It doesn't take into account that the thermal tiles are denser at the bottom, so it's always predicted greater damage than what actually occurs. In any case, as I've said, the impact on *Columbia* is in-family with similar events on previous flights."

"I'm sorry, but that's a lousy rationale," Seriale-Grush said. "Things aren't supposed to be hitting the Shuttle at all. Just because it's happened before without consequences doesn't mean there's no danger."

"Look," Delaney hissed, "I was there when they invented those tiles and I've got a dozen tile-related patents to my name, so I know what I'm talking about."

"Nobody is questioning your expertise, Peter," said Ramon, trying to moderate, "but Joyce raises an important point."

Rocha spoke up. "Well, *I'm* going to question. Peter's expertise is in the tiles, but the film analysis indicates it was more likely the foam hit the RCC panels," he said, referring to the reinforced carbon-carbon leading edge of the Shuttle's wing.

"The RCC is even more resilient to damage than the tiles," Delaney said. "If that's what you saw, it's the best thing that could've happened."

"Peter, I grant your expertise in what you know and your experience with tiles," Rocha said, his voice starting to rise. "But you are not a structural dynamicist. You are not a stress expert. You are not an image specialist for enhancing pictures. You are none of these things. So how can you know?"

Delaney started to respond, but Ramon held up a hand. "That is the fundamental issue here. None of us actually knows." He pointed at the screen. "Those last two bullets on the slide: 'Flight condition is significantly outside of test database/Volume of foam is 1920cu vs 3 cu in for test.' *That* is the key issue. The estimated size of the debris that hit *Columbia* is *640 times* greater than the data used to calibrate the Crater model on which we are trying to base our damage assessment. This entire exercise has been invalid. We will need to do the analysis all over again when we get the images of the vehicle in orbit."

Everyone turned to look at Ramon.

"What images?" Delaney asked.

"Joyce and Rodney and I talked about it, petitioning outside agency assistance for imagery from national technical means." Ramon was using the politically correct words for spy satellites and high-resolution military telescopes. "I emailed the MMT, emailed Maria Garabedian, after we talked. Are you saying nobody's heard anything?"

Ramon called Garabedian, the chair of the Mission Management Team, as soon as he got back to his office. It went to her voicemail. He put down the phone, thought for a moment, and then started writing an email asking for on-orbit imagery to be put on the agenda for the MMT meeting first thing Monday morning.

✡

Aboard Columbia
Flight Day 5
January 20, 2003

Yael Dahan gazed down upon the Holy Land from the heavens.

From orbit, Israel looked exactly as it did on a map. It had come into view and would be gone again in less than a minute, testament both to the speed of her spacecraft and the size of her homeland. She pressed her hand against the window, and just like that, all of it—from the Mediterranean to the Sea of Galilee to the Dead Sea—six-and-a-half million people and three thousand years of history, was gone. It was a humbling revelation.

She recited the Shema prayer. "*Shema Yisrael Adonai Eloheinu Adonai echad …*"

✡

NASA Johnson Space Center, Building 30
January 20, 2003

Maria Garabedian convened the Mission Management Team meeting at precisely 8:00am. Among the attendees were Peter Delaney and Mission Evaluation Room manager Don McCormack. A number of others participated by teleconference including Ron Dittemore, the Space Shuttle Program manager, and Wayne Hale, a manager at the Kennedy Space Center. Ilan Ramon, Joyce Seriale-Grush and Rodney Rocha sat at the back of the room.

"Good morning," Garabedian said. "Flight ops don't respect stat holidays, so I appreciate everyone being here."

Ramon watched in amazement as Garabedian prosecuted the meeting with brutal efficiency. She seemed to revel in briskness, speaking in a stilted syntax of shorthands and acronyms like some NASA auctioneer. A/C problem in the SPACEHAB? Check. Leak in the WLCS? Check. Ku-band antenna glitch? Check.

Discussion of the foam strike was left to the end.

"We received data from Rodney Rocha's team on the potential range of sizes and impact angles and where it might have hit, and Peter Delaney's team have done an analysis," Don McCormack reported. "While there is potential for tile damage, our thermal analysis does not indicate burn-through, only localized heating."

"No damage and localized heating means tile replacement," Garabedian summarized.

"Now, the foam might have hit the RCC," McCormack continued, "but there shouldn't be anything more than coating damage."

"So, I'm hearing from Don and Peter there will be no burn-throughs, so no safety-of-flight issues." Garabedian looked at the wall clock. "All right, it's 8:30. Thanks, everyone."

Rodney Rocha turned to Ramon in disbelief. "This is ridiculous. Is that all they're going to say about it? And what about the imagery request?"

The crowd filed out of the room. Ramon got up and followed Garabedian to the elevator.

"Excuse me, Maria," Ramon said. "May I please have a word with you?"

"What do you want?"

"I had emailed you about on-orbit imagery. Why was it not discussed?"

"Is there a mandatory requirement for imagery?" Garabedian asked.

"Mandatory?" Ramon blinked. "I'm not sure what you mean."

"Is there a mandatory requirement for imagery? Because I didn't see anything in that analysis that would indicate a mandatory need."

Ramon thought he understood. "Maria, this puts my team in an impossible situation. We need images to be able to accurately assess potential damage, but you're telling me that we need to prove the damage is bad enough to justify taking images."

The elevator doors opened and Garabedian stepped inside. "I can't help you until you show me a mandatory requirement," she said as the doors closed.

Ramon's mind churned as he drove back to his office in Building 4. He sat at his desk for a long while in contemplation, and then he made a decision. It took some time to find the right contact, but when he did, he started writing an email.

✡

Aboard Columbia
Flight Day 6
January 21, 2003

"Jerusalem, this is Houston," said the voice of the NASA public affairs officer. *"Please call* Columbia *for a voice check."*

Yael Dahan, along with commander Ben Hernandez, flight engineer Kalpana Chawla and mission specialist David Brown, floated together in the middeck of *Columbia*. They stared at a small camera mounted on the bulkhead.

"Hello, Columbia," called the voice of Israeli Prime Minister Ariel Sharon. *"I am here with technology minister Limor Livnat, and you should know that our conversation is being broadcast live across the country."*

"Thank you, Mr. Prime Minister." Hernandez spoke into the microphone. "It is an honor to be speaking with you and Minister Livnat today."

"The honor is ours, Commander Hernandez," Sharon continued. *"I wish you continued success in your mission, and upon your return I would like to invite your crew to visit us in Israel. I can assure you that you will find yourselves among friends."*

"Thank you, Mr. Prime Minister. We appreciate the invitation. And now,

I would like to turn it over to Yael Dahan." Hernandez passed her the microphone.

"*Yael Dahan,*" Sharon said, "*on behalf of our entire nation, I cannot tell you enough how wonderful it is to know that a daughter of Israel is up there among the stars.*"

"Thank you, Mr. Prime Minister."

"*How does Israel look from space?*" asked Livnat.

"It is beautiful and small and fragile, and peaceful," Dahan replied. "And that is my greatest hope, for peace. Peace in our homeland, peace with our neighbors, peace throughout the world."

"*I understand you brought some special artifacts with you to space,*" Sharon said.

"Yes, Mr. Prime Minister." Dahan turned to her colleagues. "Begging the pardon of my crewmates, I will now say a few things in Hebrew."

"Mr. Prime Minister, I have one particular artifact for which I received special permission to bring. This artifact is very special."

Yael Dahan held up a tiny Torah scroll, bringing it into view of the camera.

"We are usually not permitted to show these, but today I am filled with excitement while I hold this in my hand. This little Torah scroll you see here, almost sixty years ago when he was only a boy at Bergen-Belsen, our mission scientist Joachim Joseph—Yoya—received it from the Rabbi of Amsterdam who was preparing him for his bar mitzvah. I am thankful to Yoya and very touched to have it here with me in space."

✡

Ramat Aviv Gimmel, Israel

"*This little Sefer Torah,*" Yael Dahan said on the television, "*shows the ability of the Jewish people to survive anything, even the darkest of times, and to always look forward with hope and faith for the future.*"

As Joachim Joseph watched, the little Torah slipped from her hand, and for a moment, floated free. Rabbi Dasberg's Torah. In the heavens. Free.

"Yoya."

Joseph turned. Sunlight through the window caught the gray in Stella's hair, giving the appearance of a halo. She was holding a camera.

"Go over there." She waved her free hand. "By the TV."

Slowly, Joseph got up from the chair and went to stand by the television, resting his hand on the set. The little Torah was still there. And Stella took the picture.

✡

NASA Johnson Space Center
January 21, 2003

Being called to Maria Garabedian's office in Building 1 was, in some ways, like being summoned to the principal's office. Ilan Ramon was in trouble.

"Why did you email the NIMA POC about on-orbit imagery?" she asked, referring to the National Imagery and Mapping Agency. "Those requests are supposed to go through proper channels. Through me."

Ramon sighed. As a former fighter pilot, nobody needed to tell him the importance of following the chain of command. But even he found the management culture at JSC to be closed and insular compared to the Israeli Air Force. He believed the safety of a crew under his watch was in danger, and he had to act.

"We did go through you," Ramon said quietly. "Twice. There was no response."

"Because neither you nor anyone on your team ever articulated a mandatory requirement for imagery," Garabedian said.

"We thought the rationale was obvious." He waved a hand. "We have all these safety posters everywhere saying things like, 'If it isn't safe, say so.' Well, Maria, we really think it's that serious."

Garabedian's eyes narrowed. "My husband is an astronaut. Don't you ever imply that I don't care about safety."

"Yes, of course. I apologize."

"Listen, Ilan," Garabedian said. "This is a busy flight, with all those science payloads. There is no mandatory requirement for imagery. And you know, even if there really is damage, there's nothing we can do about it."

"Are you going to turn off the imagery request?" Ramon asked, deflated.

Garabedian thought for a moment. "No, I think *you* should do it. Tell them the vehicle's in excellent shape, and that in the future we will better coordinate to ensure that when a request is made it's done through proper channels."

Ramon found himself shaking when he got back to his car. Gripping the steering wheel, he took a few deep breaths. He could not bring himself to go back to his office. After a while, he picked up his cell phone and made a call.

"Hello, Rachael."

"My goodness Ilan, you sound upset. Are you all right?"

"I've been better. Listen, I know this is very short notice, but could we meet for lunch?"

"Of course, sweetie. How about Pho Hoang in an hour?"

✡

She was the Chinese-American girl with the almost Jewish name.

"What a treat to be able to see you for lunch," Rachael Chen said.

Ilan Ramon gave his wife a kiss before sitting down. "Thank you for making the time."

"You sounded upset on the phone," Chen said, "and believe me, it's no trouble. I spend far more time in sales meetings than any engineering director ever should."

The waiter came and wrote their order for two bowls of beef noodle soup. He then gathered up the menus and took Ramon's cane.

"Excuse me, please." Ramon pointed at his cane. "I need that."

"Oh, sorry sir."

Chen shook her head, then said, "So, tell me what happened."

Fifteen months in an Iraqi prison had not been kind to Ilan Ramon. When he was finally released in the fall of 1982, he weighed seventy pounds and had to be carried out on a stretcher. He spent three months at the Chaim Sheba Medical Center in Ramat Gan before being sent to the Walter Reed Medical Center in the U.S. for specialized musculoskeletal reconstructive surgery.

It was there that he met Rachael Chen. Her father was a U.S. Army colonel who was at Walter Reed for a prosthetic fitting. She noticed he was alone in his hospital room, and one day, brought him a steamed bun to share.

Chen went to the University of Maryland to study geology and Ramon followed her there, pursuing a degree in electrical and computer engineering. Upon graduation, Chen was hired by a "dinosaur juice company" (her words) in Houston and Ramon followed her again, eventually getting a job with Rockwell. One night, they went out to watch the Schwarzenegger film *Total Recall* and shortly thereafter, completely on a whim, Ramon submitted his resume to NASA. He was hired less than a year later.

"I don't believe this," Chen said. "Garabedian expects *you* to do her dirty work for her?"

"I guess so."

"Do you have time for this?" Chen asked.

"Time for what?"

"Well," Chen said slowly, "you're a very busy person, you know. You might not have time to get to this until later today, maybe even tomorrow."

Ramon stared across the table at the beautiful Chinese-American woman with the almost Jewish name. "I love you," he whispered.

✡

Ramon had just gotten up from his desk when the phone rang. He was about to let it go to voicemail when he noticed the Colorado area code on the call display.

"Is this Mr. Ilan Ramon?" asked a male voice.

"Yes, this is he."

"Good afternoon, sir. This is Lt. Col. Timothy Lee at Peterson Air Force Base. I'm calling in regard to your email canceling the imaging request."

"Yes," Ramon said.

"Well sir, I'm afraid this is a bit awkward, but—the images have already been obtained."

Ramon gripped the handset tighter.

"What would you like us to do with them, sir? Do you still want them?"

"Yes," Ramon said immediately. "Absolutely, please."

"Understood, sir. I do need to remind you the images are classified, so they can only be transferred to and viewed by a member of your team with Top Secret clearance."

"That would be our flight dynamics officer, Richard Jones," Ramon said.

"Very good, sir. Please contact Mr. Jones, and I can set up the secure file transfer within the hour."

✡

Mission Evaluation Room
NASA Johnson Space Center, Building 30
January 22, 2003

There was a ghostly beauty to the grayscale images of *Columbia* in orbit. The white and gray delta-shaped Shuttle stood out starkly against the black of space. *Columbia* looked almost serene and, in the words of Maria Garabedian, appeared to be in excellent shape.

Except for the hole in its left wing.

"Of the dozen or so images obtained, these three provide the best views," explained Richard Jones. "The portside payload bay door obscured the other views." He used a laser pointer to indicate the dark square on the leading edge of *Columbia*'s left wing. "This is *not* a shadow or an artifact or a glitch. It appears in both of the visible light images as well as the near infrared image, in different lighting conditions and different viewing angles."

Ilan Ramon approached the screen and touched the black spot with his finger, as if it were a smudge he could wipe away. "How big is this?"

"Approximately six inches square," said Jones.

"I'm not sure I see how such a conclusion can be made from these images," Peter Delaney said.

Jones turned to Delaney. "The pictures I'm showing you have been downsampled and blurred to protect the true capabilities of the imaging assets. The Air Force assessment was based on the classified full-resolution images, which I have also seen."

Ramon's cell phone rang. He stepped to the back of the room to take the call.

"Mr. Ramon? This is Lt. Col. Lee again at Peterson. I just left a message on your office phone, but I hope you don't mind me calling your cell."

Ramon listened. "Lt. Col. Lee, I need to ask a favor," he said at last, walking back to the conference room table. "Please call me back at this number right away."

A moment later, the phone on the table rang.

"Lt. Col. Lee," Ramon said, "I have you on speaker phone in the Mission Evaluation Room with my colleagues. Please repeat for them what you just told me."

"Well sir, it's a little unusual to—"

"Lt. Col. Lee," Ramon said, "my colleagues and I believe we are dealing with a safety-of-flight issue aboard *Columbia*. Any information you are able to provide in an open forum would be extremely helpful."

There was a pause, and then the Air Force officer spoke. *"Following the execution of your imaging request, our team went back through tapes of radar tracking data, and we found something. On Flight Day 2, the day after launch, sometime between 15:30 UTC and 16:00 UTC, radar detected a small object, approximately six inches in size, drifting away from the Shuttle orbiter."*

"Jesus Christ," Rocha muttered.

Ramon pointed at the screen. "I want this analysis documented, and I want a tiger team stood up to assess the implications for re-entry. Thermal, structural, mechanical, guidance, every relevant engineering discipline. Call anyone you need, any building, any NASA Center, any contractor. We present to the Mission Management Team first thing tomorrow morning. And technical reports, *please*. Not just PowerPoint!"

✡

Mission Evaluation Room
8:00am CST, January 23, 2003

It was standing-room only in the drab, gray conference room. In attendance representing management were Maria Garabedian, MER manager Don McCormack, and Space Shuttle Program manager Ron Dittemore. Jefferson Howell, the director of the Johnson Space Center, Bryan O'Connor, the chief of safety and mission assurance at NASA Headquarters, and Wayne Hale from the Kennedy Space Center were tied in via teleconference. This time, Ilan Ramon and Joyce Seriale-Grush sat near the front.

"The timeline of the launch day in-flight anomaly was compiled by Joyce's team with the support of Richard Jones and Rodney Rocha, and is based on four lines of evidence," Don McCormack reported. "The film from ground cameras at the Kennedy Space Center, visual and infrared imagery from Air Force assets, radar tracking data also from Air Force assets, and off-line engineering analyses and computer simulations.

"At T-plus 81.7 seconds after launch, when the vehicle was at an altitude of 65,600 feet and travelling at Mach 2.46, a piece of insulating foam with a volume of 1,360 cubic inches separated from the negative-Y bipod ramp area of the external tank, and at T-plus 81.9 seconds struck the lower half of reinforced carbon-carbon panel eight on the leading edge of *Columbia*'s left wing. From the relative impact velocity of 840 feet per second, as well as the size and density of the foam and the angle of impact, the imparted kinetic energy was sufficient to breach the RCC panel, resulting in a six-inch hole in the leading edge."

Audible gasps and whispers of "My God" and "oh, shit" drifted through the room.

"Are there any questions or comments at this point?" McCormack asked.

"The USAF imagery was obtained through informal channels," Maria Garabedian said. "We'll need to be more stringent about the JSC-NIMA interface in the future."

"Yes, thank you," Ron Dittemore said. "What are the implications for re-entry?"

"I'll turn it over to Joyce," McCormack said.

"The implication for re-entry is that it's not happening," said Joyce Seriale-Grush. "The thermal team estimates plasma will burn through the wing leading edge spar between EI-plus 450 seconds and EI-plus 970 seconds, resulting in catastrophic structural failure of the left wing, associated loss of flight control ..." Her voice wavered. "And loss of vehicle and crew."

EI was "entry interface," the point about 80 miles altitude when the Shuttle started encountering the effects of the atmosphere. The implication was obvious. *Columbia* would die long before it got anywhere near the safety of a runway.

✡

Ramat HaSharon, Israel
6:26pm IST, January 23, 2003

TV was usually forbidden at meal times, but Omer Bitten made an exception for the duration of his wife's mission. As he set the dinner table, words scrolling on a ticker at the bottom of the screen caught his attention.

"Noa, can you turn that up, please?"

"...and we have unconfirmed reports of some kind of a problem on the Space

Shuttle Columbia. *Unnamed sources are telling us the problem is very serious and may even cut the mission short."*

The phone rang. Noa picked up, then passed the handset. "It's for you, daddy."

"Who is it?" he asked.

"It's Mr. Aby Har-Even."

✡

Mission Evaluation Room
NASA Johnson Space Center, Building 30
2:27pm CST, January 23, 2003

"The first priority is conservation," Ilan Ramon said. "We need to conserve every resource, every consumable, in order to buy ourselves time to figure out what to do. So, let's start with power."

"My team is working on a power-down procedure," said Max Leistung, the lead power engineer. "Our goal is to bring peak power down to 9.5 kilowatts, maybe less."

"OK. Food and water?"

"I actually have good news for you, Ilan," said Katie Rogers, the operations lead for environmental controls and consumables. "As long as the crew restricts their physical activities, we've got enough food up there to last more than a month. Assuming the minimal power level, we should still get about three gallons of potable water per crewmember per day as a by-product of the fuel cells."

"That is good news, Katie. Thank you. What about oxygen?"

"We're good for oxygen for thirty-one days," Rogers said. "Actually, the most serious limitation is not too little of something, but too much."

"You mean carbon dioxide," said Joyce Seriale-Grush.

Rogers nodded. "There are 69 cans of LiOH aboard *Columbia*." She pronounced it "lye-oh," referring to the lithium hydroxide canisters used to scrub carbon dioxide from the air. "To estimate how long we could stretch those, I need more information about crew metabolic rates and what is the highest acceptable CO_2 concentration."

"Who would be the best person to ask?"

"Jon Clark."

The room fell silent. Jon was the chief of the Medical Operations Branch at JSC. He was also the husband of *Columbia* astronaut Laurel Clark.

"We can't talk to Jon now," said Peter Delaney. "He's an emotional wreck."

"I don't agree," Seriale-Grush said. "The worst thing we can do is *not* talk to him. It's not as if we're going to hurt his feelings by accidentally reminding him that his wife is stranded in orbit on a broken spaceship. He'll want to help."

"In that case, I'll go talk to him," Delaney offered.

"No, don't trouble yourself," Ramon said quickly. "I'll do it. In the meantime, Max, we need your team to finish that power-down procedure as soon as possible."

✡

Clear Lake, Texas
4:03pm CST, January 23, 2003

Ilan Ramon navigated through an obstacle course of media vans before pulling into the driveway of the Clark residence. Jonathan and his eight-year-old son Iain greeted him.

"Hello, Jon." Ramon embraced him. Iain's arms were wrapped around his father's waist.

"Please, come in," Clark said.

They sat at the dining room table. The window curtains were drawn.

"Jon," Ramon said, "I need to pick your brain. We've got 69 LiOH cans on board, and we need to know how long we can stretch them. How much CO_2 can the crew tolerate over an extended period of time?"

Clark thought for a moment.

"Well, the first thing is to reduce the metabolic rate of the crew. Let's say that we've got them on a 12-hour awake and 12-hour asleep cycle. We assume absolutely minimal physical activities. The currently accepted CO_2 partial pressure for Shuttle and Station is six millimeters of mercury. Mission rules require flight termination if CO_2 goes above 15 millimeters. I've seen papers saying that levels as high as 26 millimeters might be tolerable without long-term effects. So, 15 millimeters should be all right, but it certainly won't be a pleasant experience."

"What are the symptoms?" Ramon asked.

"Shortness of breath, fatigue, headaches. Likely cognitive impairment."

Ramon opened his laptop and brought up a spreadsheet provided by Katie Rogers. "All right, we assume crew metabolism consistent with 12-hour sleep and wake cycles and maximum CO_2 of 15 millimeters, with an assumed absorption capacity per LiOH can, which drives the canister changeout schedule …" He created a chart, then turned the screen to Clark.

"Get Katie to check that, but it looks reasonable to me."

"We're nearing the end of Flight Day 8. This tells us we have until Flight Day 30 before CO_2 levels become unacceptable. That takes us to Friday, February 14th."

"Valentine's Day," said Clark, his voice breaking.

Ramon reached across the table and took Clark's hand. "Then we'll have Laurel home for Valentine's Day. We'll have them all home."

Clark managed a weak smile. "You sound pretty confident."

"I am," Ramon said, "because you're helping."

✡

"How do we bring them home?" Don McCormack asked. "What options do we have?"

"Can they make it to ISS?" asked Maria Garabedian.

"Impossible." Richard Jones shook his head. "*Columbia* and Space Station are in different orbital inclinations. Russian Soyuz won't work for the same reason."

"So, we'll have to go up and get them," McCormack said.

"Yes, and for that we might just have a chance," Ilan Ramon said. "Angela?"

Angela Brewer, the processing flow director for the Shuttle *Atlantis*, was on the phone from the Kennedy Space Center. *Columbia*'s sister ship, she explained, was already in the Orbiter Processing Facility undergoing preparations for a launch on March 1st. "Atlantis *is in OPF-1 with its three main engines already installed, but no cargo yet in the payload bay. The solid rocket boosters are already attached to the external tank in the VAB,*" Brewer continued, referring to the Vehicle Assembly Building. "*By working three round-the-clock shifts seven days a week, expediting vehicle checks and consolidating or skipping less critical tests,* Atlantis *could be ready for launch by February 9th.*"

"This sounds promising," said Don McCormack, "but it's predicated on two big assumptions. First, that in the expedited launch processing we make no mistakes and don't break anything on *Atlantis*, and second—maybe more importantly—that we are willing to expose *Atlantis* to the same risk of debris strike that's crippled *Columbia*."

Peter Delaney spoke up. "I think it's a mistake, launching again without fully understanding what happened the last time. Do we really want to throw another crew up there?"

"I can guarantee you," Joyce Seriale-Grush said slowly, "that we're going to have astronauts lined up around the block to volunteer for this mission."

✡

Omer Bitten and Noa Dahan sat at the dining table, staring at the television.

"*It is a solemn day at NASA as the space agency recognizes the anniversaries of the* Challenger *explosion in 1986 and the Apollo 1 launch pad fire in 1967, while struggling with the current crisis of seven astronauts stranded in space aboard the damaged* Columbia.

"*In the midst of the darkness, there was a welcome ray of hope as NASA approves a daring rescue mission. The Space Shuttle* Atlantis *was rolled out of the Vehicle Assembly Building this morning and began its slow, six-and-a-half hour journey to the launch pad."* Under a "recorded earlier" caption, the Shuttle orbiter stacked with its external tank and twin solid rocket boosters rode atop the massive gray crawler vehicle, moving at a stately two miles per hour. "*NASA will complete launch preparations at the pad, working towards liftoff on Sunday, February 9th on a mission to rescue the crew of* Columbia."

"Noa, would you like some food?" Omer asked. She shook her head.

"*We have a video from NASA that shows how the rescue will work.* Atlantis *will rendezvous with* Columbia *about a day after launch."* On the animation, *Columbia* was upside down with its payload bay towards the Earth. *Atlantis* approached from behind and below *Columbia*, payload bay facing upwards, the vehicle oriented perpendicular to its sister ship. "*The ninety-degree orientation will enable the two Shuttles to get as close together as possible, less than twenty feet apart, without their tails hitting each other."*

"*Once in position, two spacewalking astronauts from* Atlantis *will connect a tether to* Columbia *to facilitate transfers between the ships. They will first provision* Columbia *with extra spacesuits and carbon dioxide scrubbers, and then they will begin transferring crewmembers from* Columbia *to* Atlantis. *The process is expected to take up to nine hours."*

Omer squeezed Noa's hand. "You need to eat. Let me get you some food."

✡

Aboard Columbia
Flight Day 17
February 1, 2003

There were some in the ultra-Orthodox community, probably the same ones that had issues with Yael Dahan's gender, who also complained that she would be working on Shabbat while in space. She would be pleased to tell the Haredis this was no longer a problem.

After a brief flurry of activity to power down the vehicle almost ten days ago, there was now little for the crew of *Columbia* to do except wait and try not to move or breathe too much. At the start of every 12-hour cycle, Dahan emerged from her bunk to use the facilities, eat a cold food pack, and drink her water ration. And that was it. There was literally nothing else to do for the next eleven-and-a-half hours except eat and drink, and finally to sleep again.

Dahan and her crewmates spent hours staring out the windows at the Earth or the blackness of space. But they couldn't watch movies or listen to music because their battery-powered electronics were dead, and those needing plug-in power had been turned off and stowed. Emails could not be sent or received for the same reason.

She missed Noa and Omer terribly.

History would record that the first Israeli astronaut spent most of her mission floating in her bunk, unintentionally observing Shabbat.

✡

Mission Control Houston
NASA Johnson Space Center, Building 30
8:52pm CST, February 9, 2003

"This is Shuttle Launch Control, we are at T-minus 9 minutes and holding. We are awaiting the go/no-go poll of the launch controllers to come out of the hold."

Ilan Ramon watched Steve Stich's flight control team in action from the glassed-in VIP area behind and above the Mission Control room. The screen showed an image of *Atlantis* on the pad at Kennedy, glowing in the darkness under the illumination of spotlights.

"Hi, Ilan." Maria Garabedian came into the VIP box, shuffling across the row of chairs. She pointed to the spot beside Ramon. "Is this seat taken?"

"Yes. Joyce will be joining us shortly."

Garabedian moved Ramon's cane aside and sat down.

"Houston, Launch Control. We are 'no-go' on Range due to an unauthorized aircraft in the launch danger area."

Joyce Seriale-Grush came in. She looked at Garabedian for a moment, then sat down beside her. "What's going on?"

"Still holding, due an unauthorized aircraft in the range," Ramon said.

"I hope that guy has an engine failure," Garabedian muttered.

✡

Ramat HaSharon, Israel
4:57am IST, February 10, 2003

The extended family gathered in the predawn darkness to watch the launch. Noa Dahan served tea to her grandparents Michal and Eitan. Omer Bitten chatted quietly with his sister Neta and their parents Rivka and Moshe. The matriarch of the family, Noa's 87-year-old great-grandmother Anat, was dozing in an armchair.

On the television, the illuminated numbers on the countdown clock at the Kennedy Space Center were changing again. Omer turned up the volume.

"...after security forces escorted an unauthorized aircraft out of the launch area." The picture changed to a view of the launch pad. *"We are now less than seven minutes away from the launch of Atlantis."*

✡

Mission Control Houston
NASA Johnson Space Center, Building 30
9:01pm CST, February 9, 2003

"Atlantis, *you are 'go' to close and lock your visors.*"

"*Roger, Launch Control*," said *Atlantis* commander Mike Bloomfield. "*And please tell the crew of* Columbia ... *tell them, we're coming.*"

The screen showed a view of *Atlantis* on the launch pad, steam rising and lights glistening in the darkness.

"*T-minus 31 seconds. We have a 'go' for auto sequence start. The five computers on* Atlantis *are now in control.*"

The screen switched to a close-up shot of the engine nozzles at the base of *Atlantis* beneath its tail.

"*... eight, seven, we have a 'go' for main engine start ...*"

Orange-red flames spewed as the engines roared to life, quickly turning a translucent bluish-white as the combustion of the liquid hydrogen fuel became complete.

"*... three, two ...*"

The flame suddenly disappeared.

"*... and ... we have main engine cut-off.*"

Ramon's eyes widened. Joyce Seriale-Grush and Maria Garabedian gasped.

"*We have an RSLS abort. GLS safing and APU shutdown are in progress.*"

Ramon struggled to follow the acronym-filled chatter between Mission Control, the Launch Control Center, and the crew aboard the Shuttle. There were references to the ground launch sequencer and the redundant set launch sequencer and the auxiliary power units. The screen switched to a close-up of *Atlantis*. He saw water being sprayed on the engine nozzles.

"*Flight, Booster.*"

"*Go ahead, Booster*," said Steve Stich.

"*Flight, I'm getting a report from the LCC that the MPS fire detectors have tripped.*"

"*Copy, Booster*," Stich said with deliberate calm. "*Flight controllers, listen up. We are in a Mode One Egress situation.*"

Seriale-Grush put a hand to her mouth.

"The main propulsion system fire detectors went off," Ramon said grimly. "They are evacuating the crew."

✡

Ramat HaSharon, Israel
5:36am IST, February 10, 2003

The family shouted and pointed at the television. Omer Bitten waved his arms and asked for quiet.

"... hearing now from NASA that Atlantis *suffered a major engine malfunction less than two seconds from launch. The astronauts have been evacuated and are reported to be uninjured and safe."*

"Oh, the *fuss*," cackled 87-year-old Anat Dahan. "Why can't they put more gas in that thing and *go* already!"

The illuminated countdown clock was on TV. All the digits were zero.

✡

Mission Evaluation Room
NASA Johnson Space Center, Building 30
11:23pm CST, February 9, 2003

"What the fuck just happened?" Maria Garabedian shouted.

"The preliminary assessment from Marshall and Rocketdyne indicates a catastrophic failure of the high-pressure liquid hydrogen turbopump in the number two engine," Steve Stich said, "triggering the RSLS abort at T-minus 1.9 seconds." He spread his hands. "I can't ... I can't even describe how bad this could've been. If this'd happened two or three seconds later, after we lit the solid boosters, we could have lost the vehicle, the pad, the crew ... everything."

"How long to replace SSME-2?" Garabedian asked.

"We need to change out all three engines," said Angela Brewer on the speaker phone from Kennedy Space Center, *"because they all fired and the subsequent water damage."*

"How long?"

"Three weeks. Minimum."

"The crew will be dead in five days," Garabedian said.

"Yes, thank you," Rodney Rocha muttered.

Garabedian whirled. "Has it ever occurred to you, Rodney ... Has it occurred to anyone, that maybe ... maybe it would have been better if we didn't know? The crew would have had sixteen wonderful days up there, a terrific mission, and then on re-entry they just, they just ..."

A terrible, oppressive silence gripped the Mission Evaluation Room.

After a while, Ramon spoke in a quiet voice. "They'll need to do it. The crew will need to repair the damage somehow, and attempt to come home themselves."

Every pair of eyes turned to Ramon.

"How?" Garabedian asked. "They have no repair materials. They are physically and mentally exhausted." She shook her head. "Ilan, you're asking for the impossible."

Ramon closed his eyes. When he spoke again, it was in such a soft voice that people strained to hear. "I am impossible."

"I'm sorry?"

"I am impossible," Ramon repeated. "My mother was a Holocaust survivor. I was born to a woman who wasn't supposed to be alive. When I was eighteen, I had to jump out of an airplane without an ejection seat. When I was twenty-seven, I was blown out of the sky over Iraq. The first time I came to America, I learned to fly the F-16. The second time I came to America, I learned to walk again. And then I learned other things, too."

After a moment of silence, Joyce Seriale-Grush said quietly, "Are you going to say something about failure not being an option?"

Ramon managed a weak smile. "Failure is always a possibility. But giving up, that is not an option. For my part, I will never give up, and I mean never."

People looked at each other, and nodded. In ones and twos, and then in small groups, the engineers stood. They all got up, and with quiet, dignified resolve, went back to work.

✡

Johnson Space Center, Building 1
11:30am CST, February 10, 2003

"To paraphrase my colleague Ilan Ramon," Don McCormack said, "I think we have our Mission Impossible."

"Let's hear it," said Ron Dittemore, the Space Shuttle Program manager.

Ramon watched Joyce Seriale-Grush move to the front of the room. She looked exhausted, but pressed ahead.

"Our team has devised a repair scenario that we believe to be logistically feasible, making use of existing materials aboard *Columbia*. However, given the critically short timeline, the physiological condition of the crew, and the high number of uncertainties, our team considers the scenario to be high risk with low probability of success."

Seriale-Grush put up series of screen shots from a computer animation. "The crew will fill a bag with whatever pieces of metal they can scavenge from the cabin—metal tools, small bits of titanium, cutlery … any metal they can find. Two astronauts will conduct an EVA, taking the metal scraps and the middeck ladder to use as a work platform, to the site on the left wing."

She pointed to a rendering of two spacesuited figures at the end of a ladder, hovering over an area of the wing highlighted by a yellow square. "They will stuff the bag of metal into the hole, and then they will put a second water-filled bag over it and secure everything as best they can with kapton tape. We will maneuver *Columbia* to orient the left wing towards deep space, cold-soaking the patch and freezing the water. *Columbia* will then attempt a modified re-entry profile, one that minimizes the heating of the left wing, hoping to survive long enough to reach bailout altitude."

There was stunned silence.

"A bag of scrap metal and a bag of ice? That's not going to stop three thousand degree plasma!" Maria Garabedian exclaimed.

"No, it's not," Rodney Rocha said, in a trembling voice that betrayed despair. "All we're trying to do is buy time, delay the burn-through of the wing spar, delay the structural failure of the wing for as long as possible. Maybe—just maybe … long enough for the crew to bail out."

Dittemore stared at the screen. Finally, he asked, "What needs to happen next?"

"Four things," Ramon said. "First, we need a team to come up with a detailed EVA procedure for the crew. Second, we need a team to develop the software load for the modified re-entry profile. Third, we need to interface with the Navy for the rescue and recovery effort."

"Because—"

"The re-entry trajectory will be based on the profile for a landing at Edwards Air Force Base in California," Ramon explained. "After the crew has bailed out, we will need to ditch *Columbia* into the Pacific."

"Because we don't want debris falling over Texas. Understood. What's the fourth thing?"

"Someone will need to brief and to also … um, 'manage' the management, here as well as at Headquarters in Washington."

"Let me take care of the politics." Dittemore pointed at the screen. "I need you to make *that* happen."

✡

Ramat HaSharon, Israel
7:47pm IST, February 10, 2003

Omer Bitten lay in bed. He was awake but unmoving, his arms clutching a pillow.

The phone rang. He heard Noa Dahan calling to him, but did not respond. After a moment, he heard his stepdaughter pick up the phone and say something.

She came into the master bedroom.

"Who was that?" he asked.

"Mr. Har-Even," she replied.

"What did he say?"

When Noa didn't respond, Omer rolled over to face her. "What did Mr. Har-Even say?"

"He said *eema* is going to fix the Space Shuttle."

✡

Aboard Columbia
Flight Day 27
13:13 UTC, February 11, 2003

For the first time in weeks, Yael Dahan felt truly awake and alert. She and Dave Brown were wearing masks and inhaling pure oxygen. This pre-breathe protocol was standard preparation for spacewalks, needed to purge nitrogen from their bodies to prevent the bends. But for Dahan and Brown, the contingency EVA crewmembers, it was also a welcome respite from the CO_2-induced malaise that had tormented them for the past nineteen days.

Kalpana Chawla and Mike Anderson were taping towels over one end of the ladder. Willie McCool did the same with the boots of the spacesuits. Laurel Clark floated about with a large stowage bag, filling it with whatever bits of metal she could scavenge from the crew cabin.

Dahan watched her crewmates with concern. In contrast to her regained state of alertness, she saw they were clearly lethargic and perhaps even cognitively impaired.

Ben Hernandez and Willie McCool helped Dahan and Brown don their bulky spacesuits and enter the airlock. Anderson and Clark passed them the ladder, the bag of scrap metal, and some empty water and stowage bags. They began to close the hatch.

"Jesus Christ, *stop!*" Brown suddenly exclaimed. He held out his hands. "Gloves, people. *Gloves!*"

Dahan stared down at her own bare hands, shocked. Seven sets of eyes, seven people with checklists, seven of the smartest people in the world, had somehow managed to miss something that obvious. It was not an auspicious start to the spacewalk.

✡

Mission Control Houston
NASA Johnson Space Center, Building 30
8:49am CST, February 11, 2003

"Flight, EVA," said Victor Tsang, the extravehicular activity officer. "They are coming out now."

"Copy, EVA," said Ilan Ramon.

The screen showed a shot from a hand-held camera operated by flight engineer Kalpana Chawla, looking out the aft flight deck windows that had a view into the payload bay. Since the contingency spacesuits worn by Yael Dahan and Dave Brown had no cameras, this was the only way Mission Control could see them, and even this view would disappear when the astronauts went over the side of the payload bay to attempt the wing repair.

A white-suited figure emerged from the airlock.

　　　　　　　OTHER COVENANTS

"Columbia, Houston for Yael," CAPCOM Stephanie Wilson said. "Congratulations on becoming the first Israeli to walk in space."

✡

Ramat HaSharon, Israel
4:54pm IST, February 11, 2003

On the television, a white-suited figure emerged from the airlock.

"... are coming out of Columbia now. *Yael Dahan is wearing the all-white spacesuit, and her colleague the American astronaut Dave Brown can be differentiated by the red stripes on the legs of his spacesuit."*

"Look, it's *eema!*" Noa Dahan pointed.

Omer Bitten nodded.

✡

Aboard Columbia
Flight Day 27
15:08 UTC, February 11, 2003

Yael Dahan and Dave Brown floated from the airlock to a tool storage container located at the forward-left corner of the payload bay. Brown retrieved a portable tool caddy called a mini-workstation and attached it to the front of his spacesuit. Dahan took out a payload retention device, a pair of scissors, and a roll of kapton tape from storage and mounted them to the caddy on Brown's suit.

"All right, I'll get Laurel's bag of goodies." Brown went back to the airlock, returning a few minutes later with the metal scraps. As Brown held the bag open, Dahan threw in the remaining metal tools from the container. They returned to the airlock to fetch the ladder.

"All set," Brown said. "I think we've got everything."

Dahan keyed her radio. "Houston, we are proceeding to the work site."

The two spacewalkers floated to the port-side longeron sill, tethering themselves to a slide wire that ran the length of the payload bay. Each holding an end of the ladder, they used their free hands to pull themselves along a set of handrails. It was a gruelling traverse. The stiffness of their inflated gloves and suits made it a physical effort just to maintain a grip.

Dahan and Brown stopped about two-thirds of the way down the length of the payload bay, and climbed over the portside door. They flipped the ladder over the edge and carefully lowered it until the towel-wrapped end touched the left wing, securing the top rung to a door latch using the payload retention device.

"So, there's our work platform." Brown was breathing heavily. "Let's ...

let's harvest ourselves some thermal blanket."

"Are you all right?" Dahan asked.

"F-fine. Let's go."

They returned to the longeron handrails and continued to the back of the payload bay. *Columbia*'s tail and bulbous engine pods towered over them. After several frustrating attempts, Dahan finally managed to cut a jagged eight-by-seven inch piece of insulation blanket from the aft bulkhead. They returned to the ladder hanging over the edge of the payload bay.

Dahan climbed down. The gray leading edge of *Columbia*'s left wing filled her vision. Except it was not all gray. There, on the curved bottom of the now infamous RCC panel eight, was a gaping black hole. Her eyes widening as the extent of the damage.

"Houston, I am looking at the RCC panel, and the breach looks bigger than six inches, maybe more like seven at least."

"*Can you be more precise?*" asked Mission Control.

"I don't have a tape measure, Houston," Dahan said, immediately regretting her tone.

Brown was now on the ladder behind her. "Will you look at that?"

"Houston, we are proceeding with the repair. We'll do the best we can."

Brown handed Dahan an empty stowage bag. She gently stuffed it into the hole, leaving the mouth open to the outside. Brown started passing her pieces of metal from the other bag, which she in turn placed carefully into the cavity.

"All right, that's the last of Laurel's goodies," Brown said. "I'll be back with the hose."

Dahan took deep breaths, fighting fatigue and willing herself to stay awake as she waited for Brown to return with the water line. The Earth passed beneath her, and she watched the approaching west coast of Africa with tired apathy.

Brown handed Dahan a water container with the hose already attached. She gently placed the container into the hole over the bag of metal.

"All right, K.C.," Dahan called to flight engineer Kalpana Chawla inside *Columbia*. "You can start the water."

As the container inflated, Dahan pushed and kneaded the bag like a lump of dough, trying to achieve a good fit. The expanding container began to press against the edges of the hole.

"Hey K.C., you can stop now," said Dahan.

There was no response. The bag kept growing.

"Kalpana, *stop*, please," Brown called out in a louder voice. The flow of water halted.

"She's exhausted," Dahan said on a private channel.

Dahan pulled the hose from the water bag. Brown handed her the crude patch of insulation blanket, which she put over the water bag, tucking the sides against the edges of the hole as best she could. Finally, she secured the blanket with strip after strip of yellow-gold kapton tape.

"Houston, I think we're done," she said at last.

"How does it look?" asked Mission Control.

Dahan surveyed their work. It actually looked ridiculous, like the parcels overwrapped with packing tape she handled the summer she worked at the Israel Postal Company. She tried to recall the English expression. "Jerry-rigged, Houston. It looks totally jerry-rigged."

"Understood."

"We've done the best we can, Houston. We've done everything we can."

✡

Mission Control Houston
NASA Johnson Space Center, Building 30
12:47pm CST, February 11, 2003

"They're back inside, Flight," said Victor Tsang.

"Copy, EVA," said Ilan Ramon. "And CAPCOM, please send our thanks and congratulations to the crew for a job well done."

✡

Ramat HaSharon, Israel
8:52pm IST, February 11, 2003

"She did it!" Noa Dahan shouted. *"Eema did it!"*

Omer Bitten nodded, managing a weak smile.

✡

Mission Evaluation Room
NASA Johnson Space Center, Building 30
4:02pm CST, February 11, 2003

"Well done, everyone," Ilan Ramon said. "Now, we bring them home. Status, please."

"Columbia is in the cold-soak attitude," reported Mike Sarafin, the guidance and navigation lead. "The vehicle is oriented with the port wing towards deep space, away from Earth albedo."

"Thank you," Ramon said. "Richard, where are we with re-entry?"

"Given the need to cold-soak for as long as possible and the Friday deadline for consumables," said Richard Jones, "the only re-entry opportunity is Thursday evening, Houston time. Deorbit burn will take place over the Indian Ocean at 04:05 UTC, that's 10:05 pm here in Houston. The vehicle will re-enter 45-degrees nose-up, versus the nominal 40-degree angle of attack. The ditching zone is a 2.5 mile by 1.3 mile ellipse in the Pacific Ocean, centered about 30 miles southwest of Los Angeles. The vehicle is expected to descend to the safe bailout altitude of 34,000 feet about 18 miles short of the ditching zone."

"OK, thanks. What about software?"

"We're using the Ops 3 flight control software from STS-111 as a template," said the software engineer David Deschênes, referring to the last Space Shuttle mission to have landed at Edwards Air Force Base in California. "Changing the reference alpha to 45-degrees is requiring a significant change to the code. We'll have *something* ready for uplink by Thursday, but I don't have to tell you the code will hardly have been verified. There could be a bug in there that could send them to Mars."

"Wouldn't that be something," Joyce Seriale-Grush muttered.

✡

Ramat HaSharon, Israel
4:57pm IST, February 13, 2003

As the Sun went down, the street in front of the Bitten-Dahan home began to fill with media vans. Family, friends and neighbors gathered for the all-night vigil before the re-entry of *Columbia*. Omer Bitten's sister Neta stayed at his side while his parents Moshe and Rivka prepared snacks in the kitchen. Yael's parents Eitan and Michal were in front of the television, and great-grandmother Anat was, once again, dozing in an armchair.

The doorbell rang, and Omer went to get it. Rabbi Eli Levin from Beit Knesset Darchei Noam entered and greeted him warmly, then joined the crowd by the TV in the family room.

" ... *recovery task force will be led by the* USS Essex *out of San Diego, with support from ships of the U.S. Coast Guard and the Maritime Search and Rescue Unit of the Mexican Navy.*" A map appeared on the screen. "*The crew will bail out over the Pacific, when* Columbia *is below 34,000 feet altitude. This will occur around 9:04 pm local time, or 7:04 am in Israel.*"

✡

Aboard Columbia
Flight Day 29
01:07 UTC, February 13, 2003

The crew installed their seats in preparation for deorbit burn and re-entry. On the flight deck, Ben Hernandez and Willie McCool would assume their respective commander and pilot positions, with Yael Dahan and Kalpana Chawla sitting behind them. Below in the middeck would be Dave Brown, Mike Anderson and Laurel Clark.

Brown and Anderson were installing the escape pole that would deploy after they blew the hatch, curving outwards and downwards away from the vehicle. Its purpose was to prevent the astronauts from—ironically—hitting *Columbia*'s left wing as they bailed out. Brown would serve as the jumpmaster, helping his crewmates slide down the pole to presumed safety.

"Houston, *Columbia*," Hernandez reported. "Power-up is nominal, and the Ops 3 Mod 1 flight control software is loaded."

✡

Ramat Aviv Gimmel, Israel
3:37 am IST

Joachim Joseph was asleep in front of the TV.

"We are waiting for a 'go' from NASA for the so-called deorbit burn. This is the engine firing that will take the Shuttle out of orbit and start its plunge into the atmosphere."

Stella gently touched him on the shoulder. He snapped awake.

"Yoya, please come to bed," she said.

"I'm not tired!" Joseph whined like a petulant child.

"Of course you're not." She kissed him on the cheek. "Please come to bed. Don't worry, my sweet. I will not let you miss this."

✡

Mission Control Houston
11:05 pm CST

"STS-107 flight controllers, may I have your attention please. I would like to invite anyone who wishes to do so to take a moment … to pray, or reflect, or contemplate—whatever is your belief or custom or practice, for the safe return of our colleagues."

Ilan Ramon recited the *Tefilat HaDerekh* silently to himself, then opened his eyes and scanned the room. Some of his colleagues had their hands clasped in front of them. Other sat in silence with their eyes closed. Some just stared ahead in quiet contemplation.

"All right, everyone," he said at last. "Let's bring them home."

✡

The view out the windows began to change from the inky blackness of space to a diffuse orange-yellow glow. Over the course of a few minutes, the glow steadily brightened to the white hot intensity of a blast furnace. Swirls of fiery plasma streaked across the windows.

But the flight deck was quiet. Except for the occasional perfunctory report from Ben Hernandez to Mission Control, no one said a word.

Yael Dahan thought about the jerry-rigged repair on the left wing. The kapton tape and insulation blanket would have burned away quickly, melting like butter on a frying pan. But every minute, every second the remaining mass of ice and metal delayed the plasma's progression to the wing spar, was another second closer to their bailout altitude.

Dahan closed her eyes and slowly counted to ten. *Echad, shtayim, shalosh...* She was still alive when she reached ten. So she counted again. And again.

If they could live for ten seconds, they could live for another ten. And another. And another. That was how they were going to make it. Ten seconds at a time.

✡

Mission Control Houston

On the screen, *Columbia*'s re-entry track was plotted on a map as a green curve, arcing from the southern Indian Ocean to the Pacific seaboard of the southwestern United States. The red triangle indicating *Columbia*'s position crept towards the coast of California.

"Altitude 90,000 feet, speed 4,308 miles per hour," reported Richard Jones.

"Flight, MMACS," called Jeff Kling, the mechanical and systems officer.

"Go ahead, MMACS," Ilan Ramon responded.

"Flight, we've just lost four temperature transducers on the left side of the vehicle, two of them on system one and one in each of systems two and three."

"Copy," said Ramon. He turned to Joyce Seriale-Grush. Her face was ashen.

"It's started," she whispered.

✡

Aboard Columbia

"Altitude 43,000 feet, speed 806 miles per hour," Willie McCool called out.

Yael Dahan turned and saw blinking red-and-white aircraft lights out the left-side window, just past Kalpana Chawla's helmet.

"Houston, *Columbia*," Ben Hernandez radioed. "It looks like we have company."

"Roger, Columbia," said Stephanie Wilson. *"That would be your buddy Mike Bloomfield. He promised to come for you, and here he is."*

✡

Mission Control Houston

A new window appeared on the screen, showing the feed from a night-vision camera aboard the T-38 chase plane flown by astronaut Mike Bloomfield. *Columbia* appeared as a ghostly image in shades of green against a black sky with greenish-white speckles of stars.

Audible gasps went through the room. Some of the flight controllers stood from their consoles like an honor guard.

The hole in *Columbia's* left wing was now an obsidian gash. There were black streaks over the wing and along the fuselage, and dark splatters on the left engine pod and tail—cooled residue of molten metal. The rudder and elevon were deflected, physical manifestation of the flight control system struggling to keep the ship steady.

A chill went down Ilan Ramon's spine. *Columbia* was mortally wounded, but she was still alive, still fighting to bring her crew home. She was simply a beautiful, magnificent, heroic flying machine.

"Don't do it."

Ramon blinked. Had he said something aloud?

"Don't anthropomorphize the vehicle," Joyce Seriale-Grush said. "She doesn't like it."

✡

Aboard Columbia

A buzzing vibration shook *Columbia* as the vehicle passed below the speed of sound.

"Altitude 42,000 feet, and we are now subsonic," Willie McCool said.

"All right, everyone," Ben Hernandez called out. "Final verification of your sea survival gear, and have your breakup/LOC cue card handy."

Yael Dahan finished checking her pressure suit, parachute and survival gear as McCool reported their altitude at 40,000 feet.

"Houston, *Columbia,*" Hernandez said. "We are venting the cabin."

✡

Mission Control Houston

"Cabin venting complete," reported Katie Rogers from the EECOM console.

"Altitude 34,120 feet," said Richard Jones.

"That's close enough," Ilan Ramon said. "CAPCOM, get them out of there."

"*Columbia*," Stephanie Wilson called, "you are 'go' for Mode One Egress."

✡

Aboard Columbia

"Blow the hatch!" Ben Hernandez ordered.

There was a muffled bang as the middeck door jettisoned and the escape pole deployed. Through her helmet, Yael Dahan could hear a faint whistle of wind.

"Jumpmaster is in position," Dave Brown called from the middeck.

"Houston, *Columbia*." Hernandez made the final report. "We are initiating the bailout procedure now."

After disconnecting the oxygen and communications lines from her pressure suit, Dahan unfastened the seatbelt and threw the harness over her head. She followed Kalpana Chawla to the passageway leading to the middeck below. Chawla climbed down the ladder.

Dahan grasped the top rung. She pressed a hand against the bulkhead.

"*Todah rabbah*," she whispered, then descended the ladder.

✡

Mission Control Houston

"Flight!"

Ilan Ramon looked up, and watched *Columbia* die.

The left wing simply disintegrated. *Columbia* rolled over violently, pitched down, and then went into a flat spin. The tail snapped off, and then the right wing and the main fuselage came apart, throwing the crew cabin clear.

For a moment, the image disappeared as the debris fell out of the field-of-view of the night-vision camera. Then the camera found the targets again and started tracking downwards, following the pieces of wreckage like giant, greenish-white snowflakes tumbling towards the dark ocean below.

✡

"No!" Stella cried.

Joachim Joseph pulled his wife closer.

It was the middle of the night in Houston. On the television, a somber-faced reporter was standing in front of the large NASA sign at the entrance to the Johnson Space Center. Flowers, wreaths, balloons and cards were already piling up.

"We now have a report from NASA, from the flight dynamics officer at Mission Control, that the vehicle is destroyed. We are told that rescue forces will begin moving into the recovery zone as soon as debris has stopped falling."

✡

Mission Control Houston
11:21 pm CST

"Recovery, how many?" Ilan Ramon asked.

The screen showed a view from a night-vision camera aboard the *USS Essex*. The dark ocean blossomed with a greenish-white plume every time a piece of wreckage hit the water. On an adjacent telemetry screen, there was no more data, only the letter "S" for "static" or "NaN" meaning "not-a-number".

Joyce Seriale-Grush was crying.

Ramon wiped his eyes with the back of his hand. "How many, Recovery?"

"Three, Flight," came the answer at last. "There were three parachutes."

✡

Ramat HaSharon, Israel
9:09 am IST

"Three, three, three!" shouted 87-year-old Anat Dahan. "They keep saying three but they won't say who. Who is it?"

The doorbell rang.

Moshe Bitten answered it. "Omer, Noa. I think … I think you better come here."

An icy knot formed in Noa's stomach. She took Omer's hand, and together went to the front door.

It was Aby Har-Even. He was wearing a dark suit.

Noa Dahan covered her mouth and began sobbing.

Omer Bitten let out an anguished, almost inhuman cry of grief and despair. Har-Even and Moshe reached out to steady him as Omer's knees gave and he sank to the floor.

✡

Mission Control Houston
1:10 am CST, February 14, 2003

Ilan Ramon sat alone at the Flight Director's console. Mission Control was empty. Screens were dark, consoles were off, and lights were dimmed.

Ramon slowly took off his headset and tossed it to the console. Taking out his cell phone, he sent a text. Not entirely to his surprise, he received a response only a few seconds later. He dialed a voice number.

"You're still up," said Ramon.

"*Of course,*" Rachael Chen said. "*I don't think anyone slept tonight. Ilan, I am so sorry.*"

"Such a terrible day." His voice broke.

"*You and your colleagues did everything you could.*"

"We could have done more. We could have saved more." He knew them to be the words of the son of a Holocaust survivor.

"*Come home, Ilan.*"

"Because I *can* come home."

"*Yes, because you can. So, come home. I'll be waiting.*"

Ilan Ramon took his cane and made his way to the exit. He glanced behind him one last time, then turned out the lights and locked the doors. He was going home.

✡

Lod Air Force Base, Israel
May 12, 2003

It took almost three months for the wreckage of *Columbia* and the remains of her crew to be recovered from the bottom of the Pacific, but at long last, Yael Dahan also came home.

An honor guard carried the casket, draped with the Flag of Israel, down the cargo ramp of the Israeli Air Force C-130 transport. Noa Dahan and Omer Bitten followed the procession into a hangar where family, friends, colleagues and dignitaries had gathered.

Noa and Omer took their seats beside Prime Minister Ariel Sharon and former Prime Minister Shimon Peres. Aby Har-Even sat with NASA Administrator Sean O'Keefe. Noa saw the surviving *Columbia* astronauts—Laurel Clark, Kalpana Chawla, and Michael Anderson—and their families. Laurel Clark sat between Jon and Iain, holding their hands.

The casket was placed on a raised platform beside a podium. A large-size image of Yael Dahan's astronaut portrait, and those of Ben Hernandez, Willie McCool and Dave Brown, flanked the casket. The Chief Rabbi of Israel read

"A Woman of Valour" from the Book of Proverbs, and then *Hatishma Koli* began to play.

"Allow me, on behalf of the people of Israel, to honor the memory of Yael Dahan on this, her last road in our homeland," said Prime Minister Sharon. "Yael's image, projected from above, was a reflection of Israel at its best. As Israel's space pioneer, her memory will be engraved in our hearts forever."

Hand-in-hand, Noa and Omer made their way to the podium. He was wearing a dark suit. She wore her mother's blue NASA jacket.

Omer recited the mourner's kaddish, then started reading from a piece of paper.

"My dear Yael went in search of a better world. In the midst of our sorrow, our family takes comfort in knowing that she died doing what she loved—" he looked at the surviving astronauts—"with people she loved. Everyone who knew Yael knows it is impossible to remember her without a smile on her face, and we will continue forward with that same smile."

He switched to English. "I want to say something now, to the people at NASA. I wish I could talk to every person who worked on this mission, and tell them ..." Sobs racked his body, and he collapsed against the podium.

Noa pulled Omer closer and help him stand. Gently, she prised the crumpled piece of paper from his hand and smoothed it out on the podium.

"What my father wants to say," she began in a soft but steady voice, "is that our family wishes to thank every person at NASA who worked on this mission, who never gave up trying to bring my mother and her friends home, even when things must have seemed impossible. Because of such people, there will always be goodness and hope in the world."

Noa repeated the words in Hebrew, and then helped Omer off the stage. She looked into his eyes. Behind the tears of grief there was love—and fierce pride.

✡

Department of Geophysics and Planetary Sciences
Tel Aviv University
May 13, 2003

Joachim Joseph picked up the phone. It was Scott Janz, his MEIDEX co-investigator at the NASA Goddard Space Flight Center.

"Scott, how are you, my friend?" Joseph said. "Listen, I know I'm behind on the abstract for the IASTP Conference, but you can be sure—"

"Yoya, I am sorry to interrupt, but I'm not calling about the abstract." Janz paused. "Yoya ... they found it."

"Found what?"

"Your Torah scroll. They have recovered it from the wreckage."

A lump formed in Joseph's throat.

"The scroll and ark were sealed in plastic bags and wrapped in some towels and stuffed into a middeck locker. Someone did this deliberately, trying to protect it from the crash. There's some water damage, but it is intact. They found it, Yoya!"

"Oh, Scott ..." Joseph took a moment to compose himself. "I don't know what to say. Wonderful. Thank you. Thank you!"

"We're going to get that Torah back to you right away," Janz said. "I promise."

✡

International Atmospheric and Solar-Terrestrial Physics Conference
Binyenei HaUma Convention Center, Jerusalem
September 2003

"In summary," Joachim Joseph said, "we were successful in determining the height distribution in a set of six areas of desert dust aerosol plumes over the eastern tropical and subtropical Atlantic Ocean, using multispectral reflected radiance data collected by the MEIDEX payload aboard the *Columbia* mission.

"If there are no questions, I will conclude by acknowledging my co-investigators Zev Levin, Yuri Mekler, Peter Israelevich, Eli Ganor, Scott Janz, Ernest Hilsenrath, Mustafa Asfur, Adam Devir, Meir Moalem, and Yoav Yair, as well as all the students in Israel and America who contributed to this project over many years. This work is dedicated to the *Columbia* astronauts, without whom we would not have the data."

As Joseph disconnected his laptop from the projector, a middle-aged man in a light gray suit approached the podium.

"Professor Joachim Joseph?"

"Uh, yes. Just Yoya, please."

"Yoya, hello." They shook hands. "My name is Jeremy Issacharoff. I am from the Ministry of Foreign Affairs."

"Yes," Joseph said. "I remember your email. It is a pleasure to meet you."

"No, truly, the pleasure is mine." The polished-looking diplomat seemed at a loss for words. "As I wrote in my email ... well, I know it was a crazy thing to ask, being that you don't really know me at all, but—it would mean so much, if there were any way it could be possible? I only hope you will consider my request."

"Yes, Mr. Issacharoff," said Joachim Joseph. "I have considered your request."

✡

Beyt Knesset Menachem Zion
Jerusalem
November 2003

Four small candles were lit, and then the rabbi called the young man forward.

Thirteen-year-old Dean Issacharoff slowly approached the table and, with white-gloved hands, gently took hold of the small, water-stained Torah scroll. He began to read.

✡

Jerusalem Post, *Tuesday, December 9, 2008*
Joachim Joseph, Professor of Physics, Tel Aviv University

Joachim Joseph, professor of physics at Tel Aviv University, died Monday at his home in Ramat Aviv Gimmel. He was 77.

Joseph was born on March 31, 1931 in Berlin, Germany. During the Second World War, Joachim (or "Yoya," as he preferred to be called) and his family were sent to Bergen-Belsen. After the war, Yoya and the surviving family members sailed to Palestine to help pioneer the modern state of Israel. Young Yoya excelled in science, eventually earning a doctorate in atmospheric physics from the University of California, Los Angeles before becoming a professor at Tel Aviv University.

Yoya was a world-renowned expert on desert aerosols, becoming the principal investigator for the Mediterranean Israeli Dust Experiment that flew with astronaut Yael Dahan on the ill-fated *Columbia* mission in 2003. It was through Dahan that Yoya's death camp experience returned to bookend his life in a remarkable way. Rabbi Simon Dasberg, a fellow prisoner at Bergen-Belsen, secretly trained Yoya for his bar mitzvah, afterwards giving him the tiny Torah scroll and extracting a promise from Yoya to tell the story to the world. Almost sixty years later, Yael Dahan took the scroll with her to space. *Columbia* tragically broke apart on re-entry, but the little Torah survived and was recovered from the wreckage. Yoya's family has bequeathed the scroll to the Holocaust History Museum at Yad Vashem. The scroll will be the centerpiece of a new traveling exhibit that will visit more than a dozen countries before returning to its permanent home at the Yad Vashem museum.

Yoya is survived by his wife Stella, his daughters Iris and Gili, his sons-in-law Ronen and Pablo, and six grandchildren, Yuval, Chen, Liad, Tal, Gal, and Yam. His legacy also continues through his scientific papers and the countless students he mentored over a remarkable life.

The Book of Raisa

Alex Shvartsman

Raisa Kogan watched as the group of men marched down the perpetually busy corridor of the Birobidzhan General Hospital. Patients and staff alike scrambled out of their way, the path clearing in front of them like the waters of the Red Sea parting before Moses.

The lead man was in his sixties and wore a military uniform. The shoulder straps identified him as a *podpolkovnik*, a lieutenant colonel. He squinted at the unfamiliar Yiddish characters that adorned the walls next to the signs in Russian as he sought his destination. The three men that followed him wore civilian clothes, but their demeanor, their buzz cuts, the very attitude they projected, marked them as surely as any uniform.

Groups like theirs were a common sight. They'd barge into homes, offices, and schools at all hours of day or night, and escort away their quarries, never to be seen again. Raisa watched her co-workers tense up as the men approached. They reached for patients' charts or adjusted their stethoscopes, anything to busy themselves and avoid meeting the intruders' gazes. They sighed visibly with relief as the group passed them without slowing.

Raisa couldn't help but feel the same wave of panic rise within her as the men approached. She was on a break, resting between surgeries, a cup of lukewarm instant coffee in her hand. She sat on the bench in the corridor where she sought respite from the tiny staff cafeteria overrun with the latest batch of residents.

The *podpolkovnik* slowed as he approached, examining her like a farmer picking out a chicken for an evening's meal.

"Raisa Semyonovna Kogan?" he asked.

She swallowed hard. Raisa knew she hadn't been guilty of any crime, but that wasn't a guarantee of anything. It only took a cantankerous neighbor or a jealous coworker to phone in an anonymous tip, perhaps claiming that she had told a political joke or read an unauthorized book. The tip didn't have to be true.

"Yes?" She managed to keep her voice even.

"Comrade Kogan," the *podpolkovnik* removed his hat and offered her a nod that was nearly congenial. "You're urgently needed in the capital."

✡

Raisa felt anxious, but also tired and numb. The trip to Moscow had been as comfortable as it might have been under the circumstances: the military plane carried them there in under ten hours, as opposed to a week-long journey via the Trans-Siberian railroad. She recalled the train car that delivered her family to Birobidzhan when she was a teenager. It was packed with people uprooted from their homes, luggage that contained their meager belongings arranged to carve up the freight car into tiny family fiefdoms, fine dresses and curtains spread on the floor to provide some protection from the bitter cold that permeated the drafty car. And despite the draft, the sharp stink of sweat and human waste that lingered within.

The plane was clean and warm and comfortable. *Podpolkovnik* Selezenko reclined his seat all the way back and covered himself with a wool blanket. He was asleep in minutes, snoring lightly. Raisa tried to rest also, but she couldn't. With sleep came bad memories, and she would jolt awake fifteen minutes later, then toss and turn for another half-hour hoping sleep would reclaim her.

Neither Selezenko nor any of the others would explain why she was summoned, but she had a pretty good idea. She was a skilled neurosurgeon, so much so that prestigious hospitals in Kiev and Novosibirsk had tried to recruit her at one time or another, offering a waiver that would allow her to live and work outside of the Jewish Autonomous Oblast. She had declined all such offers.

Having been forced to move across the country once, she had no appetite for relocating again. Even so, she would travel to perform complicated surgeries: often to Khabarovsk and Vladivostok, but occasionally farther. She had operated on mayors and generals, and their family members, and her reputation grew. In retrospect, she shouldn't have been surprised at being summoned to the capital, though the urgency and the secrecy involved still made her nervous. She wondered if her patient would turn out to be a high-ranking Party member, perhaps even someone from the Politburo, or a foreign dignitary from one of the socialist countries.

They disembarked at a secure terminal at Sheremetyevo airport where Raisa's meager travel bag was transferred into the trunk of a brand-new '69 Volga which waited for them at the end of the runway.

Raisa stared out the window. She could barely recognize the neighborhoods she hadn't seen in sixteen years, half her lifetime. The faces of her school friends, blurred by the passage of time, came to her mind. She hadn't thought of them in years, and wondered if they ever thought of her. Her family had been given no warning, only a few hours to pack the essentials. She never got to say goodbye to anyone. She had written letters to two of her closest friends a few months after her family had settled in Birobidzhan, but she never received a response. She was hurt by this, but later realized her friends' parents may have thought it unsafe for their children to correspond with one of the "rootless cosmopolitans" deported to the Far East.

The car navigated the increasingly narrow Moscow streets as it reached the heart of the city and, having passed several check points, delivered her and Selezenko onto the Kremlin grounds.

✡

Raisa gawked like a tourist, having never been inside the Kremlin walls. She took in the palaces and cathedrals on the vast sixty-eight acre estate. A slight breeze caressed red flags that hung atop fifteenth-century buildings. Armed guards were positioned throughout the grounds. Selezenko presented his papers several more times before they entered one of the buildings, where both of them were searched, patted down, and passed through a device she'd never seen before but recognized from the scientific papers as a metal detector.

A guard escorted them up the stairs and across the many halls of the old palace, until they reached a series of rooms that had been repurposed into a small but incredibly well-stocked hospital.

Raisa gaped in envy at the Western equipment in the examination and operating rooms as she and Selezenko were left to wait in the hallway while someone went to summon the head physician. Some machines she had seen only in the journals and coveted for her hospital, others she didn't even recognize and had to make educated guesses about their intended purpose.

A goateed, rotund man in his fifties arrived carrying a folder. He nodded to Selezenko and extended a soft hand to Raisa.

"Welcome," he said. "I'm Dr. Petrov."

"We've heard good things," he told Raisa once she introduced herself. He thrust the folder toward her. "What do you think?"

She flipped through the stack of x-ray prints, studying the images closely.

"The tumour appears to be operable," she said. "Of course, I couldn't recommend the surgery without knowing the patient's condition, medical history, the works."

Petrov glanced at Selezenko, then back at Raisa. "No one has told you who the patient is, have they?"

She shook her head.

"This facility was designed to safeguard the health of a single individual," said Petrov. He pointed at the iconic portrait hanging on the wall alongside a hammer-and-sickle banner. "It's Comrade Stalin."

✡

Raisa was assigned a room and given some time to shower and change. She was told Stalin wanted to meet her, and he wasn't the sort of man one kept waiting, but she took her time anyway, trying to prepare herself. When she finally re-emerged, wearing the best dress she had brought and a white lab coat over it that was laid out for her in her room, she was led to the apartments just down the hall from the makeshift hospital, where yet more guards parted to let her pass.

"You may enter," said one of the guards.

She grasped the door handle and tried to compose herself. Beyond waited the man whose face she had seen on countless posters and banners, on television and in books, a man the newspapers lauded as the "Great Architect of

Communism" and the "Gardener of Human Happiness." The man ultimately responsible for the death of her father.

She pushed the door open and entered the room.

The man propped up in the four-poster bed looked nothing like the propaganda images of him she'd seen everywhere. At eighty-nine, his gray bushy eyebrows and mustache had thinned so much they practically disappeared, his once-thick hair was gone, liver spots covering his bald scalp. His face was gaunt and his body frail. Had this old man been rolled into her operating room on a gurney, she would never have recognized him.

Stalin opened his eyes and turned his head slightly toward her.

She didn't quite know whether to salute or stand at attention. But she wasn't in the army and wasn't even a member of the Communist Party, so the protocol was unclear, and nobody had bothered to instruct her. "Hello," Raisa said after the silence lasted long enough to become awkward.

If Stalin was annoyed at her breach of protocol, he didn't show it. "Hello, young lady," he said. "So, you're the brain surgeon?"

His voice was steady, stronger than his frail appearance would suggest. His Georgian accent was detectable, but softer than she'd heard in recorded speeches.

"Yes, Iosif Vissarionovich," she said.

Stalin studied her. "You're young," he said.

"I've performed similar operations many times," she said, working to keep annoyance out of her voice. She'd heard such sentiments from patients before. It was either that, or her being a woman. Some people couldn't see past age, or gender, or both. "Which is not to say the procedure is without risk," she added. "For persons of an advanced age the stress on the body can be considerable, dangerous even. As your physician, I must warn you of that."

Stalin's lips parted in a crooked smile. "Risk? Ha! A little malignant growth isn't taking me down. I'm a fighter. I had a stroke in '52 and spent half a day on the floor at my *dacha* before anyone came to check on me. Even my doctors were surprised I survived that one. But I was back at work in a matter of months."

And a few months after that the so-called Doctor's Plot—trumped up charges against a number of prominent Jewish doctors—escalated into a deportation order for most of Russia's Jews to the underdeveloped mountainous region on the border with China.

It was the last and the largest of Soviet-era ethnic deportations. The banishment of the Jews exceeded the scales of what had been done to the Poles and the Finns, the Chechens and the Koreans. Entire populations were moved across vast expanses of Siberia or the Central Asian republics at a stroke of Stalin's pen.

They started with the Jews in Moscow and Leningrad, then expanded the program to other cities and finally to the large swaths of Belarus, Moldova, and Ukraine, where two million Jews who survived the Holocaust lived in shtetls.

Those early years were hell. There wasn't enough food or fuel, but the trains kept on bringing carloads of people instead of grain. In a way, Raisa's family was among the lucky ones. They arrived early enough to be assigned a small apartment in the administrative center of what became the Jewish Autonomous Oblast. Even so, they weren't immune to the shortages. Their apartment building wasn't heated in the winter. Her father's flu turned into bronchitis, and he passed away days before the area's harsh winter reluctantly ceded to spring.

All of this roiled in Raisa's mind as she stared at the dilapidated despot before her. It was unfair that he got to live such a long life, despite the history of liberal consumption of alcohol and fatty foods denoted in his medical chart, while her father had been buried in the still-frozen earth so far from where he was born.

She watched as Stalin sank back into his pillows, exhausted by stringing several sentences together. His breathing was ragged. Raisa relented. Whatever his sins, he was an old man, surviving rather than enjoying his twilight years. Despite the best medical care available, the years of hard living were catching up with him after all.

The spell had been broken. It was possible for her to see him as merely one of her patients. She answered his questions as clearly as she could, patiently and with a practiced mix of cool professional detachment and polite empathy.

The surgery would take place the next morning. She insisted on getting a good night's rest before undertaking the procedure. As long as she could continue to see him as just another patient, she was confident it would turn out fine.

✡

When she was summoned again, she thought Stalin had more questions for her. But the guard led her out of the building and across the Kremlin grounds, now illuminated by electric streetlights. This time she arrived at an office rather than a bedroom, where another old man was sitting behind a large desk.

First Deputy Premier of the Soviet Union and head of the secret police Lavrentiy Pavlovich Beria had the look of a gentle, aging intellectual about him. The country's second most powerful man was in his late sixties but appeared spry, unlike his boss. He had a square-cut jaw and alert, deep-set eyes behind his trademark pince-nez. On his desk, sheaves of papers were moved out of the way to make room for a plate of ham sandwich and fried potatoes, which he was eating with knife and fork.

Beria finished chewing a bite of food and dabbed his mouth with a cloth napkin before he spoke.

"Comrade Kogan, thank you for undertaking the long journey in order to accommodate my request." Like Stalin, Beria hailed from the Republic of Georgia, and his Russian was accented. He spoke in a cultured, suave manner, which left Raisa feeling vaguely uncomfortable nevertheless.

"At your request, Comrade Beria?"

"Indeed! I've asked Selezenko to fetch you because your medical credentials are beyond reproach, but also because of my fondness toward and patronage of the Chosen People, you see."

"Oh?"

Raisa was uncertain as to where this conversation was going. Beria had a fearsome reputation, and was rumored to have dispatched his enemies within the Politburo as ruthlessly as the enemies of the state. There were also persistent rumors of women he had forced into his bed. Raisa hoped such monstrosities, if true, were many years behind him.

"Oh, yes. Stalin thought the Jewish doctors were trying to kill him after the stroke. He wanted to massacre your people, or to send them to Siberian gulags. It was I who pushed for the idea of relocating them to the extant Jewish Autonomous Oblast. I oversaw the opportunity for your people to grow and prosper, to uphold your traditions and literature, to speak Yiddish, and most importantly, to survive far from our dear Premier's wrathful attention."

To grow and prosper, the Jews had to tame the inhospitable land, much like their brothers and sisters in the Israeli kibbutzes. Hundreds of thousands of people died, and it took a decade before life in Birobidzhan gained any semblance of normalcy. Even now, her hospital and others in the region could barely keep up with the demand.

Raisa didn't think it would be wise to tell Beria these things. She tried her best to ensure the expression on her face was that of polite interest, hiding both her reaction to his claims of being her people's patron and the surprisingly frank way in which he spoke of his boss.

"My mother was a deeply religious woman," said Beria. "I studied the Bible in my youth, and must admit my fascination for the Good Book has been rekindled in recent years." He winked theatrically as he admitted to a stranger the sort of thing that might get another man arrested on suspicion of anti-Socialist tendencies. "I especially like the Book of Judith. Do you know her story?"

Raisa nodded again.

"Imagine that woman, holding the blade to the unconscious head of the enemy of her people. She must've been terrified, but she did what she had to do, as a hero and a patriot."

What was Beria saying? Was he testing her loyalty, trying to lure her into a trap before she could be permitted to operate on the Premier?

"It's a good thing Judith wasn't a doctor," Raisa said carefully. "Else the Hippocratic Oath would have proscribed her from doing harm."

"Of course, we couldn't have anyone parading the head of a beloved leader in front of his troops, not in our day and age. Think of the scandal. Think of the repercussions!" Beria went on as though she hadn't spoken at all. "No, that wouldn't do. Accidents, on the other hand, do happen. A tremble in the hand, a cut a single millimeter off target; who could blame a young surgeon from a small town, thrust into such a high-profile assignment? After all, brains are such delicate things." He used the tip of his knife to cut into the sandwich, slowly inserting the thin blade deeper into the bread. "The next person in charge would certainly understand and forgive, perhaps even reward, would he not?"

Raisa gathered her thoughts against the torrent of a million emotions and fears swirling in her mind. "I'm a very good surgeon," she said. "My hands are steady. I'm sure no accidents will take place—"

"I tire of this pretense, as I tire of the old bastard clinging to life and to his throne long past his expiration date." Beria's tone changed subtly, as had his facial expression. It was as though a magician had pulled a curtain, replacing a cultured academic with a butcher. He waved his knife, pointing it at her. "You will do as you're told, girl. He's not long for this world either way, and believe me, you would rather have me as a benefactor than an enemy." He stabbed the knife into the stack of fried potatoes on his plate hard enough that it clinked against the porcelain. "Do you understand me?"

Reluctantly, Raisa nodded again.

"Good. You can go now."

He picked up the fork and resumed his meal, his eyes on the top document in the stack to the side of his plate. He didn't look up as Raisa let herself out.

✡

Late into the night, Raisa roamed the rooms of the makeshift hospital. She wasn't allowed to leave, to make a phone call, or to talk to anyone other than the guards, all of whom she suspected worked for Beria, but she was given free rein in her operating room and the adjacent spaces. There were a nurse and a doctor on duty but each was allowed to sleep in the nearby quarters, which were similar to hers; they could be summoned at a moment's notice if their patient needed them.

She needed rest, but sleep was the furthest thing from her mind. Beria had ordered her to kill Stalin, and she could see no scenario where this might end well for her. If she completed the surgery in good faith, she was certain she'd end up in a *gulag* at best, or more likely be executed in the basement of the KGB headquarters at Lubyanka.

There was some temptation to go through with it, to rid the world of the great despot, and she hated herself for entertaining the thought. First, she was certain Beria would tie loose ends. Her only reward would be certain death, as there was no chance he'd leave a witness who could implicate him in the death of a leader loved—for better or for worse—by millions of Soviet citizens.

That wasn't her greatest fear, however. She imagined the outrage, the antisemitic backlash, the Doctors' Plot revisited with greater vigor. Unlike biblical Judith, there was a real possibility she would end up being used as an instrument of destruction against her own people. Even if Beria held no animosity toward the Jews as he claimed, he was pragmatic enough to take advantage of any popular sentiment against them if it helped cement his place as Stalin's successor.

Hours of rumination later, she still couldn't see a viable way out. She studied the well-stocked shelves of a medicine cabinet through glass doors. Perhaps the solution was to incapacitate herself in some non-permanent way. If she couldn't perform the surgery, Beria might find another pawn to carry out his plan. He might still dispose of her, but there would be no risk to her people.

She opened the cabinet and rummaged through the medications, reading the labels. She tried to figure out what sort of harm she might be able to inflict upon herself with a strange detachment, as though she were completing an assignment for Pharmaceutical Sciences class back in medical school.

There was a commotion behind her. The doctor on duty, summoned by one of the guards, rushed past her, rubbing sleep from his eyes.

"What's happening?" Raisa asked. Before her colleague could answer, she shoved the pill tubes she was holding back onto the shelf and hurried after him.

The guards allowed both doctors through to Stalin's bedroom.

✡

"He had a pulmonary arterial hypertension episode last night," Raisa told Beria.

She had showed up at his office of her own volition in the morning, and asked for an audience. The secret police chief ordered her to be sent in, and was just hanging up the phone when she came in.

"What does that mean in plain language?" he asked impatiently.

"His heart isn't pumping enough blood to his lungs," she said. "We've stabilized him and given him the proper medications, but the surgery will have to be postponed for at least a week. His heart isn't strong enough for it."

Beria frowned and his eyes narrowed. "You've engineered this somehow, haven't you?" He lobbed an accusation with menace in his voice.

"One can't orchestrate such an episode," she replied. "I'm a doctor, not a sorceress."

His frown deepened. "You were there. You could have done ... something."

"What would you have me do, smother him with a pillow?" Raisa said. "I'm not one of your spies, or a trained assassin. I couldn't do anything to hurt him even if I wanted to, not in front of the other doctor and the guards."

Beria took off his pince-nez, cleaned the lenses with a handkerchief, and put it back on. "You've only forestalled the inevitable," he said. "You will remain our guest until such time as the surgery becomes viable, and then you will do what I've asked of you. Now, if there's nothing else?" He motioned toward the door.

"There is, actually. Did you know the Book of Judith isn't part of the Jewish sacred texts? It appears in some versions of the Christian Bible, but many Jews consider it a made-up story, written many years after the events it purports to describe."

Beria glared at her.

"I much prefer the Book of Esther, myself," Raisa pressed on. "She saved her people without murdering anyone, but rather by exposing an evil minister to the Persian king. We celebrate her deeds every year, at Purim."

"Where are you going with this?" Beria asked.

She pulled a transmitter the size of a small wallet from the pocket of her lab coat and showed the bug to Beria. "You've damned yourself, Haman."

His face a mask of rage, Beria pulled a pistol from his desk drawer, but before he could aim it at Raisa, several armed men broke into his office.

"Arrest the traitor," Beria told them. He turned to her. "Whose ear did you poison with your lies about me? Was it Brezhnev? Andropov? There will be a reckoning for this!"

The men ignored his theatrics, their weapons trained on the minister. One of them approached and relieved him of his firearm.

"I didn't know who was in on your conspiracy," Raisa said, "so I brought the information to the one man who I knew couldn't be involved. I told Stalin himself. He didn't strike me as the kind of man to ignore the possibility of his underlings plotting against him, even long-time loyalists like you." She hefted the listening device. "Of course, it helped to have proof, but he must've suspected you all along, because he had Selezenko and several others arrested even before sending me here."

Beria made no reply as he was led away, and then Raisa was standing in his office alone, uncertain as to what she should do next. She wondered if Esther, or Judith, or any biblical women lived with the sorts of doubts about their decisions she was having about hers.

She had saved the life of a tyrant by removing another who had waited for his turn at the helm in his master's shadow. Even if the surgery was successful in removing the tumor, Stalin's days were numbered, and the rest of the Politburo would jockey for power in the vacuum left by Beria's removal. Would whomever came next be better than Beria? Could they possibly be worse?

She wondered what the 1970s would bring for her people, and all the peoples of the Soviet Union. And as she looked out of Beria's window to the stars that topped the towers of the Kremlin and glinted in the morning sunlight, she allowed herself to hope.

Author's Note:

Joseph Stalin died in 1953, after suffering the stroke mentioned in this story. In the final months of his life, antisemitism in the Soviet Union had swelled. Prominent Jewish doctors had been accused of attempting to assassinate party leaders in what became known as the "Doctor's Plot." There's evidence that Stalin planned to deport millions of Russian Jews, as he had previously done with other minorities, though this plan hasn't been conclusively proven.

The Jewish Autonomous Oblast was established in 1934. The Soviets encouraged Jews to relocate to Birobidzhan through propaganda such as articles in the Yiddish newspapers and Yiddish language films, and were moderately successful, the Jewish population of JAO peaking at approximately 20,000. It never exceeded 16% of the population, and is currently less than 1% according to recent census data. On paper, the JAO remains the world's only official Jewish territory outside of Israel.

A Tartan of Many Colors

Allan Weiss

He stood on the seaside cliff, watching his crew unload the ship beneath the snapping, gold-embroidered sails. The ship rocked in the swells of the glistening North Sea as his men passed the proceeds of their latest trading voyage from vessel to rocky beach. His salt-encrusted woollen kilt hung heavily from his waist. More salt stains streaked his black wool stockings, their checkered calfskin garters, and black leather boots. Behind him came the crunch of small feet on pebble. He unbuckled his scabbard and held it out beside him, where it was taken from his hand by the lad, who struggled to hold it off the ground.

He turned landward. As the steady wind fluttered his hair around his face, he scanned the field and trees and hills. Every feature of the landscape called to him. The gloomy forests to the south, broken by stretches of verdant glen; the frost-capped mountains to the west and north, their slopes bulged by screes and creased by corries; the gauzy mists veiling the valleys; the distant blue and white river cutting through the strath; and the waving heather below his feet—all spoke to his memory, all sang songs that echoed in the deepest roots of his mind. He nodded his head, smiling. With a rugged voice more accustomed to shouting orders than telling the tales of his heart, he spoke to the land and the racing clouds and the rooks that cawed in the firs and to his son, who still stood beside him. "Home again, at last" he said, the words broken by his satisfaction and his Highland brogue. "What a *mechiah*!"

Thus Shlomo MacIsaac surveyed his domain, savoring the transcendent pleasure of returning to the land of his birth.

✡

Shlomo was of the Dornoch MacIsaacs, a family whose lineage dated back beyond the establishment of the Twelve Clans to the very origins of the People; Uncle Saul, the clan Chief, even claimed when he'd eaten too much honeyed egg-bread to be a direct descendant of the Leader himself. The women could laugh at his sweets-induced folly, but the men worried: if the clan had need of his wits and right arm, was he still capable of leading them into battle? Or would he be incapacitated by the infirmities of age and overindulgence in pastries?

Shlomo walked briskly into the village, followed by the six men and one lad in single file; the side-curls on the younger one swung like rope-ends in a storm. As he entered the cluster of huts the clan gathered around them, shouting their hearty shaloms, while the chickens squawked and burbled. His crew were good men, and Chaim—who had been bar mitzvahed only a few months before they left—had done well in support of the expedition. Their trading partners, those barbaric heathens with their leather, *kipah*-like helmets and blond hair, had frightened Chaim at first, but, seeing their unsophisticated weapons and smelling their unwashed bodies and hearing their argle-bargle tongue, he'd soon lost his fear. He'd been astonished by the herds of sheep and goats in the Norsemen's pens, being unused to such ways.

"*Nu?*" Shlomo exclaimed as he neared his hut. "Where's my Rutheleh!"

The sheepskin flap covering the doorway lifted, and his wife emerged beaming at him and rushing into his arms. "At last!" She buried her face in his robe first, then kissed him. "What did ye bring? Besides my lad?" She grabbed Chaim and smothered him in a tight maternal hug.

"Already?" He looked behind and waved Nathan over. The mate had been granted the privilege of shlepping the ivory casket that had cost them a whole cask of the *treyf* oil they'd gotten from the southerners. The stuff was larded with lard but valuable on the open market. Nathan handed him the casket, and Shlomo in turn presented it to Ruth. "Nice?"

She gave him a sly look. "A box? Aye, it's nice, but . . . "

"Try opening it."

She found the clasp, pried open the lid, and her eyes widened as her treasure was revealed. "Oh, Shlomo!" She pulled out the coils that gleamed yellow under the sun's sparse rays.

"*Gelt.* Wear them in good health."

Half-laughing with glee, she slipped them onto her wrists, pushing back the sleeves of her tunic. They looked very, very fine against her pale skin.

"Does she like them?" Nathan asked, grinning.

"I think so," Shlomo replied. He had earned and now received another kiss from his appreciative wife. And they would reward each other later in due course. "Now to enjoy some real food," he said, and waved the men away to deliver their bounty to the Chief for distribution. He and Chaim ducked beneath the door-cloth held aside by Ruth, to be greeted by the smells of baked and broiled and smoked delights.

As he doffed his cloak, Ruth, her black eyes sparkling, directed him to the table he'd chopped out of an oak tree when they first wed, and proceeded to fill his tin plate—the fruit of an earlier expedition—with a stew of venison and neeps. Beside it she placed one of her special treats: an oat ring-roll coated with caraway seeds. "Ye get only one," she insisted. "Save the rest for later."

"*Och oy*," Shlomo complained. He turned to Chaim. "Ye say the *brochah*; ye're a man now, not a bairn any longer."

In his cracking voice, the boy sang, "*Baruch atoh adonai*," and completed the blessing with only a few prompts from his father. Then Shlomo dug in with his wooden spoon, as Ruth and Chaim waited for him to take his first bite before eating. After four months at sea, and an almost unvarying diet of oat cakes and smoked fish, this was paradise, a diner's Eden.

"Papa?" Shlomo braced himself for one of Chaim's innumerable questions. "Why do we have two languages, one for blessings and *shul* and one for other times?"

"The Hebrew Moshe gave us is too holy for profane use. So we use the *goyische* tongue for that." Chaim seemed to want to ask more, but Shlomo stopped him with the usual: "It is our way."

✡

The knock on his doorpost came well after they were finished their supper; the People knew that one never interrupted a meal. Shlomo was not at all surprised by the sound, nor by the sight of Yakov MacAsher looming above him. Yakov made up in height what he lacked in breadth, compensating at clan meetings for Saul MacIsaac's short stature. Shlomo had expected to hear serious news upon his return.

"*Shalom*," Yakov said through his mouth-obscuring beard.

"*Shalom*. What have ye to tell me?"

"Come." Shlomo flung his cloak over his shoulders once more. "We have things to discuss," Yakov continued ominously.

"No hints?"

"No hints." Yakov led him to the double-sized hut of the Chief, Saul's private and official home, and opened the squealing wooden door for him. Saul insisted on such indulgences as doors and bronze hinges, and satin *kipah*s. Oil lamps guttered in the dim hall, filling the upper half of the room with black smoke that swirled slowly up to and through the hole above. Shadowed figures rose at Shlomo's entrance: the leading men of the clan, stern expressions beneath their beards and skullcaps. Shalom MacIsaac and his sons Ephraim and Aaron sat on the other side of Saul; Solomon and Hamische and young Baruch the tailor were opposite Saul; and of course Saul's son Shimson, the thick-armed blacksmith, sat at his father's side. Avraham MacCohen, the priest who normally considered himself above mere political questions, was also in attendance. Saul looked as if he'd aged far more than the mere months since Shlomo's departure.

The men exchanged their shaloms and handshakes, but there was no spirit in the greetings, either verbal or physical. Saul motioned him to an open spot on the bench to his left. "Welcome home, *landsman*," he said. "It's truly good to have ye back." His voice was scratchy; his "r" barely rolled, and his gutturals were soft, like a wee lad's. "We've been awaiting ye."

"*Tsuris?*" Shlomo asked.

Saul nodded. "Ye ken there's trouble, but ye dinna ken the worst on it." He moved his behind to a more comfortable spot on the lone chair in the room, the one reserved for a Chief's *tuchus*. "Ye ate well?"

"Aye."

"Enjoy it while ye can." Saul paused, for effect it seemed. "It's good that ye've brought so much wealth back from yer travels, but we canna eat gold or stones or bonny cloths."

"What do ye mean?"

"It's the Sassenachs." Of course; who else would give them so much trouble? "They want to cease trading edibles with us."

"What? Why?"

Saul waggled his head. Yakov said, "They told us, no more corn. 'Grow yer own,' they said. They ken the land; they ken it boasts more rock than soil. And no more salted meat. Our gold is not enough."

"It's *meshuggah*," Shlomo said. Heads nodded in agreement. "What do they want? Our rock?"

"They hate us," Saul said. "They resent that Adonai made his Covenant with us, not them. And if they can't be Covenanters, they will hate those who are." He pointed in a vague direction. "The Leader landed on one of *our* islands, not to the south! God Himself steered the basket past the shores of their *ferkakte* land, scorning their cliffs, and northward to our lands."

"It's not so simple, Saul," Shlomo said, and Solomon and Hamische grunted assent. "They're pagans. Blue-painted heathens. They care naught for the Laird nor His messenger."

"It eats at them that Adonai chose us!" Saul insisted.

Shlomo shook his head. Long had the tale been told that had given the Scots their identity as the Chosen Ones; for the ancient Leader arrived upon the shores of the northwestern islands. A fisherman found the Holy Bairn lying in a basket woven of strange reeds, and brought him home to raise as his own, naming him Robert for his shining face; the poor lad had been oddly mutilated and was much pitied for it, but when he grew he heard the voice of the Laird, and spoke of the practice as a Covenant with God, and so others had followed him, becoming Sons of the Covenant. In their faith, the Covenanters had switched from trousers to kilts to ease the work of the priests with their ritual dirks. The young man then became known among the People as Robert the Briss; and when he reached his prime, Robert climbed to the top of Ben Nevis, stayed for forty days and forty nights, and returned with a new name, Moshe Ben Nevis, and a Book of Laws—including the Ten Dinnas—and to tell the People of their true identity as God's own, and of their true ancestry and tongue; and the islands where he had arrived were forever after known as the Scottish Hebraides.

But Shlomo doubted spiritual jealousy was the motivation for the Sassenachs' hostility. More likely, they simply wanted the Scots' more material possessions, and the Scots—a trading people whose ungenerous land had made them tight-fisted—had much gold.

Gold torques for their wives: a delight for now, a temptation for enemies in the future.

"We have to act," Shalom said. Contrary to his name, he was a belligerent man, a lover of battle who had inculcated that spirit in his sons. "What will we do?"

"The Twelve Clans are holding a Congress," Saul said. "We will need to act as one Nation."

"Aye," Shalom said. "But what if some dinna want to defend our land?" Shlomo knew whom he meant. One clan was notoriously soft, because they possessed the lowlands and the best soil, and had always been the favored ones.

"We will speak to them," Saul said. "We maun. *Mazel tov* to us all in the coming days!"

✡

The men discussed a few more topics of concern, and when the meeting ended Saul pulled Shlomo aside. "Ye'll come wi' me as one of my advisors. There is no kenning how this will go."

"Aye." Bring twelve of the People into a room and ye'll hear thirteen opinions, as he'd oft advised Chaim. "Can we fight? Or are our numbers too wee? And our spirit too weak?"

"As ye said, the Sassenachs are barbarians, *goyische-kop*s. They're better at murder than we are."

On his way home, Shlomo wrestled with how to break the news to Ruth that he would have to leave so soon after his return. She'd likely weep at that; so might he. As he entered his hut, she looked at him expectantly, wiping her hands nervously on her tunic. With careful, soothing words he laid it out for her, like a cracked bowl painted to hide the flaws.

"Again?" she said, barely able to keep her voice from rising. "Can ye not be left in peace to stay with yer wife and bairn a few days?" And he shared her pain, but also envisioned his wife and bairn starving under the Sassenachs' siege.

Chaim sat listening, silently at first. Then he declared, "I want to come." So desperate to be a man, and so sad he had to be a lad still.

"Nae!" Shlomo and Ruth cried almost in unison. Shlomo said, "Ye'll stay here and take care of this house," he continued, then added, "like a man!" That did it; Chaim subsided, and even seemed pleased. It paid a trader to know how to manipulate others.

✡

The men set out the next day, riding the horses they'd traded so much gold for—and had traded for with the very Sassenachs now besetting the People once more. So many wars had been fought over the centuries with the southerners, till the pagans learned how much could be gained by following the People's trading way of life. Obviously, they'd had their fill of peaceful commerce, and wanted not just a great deal but everything.

Saul led, although Shlomo could see that his strength to control his horse and stay awake was no longer great; they had to rest often for his sake. If there was a fight, how would Saul cope, let alone lead them? What the People needed was a true leader, a guide like Moshe. Twelve clans and no king: it was daft, like setting a course for the shoals.

Along with Shlomo, Saul had brought Shimson, Shalom and his lads, and Yakov. They spoke little on the journey, except to establish their own position in the coming debate and argue about points of Law, a subject about which Shlomo cared little. When Robert came down from his mountain after speaking with the Laird, he carried with him not only a language and faith but also a code governing how the People might live, work, and eat. He had made them a farming and trading People, and brought strict guidelines on how they might feed themselves: fish were proper, shellfish were not; the deer and sheep they hunted were acceptable, the boars were not; he had even distinguished between the kinds of bird they could legitimately consume: chickens, yes; hawks, no.

But what if the People were starving? Would the laws still apply?

The delegation rode in the chill winds pouring down the hills, their horses stepping through heather and moss and across burns. The terrain ensured they would enjoy few stretches of flat land, but instead constantly climbed and descended. In these autumn days, the sun sank early beyond the mountains; once it was too dark to proceed safely, they would hoist their tents, which were indeed sails in their more active lives, and each crawled into his own and out of the freezing mists that clung to the ground and their cloaks. This was not the first time Shlomo regretted the Leader's choice to surrender trousers in favor of a spiritually, but not physically, more suitable garment.

Chaim had asked him over the years about the kilt and other traditions. "Why do we eat different foods at the Spring Feast?" "Why is the Sabbath that day and not another?" And the answer had always been the same: this is our way, passed down by the Leader.

Finally, one morning after climbing yet another hill, they saw on the field below the tents of the Congress: delegations from all the clans, big and small, near and distant, plus the larger tent to house the meeting. The tents almost fully encircled a bonfire, though an empty space on the heath had been left vacant for new arrivals, and a creek sparkled beyond them, while white-peaked mountains stretched beyond that. Each tent bore the emblem of its clan, with embroidered lions, altars, rams, sheafs of oats, scrolls, and other motifs. On the MacIsaacs' own tents were pictured the stylized dirks, although no one knew the origins of the association between the name and the symbol. Every tent bore the *Mogen Saul*, the six-pointed star that, in all their clannish division and even hostility, linked them as one.

Men and a few women stood or strolled about, the latter cooking at the bonfire and the former chatting in small groups. One man stood by the creek, practicing his swordplay beside a double rank of tethered horses.

"Come," Saul said, "let's greet our *landsmen*."

The Dornoch MacIsaacs rode to their reserved spot, beside the Abnerden MacIsaacs, a branch of the clan with whom they'd oft exchanged visits, and raised their tents with the help of others who came to chat and learn. Names flew back and forth, and Shlomo saw men and boys he hadn't seen in many years. And here was cousin Yeshuah and his son Dovid, who had oft played with Chaim during those visits. The Abnerden MacIsaacs lived closer to the border with the Sassenachs, if that wilderness of hills and passes could be considered a border.

"Look at ye!" Shlomo said. "A fine lad."

Dovid smiled. Yeshuah put his arm around his son. "Good to see ye, Shlomo," he said. "Good to see the whole Congress."

"What is yer sense of it, Yeshuah?"

"The Sassenachs want trouble. We might have to give it to them. Go to yer mother," he said to Dovid. When the lad was gone, Yeshuah continued, "They're blocking all trade from the south, not just their own victuals but any they get from across the sea: seeds, nuts, the whole *megillah*." He shook his head. "They're trying to take the food from our mouths, Shlomo."

"Canna we trade around them?"

"And build a thousand more ships? Nae, we might have to take their food before they can keep ours away completely."

✡

The meeting was held early in the morning; nearly a hundred men jammed inside the sheepskin confines, their combined heat making a fire unnecessary. Naturally, the meeting began with the required blessings, as the priest of the host clan, the MacDaniels, intoned the *brochah*s on the People, the sun, and the fact there was a world at all. Moishe MacDaniel then stood and addressed them.

"Ye ken why we are here. Ye ken the danger we face from the Sassenachs, who have besieged our land with their refusal to let food be traded by their own people or those of other lands through their own. We hear that their ships are moving near our shores, by Edenberg and Dayandee, and we fear they will block all who sail from other places to trade with us."

Zebulon MacNathan spoke next. "I warned ye, did I not? I warned ye we shouldna trust the Sassenachs. It was argued that we maun trade or fight; but if we trade, we become their slaves, while if we fight, we have the arm and sword of the Laird Himself on our side. If it be the will of Adonai that we are to triumph, then so shall it be, and so it could have been had ye listened."

Moishe summoned Saul to take the floor. Saul rose clumsily, his legs nearly giving way as he came to his feet, and his voice was quiet, his speech slurred. "It is now as Zebulon has said. It may have been the right policy before, not to appease the Sassenachs but to deal fairly with them. But this is a different matter. Their envy makes them hate, and their hate makes them warlike." He coughed. "We maun make common cause, of all the clans, and defend ourselves and our home!"

Yeshuah responded, "'Tis not envy, cousin. There may be some of that,

I'll grant. But they have their own gods and want none of our'n. They want our lands, they want our waters and their plenty, and they want to keep the Norsemen away. For they think that if we trade with the yellow-hairs, and be their friends, we might make common cause with *them* against the Sassenachs."

Moishe now recognized Asher MacYosef, who stood up and, to Shlomo's eyes, seemed to flaunt his elaborately decorated kilt. He was a fat man in a lean land, soft-featured and bulbous in belly and limb. If only fate had granted others the benefits enjoyed by these arrogant Sons of the Leader. "*Landsmen,* I have heard yer complaints and yer views. But the Laird helps those who help themselves, as the Leader says in his Proverbs, and hurts those who hurt themselves. Can we be sure that we will be victorious in a war with the Sassenachs? Have we the strength? Or should we speak to them and come to an understanding? For if—"

"With savages?" Shimson cried. "Reason with barbarians?"

Moishe called for order. "Let him speak!"

"Let us go as one People," Asher continued, "and in our strength as a People let us speak with one voice. Or we may be calling down disaster upon our heads."

Shlomo joined the chorus of angry shouts that greeted the words of Asher MacYosef. The MacYosefs had always been favored, not by God but by the ancestors. Moshe Ben Nevis led his followers south from their distant islands, attracting more and more People with his teachings and divine inspiration; he taught not only the Law but how to read it. He taught the Holy Tongue. When a local tribe would not let them pass, with God's help he parted Loch Lomond so that they might continue their journey, and eventually the People possessed the whole of the Highlands and Lowlands, from east to west and south to the borderlands with the Sassenachs. He begat Isaac, and Isaac begat Yakov, and Yakov begat the twelve sons who fathered the Twelve Clans. But Yakov favored Yosef above all his other sons, and granted him the best lands. The MacYosefs were always the fattest, the most complacent. Like the sheep raised and slaughtered by the Norsemen.

Others spoke; some shared Asher's view that dialogue should precede confrontation, but those were listened to more attentively, perhaps because they spoke without the detested clan name. Yet the debate remained rancorous. Shlomo said to his Chief, "It has ever been thus, Saul MacIsaac; the People fight with each other more than with their foes. We are indeed a stiff-necked people, as the Leader said."

"Aye," Saul replied, his voice tired.

The meeting broke up, or broke down, as it came close to the time to eat. It was then that the stomach rightly ruled the mouth and the head, and the People gathered for a feast about the bonfire. Porridge, venison and neep stew, and ring-rolls, with small-beer to wash down the delicious fare. The MacIsaacs sat together. Yeshuah was furious, unable to conceal his disdain for the MacYosefs. "They live near the Sassenachs. Ye'd think they'd be feeling more in danger, but they dinna ken and have never kenned what danger or want is. Aye, they're a womanish lot."

Saul nodded. Dovid merely listened to his father's words, wisely remaining silent like a good lad. Shlomo said, "We have to act, even without them."

Saul said, "Even fewer numbers than we might have had? 'Tis a worry."

"'Tis no choice," Shlomo commented, and tossed a chunk of gristle into the fire.

After the meal, the Congress turned to other, less divisive topics before reopening the main issue: some involving internal trade among the clans, some theological as men tried to reconcile daily practice with what was in the Holy Book of the Leader, and inevitable boundary disputes to arbitrate. Finally, at the end, the Congress returned to the vital question of the day. Moishe MacDaniel, in his capacity as host and Chair, said, "It is time to decide what we shall do. There are two options before us: to take up arms and move south as one People, or to send a delegation to the Sassenachs in hopes they will listen to reason. Let us vote."

It was a complicated procedure, as so many things involving the People were: secret ballots, special votes by clan Chiefs on behalf of their members—Shlomo threw his dirk repeatedly into the dirt as the process dragged. Such a waste of time, while the Sassenachs took food from their families' mouths! The vote was counted, and the vast majority elected to move against the southerners. As soon as Moishe read out the results, the MacYosefs, without another word, ostentatiously walked out as a body. The priest intoned a quick *brochah* to end the Congress, and quoted the Proverbs of the Leader: "They that be slain with the sword are better than they that be slain with hunger." *Omain*!

Outside, in the frosty wind, they all watched as the MacYosef delegation struck their tents and headed to their horses. "*Och oy*," Shlomo said to Saul. "They're away."

Shimson spoke in his father's place. "Aye, and well rid of them." But it was a glib comment, and a dark mood fell over them. Some men yelled obscenities toward the MacYosefs' backs, some spat in their direction, some merely shook their heads, saying, "*Oy, oy, oy.*"

Yeshuah MacIsaac said, "That's that, then, is it?"

"Aye."

"It will be some time before we're ready. And there's no kenning who will be with us, who not, other than those slugs," he said, nodding toward the mounted and fleeing MacYosefs.

"Aye," Shlomo repeated. "What we really need is another Moshe, another Briss, to lead and guide us."

"A king."

"Aye. Failing that, we'll need to be as one, as we have never been before."

"Come." He took Shlomo's upper arm and steered him out of earshot of Dovid. "My lad is not a warrior. He writes poems, songs. A smart lad, but that's not what we need now. Ye and Shimson—well, ye twa can teach him."

"A good thought." They returned to the others and Yeshuah said to his son, "Ye haven't seen yer cousin in many a year. Would ye like to go visit?" Dovid shrugged. "Good. It's settled."

Thus, as they rode to the territory of the Dornoch MacIsaacs, their delegation was greater by one. Dovid spoke only when necessary; otherwise, he was mute, if not morose, and Shlomo could get nothing out of him regarding his feelings or opinions. He was indeed a strange lad, more suited to be a priest than a warrior, and teaching him to be one might be a harder task than defeating the Sassenachs in battle.

✡

It was now Shlomo's duty to break even worse news to Ruth, who stood awaiting them in the doorway of their hut as they returned to the village. The keen-eyed men who kept watch on the clan boundaries had informed the village about their approach. Still, Ruth let out a surprised, "Hah!" when she saw Dovid riding behind Shlomo. She watched every movement of man and lad as they dismounted; meanwhile, Chaim dropped the adze he was wielding on a log by the hut and came toward them. Ruth hugged and kissed Shlomo and hugged and fussed over Dovid. "Such a big man now! Such a *mensch*!" The two cousins greeted each other with smiles and play-punches, ran off, and now Dovid found his tongue while the lads caught up on years of unshared lives.

"We maun speak," Shlomo said as they entered.

"Tell me," Ruth said. Her motions were scattered; she seemed to be automatically reaching for some food to offer, and stifling the compulsion at the same time.

"We march against the Sassenachs."

Ruth gasped, although she must have expected it. "'We.'"

"The clans. Any who can carry a sword." Ruth's eyes strayed to the rear wall and then back to Shlomo. "Dovid and Chaim, too."

"Nae!" Ruth cried. "Nae! Ye'll not take the lad!" She stood before him as if to protect Chaim from the inevitable. "Nae!"

"Ruth, we either fight for our lives or we starve."

Now she fell as silent as Dovid had been, and when the lads came in she served them a meal like a machine, one of those water-clocks he'd seen at a fair. Shlomo could see her biting back tears, swallowing the bitter even as they all swallowed her sweets. There was nothing to say, nothing he could say, because the last thing he wanted was to put his own lad in harm's way, to bring him and his mother pain.

Yet even the Leader had had to fight. The People had fought numerous battles as they made their way south and took the land that the Laird had promised them on top of that mountain. That had been part of the Covenant: obey the Law, and the land of the Scots would be theirs. The right arm of God would guide and protect and defend them, and slay their enemies, so that wherever the pagan tongue, the *Goylich*, was heard, the People would live and prosper.

Now, they had to save what the Laird had promised and given them.

✡

The coming weeks and months meant no trading, just training—Shlomo's every nerve missed the sea. As Shimson beat their adzes and ploughshares and wood-axes into swords and people-axes, Shlomo tried to teach his son and young cousin how to wield their new weapons. Chaim practised enthusiastically, but Dovid was a stubborn lad, unwilling to learn. Shlomo couldn't help worrying, as he saw the two in rapt conversation, that the peaceable cousin might drain the needed fighting fire from Chaim. Like it or not—and neither he nor Ruth liked it at all—they would have to become fighters.

Meanwhile, the Sassenach ships infested the coasts, intercepting foreign traders, and the land trade dried up almost to nothing. The MacYosefs were fine; theirs was the most fertile land, and while they shared some of their wealth with the other clans out of sheer moral necessity, even they could not feed an entire Nation. It was a hard winter; in the village, starvation was not unknown, and death stalked those who had not been able to build up their stores of oat, neep, venison, and wild ram.

The priest sacrificed and prayed, lending his Hebrew voice to the martial cries of the training men. Fields of snow, normally dampeners of sound, rang with the clank of steel on steel. When the weather turned, and the mad winter winds howled, the men collected in one hut or another to plot tactics and strategy. Chaim's muscles grew, Dovid's hardly at all; he looked like the same lad who had arrived. And through it all, Saul was more listener than speaker, till Shlomo and Shimson became the de facto Chiefs. Many years ago, some said, a renegade priest argued that there had been two Gods in the distant past: the Creator God and the Warrior God. Maybe, with no king, the clans required different clan Chiefs for times of peace and times of war.

In the spring, when it was time to march south, Ruth refused to make their departure any easier. She was not a fool, and knew that the People had to fight for food, but that did not mean she had to like it. "Ye bring back my son hale," she said to Shlomo, not meeting his eyes, then turned her back on them as Shlomo, Nathan, Chaim, Dovid, and 200 men from the village and the surrounding territory commenced their trek.

Those who had horses rode or hitched them to the wagons that carried what food could be spared. Saul was even less steady on his mount, and soon had to become cargo. "We should have left him t'home," Shlomo said to Shimson, who didn't want to agree but couldn't disagree, either. Overall, the men of the Dornoch MacIsaac clan were a sorry lot in numbers and fighting form: farmers turned into warriors in too brief a time. If the Laird did not lend an arm, the fight was a waste of time and blood.

They marched hardy, though, not letting bad weather or distance deter them. When any flagged, it was Yakov and his lads who inspired them; the priest had come, and MacCohen led Sabbath services and gave counsel to those whose morale drooped. And he would say the kaddish for those who would need it. The dirk-decorated tents sheltered as many as they could, but most had to sleep out in the hoary, damp nights of the Scottish spring with no more than a bear or deer-skin to protect them. Was this what the Leader's people had endured in their trek south? And how much did having a Leader give them the strength to do it? Yet the clan still marched toward the spot near Edenberg where the People would converge, and fight for their lives.

Then, two days before they reached their destination, Chaim and Dovid disappeared.

Shlomo, panicking, raced around the encampment. "Have ye seen them? Where be the lads?" No one had seen them leave; no one had noticed anything. Had they run home? The shame would kill him before the Sassenachs did. It was unbearable; he avoided the looks of the others, even Saul, who patted his arm and made reassuring noises. "There's a good explanation," he said, and may well have believed it himself. A sweet old fool.

Shlomo didn't sleep at all that night. What would he say if the lads hadn't gone home? What could he tell Ruth? And Yeshuah, when they met by the River Liat? There was no worse fate for the two. Better to die by the sword than by hunger, and better to die by hunger than survive by cowardice.

But Shlomo marched anyway, though he wanted to sink into the fens; at least someone had to uphold the honor of the family. His sword and dirk grew heavier with each step. At last, the Dornoch MacIsaacs crested the final hill, and now instead of tents of peace and debate the valley below was filled with the wind-fluttering tents of war: thousands of them, gathered here to battle together, side by side in a desperate bid to save their bodies before hunger weakened them past all hope of victory. The golden threads proclaimed the clans' identities and courage—all the clan emblems glittering in the clouded light, except one. Not one tent bore the lion of the MacYosefs.

With no spirit at all, no feeling in his limbs or soul, Shlomo erected his tent alongside those of the other MacIsaacs. So far, he saw no sign of Yeshuah, the father who would soon share his incurable shame. That was Shlomo's lot, then: delivering painful words to beloved folk. *I dinna ken where they've gone*, he'd say; *we can hope for the best*. The men deposited Saul in his tent, where he groaned in pain and berated Shimson and others out of his own shame. But the weakness of age was in the nature of things, and not to be thought a failing.

The army of the People swarmed the valley, many in armor, many not. A separate encampment of mercenaries from Eire, who were themselves hungry and desperately needed the People's gold, covered a slope of the western hill. It was Saul who would consult with the other Chiefs to determine who would fight where and do what, and Shlomo hoped the messages were clearly conveyed to all.

Finally, Yeshuah approached him, smiling broadly; he'd only just arrived. "Cousin! *Shalom!*"

Shlomo swallowed. "*Shalom.*"

"Where are the lads?" He looked past Shlomo's right shoulder.

"I dinna ken. We—"

"What in the name of the Briss is that?" Other men, too, were looking in the same direction. Shlomo turned. In the distance, a vast, dense cloud billowed on the ground, moving toward them, like the tents covering the land in roiling white, though without gaps. Shlomo watched it approach, certain he was witnessing a miracle. The Laird was coming to their aid!

But as it neared, Shlomo and others saw it for what it was, and gasps and cries broke out. For this was no cloud; it was a herd. White-fleeced heads and bodies bobbed and flowed over the valley. And before them walked two figures, each carrying a tall staff. As soon as he recognized them, Shlomo moved forward, his legs stiff, numb.

"What is this, lad?" he asked, sensing the eyes of a multitude at his back. "Chaim?" Out of the corner of his eye he saw Yeshuah come stand by his side. "Dovid?"

Chaim said, "Blessed are the peacemakers."

Dovid said, "The Laird is my shepherd."

Now Shlomo raised his voice. "What is the meaning of this?" In the silence, hundreds, maybe thousands of sheep bleated; stopped now, they began to feed on the young heather.

Chaim said, "This is how we will feed ourselves. The yellow-hairs are wise. These we, well, 'found' among the Sassenachs."

"This is not our way!" To gain their lives at the cost of their souls—it was not to be! Shlomo's shame was boundless.

"It is, Papa." Dovid nodded behind him. As the cousin moved his staff, the sheep seemed to flow with it. Chaim continued, "Moshe was our shepherd, leading us. It is his way, and therefore our'n."

Shlomo had nothing to say to that. Neither did Yeshuah, or any of the other men. There was no king to guide them, and tell them what to do. Yet what the boy had said sounded right. For a change, the multitude of People had no arguments to make. As one, they stared at the masses of sheep, and recognized, or so Shlomo believed, their salvation.

Dovid, without another word, walked north through the encampment, and the sheep followed, avoiding the tents but seeming ready to walk to the ends of the People's land, even as far as the islands where the People had begun. Led by Dovid, they appeared willing to cross the valleys and waters, and climb the hills, even to the top of Ben Nevis if need be. And so, Shlomo thought, the People would follow, too.

No, the People had no king—but as he watched Dovid, he thought, *not yet.*

✡

OTHER COVENANTS

Thus did the People find a new and ancient way, adding herding to their duties and blessings. Though trade declined in the days of the Sassenachs' blockade, and farms even in the valleys supplied little, the flocks provided sustenance for the clans.

And it was Ruth, or so it is said, who came up with the idea to take a length of the sheep's intestine and fill it with delectables, and called the dish "*kishke*" after the *Goylich* word for the gut. And so *kishke* became the Scots' national dish, and every year, on Rosh Hashanah, the New Year, it is not just eaten but honored by the People as both their savior and a symbol of the protection of the Laird, and the wise leadership of their king.

The Time-Slip Detective

Lavie Tidhar

The Girl in the Window

I saw her first in a reflection in a shop's window.

Along Ibn Gvirol, heading to the square, just before the car park where Rabin was shot.

She wore a white cotton dress and sandals, her hair was auburn, our eyes met and hers opened wide in surprise. I glanced quickly away. Then I turned around to see her but there was no one there. When I looked back into the shop's window, even her reflection was gone.

Tidhar

It had been strange but the moment passed. I chalked it up to the heat, my mind playing tricks on me. I was in the center for an interview with a writer, a young novelist who has had some success overseas. His name was Tidhar, Lavie Tidhar, and he had won an international award, the World Fantasy Award, the week before, and so the paper wanted me to talk to him for a feature. I had spoken to him on the phone a couple of days earlier, in preparation, and he told me of his obsession with old Hebrew pulp fiction. In particular he was interested in the old David Tidhar detective stories, which had come out in the 1930s. The coincidence of sharing the detective's family name fascinated him. His original family name had been Heisikovitch; his family had changed the name in the 1970s, just before he was born, part of a long tradition of immigrants changing to Hebrew names. He and the detective were not related.

Though we had agreed to meet by Rabin Square, he didn't show. When I rang him he apologized and said his wife was unwell and could we reschedule, and so we did. I was still thinking about the girl I saw; there had been something so old-fashioned about her dress, it was like what my grandmother used to wear when she was a girl, and had come to Israel all those years ago from Transylvania. I grabbed a shawarma in Dabush and then, wiping the grease from my face, decided to escape the heat and the noise and so went into Landwer.

It is an old coffee house, Landwer, perhaps the oldest still surviving in Tel Aviv. I went inside into the cool of air conditioning and sat by the window and ordered an iced coffee. In my hands I held a David Tidhar pamphlet, I had found one at great expense and had brought it along with me for the interview, but had not actually read it. The detective's photo stared at me from the cover in faded black and white as I opened the book and began to read.

Erzebet and the Detective

The famous detective, David Tidhar, was in the cafe. He wore his trademark fedora hat and a long trenchcoat, despite the heat. The waitress was fawning over him, and a young boy ran up to him and asked for an autograph, which the detective gracefully signed. Are you working on a case? the boy asked, and the detective smiled and patted his head and said he was just ordering a cappuccino.

Only the month before, Tidhar had single-handedly foiled an international group of diamond smugglers operating out of Jerusalem. Dressed as a woman, he pursued them to Paris, where he revealed himself dramatically at the Moulin Rouge club in the Place Pigalle. Now the gang were safely behind bars. *Haynt* was filled with tales of his exploits, as were the Hebrew tabloids. Even now, you could see a couple of *shmekes*, working for the tabloids, waiting outside with their cameras.

The detective was waiting. He kept his eyes on the doors of the cafe. Landwer, on Ibn Gviron St., named for the Golden Age poet, and across the road from the Kings of Israel Square—named for the kings of Israel. A Zeppelin was parked in the sky above the square, the large Star of David on its gondola clear to be seen. Silent electric cars passed in the street outside and men in hats doffed them politely as the girls passed.

Then she walked in.

She wore a light summer dress—it had been all the rage in Paris the year before. She wore sandals on her feet. Her skin was pale, not brown like some of those farmer girls from the Galilee. For a moment she stood in the doorway, a little anxious, watching the people sitting inside. Soft music played—Chopin, on Landwer's electric radio. It was the first cafe in Herzlberg to have an electric radio installed, long ago. A landmark, an institution, Landwer was. The detective, David Tidhar, half rose in his seat. The girl saw him and a look, as though of relief, momentarily flashed on her face. She walked to him. He stood up fully and pulled up a chair for her, and waited for her to sit. She sat. They both did.

- You are the detective? In her hand she was holding a pamphlet. It was familiar. It detailed the detective's latest exploits, as published every week by his faithful biographer, Shlomo Ben-Yisrael. Like any other volume in the *Hebrew Detective Library*, it comprised thirty-two pages and carried the detective's likeness prominently on the cover. The last two pages carried adverts for Ascot Cigarettes (*Smoke Like A Man!*), Elite instant coffee (*Quicker – Better*), and for the King David Dirigible Company (*Comfort in the Skies!*)—one vessel of which was floating outside, above the square.

The pamphlet was priced at 200 pruta. Thousands of such identical copies were rushed off the presses every week, to be sold at kiosks across the country. While it is frowned upon by some educational types as nothing but cheap entertainment, our youth cannot, understandably, get enough of it.

- I am he, the detective said. His eyes looked at the girl keenly. His gaze was soft, but one had the sense it could turn cold and hard when faced with a wrong-doer. One heard stories, from the day before our country became the peaceful and civilized place it is now, when it was not yet called Tel Aviv, the Fount of Spring, but rather Palestine. How he had killed more than forty Arab marauders with his bare hands, how he stalked a gang of murderous Bedouins and assassinated each one in cold blood, all in service of the dream.

- You are Erzebet? he said.

- Yes, the girl said. If the detective noticed the non-Hebrew form of her name, he made no comment. Gravely, he signaled to the waitress to bring his new companion a hot chocolate. She scampered to comply.

The detective reached into his coat and brought forth a tobacco pouch and a pipe. It was a Bruyere pipe, made by Parker of London. The detective packed the tobacco carefully into the pipe and lit it with a match. He blew out fragrant smoke and gazed at the girl, Erzebet, through the smoke. He waved the match to extinguish the flame and dropped it into the ashtray on the table.

- What did you wish to see me in regard to, Miss Erzebet? the detective said. His eyes seemed to twinkle. The girl still held the pamphlet, awkwardly. Its title this week was *The Time-Slip Detective*.

- Do you ever think none of this is real? she said. Her voice was quiet, but there was a quiet desperation in it, which carried. The detective's eyes lost their sparkle. Had become, indeed, hard. His silence seemed to infuriate the girl. This! she said. All this! Her hand rose, swept across the table, sending cups and saucers of delicate Viennese china to the floor, where they broke with an obscene sound. The girl stood up, still shouting. All of this! She was waving the pamphlet. It was stained red. The girl must have cut herself on the glass, a thin gash had opened in her pale flesh, and she was bleeding.

- Sit down, the detective said and, again, Sit down!

The girl sat down. Her shoulders shook.

- I don't know what to do, she said. I see them, even now, I see them. Look! she pointed at the window. Pointed at her reflection.

Kfir

I looked at the window. I don't know what made me, the air-conditioning was very cold, it made my hair stand on end, the book felt grimy in my hand. When I looked into the reflection I saw her, instead of myself, sitting in the same place I was occupying. I was startled, it felt to me as if I were reading a book. What is your name? I said, and at the exact same moment I saw her lips move, forming the same question, though I could hear no sound come out. Kfir, I said, urgently—

Erzebet

- Erzebet, *meine nammen iz Erzebet*, the girl said, *Vas iz Kfir?*

The Wrong Door

- That's my name, I said, Kfir, and, Erzebet, what kind of a name is Erzebet?

It almost felt to me, trying to read her lips, that she was speaking Yiddish. But that was madness, as mad as a zeppelin with a Star of David on its gondola, hovering over Tel Aviv. Behind her I could see a man dressed in a raincoat and a fedora, like something out of an old pulp novel. He was staring at me. I pushed back my chair, it crashed to the floor. The girl's hand, I saw in the reflection, was bleeding. I turned around, and around. It was too cold inside. I felt trapped inside the glass. Patrons backed away from me. I have to get some fresh air, I said, to no one in particular. I reached into my pocket, brought out a handful of coins, left them on the table. I had to get out. I staggered out, but I must have taken the wrong door by mistake.

Trapped

The detective said, How long has this been going on?

- I keep seeing them, the girl said. The sound of desperation in her voice was real. It's like being trapped in a cinemascope reel and not being able to get out. You have to help me. Please.

- You should not have come to me, the detective said, and there was something sad, but also cold, in his voice. Come with me, he said. He paid for the drinks though they had not yet come. He put away his pipe and stood up. Warmth left him, then. He was cold. He was a man of the law. I said come with me! He took the girl by the hand and she cried out, it was the one she had cut. The detective paid her no mind, he dragged her from the table, towards the door. My car is parked outside, he said. It was a Susita, from the Autocars Manufacturing Company of Haifa. The girl did not resist him. The detective pushed the door open and they went outside, into the glare of the sun.

Gunshots

The sun hit me and for a moment I was blind. I blinked back tears. When I opened them fully I saw the city, but it was not the same city. A zeppelin hovered over Rabin Square, an impossible Star of David on its gondola. The people were dressed in European fashions, men in light suits and hats, women in dresses. Their cars moved like tiny beetles along the road, not making any sound. A car whose chassis was made of fiberglass was parked nearby. I heard the door opening again behind me. I turned and caught sight of a man in a fedora hat and a trenchcoat. He saw me at the same time I saw him. Something in his demeanor warned me. I fell and saw his arm rising, a handgun held in his hand. The shot was near silent. The gun was of a type I had never seen.

- You should not have come here, he said, and his voice was like that of a biblical prophet, promising doom. He raised his hand again to fire. A small figure came behind him. The girl I'd seen. Erzebet. No! she said. She pushed his arm and his shot went high. She ran to me. We have to go! she said. She took me by the hand. We ran. Behind us I heard the man shouting. He sounded incensed. I will *shtup* you in the *tuches*, you little *feigale*! he said.

- *Kacken zee ahf deh levanah*! Erzebet shouted back. We ran around the corner and his third gunshot hit a streetlamp and showered us with glass.

I *think* he threatened to fuck me in the ass, and I *think* Erzebet told him to go take a shit on the moon. But I can't be sure. Quickly! Erzebet said. I could half understand her, she spoke Hebrew intermingled with Yiddish, words I half-remembered from my grandparents' house. A street car! she said. I gaped as a silent tram appeared from Frishman and along Ibn Gvirol. The doors opened and we jumped inside.

Herzlberg

- I'd heard stories, she told me, later. We were in a house on the Yarkon. It is not so much a river as a brook. Its water was clean, I could see fish swimming inside, and children were bathing across the water from us, shouting and laughing. Where I come from that same river is filthy, though there had been recent efforts to clean it. I remembered the case of a girl who had been thrown into the river, her grandfather had murdered her and put her body into a suitcase and thrown it in the river.

- What sort of stories? I asked.

- Of people like you. Of another place, like this one. He will find us, you know. He is the foremost detective of the era, a hero. I should not have gone to him. We do not have much time.

- It's so peaceful here, I said.

- It is wonderful, she said. She leaned into me. How I hate to see that other place! she said.

- You're still bleeding, I said. Here, let me... awkwardly I tried to clean her hand, to bandage it.

- Leave it be, she said. She stroked my hair. Your clothes are so strange ... she said. She smelled of fresh milk and sweat. Her skin was so pale. There are many problems where I come from, I said. I stroked her hair. We sat very close together. It felt unreal, the heat and the humming of bees, in the middle of the city. But this was not my city. We have wars, I said. Terrorism. We fight with the Palestinians.

- Palestinians?

- The people who used to live here, I said.

- Oh, she said. We don't have them.

Her lips were close to mine. She was warm, but she shivered in my arms. Oh, Kfir, she said. She kissed me and I kissed her back. What do you mean, I said. You don't have them.

- It was Herzl's dream, she said. This. All this. Altneuland, he called it. Old New Land. We call it Tel Aviv.

- That's what we call the city, I said, and she laughed. That's silly, she said. We call it Herzlberg.

- But what happened to the Arabs? I said. To everyone who lived here before you came?

She shrugged. They would have ruined the dream, she said. And I remembered Herzl's book, the electric lights and the well-planned cities and the airships passing high above in their slow majestic flight, from the snow peaks of Mount Hermon to the shores of the Red Sea. A land of happy, modern Jews.

- There was no room for them, she said. So they had to go.

She kissed me again. She was on top of me, I was lying on my back in the grass. I heard a sound then, like a distant explosion. That woke me, I think. She grew less substantial in my hands. I felt a sudden fear grasp me. A place so clean, so ordered. She kissed me again, began to pull my t-shirt off. And I thought of soldiers in green uniforms getting on a bus, of Politicians shouting with spittle flying, of the sound of the siren on Memorial Day, and she grew less substantial still, and I heard car doors opening and shutting, and I thought of an El Al flight, of the long queue for the security checks, the endless questioning, the body scanners, the cramped rows and bad kosher food and black-clad Chasidim changing nappies, of the calls of the mosques in Jaffa and of Victory Ice-Cream up on the hill, and she grew less substantial still, and I heard footsteps, coming close, not hurrying, and saw the shadow of the detective fall on the grass beside me, and I saw him raise his hand.

For a moment our eyes met. He nodded, once. He was just an outline by then. Don't come back, he said. I heard the gunshot, but when I opened my eyes it was just some Filipino construction workers, having an impromptu picnic by the Yarkon, next to an Arab family who were setting up a barbeque, while two young mothers jogged past and someone with more enthusiasm than sense was trying to row a boat on the river.

The river smelled. And I walked home.

Tel Aviv

It's getting better now. The news helps—Channel 2, Reshet Bet on the radio once an hour, CNN, the newspapers. Rockets over Gaza, an exploding bus in Tel Aviv; the deaths and mutilations anchor me, a rope to pull me back into the right place and time. The sight of a concrete apartment block blown open with mortar, a child's plastic doll on the ground, its blue eyes staring into the camera. A mass funeral, a coffin draped with a flag, men waving guns in the air, and I realize with a start that I can't even tell who they are, Muslim or Jew.

The news helps, and I immerse myself in the second-hand bookshops, the moldy lurid paperbacks from the 1960s, with unlikely author names like Mike Longshott and Kim Rockman and the pictures of scantily clad women, two feet tall Korean secret agents, monsters, ghosts, Nazis and cowboys; and I avoid that damned Hebrew Detective, David Tidhar.

✡

I hope to never see another bloody zeppelin.

Biographical Notes to "A Discourse on the Nature of Causality, with Air-planes" by Benjamin Rosenbaum

Benjamin Rosenbaum

On my return from PlausFab-Wisconsin (a delightful festival of art and inquiry, which styles itself "the World's Only Gynarchist Plausible-Fable Assembly") aboard the *P.R.G.B. Śri George Bernard Shaw*, I happened to share a compartment with Prem Ramasson, Raja of Outermost Thule, and his consort, a dour but beautiful woman whose name I did not know.

Two great blond barbarians bearing the livery of Outermost Thule (an elephant astride an iceberg and a volcano) stood in the hallway outside, armed with sabers and needlethrowers. Politely they asked if they might frisk me, then allowed me in. They ignored the short dagger at my belt—presumably accounting their liege's skill at arms more than sufficient to equal mine.

I took my place on the embroidered divan. "Good evening," I said.

The Raja flashed me a white-toothed smile and inclined his head. His consort pulled a wisp of blue veil across her lips, and looked out the porthole.

I took my notebook, pen, and inkwell from my valise, set the inkwell into the port provided in the white pine table set in the wall, and slid aside the strings that bound the notebook. The inkwell lit with a faint blue glow.

The Raja was shuffling through a Wisdom Deck, pausing to look at the incandescent faces of the cards, then up at me. "You are the plausible-fabulist, Benjamin Rosenbaum," he said at length.

I bowed stiffly. "A pen name, of course," I said.

"Taken from *The Scarlet Pimpernel?*" he asked, cocking one eyebrow curiously.

"My lord is very quick," I said mildly.

The Raja laughed, indicating the Wisdom Deck with a wave. "He isn't the most heroic or sympathetic character in that book, however."

"Indeed not, my lord," I said with polite restraint. "The name is chosen ironically. As a sort of challenge to myself, if you will. Bearing the name of a notorious anti-Hebraic caricature, I must needs be all the prouder and more subtle in my own literary endeavors."

"You are a Karaite, then?" he asked.

"I am an Israelite, at any rate," I said. "If not an orthodox follower of my people's traditional religion of despair."

The prince's eyes glittered with interest, so—despite my reservations—I explained my researches into the Rabbinical Heresy which had briefly flourished in Palestine and Babylon at the time of Ashoka, and its lost Talmud.

"Fascinating," said the Raja. "Do you return now to your family?"

"I am altogether without attachments, my liege," I said, my face darkening with shame.

Excusing myself, I delved once again into my writing, pausing now and then to let my Wisdom Ants scurry from the inkwell to taste the ink with their antennae, committing it to memory for later editing. At PlausFab-Wisconsin, I had received an assignment—to construct a plausible-fable of a world without zeppelins—and I was trying to imagine some alternative air conveyance for my characters when the Prince spoke again.

"I am an enthusiast for plausible-fables myself," he said. "I enjoyed your 'Droplet' greatly."

"Thank you, Your Highness."

"Are you writing such a grand extrapolation now?"

"I am trying my hand at a shadow history," I said.

The prince laughed gleefully. His consort had nestled herself against the bulkhead and fallen asleep, the blue gauze of her veil obscuring her features. "I adore shadow history," he said.

"Most shadow history proceeds with the logic of dream, full of odd echoes and distorted resonances of our world," I said. "I am experimenting with a new form, in which a single point of divergence in history leads to a new causal chain of events, and thus a different present."

"But the world *is* a dream," he said excitedly. "Your idea smacks of Democritan materialism—as if the events of the world were produced purely by linear cause and effect, the simplest of the Five Forms of causality."

"Indeed," I said.

"How fanciful!" he cried.

I was about to turn again to my work, but the prince clapped his hands thrice. From his baggage, a birdlike Wisdom Servant unfolded itself and stepped agilely onto the floor. Fully unfolded, it was three cubits tall, with a trapezoidal head and incandescent blue eyes. It took a silver tea service from an alcove in the wall, set the tray on the table between us, and began to pour.

"Wake up, Sarasvati Sitasdottir," the prince said to his consort, stroking her shoulder. "We are celebrating."

The servitor placed a steaming teacup before me. I capped my pen and shooed my Ants back into their inkwell, though one crawled stubbornly towards the tea. "What are we celebrating?" I asked.

"You shall come with me to Outermost Thule," he said. "It is a magical place—all fire and ice, except where it is greensward and sheep. Home once of epic heroes, Rama's cousins." His consort took a sleepy sip of her tea. "I have need of a plausible-fabulist. You can write the history of the Thule that might have been, to inspire and quell my restive subjects."

"Why me, Your Highness? I am hardly a fabulist of great renown. Perhaps I could help you contact someone more suitable—Karen Despair Robinson, say, or Howi Qomr Faukota."

"Nonsense," laughed the Raja, "for I have met none of them by chance in an airship compartment."

"But yet . . . ," I said, discomfited.

"You speak again like a materialist! This is why the East, once it was awakened, was able to conquer the West—we understand how to read the dream that the world is. Come, no more fuss."

I lifted my teacup. The stray Wisdom Ant was crawling along its rim; I positioned my forefinger before her, that she might climb onto it.

Just then there was a scuffle at the door, and Prem Ramasson set his teacup down and rose. He said something admonitory in the harsh Nordic tongue of his adopted country, something I imagined to mean "come now, boys, let the conductor through." The scuffle ceased, and the Raja slid the door of the compartment open, one hand on the hilt of his sword. There was the sharp hiss of a needlethrower, and he staggered backward, collapsing into the arms of his consort, who cried out.

The thin and angular Wisdom Servant plucked the dart from its master's neck. "Poison," it said, its voice a tangle of flutelike harmonics. "The assassin will possess its antidote."

Sarasvati Sitasdottir began to scream.

✡

It is true that I had not accepted Prem Ramasson's offer of employment—indeed, that he had not seemed to find it necessary to actually ask. It is true also that I am a man of letters, neither spy nor bodyguard. It is furthermore true that I was unarmed, save for the ceremonial dagger at my belt, which had thus far seen employment only in the slicing of bread, cheese, and tomatoes.

Thus, the fact that I leapt through the doorway, over the fallen bodies of the prince's bodyguard, and pursued the fleeting form of the assassin down the long and curving corridor, cannot be reckoned as a habitual or forthright action. Nor, in truth, was it a considered one. In Śri Grigory Guptanovich Karthaganov's typology of action and motive, it must be accounted an impulsive-transformative action: the unreflective moment which changes forever the path of events.

Causes buzz around any such moment like bees around a hive, returning with pollen and information, exiting with hunger and ambition. The assassin's strike was the proximate cause. The prince's kind manner, his enthusiasm for plausible-fables (and my work in particular), his apparent sympathy for my people, the dark eyes of his consort—all these were inciting causes.

The psychological cause, surely, can be found in this name that I have chosen—"Benjamin Rosenbaum"—the fat and cowardly merchant of *The Scarlet Pimpernel* who is beaten and raises no hand to defend himself; just as we, deprived of our Temple, found refuge in endless, beautiful elegies of despair, turning our backs on the Rabbis and their dreams of a new beginning. I have always seethed against this passivity. Perhaps, then, I was waiting—my whole life—for such a chance at rash and violent action.

✡

The figure—clothed head to toe in a dull gray that matched the airship's hull—raced ahead of me down the deserted corridor, and descended through a maintenance hatch set in the floor. I reached it, and paused for breath, thankful my enthusiasm for the favorite sport of my continent—the exalted Lacrosse—had prepared me somewhat for the chase. I did not imagine, though, that I could overpower an armed and trained assassin. Yet, the weave of the world had brought me here—surely to some purpose. How could I do aught but follow?

✡

Beyond the proximate, inciting, and psychological causes, there are the more fundamental causes of an action. These address how the action embeds itself into the weave of the world, like a nettle in cloth. They rely on cosmology and epistemology. If the world is a dream, what caused the dreamer to dream that I chased the assassin? If the world is a lesson, what should this action teach? If the world is a gift, a wild and mindless rush of beauty, riven of logic or purpose—as it sometimes seems—still, seen from above, it must possess its own aesthetic harmony. The spectacle, then, of a ludicrously named practitioner of a half-despised art (bastard child of literature and philosophy), clumsily attempting the role of hero on the middledeck of the *P.R.G.B.* Śri *George Bernard Shaw*, must surely have some part in the pattern—chord or discord, tragic or comic.

✡

Hesitantly, I poked my head down through the hatch. Beneath, a spiral staircase descended through a workroom cluttered with tools. I could hear the faint hum of engines nearby. There, in the canvas of the outer hull, between the *Shaw*'s great aluminum ribs, a door to the sky was open.

From a workbench, I took and donned an airman's vest, supple leather gloves, and a visored mask, to shield me somewhat from the assassin's needle. I leaned my head out the door.

A brisk wind whipped across the skin of the ship. I took a tether from a nearby anchor and hooked it to my vest. The assassin was untethered. He crawled along a line of handholds and footholds set in the airship's gently curving surface. Many cubits beyond him, a small and brightly colored glider clung to the *Shaw*—like a dragonfly splayed upon a watermelon.

It was the first time I had seen a glider put to any utilitarian purpose—espionage rather than sport—and immediately I was seized by the longing to return to my notebook. Gliders! In a world without dirigibles, my heroes could travel in some kind of immense, powered gliders! Of course, they would be forced to land whenever winds were unfavorable.

Or would they? I recalled that my purpose was not to repaint our world anew, but to speculate rigorously according to Democritan logic. Each new cause could lead to some wholly new effect, causing in turn some unimagined consequence. Given different economic incentives, then, and with no overriding, higher pattern to dictate the results, who knew what advances a glider-based science of aeronautics might achieve? Exhilarating speculation!

I glanced down, and the sight below wrenched me from my reverie:

The immense panoply of the Great Lakes—

—their dark green wave-wrinkled water—

—the paler green and tawny yellow fingers of land reaching in among them—

—puffs of cloud gamboling in the bulk of air between—

—and beyond, the vault of sky presiding over the Frankish and Athapascan Moeity.

It was a long way down.

"*Malkat Ha-Shamayim*," I murmured aloud. "What am I doing?"

"I was wondering that myself," said a high and glittering timbrel of chords and discords by my ear. It was the recalcitrant, tea-seeking Wisdom Ant, now perched on my shoulder.

"Well," I said crossly, "do you have any suggestions?"

"My sisters have tasted the neurotoxin coursing the through the prince's blood," the Ant said. "We do not recognize it. His servant has kept him alive so far, but an antidote is beyond us." She gestured towards the fleeing villain with one delicate antenna. "The assassin will likely carry an antidote to his venom. If you can place me on his body, I can find it. I will then transmit the recipe to my sisters through the Brahmanic field. Perhaps they can formulate a close analogue in our inkwell."

"It is a chance," I agreed. "But the assassin is half-way to his craft."

"True," said the Ant pensively.

"I have an idea for getting there," I said. "But you will have to do the math."

The tether which bound me to the *Shaw* was fastened high above us. I crawled upwards and away from the glider, to a point the Ant calculated. The handholds ceased, but I improvised with the letters of the airship's name, raised in decoration from its side.

From the top of an *R*, I leapt into the air—struck with my heels against the resilient canvas—and rebounded, sailing outwards, snapping the tether taut.

The Ant took shelter in my collar as the air roared around us. We described a long arc, swinging past the surprised assassin to the brightly colored glider; I was able to seize its aluminum frame.

I hooked my feet onto its seat, and hung there, my heart racing. The glider creaked, but held.

"Disembark," I panted to the Ant. "When the assassin gains the craft, you can search him."

"Her," said the Ant, crawling down my shoulder. "She has removed her mask, and in our passing I was able to observe her striking resemblance to Sarasvati Sitasdottir, the prince's consort. She is clearly her sister."

I glanced at the assassin. Her long black hair now whipped in the wind. She was braced against the airship's hull with one hand and one foot; with the other hand she had drawn her needlethrower.

"That is interesting information," I said as the Ant crawled off my hand and onto the glider. "Good luck."

"Good-bye," said the Ant.

A needle whizzed by my cheek. I released the glider and swung once more into the cerulean sphere.

Once again I passed the killer, covering my face with my leather gloves—a dart glanced off my visor. Once again I swung beyond the door to the maintenance room and towards the hull.

Predictably, however, my momentum was insufficient to attain it. I described a few more dizzying swings of decreasing arc-length until I hung, nauseous, terrified, and gently swaying, at the end of the tether, amidst the sky.

To discourage further needles, I protected the back of my head with my arms, and faced downwards. That is when I noticed the pirate ship.

It was sleek and narrow and black, designed for maneuverability. Like the *Shaw*, it had a battery of sails for fair winds, and propellers in an aft assemblage. But the *Shaw* traveled in a predictable course and carried a fixed set of coiled tensors, whose millions of microsprings gradually relaxed to produce its motive force. The new craft spouted clouds of white steam; carrying its own generatory, it could rewind its tensor batteries while underway. And, unlike the *Shaw*, it was armed—a cruel array of arbalest-harpoons was mounted at either side. It carried its sails below, sporting at its top two razor-sharp saw-ridges with which it could gut recalcitrant prey.

All this would have been enough to recognize the craft as a pirate—but it displayed the universal device of pirates as well, that parody of the Yin-Yang: all Yang, declaring allegiance to imbalance. In a yellow circle, two round black dots stared like unblinking demonic eyes; beneath, a black semicircle leered with empty, ravenous bonhomie.

I dared a glance upward in time to see the glider launch from the *Shaw's* side. Whoever the mysterious assassin-sister was, whatever her purpose (political symbolism? personal revenge? dynastic ambition? anarchic mania?), she was a fantastic glider pilot. She gained the air with a single, supple back-flip, twirled the glider once, then hung deftly in the sky, considering.

✡

Most people, surely, would have wondered at the *meaning* of a pirate and an assassin showing up together—what resonance, what symbolism, what hortatory or aesthetic purpose did the world intend thereby? But my mind was still with my thought-experiment.

Imagine there are no causes but mechanical ones—that the world is nothing but a chain of dominoes! Every plausible-fabulist spends long hours teasing apart fictional plots, imagining consequences, conjuring and discarding the antecedents of desired events. We dirty our hands daily with the simplest and grubbiest of the Five Forms. Now I tried to reason thus about life.

Were the pirate and the assassin in league? It seemed unlikely. If the assassin intended to trigger political upheaval and turmoil, pirates surely spoiled the attempt. A death at the hands of pirates while traveling in a foreign land is not the stuff of which revolutions are made. If the intent was merely to kill Ramasson, surely one or the other would suffice.

Yet was I to credit chance, then, with the intrusion of two violent enemies, in the same hour, into my hitherto tranquil existence?

Absurd! Yet the idea had an odd attractiveness. If the world was a blind machine, surely such clumsy coincidences would be common!

✡

The assassin saw the pirate ship; yet, with an admirable consistency, she seemed resolved to finish what she had started. She came for me.

I drew my dagger from its sheath. Perhaps, at first, I had some wild idea of throwing it, or parrying her needles, though I had the skill for neither.

She advanced to a point some fifteen cubits away; from there, her spring-fired darts had more than enough power to pierce my clothing. I could see her face now, a choleric, wild-eyed homunculus of her phlegmatic sister's.

The smooth black canvas of the pirate ship was now thirty cubits below me.

The assassin banked her glider's wings against the wind, hanging like a kite. She let go its aluminum frame with her right hand, and drew her needlethrower.

Summoning all my strength, I struck the tether that held me with my dagger's blade.

My strength, as it happened, was extremely insufficient. The tether twanged like a harp-string, but was otherwise unharmed, and the dagger was knocked from my grasp by the recoil.

The assassin burst out laughing, and covered her eyes. Feeling foolish, I seized the tether in one hand and unhooked it from my vest with the other.

Then I let go.

✡

Since that time, I have on various occasions enumerated to myself, with a mixture of wonder and chagrin, the various ways I might have died. I might have snapped my neck, or, landing on my stomach, folded in a V and broken my spine like a twig. If I had struck one of the craft's aluminum ribs, I should certainly have shattered bones.

What is chance? Is it best to liken it to the whim of some being of another scale or scope, the dreamer of our dream? Or to regard the world as having an inherent pattern, mirroring itself at every stage and scale?

Or *could* our world arise, as Democritus held, willy-nilly, of the couplings and patternings of endless dumb particulates?

While hanging from the *Shaw*, I had decided that the protagonist of my Democritan shadow-history (should I live to write it) would be a man of letters, a dabbler in philosophy like myself, who lived in an advanced society committed to philosophical materialism. I relished the apparent paradox—an intelligent man, in a sophisticated nation, forced to account for all events purely within the rubric of overt mechanical causation!

Yet those who today, complacently, regard the materialist hypothesis as dead— pointing to the Brahmanic field and its Wisdom Creatures, to the predictive successes, from weather to history, of the Theory of Five Causal Forms—forget that the question is, at bottom, axiomatic. The materialist hypothesis—the primacy of Matter over Mind—is undisprovable. What successes might some other science, in another history, have built, upon its bulwark?

So I cannot say—I cannot say!—if it is meaningful or meaningless, the fact that I struck the pirate vessel's resilient canvas with my legs and buttocks, was flung upwards again, to bounce and roll until I fetched up against the wall of the airship's dorsal razor-weapon. I cannot say if some Preserver spared my life through will, if some Pattern needed me for the skein it wove—or if a patternless and unforetellable Chance spared me all unknowing.

✡

There was a small closed hatchway in the razor-spine nearby, whose over-hanging ridge provided some protection against my adversary. Bruised and weary, groping inchoately among theories of chance and purpose, I scrambled for it as the boarding gongs and klaxons began.

The *Shaw* knew it could neither outrun nor outfight the swift and dangerous corsair—it idled above me, awaiting rapine. The brigand's longboats launched—lean and maneuverable black dirigibles the size of killer whales, with parties of armed sky-bandits clinging to their sides.

The glider turned and dove, a blur of gold and crimson and verdant blue disappearing over the pirate zeppelin's side—abandoning our duel, I imagined, for some redoubt many leagues below us.

✡

Oddly, I was sad to see her go. True, I had known from her only wanton violence; she had almost killed me; I crouched battered, terrified, and nauseous on the summit of a pirate corsair on her account; and the kind Raja, my almost-employer, might be dead. Yet I felt our relations had reached as yet no satisfactory conclusion.

It is said that we fabulists live two lives at once. First we live as others do: seeking to feed and clothe ourselves, earn the respect and affection of our fellows, fly from danger, entertain and satiate ourselves on the things of this world. But then, too, we live a second life, pawing through the moments of the first, even as they happen, like a market-woman of the bazaar sifting trash for treasures. Every agony we endure, we also hold up to the light with great excitement, expecting it will be of use; every simple joy, we regard with a critical eye, wondering how it could be changed, honed, tightened, to fit inside a fable's walls.

✿

The hatch was locked. I removed my mask and visor and lay on the canvas, basking in the afternoon sun, hoping my Ants had met success in their apothecary and saved the Prince; watching the pirate longboats sack the unresisting *P.R.G.B.* Śri *George Bernard Shaw* and return laden with valuables and—perhaps—hostages.

I was beginning to wonder if they would ever notice me—if, perhaps, I should signal them—when the cacophony of gongs and klaxons resumed—louder, insistent, angry—and the longboats raced back down to anchor beneath the pirate ship.

Curious, I found a ladder set in the razor-ridge's metal wall that led to a lookout platform.

A war-city was emerging from a cloudbank some leagues away.

I had never seen any work of man so vast. Fully twelve great dirigible hulls, each dwarfing the *Shaw*, were bound together in a constellation of outbuildings and propeller assemblies. Near the center, a great plume of white steam rose from a pillar; a Heart-of-the-Sun reactor, where the dull yellow ore called Yama's-flesh is driven to realize enlightenment through the ministrations of Wisdom-Sadhus.

There was a spyglass set in the railing by my side; I peered through, scanning the features of this new apparition.

None of the squabbling statelets of my continent could muster such a vessel, certainly; and only the Powers—Cathay, Gabon, the Aryan Raj—could afford to fly one so far afield, though the Khmer and Malay might have the capacity to build them.

There is little enough to choose between the meddling Powers, though Gabon makes the most pretense of investing in its colonies and believing in its supposed civilizing mission. This craft, though, was clearly Hindu. Every cubit of its surface was bedecked with a façade of cytoceramic statuary—couples coupling in five thousand erotic poses; theromorphic gods gesturing to soothe or menace; Rama in his chariot; heroes riddled with arrows and fighting on; saints undergoing martyrdom. In one corner, I spotted the Israelite avatar of Vishnu, hanging on his cross between Shiva and Ganesh.

Then I felt rough hands on my shoulders.

Five pirates had emerged from the hatch, cutlasses drawn. Their dress was motley and ragged, their features varied—Sikh, Xhosan, Baltic, Frankish, and Aztec, I surmised. None of us spoke as they led me through the rat's maze of catwalks and ladders set between the ship's inner and outer hulls.

I was queasy and light-headed with bruises, hunger, and the aftermath of rash and strenuous action; it seemed odd indeed that the day before, I had been celebrating and debating with the plausible-fabulists gathered at Wisconsin. I recalled that there had been a fancy-dress ball there, with a pirate theme; and the images of yesterday's festive, well-groomed pirates of fancy interleaved with those of today's grim and unwashed captors on the long climb down to the bridge.

The bridge was in the gondola that hung beneath the pirate airship's bulk, forwards of the rigging. It was crowded with lean and dangerous men in pantaloons, sarongs and leather trousers. They consulted paper charts and the liquid, glowing forms swimming in Wisdom Tanks, spoke through bronze tubes set in the walls, barked orders to cabin boys who raced away across the airship's webwork of spars.

At the great window that occupied the whole of the forward wall, watching the clouds part as we plunged into them, stood the captain.

I had suspected whose ship this might be upon seeing it; now I was sure. A giant of a man, dressed in buckskin and adorned with feathers, his braided red hair and bristling beard proclaimed him the scion of those who had fled the destruction of Viking Eire to settle on the banks of the Father-of-Waters.

This ship, then, was the *Hiawatha MacCool*, and this the man who terrorized commerce from the shores of Lake Erie to the border of Texas.

"Chippewa Melko," I said.

He turned, raising an eyebrow.

"Found him sightseeing on the starboard spine," one of my captors said.

"Indeed?" said Melko. "Did you fall off the *Shaw*?"

"I jumped, after a fashion," I said. "The reason thereof is a tale that strains my own credibility, although I lived it."

Sadly, this quip was lost on Melko, as he was distracted by some pressing bit of martial business.

We were descending at a precipitous rate; the water of Lake Erie loomed before us, filling the window. Individual whitecaps were discernable upon its surface.

When I glanced away from the window, the bridge had darkened—every Wisdom Tank was gray and lifeless.

OTHER COVENANTS

"You there! Spy!" Melko barked. I noted with discomfiture that he addressed me. "Why would they disrupt our communications?"

"What?" I said.

The pirate captain gestured at the muddy tanks. "The Aryan war-city—they've disrupted the Brahmanic field with some damned device. They mean to cripple us, I suppose—ships like theirs are dependent on it. Won't work. But how do they expect to get their hostages back alive if they refuse to parley?"

"Perhaps they mean to board and take them," I offered.

"We'll see about that," he said grimly. "Listen up, boys—we hauled ass to avoid a trap, but the trap found us anyway. But we can outrun this bastard in the high airstreams if we lose all extra weight. Dinky—run and tell Max to drop the steamer. Red, Ali—mark the aft, fore, and starboard harpoons with buoys and let 'em go. Grig, Ngube—same with the spent tensors. Fast!"

He turned to me as his minions scurried to their tasks. "We're throwing all dead weight over the side. That includes you, unless I'm swiftly convinced otherwise. Who are you?"

"Gabriel Goodman," I said truthfully, "but better known by my quill-name — 'Benjamin Rosenbaum.'"

"Benjamin Rosenbaum?" the pirate cried. "The great Iowa poet, author of 'Green Nakedness' and 'Broken Lines?' You are a hero of our land, sir! Fear not, I shall—"

"No," I interrupted crossly. "Not that Benjamin Rosenbaum."

The pirate reddened, and tapped his teeth, frowning. "Aha, hold then, I have heard of you—the children's tale-scribe, I take it? 'Legs the Caterpillar?' I'll spare you, then, for the sake of my son Timmy, who—"

"No," I said again, through gritted teeth. "I am an author of plausible-fables, sir, not picture-books."

"Never read the stuff," said Melko. There was a great shudder, and the steel bulk of the steam generatory, billowing white clouds, fell past us. It struck the lake, raising a plume of spray that spotted the window with droplets. The forward harpoon assembly followed, trailing a red buoy on a line.

"Right then," said Melko. "Over you go."

"You spoke of Aryan hostages," I said hastily, thinking it wise now to mention the position I seemed to have accepted *de facto*, if not yet *de jure*. "Do you by any chance refer to my employer, Prem Ramasson, and his consort?"

Melko spat on the floor, causing a cabin boy to rush forward with a mop. "So you're one of those quislings who serves Hindoo royalty even as they divide up the land of your fathers, are you?" He advanced towards me menacingly.

"Outer Thule is a minor province of the Raj, sir," I said. "It is absurd to blame Ramasson for the war in Texas."

"Ready to rise, sir," came the cry.

"Rise then!" Melko ordered. "And throw this dog in the brig with its master. If we can't ransom them, we'll throw them off at the top." He glowered at me. "That will give you a nice long while to salve your conscience with making fine distinctions among Hindoos. What do you think he's doing here in our lands, if not plotting with his brothers to steal more of our gold and helium?"

I was unable to further pursue my political debate with Chippewa Melko, as his henchmen dragged me at once to cramped quarters between the inner and outer hulls. The prince lay on the single bunk, ashen and unmoving. His consort knelt at his side, weeping silently. The Wisdom Servant, deprived of its animating field, had collapsed into a tangle of reedlike protuberances.

My valise was there; I opened it and took out my inkwell. The Wisdom Ants lay within, tiny crumpled blobs of brassy metal. I put the inkwell in my pocket.

"Thank you for trying," Sarasvati Sitasdottir said hoarsely. "Alas, luck has turned against us."

"All may not be lost," I said. "An Aryan war-city pursues the pirates, and may yet buy our ransom; although, strangely, they have damped the Brahmanic field and so cannot hear the pirates' offer of parley."

"If they were going to parley, they would have done so by now," she said dully. "They will burn the pirate from the sky. They do not know we are aboard."

"Then our bad luck comes in threes." It is an old rule of thumb, derided as superstition by professional causalists. But they, like all professionals, like to obfuscate their science, rendering it inaccessible to the layman; in truth, the old rule holds a glimmer of the workings of the third form of causality.

"A swift death is no bad luck for me," Sarasvati Sitasdottir said. "Not when he is gone." She choked a sob, and turned away.

I felt for the Raja's pulse; his blood was still beneath his amber skin. His face was turned towards the metal bulkhead; droplets of moisture there told of his last breath, not long ago. I wiped them away, and closed his eyes.

We waited, for one doom or another. I could feel the zeppelin rising swiftly; the *Hiawatha* was unheated, and the air turned cold. The princess did not speak.

✡

My mind turned again to the fable I had been commissioned to write, the materialist shadow-history of a world without zeppelins. If by some unlikely chance I should live to finish it, I resolved to make do without the extravagant perils, ironic coincidences, sudden bursts of insight, death-defying escapades and beautiful villainesses that litter our genre and cheapen its high philosophical concerns. Why must every protagonist be doomed, daring, lonely, and overly proud? No, my philosopher-hero would enjoy precisely those goods of which I was deprived—a happy family, a secure situation, a prosperous and powerful nation, a conciliatory nature; above all, an absence of immediate physical peril. Of course, there must be conflict, worry, sorrow—but, I vowed, of a rich and subtle kind!

I wondered how my hero would view the chain of events in which I was embroiled. With derision? With compassion? I loved him, after a fashion, for he was my creation. How would he regard me?

If only the first and simplest form of causality had earned his allegiance, he would not be placated by such easy saws as "bad things come in threes." An assassin, *and* a pirate, *and* an uncommunicative war-city, he would ask? All within the space of an hour?

Would he simply accept the absurd and improbable results of living within a blind and random machine? Yet his society could not have advanced far, mired in such fatalism!

Would he not doggedly seek meaning, despite the limitations of his framework?

What if our bad luck were no coincidence at all, he would ask. What if all three misfortunes had a single, linear, proximate cause, intelligible to reason?

✡

"My lady," I said, "I do not wish to cause you further pain. Yet I find I must speak. I saw the face of the prince's killer—it was a young woman's face, in lineament much like your own."

"Shakuntala!" the princess cried. "My sister! No! It cannot be! She would never do this—" she curled her hands into fists. "No!"

"And yet," I said gently, "it seems you regard the assertion as not utterly implausible."

"She is banished," Sarasvati Sitasdottir said. "She has gone over to the Thanes—the Nordic Liberation Army—the anarcho-gynarchist insurgents in our land. It is like her to seek danger and glory. But she would not kill Prem! She loved him before I!"

To that, I could find no response. The *Hiawatha* shuddered around us— some battle had been joined. We heard shouts and running footsteps.

Sarasvati, the prince, the pirates—any of them would have had a thousand gods to pray to, convenient gods for any occasion. Such solace I could sorely have used. But I was raised a Karaite. We acknowledge only one God, austere and magnificent; the One God of All Things, attended by His angels and His consort, the Queen of Heaven. The only way to speak to Him, we are taught, is in His Holy Temple; and it lies in ruins these two thousand years. In times like these, we are told to meditate on the contrast between His imperturbable magnificence and our own abandoned and abject vulnerability, and to be certain that He watches us with immeasurable compassion, though He will not act. I have never found this much comfort.

Instead, I turned to the prince, curious what in his visage might have inspired the passions of the two sisters.

On the bulkhead just before his lips—where, before, I had wiped away the sign of his last breath—a tracery of condensation stood.

Was this some effluvium issued by the organs of a decaying corpse? I bent, and delicately sniffed—detecting no corruption.

"My lady," I said, indicating the droplets on the cool metal, "he lives."

"What?" the princess cried. "But how?"

"A diguanidinium compound produced by certain marine dinoflagellates," I said, "can induce a deathlike coma, in which the subject breathes but thrice an hour; the heartbeat is similarly undetectable."

Delicately, she felt his face. "Can he hear us?"

"Perhaps."

"Why would she do this?"

"The body would be rushed back to Thule, would it not? Perhaps the revolutionaries meant to steal it and revive him as a hostage?"

A tremendous thunderclap shook the *Hiawatha MacCool*, and I noticed we were listing to one side. There was a commotion in the gangway; then Chippewa Melko entered. Several guards stood behind him.

"Damned tenacious," he spat. "If they want you so badly, why won't they parley? We're still out of range of the war-city itself and its big guns, thank Buddha, Thor, and Darwin. We burned one of their launches, at the cost of many of my men. But the other launch is gaining."

"Perhaps they don't know the hostages are aboard?" I asked.

"Then why pursue me this distance? I'm no fool—I know what it costs them to detour that monster. They don't do it for sport, and I don't flatter myself I'm worth that much to them. No, it's you they want. So they can have you—I've no more stomach for this chase." He gestured at the prince with his chin. "Is he dead?"

"No," I said.

"Doesn't look well. No matter—come along. I'm putting you all in a launch with a flag of parley on it. Their war-boat will have to stop for you, and that will give us the time we need."

So it was that we found ourselves in the freezing, cramped bay of a pirate longboat. Three of Melko's crewmen accompanied us—one at the controls, the other two clinging to the longboat's sides. Sarasvati and I huddled on the aluminum deck beside the pilot, the prince's body held between us. All three of Melko's men had parachutes—they planned to escape as soon as we docked. Our longboat flew the white flag of parley, and—taken from the prince's luggage—the royal standard of Outermost Thule.

All the others were gazing tensely at our target—the war-city's fighter launch, which climbed toward us from below. It was almost as big as Melko's flagship. I, alone, glanced back out the open doorway as we swung away from the *Hiawatha*.

So only I saw a brightly colored glider detach itself from the *Hiawatha*'s side and swoop to follow us.

Why would Shakuntala have lingered with the pirates thus far? Once the rebels' plan to abduct the prince was foiled by Melko's arrival, why not simply abandon it and await a fairer chance?

Unless the intent was not to abduct—but to protect.

"My lady," I said in my halting middle-school Sanskrit, "your sister is here."
Sarasvati gasped, following my gaze.

"Madam—your husband was aiding the rebels."

"How dare you?" she hissed in the same tongue, much more fluently.

"It is the only—" I struggled for the Sanskrit word for 'hypothesis,' then abandoned the attempt, leaning over to whisper in English. "Why else did the pirates and the war-city arrive together? Consider: the prince's collusion with the Thanes was discovered by the Aryan Raj. But to try him for treason would provoke great scandal and stir sympathy for the insurgents. Instead, they made sure rumor of a valuable hostage reached Melko. With the prince in the hands of the pirates, his death would simply be a regrettable calamity."

Her eyes widened. "Those monsters!" she hissed.

"Your sister aimed to save him, but Melko arrived too soon—before news of the prince's death could discourage his brigandy. My lady, I fear that if we reach that launch, they will discover that the Prince lives. Then some accident will befall us all."

There were shouts from outside. Melko's crewmen drew their needlethrowers and fired at the advancing glider.

With a shriek, Sarasvati flung herself upon the pilot, knocking the controls from his hands.

The longboat lurched sickeningly.

I gained my feet, then fell against the prince. I saw a flash of orange and gold—the glider, swooping by us.

I struggled to stand. The pilot drew his cutlass. He seized Sarasvati by the hair and spun her away from the controls.

Just then, one of the men clinging to the outside, pricked by Shakuntala's needle, fell. His tether caught him, and the floor jerked beneath us.

The pilot staggered back. Sarasvati Sitasdottir punched him in the throat. They stumbled towards the door.

I started forward. The other pirate on the outside fell, untethered, and the longboat lurched again. Unbalanced, our craft drove in a tight circle, listing dangerously.

Sarasvati fought with uncommon ferocity, forcing the pirate towards the open hatch. Fearing they would both tumble through, I seized the controls.

Regrettably, I knew nothing of flying airship-longboats, whose controls, it happens, are of a remarkably poor design.

One would imagine that the principal steering element could be moved in the direction that one wishes the craft to go; instead, just the opposite is the case. Then, too, one would expect these brawny and unrefined air-men to use controls lending themselves to rough usage; instead, it seems an exceedingly fine hand is required.

Thus, rather than steadying the craft, I achieved the opposite.

Not only were Sarasvati and the pilot flung out the cabin door, but I myself was thrown through it, just managing to catch with both hands a metal protuberance in the hatchway's base. My feet swung freely over the void.

I looked up in time to see the Raja's limp body come sliding towards me like a missile.

I fear that I hesitated too long in deciding whether to dodge or catch my almost-employer. At the last minute courage won out, and I flung one arm around his chest as he struck me.

This dislodged my grip, and the two of us fell from the airship.

In an extremity of terror, I let go the prince, and clawed wildly at nothing.

I slammed into the body of the pirate who hung, poisoned by Shakuntala's needle, from the airship's tether. I slid along him, and finally caught myself at his feet.

As I clung there, shaking miserably, I watched Prem Ramasson tumble through the air, and I cursed myself for having caused the very tragedies I had endeavored to avoid, like a figure in an Athenian tragedy. But such tragedies proceed from some essential flaw in their heroes—some illustrative hubris, some damning vice. Searching my own character and actions, I could find only that I had endeavored to make do, as well as I could, in situations for which I was ill-prepared. Is that not the fate of any of us, confronting life and its vagaries?

Was my tale, then, an absurd and tragic farce? Was its lesson one merely of ignominy and despair?

Or perhaps—as my shadow-protagonist might imagine—there was no tale, no teller—perhaps the dramatic and sensational events I had endured were part of no story at all, but brute and silent facts of Matter.

From above, Shakuntala Sitasdottir dove in her glider. It was folded like a spear, and she swept past the prince in seconds. Nimbly, she flung open the glider's wings, sweeping up to the falling Raja, and rolling the glider, took him into her embrace.

Thus encumbered—she must have secured him somehow—she dove again (chasing her sister, I imagine) and disappeared in a bank of cloud.

✡

A flock of brass-colored Wisdom Gulls, arriving from the Aryan war-city, flew around the pirates' launch. They entered its empty cabin, glanced at me and the poisoned pirate to whom I clung, and departed.

I climbed up the body to sit upon its shoulders, a much more comfortable position. There, clinging to the tether and shivering, I rested.

The *Hiawatha MacCool*, black smoke guttering from one side of her, climbed higher and higher into the sky, pursued by the Aryan war-boat. The sun was setting, limning the clouds with gold and pink and violet. The war-city, terrible and glorious, sailed slowly by, under my feet, its shadow an island of darkness in the sunset's gold-glitter, on the waters of the lake beneath.

Some distance to the east, where the sky was already darkening to a rich cobalt, the Aryan war-boat which Melko had successfully struck was bathed in white fire. After a while, the inner hull must have been breached, for the fire went out, extinguished by escaping helium, and the zeppelin plummeted.

Above me, the propeller hummed, driving my launch in the same small circle again and again.

I hoped that I had saved the prince after all. I hoped Shakuntala had saved her sister, and that the three of them would find refuge with the Thanes.

My shadow-protagonist had given me a gift; it was the logic of his world that had led me to discover the war-city's threat. Did this mean his philosophy was the correct one?

Yet the events that followed were so dramatic and contrived—precisely as if I inhabited a pulp romance. Perhaps he was writing my story, as I wrote his; perhaps, with the comfortable life I had given him, he longed to lose himself in uncomfortable escapades of this sort. In that case, we both of us lived in a world designed, a world of story, full of meaning.

But perhaps I had framed the question wrong. Perhaps the division between Mind and Matter is itself illusory; perhaps Randomness, Pattern, and Plan are all but stories we tell about the inchoate and unknowable world which fills the darkness beyond the thin circle illumed by reason's light. Perhaps it is foolish to ask if I or the protagonist of my world-without-zeppelins story is the more real. Each of us is flesh, a buzzing swarm of atoms; yet each of us also a tale contained in the pages of the other's notebook. We are bodies. But we are also the stories we tell about each other. Perhaps not knowing is enough.

Maybe it is not a matter of discovering the correct philosophy. Maybe the desire that burns behind this question is the desire to be real. And which is more real—a clod of dirt unnoticed at your feet, or a hero in a legend?

And maybe behind the desire to be real is simply wanting to be known. To be held.

The first stars glittered against the fading blue. I was in the bosom of the Queen of Heaven. My fingers and toes were getting numb—soon frostbite would set in. I recited the prayer the ancient heretical Rabbis would say before death, which begins, "Hear O Israel, the Lord is Our God, the Lord is One."

Then I began to climb the tether.

And In This Corner...!

D.K. Latta

The giant roared defiantly at the thin circle of men around him, the setting sun stretching their shadows like willow leaves across the parched earth. He was at least five cubits tall—easily head and shoulders taller than the tallest man there—with broad, bull shoulders and limbs like tree trunks. He wore a simple skirt about his loins, frayed sandals upon his huge feet, and his black beard was braided into a tail that flopped against his hairy chest. His eyes were ringed with black eyeliner in a vaguely Egyptian fashion that lent an even greater ferocity to his glare.

He bared his teeth in a terrifying grin. "Who dares stand before Hanun the Bull?" he shouted, spittle flying from his lips. He pounded a massive fist against his chest. "Who wants to make their wives into widows?"

There were no widows tonight—not yet. But three men who had already taken up his challenge lay slumped by the crackling bonfire, bruised and possibly concussed.

When none stepped forward, Hanun threw back his head. "Hah! I thought I would find at least one true man among you. You break your backs in the quarries by day, yet simper over your stew bowls at night, eh?"

"I'll challenge you."

The voice was soft, barely above a whisper, yet it cut through the twilight and silenced the murmuring throng. Hanun stiffened, then turned toward the speaker.

"You?" he laughed.

Pushing through the ring of men was a slight fellow, shorter than most there and barely reaching the chest of the giant. He was dressed simply in a worn tunic. His dark curly hair was unruly and his chin graced by a scruffy beard.

The group of men stirred and nudged each other, the sight of the small man standing before the giant causing some to snicker openly.

"I am Isaac," shouted the smaller man. "And by God's grace I will beat you, giant."

Hanun cocked his head, as though considering the matter. "The only wager I can imagine here is how long it takes me to squash you." He looked around at the crowd. "One blow? Two? Or does he look tough enough to endure three?" The crowd joined in the mockery, and instantly bets were shouted out and odds taken, a lithe dark-haired woman at the centre of the haggling. Hanun turned back toward Isaac. "I'll kink my back just trying to bend over and hit you, little one. So just this once let us agree to weapons." One-handed he hefted an old tree branch that an average man would struggle to raise with two hands. "Just so I can reach you down there."

"Very well," said Isaac blithely. And then to everyone's surprise he reached not for a stick or even a sword, but uncoiled from about his wrist a leather strap. He snapped it loose, revealing it to be a sling. From out of a pouch about his waist he drew a small object.

Hanun started laughing again. "Do I have a bird's nest on my head? That's all that toy is good for—killing birds." Then mirth discarded, he strode grimly toward the little figure, branch held aloft as a club.

If the crowd expected Isaac to bolt, to run, his bravado deserting him when faced with such inevitable punishment, they were wrong. Instead, the smaller man stood his ground, spinning his sling around and around, faster, faster, till it was a blur. Then, just as Hanun loomed over him, Isaac flicked the sling and the tiny object shot through the air, impacting the very center of Hanun's forehead. The big man's head snapped back. His club dropped from his fingers as he clutched his brow. He let out a howl of almost animalistic anguish.

Like a felled tree, he toppled back into the cluster of onlookers.

✡

Isaac picked his way along the road, the full moon turning to the hue of dirty ivory, the parched yellow grass scrabbling over the hills. He had not realized how late it had grown, and there was a chill falling with the darkness.

He stiffened, hearing the nearby scuffle of feet on dry earth. "Who's there?" he called.

Suddenly, out of the darkness, loomed a massive figure. "Did you think to best The Bull and simply walk away?" growled the giant, Hanun.

Isaac stared up at the towering figure, more shadow than man with the moon at his back.

"Did you think you could escape—" The giant caught him up in his big arms and pulled him to his chest. "—without a kiss?"

The two men hungrily locked mouths together, silencing their laughter.

"Save it for the privacy of a tent," chided a woman's voice. A lithe, dark-haired woman emerged from the darkness—the same woman who had been collecting bets at the quarry worker's camp.

Hanun put Isaac down. "You've seen us kiss before, Yamtisy."

"But you wouldn't want any of those quarry workers out for a late night stroll to see. They might wonder why two men who seemed mortal foes an hour ago were tonguing like Gomorrites now."

Hanun made to argue, then shrugged, conceding the point.

"So how much did we take?" asked Isaac.

Yamtisy shrugged. "As much as can be expected. Everyone bet on Hanun, obviously—but it's not like quarry men have a lot of spare coin to wager in the first place."

"And no one questioned your recovery?" asked Isaac of the giant.

"No. I just lay insensible for a while, then sat up, cursing, and staggered off." Then he rubbed his brow peevishly. "But what sort of stone did you hit me with? It's just supposed to be play-acting!"

"It was just a date, you big baby," laughed Isaac. "But if we're going to criticize each other's play-acting ... " Isaac clasped his brow, let out an exaggerated groan, and started staggering drunkenly about in a parody of Hanun's earlier performance. Yamtisy started laughing. Hanun huffed indignantly for a moment, but then even he chuckled amiably.

"Shhh," hissed Yamtisy suddenly.

They stopped, hearing what sounded to be the clopping of horse hooves. They waited by the side of the road as a dark shape swelled out of the night. The rider reined in his mount, clearly as startled to see pedestrians at this hour as they were to spy a rider.

"Hail," he said unsurely. Metal glinted about his body in the moonlight, and more metal rattled at his hip. A fighting man, it seemed.

"Evening," said Hanun neutrally.

The man studied the trio, darkness making it difficult to gauge true perspective. Hanun, standing a bit back from the road, appeared to simply be a large adult with two youths at his side. "Is this the Eastern road?" he asked, pointing the way from which they had come.

"Aye," Hanun agreed.

"Good. I hear the Israelites and the Philistines are at it again."

"I've heard something of that," said Hanun. "But is that good news?" he asked.

The rider laughed and rattled the sword at his hip. "It is if you're a fighting man. One side or the other will have me, I'm sure." He looked Hanun up and down. If he could not perceive his true height, he could at least discern that Hanun was a powerful figure. "You should think of joining up yourself—there's always profit to be had when kingdoms war. Well, good night." He twitched his reins and moved past them.

"And to you," Hanun called.

✡

The three lay stretched out beneath the stars, their small fire subsiding into crimson embers. Hanun and Isaac had spread their bed rolls next to each other, while Yamtisy slumbered on the other side of what remained of the fire.

Isaac netted his fingers beneath his head and stared at the inky heavens.

"I want to get off the road, Hanun," he said at last. "Settle down."

The big man grunted. "What brought this on?"

"What Yamtisy said, I guess—about hiding our relationship. Wouldn't it be nice to have our own place, where we could just be who we are? We've talked about that before: buying some land, acquiring a flock of sheep to herd."

Hanun propped up on his elbows. "You found a nice little heiress to marry, have you?" he teased.

"No, of course not." Then he shot the bigger man a look that was barely visible in the darkness. "And you're a fine one to talk."

Hanun scowled. "I haven't been with a woman in over two years."

"We've been together four."

He snorted. "I thought we'd moved past that. I said it was a mistake."

Isaac waved a hand. "I have. We have. That's not my point. It's just—we go from town to town, scamming enough to get to the next town, where we do it all over again. I want something more. Something stable."

Hanun was silent for a time, then asked: "What about Yamtisy? We can't just drop her."

Isaac sighed. "Fine—she can help us run our sheep farm if she wants. Happy?"

Hanun laughed and leaned forward, attempting to kiss Isaac in the darkness, but bussing his cheek instead. Impatiently, the smaller man pushed him away. "It's just a fantasy anyway. Scamming a few miners and farmers isn't going to give us enough capital for a farm and a flock, not at this rate." And then, somewhat petulantly, he rolled over and made a show of going to sleep.

✡

"I was thinking about what you said last night," said Hanun as the trio sat about their camp, finishing what there was of their breakfast—dried roots, dates, and a bit of smoked meat that would have to hold them until they made the next town. There was a light breeze stirring the dry heat in the air and a raven cawed as it circled above. Hanun dug out an obdurate string of gristle from between his teeth and flung it at the smoldering embers. "About making some real money. You remember that rider last night who mentioned the Israelites and the Philistines are fighting, yes? Why not do our routine there? Tempers'll be high; patriotism, religious pride. Play the crowds right and it'd practically be treasonous for them *not* to wager on the outcome."

The dark-eyed Yamtisy stared at him thoughtfully, then shot a look at Isaac. "You know—he's not wrong. Soldiers have salaries, and there'll be thousands of them."

"Are you both crazy?" demanded Isaac. "With small crowds, if it goes wrong the worst that happens is we get chased out of town. Mess up in front of armies, with kings watching—and we end up with our heads on pikes."

"What could go wrong?" insisted Hanun. "We've done this hundreds of times and never had a problem. I mean, you're an Israelite, right?"

Isaac hesitated, then nodded.

"And my father was a Philistine..."

"I thought your father was a Samaritan?" said Yamtisy.

The giant waved his hand dismissively. "My mother was a bit vague about details. But the point is: *look at me.* The Philistines aren't going to turn me down, are they? And Isaac could present himself to the Israelites as some sort of, I don't know—a messenger from God. I mean, your people believe in that stuff, right? Dreams and heavenly agents? If you say God came to you in a dream—people take it seriously."

"I think it's a little more complicated than that," Isaac said drily.

"Which god?" Yamtisy asked, trying to follow the discussion.

"The Israelites believe in the one God," Hanun said off-handedly.

"The god who won what?"

He held up one big finger. "No—just one God."

Her brow crinkled. "Who looks after the harvest?"

"The one God."

"And the storms?"

"Same."

"And the, I don't know—the artists? And the sailors?"

"All him."

"That's crazy. How could he do all that?" She shook her head. "Where I come from we have gods for everything—*that's* something you can get your brain around."

"Don't they also have crocodile and hyena heads?" said Isaac wryly. Before she could respond he said, "Look—this is beside the point. The bigger the stage, the greater the danger we'll be recognized. Suppose one of those quarry men from last night signs up with an army on one side or the other. He sees us, recognizes us, and tells someone..."

"So we resurrect an older routine, one we haven't used around here. What was that variation we did in Sheba a few years back? You pretended to be a young shepherd or something."

Isaac pursed his lips. "I'm hardly going to pass for a youth now."

Yamtisy looked at him thoughtfully. "Shave off that beard of yours and you've still got a bit of a baby face." She pinched one of his cheeks playfully and laughed as he swatted at her hand.

"I don't know..." he muttered uncertainly.

Hanun stared at him, eyes gleaming. "With this one performance we could earn enough to buy those sheep you were pining for—we could buy a herd of oxen, too, probably." He stroked his long, braided beard thoughtfully. "What were the names we used in Sheba? Daniel, wasn't it?"

Isaac shook his head. "David."

"*That's* right," Hanun said, nodding to himself with a grin. "I remember now: David... and Goliath!"

✡

Isaac shifted nervously, scratching at his clean-shaven cheeks. Somewhat to his chagrin, with the hair gone from his face, he did pass surprisingly well for a lad of maybe fourteen or fifteen summers. In truth he had seen twenty-six.

Ever since he and Hanun had started the gimmick of the giant challenging all comers and the little man defeating him against the odds—literally, with the betting odds against him—it had mostly been a fast and quick variation.

A day or two in any given village. Sometimes he would just show up, as he had the other night with the quarry workers; sometimes he would arrive with a story, perhaps portraying a man seeking revenge against a giant who had wronged him.

But this variation had called for more diligence, to properly insinuate themselves into their respective communities. For two weeks he had hung around the Israelite camp, doing odd jobs, being seen as a helpful but innocuous figure—almost a mascot. He entertained the weary, homesick soldiers by singing songs. While Hanun and Yamtisy had gone over to the Philistine camp. Already stories were told of the Philistine giant who could best all comers, sending a shudder of fear through the Israelite ranks. Though this giant, Goliath as he was known, hadn't actually killed anyone. Indeed initially most of his bouts of strength had been demonstrated in matches with other Philistines, in semi-friendly bouts to blow off steam while troops sat around between engagements. Isaac suspected the Philistine commanders were reluctant to put him on the front lines in actual battle, where a stray arrow could find him as easily as any other man.

Hanun's—Goliath's—value was more propagandistic than strategic.

Only recently had they started to bring him out against the Israelites. The two sides would arrange one-on-one combats to distract the restless troops while the leaders plotted more significant strategies. These combats inevitably resulted in Hanun victorious and his Israelite foes staggering from the field, or carted off on stretchers. Sending soldiers out only to be defeated by him was demoralizing to the Israelites. But to outright refuse to participate would be humiliating.

Which had eventually led to Isaac standing nervously in a large, musty tent before a sullen-eyed old man with silver hair and a speckled beard. The man lounged upon a high back chair, absently stroking a gray-brown cat that was curled beside him in another, less ornate chair.

"What is this?" the man growled, his words a bit thick from an early morning indulgence in alcohol.

His hawk-faced advisor bowed before him. "King Saul, this is David, a shepherd boy. You've heard him sing once or twice."

That caused one heavy lid to rise slightly as the king looked curiously at the supposed youth. Then he squinted at his advisor and spread his hands as if to say: so?

The advisor coughed. "David... had a dream."

Saul stirred just a little. Dreams he understood. He spent good money on dream interpreters. They had helped to build him a kingdom. He leaned forward, an elbow on his knee. "What dream have you had, uh, David was it?"

"My King" Isaac said, not having to feign the nervousness that constricted his throat and, conveniently, gave his tones a high, more youthful timbre. "While I slept beneath a tall tree, I dreamed an angel of the Lord appeared to me and said that I, littlest and least worthy of your people, would cast a yoke from about our necks."

Saul stared, as though awaiting him to elaborate. Finally he glanced at his advisor. "What yoke?" he muttered.

Isaac realized this might prove trickier than he thought. To be effective, the dream should be vague, yet obvious—allowing King Saul to feel he was divining the meaning himself. "And, uh," he added quickly, "the tree beneath which I slept cracked and fell over, and I saw that its base had been chewed away by termites—the mighty tree toppled by the smallest of God's creatures."

Saul's eyes widened. "Wait—what? A *tree* fell on you?"

"In his dream, sire," the advisor explained patiently.

"Oh," he said, finding that more plausible than this slender youth somehow emerging unscathed from under a fallen tree. Then he glanced questioningly at his advisor, still struggling to understand.

"The tree is, um, no doubt the ill fortunes of your people," the hawk-faced man said haltingly. "And the termites represent, ah, the number of days before—"

Impatiently, Isaac blurted: "I think God wants me to fight Goliath!"

Saul and his advisor turned to stare, mouths agape.

Isaac froze.

Then Saul threw back his head and roared the laugh of a man who had had too little to find amusing in recent weeks. He patted his advisor on the arm gleefully and wiped tears from his eyes. "I needed that. What a delightful boy." He leaned forward, grinning. "And aren't you a brave one to offer," he said, as though Isaac looked five and not fifteen.

Isaac bit his lip, worried he may have blown his one and only opportunity to impress the king.

"Your Majesty," came a hesitant voice from behind him. King Saul frowned, not used to such audacity, and Isaac glanced back to see one of the sentries by the entrance stepping forward with trepidation. The sentry eyed Isaac curiously, then looked back to his king. "Sir—my cousin once told me of an incident some leagues from here where a very small man slew a much larger one, much to the surprise of the onlookers. I know not if this is he—I thought my cousin said it was an adult man, but I may have misheard the tale."

The amusement left Saul's eyes as he regarded Isaac with renewed interest. "Is this true, lad? Have you slain giants before?"

Isaac opened his mouth, then closed it. He had been the one worried their past would catch up with them. But now it seemed like it might actually make his story more plausible. "Uh...yes?" Even to his own ears it came out almost a question.

Saul looked at his advisor, who raised an eyebrow in response. Then, as if anticipating his king's next question, the hawk-faced man addressed the supposed shepherd boy: "A giant as large as this Goliath?"

Again, Isaac had only a second to read the room, to choose the most advantageous response. He needed to gain the king's faith, but he still wanted the odds to favor Goliath if they were to make a profit. "Uh... no, milord. No, not quite as big. But—what kills a cat may also kill a lion," he added sagely.

Saul looked momentarily perturbed by the metaphor, protectively laying a hand on the gray-brown cat obliviously grooming itself beside him.

"Uh, figuratively speaking," Isaac amended. "Nor can I guarantee I will actually kill Goliath. But I swear, by God above, that I will lay him out upon the ground."

✡

After he left the tent, Isaac grew nervous.

Things had gone remarkably well. Hanun had successfully established himself and his reputation among the Philistines. And King Saul was taking the story of Isaac triumphing over an earlier large man, in conjunction with his supposed heaven-inspired dream, as a sign that Isaac—well, David—should be allowed to face the mighty behemoth of the Philistines. And if all had proceeded as they intended, Yamtisy was embedded in the Philistine camp, ready to accept any and all bets from Philistines eager to profit off of what was so obviously a sure thing.

But Isaac was worried nonetheless. He had been concerned about the scale of things, pulling their usual scam before men numbering in the thousands, with tempers and passions high.

What troubled him most was his improvisation of admitting to having previously fought a giant. It was necessary in the moment, helping to win over King Saul. But what if word of it got back to Hanun? There was more interaction between the two camps than was officially acknowledged. Many of the Israelites and Philistines were reluctant conscripts and restless to get home, and there was smuggled contraband, even games of dice, between opposing soldiers when far from the supervision of their commanders.

Isaac had seen neither Hanun nor Yamtisy in the two weeks he had been in the Israelite camp. What if Hanun heard some muddled rumour that Isaac was admitting to a previous fight? Might he think it was like that time near Damascus when they had pretended to be step-brothers fallen out over an inheritance? If Hanun started improvising, telling people he had fought little David before because he assumed that was the way Isaac was now playing it, and that got back to Saul and the Israelites who assumed David had never met Goliath...?

Things could get problematic. It wasn't simply about keeping their stories straight *before* the fight. If, even after the fight, contradictions in what they said started getting reported, it could still go badly. An angry king had a larger reach than a few drunken louts in a village.

Isaac brooded about it most of the remainder of the day, the worry sitting in his stomach like too much unleavened bread. Finally, he knew he would not be able to relax until he had clarified things with Hanun. If they wanted to keep their heads, they would have to make sure they put their heads together.

✡

That night, he sneaked over to the Philistine camp under the vague glow of a crescent moon. He was aware there was some unsanctioned back and forth, trading and prostitutes and the like. But that did not make the journey any less nervewracking as he kept low to the ground, half worried he'd put his hand on a scorpion in the darkness. He had thrown on a woman's abaya cloak, taking advantage of his small size and slight build, and thinking that a woman, if seen sneaking into the Philistine camp, would arouse less suspicion than a man.

He made it across and was somewhat surprised to realize it looked no different than the Israelite camp. Lots of tents, lots of men lounging about campfires, most sullen and half-inebriated after months of seemingly pointless fighting.

He jumped as a figure stumbled up to him, emerging from between two low-slung tents. "Well, well," he slurred, "what have we here, pretty one?"

Isaac frowned, momentarily confused—before remembering his feminine guise. Pitching his voice an octave higher, he spoke softly, so as not to draw undue attention. "I'm looking for the tent of Goliath." He figured naming Goliath would cause the lout to back off, assuming "she" was already spoken for by the fiercest man in the camp—and Isaac did, after all, need directions.

The man blanched a bit in the watery light and stepped back diplomatically. "Of course, ma'am—no offense." He gestured toward a larger tent. "There." Then he looked at Isaac and a wry grin turned his lips. "Though you may be a bit late." Turning unsteadily, he staggered away.

Isaac frowned. Late for what? Shrugging, he turned and hurried toward Hanun's tent. The sooner he had assured himself Hanun knew to stick to the original plan, the sooner he could be on his way back to the Israelite camp and its relative security. Aside from anything else, he was still an Israelite and this was the camp of the enemy.

He hesitated before the tent flap and glanced about, not wanting to be observed. Then he frowned as he realized noises were coming from inside. Grunts, as though Hanun was exerting himself. Was he as nervous as Isaac, and unable to sleep, had he turned to exercise? Then he heard another grunt. Only this one did not sound like it came from Hanun's throat.

Isaac threw back the flap and stepped in. "What the Hell?" he demanded.

Hanun was upon his sleeping mats, naked, his massive form curled about a small, lithe, equally naked figure that it took him a moment to identify.

Hanun glanced over—and his eyes flared. "Isaac!" he exclaimed. Yamtisy grabbed a loose animal skin and pulled it over her nakedness.

"Damn you," snarled Isaac. And this, after he had forgiven the man for his infidelity two years before with that tavern girl outside Aleppo!

"It's—it's not what you think," said Hanun, his very nakedness rather belying that assertion. "We..."

Isaac felt sick. He couldn't bear to hear any more and stormed out into the night. Dimly, he heard Hanun race to the tent entrance and begin calling his name, but stopped himself mid-call, remembering where they were. Isaac kept running.

If he was seen returning to the Israelite camp, he was assumed to be a prostitute and ignored.

✡

Drums thundered beneath the midday sun; like an approaching herd of horses, building to a frightening crescendo—then abruptly, they went silent. A dry wind hissed across the parched earth, providing the only voice heard upon the preternaturally quiet field. A few thousand men stood upon one side, a few thousand stood upon the other, immobile save for the occasional jangle of a sword, or the dull clink of a breastplate. Overhead, the sun broiled almost white, ensconced in an azure sky.

The man known by most as Goliath stood at the forefront of the Philistine army, head and shoulders above those around him. Light flared off his armor as he took one great step forward, then another, till he stood alone between the two rival forces. His sword was sheathed at the hip, his big hand resting on the hilt.

The Israelite forces stirred at last, a low murmuring susurrated between them as they stared with almost superstitious awe at this living avatar of Philistine might. Then there was a shuffling among the forefront of the army, an almost barely perceptible rippling like a pond before a frog breaches.

And then, a small figure disgorged into the field, slender of limb, and dressed only in a humble shepherd's smock. There was an increased murmuring among the Israelites, and wafting across the field, laughter echoed from the Philistine forces.

The one many knew as David stepped forward, at first cautiously, then more boldly, till he too stood away from his comrades.

And soon, "David" faced "Goliath" in the middle of the field.

The armies on either side were too far away to see the odd look in Goliath's eyes, nor if they had would they have understood why there was a softness to them, as if the giant looked at the smaller man beseechingly—as if he wanted to speak to him. David, meanwhile, had a cold, almost expressionless look upon his face, in marked contrast to the guileless innocence he had often demonstrated when wandering the Israelite camp.

A drum sounded. A single, sharp, beat.

And then another.

Stiffly, almost as though play-acting a part he no longer found entertaining, Goliath unsheathed his sword.

David uncoiled his sling.

The drum sounded again.

Even the wind seemed to still.

Goliath hefted his sword uncertainly.

David looked at the giant, then at the sling in his hand, then back at the giant. He raised his arm—and flung the sling upon the dry, packed earth. "To Hell with this!" he shouted, glaring at Goliath. "I'm done!" He turned and stormed back to the Israelite lines, shouldering his way into them, the soldiers staring dumbfounded, making no move to halt him.

Goliath seemed to reach out a hand, almost plaintively, his mouth opening and closing. Then he dropped his chin, his sword slipping from his large fingers. And he too turned back to his camp.

After a moment, the field erupted with cheers on both sides.

✡

Later scribes would recount the Israelite/Philistine conflict in histories and scriptures. When King Saul passed away a few years later, his son David assumed the throne and some imaginative writer, forgotten to history, erroneously presumed it was the same David who had been on the field that day.

While the story of David and Goliath entered the annals of legend. It became one of the most profound and moving of religious parables, cited in the ensuing millennia by pacifists and giving encouragement to the peacemakers. That legendary day when two men faced each other upon a battlefield, between two armies locked in a bitter, bloody conflict fuelled by the egos and greed of their kings and generals. And how each looked across the field into the face of a man they had been told was their enemy, and instead discovered a shared, universal brotherhood. And they gave voice to the frustrations and weariness of the assembled soldiers by simply saying: "I'm done." And then they walked away. Rabbis and priests and imams would cite the parable, arguing that though it takes a brave man to fight, sometimes it takes a braver man to decide *not* to fight.

Thus, the story of David and Goliath became a powerful story of shared humanity and of brotherly love.

Ironically, Isaac and Hanun never spoke to each other again.

Three Stars

Isak Bloom

In Anatevka, I knew a demon.

Let me start at the beginning—

The train carriage rocks. Sunlight glints off the silver *podstakanniks* holding the tea glasses. Cold tea splashes in its transparent prison. I feel sick, but it's not the motion. Yesterday's unfortunate encounters left me twisted up and strung out, like I'm coming off a week on smack. Every time the carriage lurches, my stomach does too, but there's nothing there left to throw up but acid and bile. Every time I stop thinking about how sick I feel, I think about Victor.

I can't be in your life, Lyova.

The whole time he was talking, I couldn't say anything. My throat closed up. I couldn't look at him.

You called fourteen times in two hours. I was at work! I couldn't see the messages you were sending, never mind reply.

While he was busy working and not knowing I was having another paranoid jag, I'd already decided he hated me.

We can't... we can't be together, we can't be friends, we can't be anything. I'm sorry. I just. I can't. I'm sorry.

He didn't sound sorry. In the present, my stomach drops again and I fight not to retch. There's an ache in my chest and a throbbing pain in my head. I grit my teeth and recite the *Shema*, like it'd make a goddamn difference.

Hear, O Yisrael, Hashem is Our God, Hashem is One.

It makes me feel like a putz, for letting myself flip out, for contacting Victor, for walking into that alleyway later. It doesn't help one bit. *Hashem*'s not about to break His millennias-long silence to reach down and intervene in the life of one femmy Soviet *feygeleh*, even if said little birdie asks politely and repeatedly. Not even if said little birdie was almost a rabbi, before the cantor walked in on him and his *chavrusa* engaging in what couldn't be called Talmudic study even by the most convoluted and esoteric standards. Appeals to David and Jonathan hadn't worked and yours truly, Lev Veniaminovich Morgenshtern, had to leave the yeshiva sharpish. So it goes.

Opposite me, Shlomovich is staring at his shleptop, reading some sensationalist pap from the morning edition of *Pravda*. He's listening for the train conductor's footsteps—every time he comes near our compartment, Shlomovich throws up a ward to shroud us and the conductor walks right on by, thinking the compartment empty. Shlomovich thinks it's funny. I don't, but if he were to desist, we'd be back in third class, amidst the noise and on the hard benches. Even when not spell-sick and heartbroken, I'm a little too schizo for that sort of excitement.

In my head, Victor's words replay themselves over and over, like the shmuck providing the soundtrack for my life wants me to *really* appreciate the tune he picked out.

I look at my phone, at Victor's number. My stomach lurches. I tap the number and recite the *Shema* while it's dialing.

The call goes straight to voicemail. I hang up. I call again. It goes to voicemail again. I hang up again and make a noise like a possum in distress.

Shlomovich jerks his head up like someone's tugged his puppet strings and stares at me, his yellow eyes glowing in shadowed eye-sockets.

"*Nu*," he says and then holds a meaningful silence. I look blankly at him, not able to have emotions about something other than Victor. "*Nu*, Lyovka, you taken your meds?"

"Aga, what for?" I reply, irritably. "So I can throw them up again?"

Shlomovich clucks his tongue and shakes his head. I throw up my hands.

"*Nu*, fine," I say. "I'll take the bloody meds if it makes you happy."

"It won't," says Shlomovich, philosophically. "But it'll make you less feral."

"*Nu, vashu mat*,'" I mutter. I've been working closely with the old goat for three months and I still can't bring myself to switch from the formal-you, even when telling him to fuck his mother. I reach for my backpack and fish out the pillbox. I double-check I've got all of today's pills—amisulpride, lamotrigine, duloxetine and good old methylphenidate, my only friend among the chemical devils—and then snap a picture of them with my phone, proof that I did indeed take them. I swallow them dry, choke and have to swig cold, too-sweet tea to get them down. Shlomovich suppresses a chuckle.

"There!" I say, wincing at the pain in my throat. "Happy?"

"I already said, no," says Shlomovich. "But at least you'll be done with crying jags in public, *nu*?"

A knock interrupts us. The compartment door slides open and the conductor peers in.

"Huh," he says, looking at us in puzzlement. "Must've missed you two before. Tickets, Friends?"

✡

As it turns out, Shlomovich doesn't have tickets for third class, either, so to avoid undue excitement and involvement of the ments, he slips the conductor a hundred rubles and then gets our bags and has us disembark at the next stop, a rural little platform in the middle of a birch grove with no phone reception to speak of.

"Beautiful," I say, as the train disappears into the lilac distance. "What a great turn-up for the books, *nu*? Where the fuck are we, Shlomovich?"

"The Union of Soviet Socialist Republics," he says, ponderously. "In a lovely birch grove, on a wonderful summer morning in the year 5777 since the creation of the world. Why?"

"We're *supposed* to be on our way to the Urals," I mutter. "Where you're *supposed* to take up the post of rabbi for some shitty little *shtetl* that's barely big enough to have a *semiletka*."

"They're not expecting us for another few days," says Shlomovich. "We were rather ahead of schedule, setting out yesterday. But you were keen to get away from Piter."

I tell him to go fuck his mother again, which he ignores. He pulls out his phone, stares at it intently and then shrugs.

"Not getting a signal here," he says. I snort. Shlomovich ignores that too. I sit down on the platform and dangle my legs off the edge. No train's due for another four hours. Lurking schizophrenic stupor ambushes me and I zone out. Right on cue, yesterday's conversation plays again in my mind.

You... it's like you don't think I'm a real person outside of what I do for you.

He was the only one I wanted comfort from. The memory of how he looked at me makes me go cold and tearful again.

You just take and take and take and you sink your claws in and you won't let go.

I couldn't stand the thought of him leaving. I can't stand the thought that he's gone. I feel sick. Bile rises in my throat. I taste it, sharp and painful, at the back of my mouth.

"I got a signal," Shlomovich says, suddenly. I snap away from the memory loops. "We're near Anatevka."

"Anatevka?" I say. "*Nu*, where the fuck is Anatevka?"

"About two miles east, down that dirt track," says Shlomovich, gesturing with his phone. "Come on, Lyovushka. Move your skinny ginger ass."

✡

By the time we arrive in Anatevka, I've almost thrown up again at least three times and had to sit down on a tree stump to catch my breath twice. Shlomovich says nothing and carries both our suitcases and shleptop bags and I say nothing, even though I'm very grateful.

Anatevka's got no spires with crosses rising up among the *izbas* and the five-storey concrete blocks of flats. There's a synagogue all prominent and grand, the brass *mogen dovid* on the facade all gleaming in the sunlight. I try to hide my relief, but Shlomovich's grinning like the Cheshire Cat. He takes our *kippot* from his jacket pocket and passes mine to me, along with a hand-ful of hair clips. I fix the *kippah* in place, rearrange my long hair around my shoulders like it's a *tallis* and mutter a reluctant *bracha*. The Soviets eased up on the whole no-priests-no-rabbis thing quite a lot, after Friend Lenin passed, but it's still not great fun to be among the nations. The Russians were never what one would call fans of the people *Yisrael* and never mind that Yiddish's among the forty-eight official languages of the state and the current Secretary's surname is Rabinovich.

Can't blame a yid for feeling better among his own, is all I'm trying to say.

There's a street market all along the main street and Shlomovich stops to buy some fruit. While he's picking through the produce, I lean against the stall and zone out again.

You're like a leech.

It occurs to me that it's a boring comparison. Lampreys are about as clingy and they're far more interesting.

And then—

I feel the demon's aura in my teeth. He burns in the eye-spots on my forehead, makes my Flesh eyes water, but I don't see him. I rock and stumble forward and next thing I know, Shlomovich's got an arm around my waist and the fruit merchant's handing me a bottle of water.

"She okay?" he says and Shlomovich makes that noise he always makes when people look at the hair down to my ass and the eyeliner and the pink cardigan and arrive at "girl" rather than "faggot."

"He's fine," he says. "He's... sensitive. Starborn, *nu*? His mama, she was a *shoggot*."

The fruit merchant eyes my *kippah*.

"He a yid?" he says, skeptically.

"His *other* mama, *her* daddy's surname was Kaplan," says Shlomovich, a little reluctantly. "Does *him* no good, but is a kohen's grandson enough of a yid for you?"

The fruit merchant shrugs. I'd glare, but I've not got the strength. The demon's aura is tugging at my First Sight and my stomach's rebelling.

Shlomovich pays for a net bag of clementines and walks me to a nearby bench. I lie down on it.

"What gives, *nu*?" he says.

"There's a fucking demon by the kosher butcher's," I croak. Shlomovich sits down beside me and starts to peel a clementine.

"Is there," he says, mildly, and pointedly doesn't look. I groan. "*Sheid* or *lilit*?"

"*Sheid*," I mutter. "*Lilin* don't burn like that."

Shlomovich slowly eats his clementine, then starts peeling another. My head thumps with the start of a nasty migraine.

"Fancy that," says Shlomovich, finally. He pulls his phone out and ignores me for a solid five minutes while I lie face down on the rotting wooden bench and wish for the Angel of Death to come and rescue me.

"You're right," Shlomovich says, abruptly. "There's one lurking around. Bound with Solomon's Chain."

I prop myself up on one elbow and peer at Shlomovich.

"How can *you* tell?" I say. "You've only got what Spirit's in your eyes—"

"There's an app," says Shlomovich and seeing my expression, laughs. "There's nothing a starborn can do that technology can't, Lyova. It's the twenty-first century!"

"Bugger *me*," I say. "Shlomovich, can you go chase him off? Before I like, throw up again."

"*Nu*, are you crazy?" says Shlomovich, then realizes what he said and makes a face full of regret. "Never mind. Come on, let's get you out of here."

OTHER COVENANTS

✡

Shlomovich gets us a private room at the local hostel, on the grounds that I look like I'm about to kick the bucket instead of the habit. I lie down and spasmodically think about Victor and then I open my eyes and turns out I fell asleep for three hours and there's sacred geometry drawn on my face with my second-best lipstick. Shlomovich is sitting on the windowsill, vaping. He looks at peace.

"Morning, sunshine," he says, without even looking at me. "How are you feeling?"

"What did you draw on my face?" I say, fishing in my suitcase for makeup wipes.

"Just a little pick-me-up," he says and takes a pull on his vape. "Something to take the edge off your moping."

I wipe the lipstick off my face, practically not wanting to admit that I *am* feeling less raw. The spell-sickness seems to have abated, too. I sit down on the bed again, cautiously probing my feelings to see if maybe I can avoid crying myself to sleep tonight.

Shlomovich hops off the windowsill and tosses me a bottle of pills. I fail to catch it—it bounces off my chest and lands in my lap.

"What's that?" I say.

"Your rescue medication," says Shlomovich. "Take two and pass out, Lyova. I'm... going out."

"Out?" I frown at him. Shlomovich shrugs one bony shoulder.

"I don't like *sheidim* wandering around willy-nilly," he says. "You sleep, though. I need you to get over this right quick."

"Fuck your mother," I mumble, but he's already out the door.

I shake out a single pill from the bottle and swallow it dry. Then I lie back and close my eyes and try to think of nothing as the pill does its thing.

I think of Victor lying next to me on our second date, naked and post-coital. He'd told me he felt safe with me. I can still hear the cadence of his words.

✡

I wake up again around seven, long before the sun sets. Shlomovich is no-where to be found. There's an ache in my heart and a loneliness sitting upon my chest. I pace around the room like I'm a tiger at a shitty pre-Revolution zoo and eventually decide I want a drink. Or five. Five drinks sound like just the thing.

Five drinks and maybe a dick in my ass. Wouldn't that be a way to forget Victor?

I get in the shower before I can chicken out. By the time the specter of common sense catches up with me, I'm clean and ready to take it and head out the door wearing the tartiest outfit I could throw together in five minutes.

I've got my pillbox in my trouser pocket and it's full of benzos. I pop a couple under my tongue as I walk down the street.

It doesn't take me long at all to find a bar marked with a *conspicuous* pink triangle. It's a shitty dive. I feel right at home.

I order the most obnoxiously-named cocktail on the menu and sequester myself in a far corner. My hands are shaking and I don't know if it's the duloxetine or sudden nerves breaking through the benzo haze. My eyespots itch. I close my eyes and try to center myself, remind myself what the hell I'm doing here.

I'm trying to forget. I'm trying to move on. Something sings in my teeth like I'm getting radio transmissions through my fillings.

"Hey you," says a wavering kind of voice. I shudder and snap to. There's a boy standing over my table, looking at me all wide-eyed. He's got hair almost as long as mine, black like spilt ink and wavy like Art Deco flourishes. His hips are cocked at an appealing angle and I can see the ridges of his wings of ilium where his t-shirt doesn't reach the waistband of his jeans.

"You look lonely," he says, plonking himself down on the chair opposite me. "Mind if I join you?"

"No?" I blurt and wish I'd thought of something more interesting to say. "Go ahead—"

He cocks his head to one side and looks at me.

"Mind if I borrow your phone?" he asks. I drop my phone in response and nod. Common sense doesn't intervene. The boy grabs my phone, stares at it in puzzlement.

"What's that?" he says, turning the phone around so I can see he's asking about my lockscreen.

"It's a Virginia possum," I say. "Um. It's from the USA. They live in holes and eat garbage and make awful noises. It's *me*."

"You're both cute, I guess?" he says. "The poor thing looks like it has rabies. Do you have rabies?"

I snort.

"*Nu*, I'm schizo," I tell him. "That's like human rabies. Less foaming, though."

He laughs and I don't feel quite so bad about myself, suddenly.

"They, uh, don't carry rabies, though," I say, in the silence that follows. "Um, it's actually super interesting, *nu*? They're like—they have too low a body temperature and something about their natural aura, it won't let the rabies spirit settle in and the body's too cold to incubate the virus, anyway. So. You don't have to get stuck with needles or get runes drawn on you if one of them bites you. Uh—"

He's looking at me wide-eyed, listening to every word I say. I bite my lip, nervous. He hands me my phone back.

"It's got a passcode," he says. "Unlock it for me, *nu*?"

"What for?" I blurt and he just smiles.

"You'll see," he says, all faux-demure. I unlock my phone and pass it to him. He snaps a selfie, then spends a minute or so tapping the screen and making puzzled faces at the phone. The phone beeps angrily at him when he tries to do something arcane with it and he squeals in alarm. I accidentally laugh aloud and his ears turn red.

"I'm dignified," he pronounces and hands me back my phone. "There."

I look down. The screen's on a contact profile I don't remember making. The picture's of the boy sitting opposite me and the name's Grigoriy. I snort.

"That's a *goyishe* name," I tell him, but I'm smiling as I say it.

"Nah," says Grigoriy, happily. "It means 'watcher', *nu*? Like in the Book of Enoch."

"That's apocryphal," I say. "That means we decided it was stupid and bad so long ago that we didn't even consider it worth studying."

"You mean pseudepigraphal," says Grigoriy. "And that doesn't mean stupid and bad, it means it was weird and probably forged. Anyway, Enoch has some fantastic angelic lore."

"I know," I say. "It's probably all descriptions of starborn. Ezekiel, too."

Grigoriy leans forward, props his chin up on one hand.

"You think angels are just *shoggot*?" he says. There's an odd look in his eyes.

"Probably?" I say. "Like, what we have of *shoggot* culture, what they've actually told us, sounds pretty angelic. And I mean," I sweep aside the hair that's fallen over my forehead and show Grigoriy the three eye-spots that grace my forehead like Tsarevna Lebed's star. "I'm part starborn? One of my mums was a *shoggot*. And I'm all full of eyes. Like the traditional descriptions of the Angel of Death." I don't tell him about the magic sensitivities.

"Okay, yeah," says Grigoriy, but he sounds kind of disappointed. "But what about *starczy*? The Elder Things?"

"Fuck if I know," I tell him, rearranging my hair so it's covering up the evidence of my inhumanity. "They're like, fungus."

Grigoriy laughs, showing his teeth. One front incisor is chipped slightly. He toys with his hair.

"You're pretty," I suddenly blurt and I don't know if it's the drink or the loneliness or if there's a purer, truer emotion behind it. He goes bright red and bites his lip and I can't tear my eyes away.

"You're pretty too," he says. "I like your lipstick."

"Want some on you?" I say, before I can stop myself. He looks startled, but leans forward.

"Maybe," he says.

I lean forward and kiss him quickly. It's just a peck, really. I pull away and he grabs my upper arms. He brings his face close to mine and for a second he looks scared, but before I can reassure him, he's kissing me deep and gentle, his tongue already beyond my teeth. His lips are curiously warm, like fresh bread, and just as soft.

He breaks the kiss and we just look at each other for a few seconds. My blue lipstick's smeared over his mouth, marking newly conquered territory.

"You can say no if you want," he says, carefully, "but what do you say we... go somewhere quieter? I'd like to talk more." He smiles in a way that suggests he's proud of himself for asking and that he's got more than just talking in mind.

"Sure," I say. I don't quite dare believe my luck. "Um, like where?"

Grigoriy looks from side to side, then blushes and looks down, biting his lip again.

"My place?" he mumbles.

✡

Grigoriy's place is a little room in a big *kommunalka*. There's some kind of sad nerd party going on in the sitting room—I can hear Moishe Kozlov's nasally voice singing about methamphetamine addiction and psych wards. I stop to listen, nodding along. The benzos have made me light-headed and the music flows freely through my head.

"I think that's off The Life of *Olam Ha-Ba*," I say. "I love that album."

Grigoriy looks at me with a wry smirk. It makes him look like a trout that's trying to be cunning.

"Of course you like Kozlov," he says.

"What?" I say. "I've got bad taste."

"I didn't say that," says Grigoriy. "It just... figures." Before I can ask for clarification, he takes me by the hand and pulls me into his room.

His room's barely bigger than a closet. Most of it's taken up by a bed and a rickety little desk piled high with take-out boxes, receipts, loose condoms in foil wrappers—the miscellaneous garbage of bachelor living. A shabby shleptop lurks under all that mess.

I perch on the bed, waiting for Grigoriy's next move.

He falls in my lap, already shirtless. There's a pendant on a gold chain around his neck, aged and ancient. I open my mouth to ask him about it and he kisses me. The question slips away into the murky depths of my hindbrain.

Grigoriy runs hot, like he's feverish, but when I ask he says he's okay. He seems perturbed by the question. I make nothing of it, just press myself against him. My eyespots burn and I ignore it.

He plucks at the waistband of my trousers.

"Get these off," he says. "They look like they're cutting off some real important circulation." I'm only too happy to comply. I peel the trousers off and fling them into a distant corner. Grigoriy claps. When I move in to kiss him, he grabs my cock. I gasp and he makes a sound halfway between a laugh and a growl and pulls me on top of him.

His mouth is soft against my mouth.

His cock is hard against my leg.

We break apart and I gasp for breath. I lean against him again and he puts his arm around me. He smells of alcohol and ashes. I watch his bare chest rise and fall, ribcage working like a bellows.

I want to press this moment between the pages of a book. I want to hold it, but it runs between my fingers like water, like sand.

I reach for my phone.

I take a selfie of us, bare shoulders and abashed grins and my lipstick smeared across both our faces. It comes out all grainy and gives Grigoriy red pupils from the flash. I hop off the bed and go around the room, turning on all the lights. Grigoriy watches me, giggling into his cupped hand. It's the most adorable thing I've ever heard.

My efforts make the room uncomfortably bright. The table lamp buzzes like an angry wasp. I get back into bed with Grigoriy and try taking a selfie of us again. It comes out all yellow from the shitty incandescent light bulbs and Grigoriy's still got the demon eyes.

"I can just slap a filter over it," I tell Grigoriy while I look for one that's mostly purple. "Or I could like, live with us looking like we're jaundiced?"

"It could be an aesthetic," says Grigoriy. "Liver failure chic."

"Cirrhosis looks," I rejoin. "We're going to hell, Grisha."

"Hell's for *goyim*," he says and kisses the tip of my nose. "And I hear Gehenna's nice this time of the year."

I tweet the photo unfiltered and go to chuck the phone to one side when it makes that obnoxious noise that means I've got a PM. I consider ignoring it, but my curiosity gets the better of me.

It's from this girl, Mogila. We've been mutuals for about six months, but all I know about her is that she lives somewhere in the Urals, buys her estrogen on the gray market and dresses like it's the 1920s and she's from Chicago.

Her entire message's just the eggplant emoji. I consider a number of different responses, send her a kitty face and put my phone on silent.

I turn to Grigoriy. He's kicking off his trousers.

✡

The holy dove moves with us.
Halfway through, Grigoriy suddenly laughs in my ear.
"What?"
"I forgot," he says, between giggling, "I forgot to ask your name."
"Lev," I tell him. "I'm Lev."

✡

I wake up disoriented and fumble for my phone to check the time.
There's a message from Victor.
I delete it, unread and get back into bed with Grigoriy. I stroke his cheek. He smiles in his sleep. I wonder if Shlomovich would be amiable to taking him along.

Three Stars   235

I kiss Grigoriy's temple. He opens one eye and makes a sleepy noise at me. I pull him into an embrace and he wriggles against me.

"You're not leaving, are you?" he mumbles.

"No," I say.

"Good," he says. "Stay."

✡

I wake up in the morning just as the dawn is creeping in, because my eye-spots are burning again and I can barely breathe. Beside me, Grigoriy sleeps, his lips parted slightly. Around him is the wavy corona of an inhuman aura. My breath gets stuck in my lungs. I try to back away, misjudge the distance to the edge of the bed and fall off, entangled in the duvet.

Grigoriy stirs, awakens and sits up. He flutters his long eyelashes and looks around in puzzlement, looking for me.

"You're a demon," I croak from the floor. He looks over the edge of the bed and laughs, nervously.

"I didn't think you were sensitive..." he says, half-apologetically.

"I'm starborn," I say. "My mum was a *shoggot*. I *told* you—"

Grigoriy laughs. It's shaky.

"I'm sorry?" he says.

"That chain," I mumble, pointing at his necklace. "That's Solomon's Chain. That's the Name on that pendant."

"Er," says Grigoriy. "Yeah." He looks down, chewing on his lower lip. "I mean, I told you my name means 'watcher'—"

"I thought your parents were just weird hippies," I say, propping myself up on one elbow.

"Didn't really *have* parents," says Grigoriy. "The guy who bound me, he's the one that named me—"

While he's talking, I retrieve my trousers and pull out my pillbox. I shove a benzo in my mouth, my back to Grigoriy so he doesn't see what I'm doing. I don't think he's paying attention, anyway. He's staring into the middle distance, his mouth moving around words he can't give voice to.

"He'd kill me if he knew," he says, abruptly and looks at me, wide-eyed. "I shouldn't... I shouldn't have..."

"Who is he?" I say.

"He's... he's a big man in the local community," Grigoriy mutters. "And I'm his enforcer."

"*Unzer Shtick?*"

Grigoriy only nods. I touch his shoulder. It occurs to me that the other shoe always drops.

"I only wanted a body," Grigoriy says, in a small voice. "Being... being what I am... smoke and ash and... and just, this *wanting*. I wanted to feel whole." He looks up at me, his lower lip pinned under his chipped incisor.

I stroke his cheek. He leans against me.

"I keep Shabbos, you know," he says into my hair. He takes a deep, shuddering breath. "I mean. I try. He won't let me go to *shul*. I just wanted... I just wanted to be a *person*. But he can make me do whatever he wants. He... he makes me hurt people."

I look away, not knowing what to say.

When I look back, the chain glints in the light of the rising sun.

I reach for the clasp.

✡

memetic goff: soooooo

memetic goff: how was ur nite? ;)

i want it darker: omg mogila don't ask,,,

i want it darker: i think i broke him

memetic goff: how did u manage that. arent u a bottom.

i want it darker: fffff it's not like that. he's like a *sheid*. i might've... tried breaking his chain.

memetic goff: well fucking done

memetic goff: he alive?

i want it darker: shlomovich's checking?

✡

Grigoriy lays on his bed, out cold. His breathing is shallow. I sit beside him, holding his hand, stroking his fingers.

"I'm surprised *you're* alive," says Shlomovich from the doorway. I don't turn. "Not many men have tried to take off Solomon's Chain and lived to have grandchildren."

He sits down on the bed and looks at me.

"If I ask you *why*," he says, casually, "will I get a sensible answer?"

"*Nu*," I say and think of the *shpiel* I'd prepared between calling Shlomovich and him getting here. "He... he keeps Shabbos. He's circumcised. He's..." I look at Shlomovich. Shlomovich looks at me. His expression is mild, politely interested. I squeeze Grigoriy's hand. "He's cute and—" I falter.

"He took you home from a bar," says Shlomovich. "You two had a good time, if the marks on your neck are anything to go by. And you... you decided to do him a good turn, *nu?*"

"Something like that," I mumble, looking away. Shlomovich shakes his head.

"Lyova—" he begins and then falls silent again. "Oh, Lyovka. What will I do with you?"

"He... he doesn't want to hurt people," I tell the floor. "He sounded... he sounded so *sad*..."

"He's a demon, Lyova," says Shlomovich, kindly.

"He keeps Shabbos," I say.

Shlomovich tuts.

"By all rights," he says, "I should dispel him and send you packing back to Piter."

I say nothing. Shlomovich sighs.

"But I'm a sentimental old baggage," he says. "Always have been."

I look up at him, allowing myself to hope. Maybe the other shoe is going to bounce.

"He should wake up in a few hours," Shlomovich says. "He'll have a hell of a headache, but he'll be fine. And as for the chain..." he looks at me, eyes shining like streetlights. "Well. If he keeps Shabbos... there might be a way."

✡

The hardest thing is not seeing Grigoriy until Shabbos.

He comes to the hostel, just as the sun's on its way down. We sit together on the bed, while Shlomovich keeps watch on the skies, waiting for the first three stars to appear. I get up again, pace the room. There is nothing left to do—the candle, the wine, and the spices stand ready, awaiting the *Havdalah*. I yank on my hair out of sheer nerves. Grigoriy gets up and takes hold of me, pinning my arms to my sides.

"Hush," he says. "Don't—don't fret." He guides me to the bed again. We sit together, my head resting upon his chest.

I doze off.

"There!" yells Shlomovich, startling me awake. "Third star!"

Grigoriy shoves the pendant around his neck into my hand. I clutch it hard, the edges biting into my palm. Shlomovich passes me a faded printout on yellowed paper, a photocopy of a photocopy. Three whole paragraphs, to be recited as Shabbos ends.

Even demons rest on Shabbos.

And in that no-man's time between the end of Shabbos and the last blessing of the *Havdalah*, a binding may be transferred.

If you do it right, a binding may be stolen.

The Aramaic twists my tongue. I choke on the syllables. Beside me, Grigoriy shivers and shakes and I don't know if it's the binding or nerves or something worse.

There is no lightning-strike, no thunder. I blurt the last words. Grigoriy clutches my arm, his nails digging in.

There is a silence, unbearable and infinite.

Shlomovich meets my eye.

"*Baruch ha'mavdil bein kodesh l'chol*," he says, and pours the wine. "Come on, *malchiki*. Let's do the blessings."

✡

memetic goff: so?
i want it darker: we're on a train.
memetic goff: we?
i want it darker: me, grisha, shlomovich.
i want it darker: where do you live again?
i want it darker: shlomovich says we'll have time to visit.

✡

I text Victor a selfie of Grigoriy and me kissing and block his number.

Rise and Walk the Land

David Nurenberg

"A man should carry two stones in his pocket. On one should be inscribed, 'I am but dust and ashes.' On the other, 'For my sake was the world created.' And he should use each stone as he needs it."
—Rabbi Simcha Bunam of Pzhysha (1765-1827)

Chayim had not yet told anyone, but he had come close, so close, to making a change to his daily prayers.

He recited the *Amidah* each morning, as he had since his almost-forgotten boyhood days. He faced the warped wooden wall of his family's small house, and through its tiny window, still looked east, past the shtetl's rusty chicken coops and dusty avenues, in the direction of far-away Jerusalem. With feet together and knees bent, Chayim rocked back and forth, reciting the same Hebrew that had been on the lips of his father and grandfather and all their ancestors since the days of the Temple.

But today his lips fumbled and his voice caught on the final blessing of the *Amidah*—*Baruch Ata Adonai, mehayei ha-metim*. Blessed are You, God, who gives life to the dead.

It was as if his body were staging a quiet kind of rebellion, one Chayim didn't quite know what to do with yet. He thought of his grandfather, a rabbi, who was doubtless turning over in his gra—

Chayim succeeded in forcing *those* words from his thoughts. That much, he was still capable of.

His daily routine gave him little time for further thought. He took off his prayer shawl, gingerly folded it and returned it to his dresser, unwound his phylacteries, donned his skullcap, and put on his work clothes. In the next room he could smell the greasy stew Chava was already making for breakfast, and ate it desultorily as their four children fought over the bread with their dirty hands. He watched his youngest, Motel, cavorting around with a smile, his uncut hair flapping as he ran. Chayim found the strength, somewhere, to return his son's grin. If Chava saw, she offered no reaction.

As Chayim took up his tools, Chava put her hands to her aproned waist and said, "Make sure that Moishe the weaver pays you before you hammer one more nail into his roof, do you hear me? That *gonif* would have you work your hands raw so his children have a dry house, while your family shivers in the cold."

"Enough, woman." Chayim raised a calloused hand. "If your yammering were rubles, I'd be a rich man, and wouldn't need to charge Moishe anything."

"Oh, a big man with me, he is," Chava played to an invisible audience—the children were absorbed in their meals, and were well used to their parents'

OTHER COVENANTS

bickering. "Show that kind of *chutzpah* to Reb Moishe, will you? And to Reb Reuven, too, who still hasn't paid you for that fence yet. Rochele the matchmaker's already been snooping around here asking about our Gitl, and if she finds a young man for her, what then? What are we going to offer him as a dowry, your *shmutzik* old carpenter's vest?"

"Better that than your damned tasteless stew," said Chayim. He paused at the door to grab the large axe that hung there.

Feeling its weight in his hands, knowing what he and all the other Jews of Tautskielvska had had to use such tools for lately, gave him pause.

He softened for a moment, turned back to his wife, and forced himself to see her as the young woman he had married ten years ago, reimagined the long midnight-black hair that had since been hidden under a scarf, the shy smile beneath flashing eyes. He saw that younger woman reflected in his daughters and sons, and spoke a silent prayer to God to please protect them from the *tsuris* (was there any other word for such horrors?) while he was out this day.

"*Nu?*" asked Chava. "What are you standing there like an idiot for? Go!"

Grunting, he nodded and left the house.

2.

The daily routine of a *deker* like Chayim passed quickly. Since the *tsuris* began, it seemed every house needed patching. The bloodstains on some of the doorposts reminded him of the story of the Exodus. These days, though, the Angel of Death needed somewhat stronger persuasion.

Despite everything, Tautskielvska was still bustling. Wolf the Milkman delivered his bottles, Lazar the baker hawked fresh *challah* bread for Friday night. The Lubavitchers engaged in shouting, hand-waving debates with the Verbovers about everything from politics to theology in the middle of the street, indifferent to the curses from the wagon traffic they tied up in all directions. Gimpel, the town *schnorrer*—who had amazingly managed to stay alive during these insane times—still held his tattered hat in front of him (an even more tattered skullcap remained on his head) as he went from townsperson to townsperson, asking, "*Rachmanes,* my fellow Jews, a little *mitzvah* of charity for the needy man? Who knows, but that it might take just one act of righteousness, maybe yours, to end this madness?"

As he sawed planks and hammered nails, Chayim kept a close eye on the axe that lay nearby, but so far today had been a blessed one—he had heard no screams beyond the usual tumult of the busy day. Still, a gaggle of *yentehs* who passed by were spreading rumors that there had been another attack in the neighboring shtetl, and that a dozen people had been killed before the townsmen had dealt with the problem. Chayim had learned to cut anything those gossipmongers said in half. *Still, gevalt, that meant six more people were dead.* And where there was one attack, another would soon follow. Tautskielvska had yet to go a week without at least one incident, usually more, and this week was almost over. He couldn't help feeling that they were due.

On the hill above the whole scene, Chayim could see Rabbi Landsman, draped in a heavy black coat, staring down at them all like some meditative crow. He paced back and forth along the gates of the synagogue as if they were battlements.

Chayim shivered, instinctively making a *phyg* by sticking his thumb up between his first and third fingers, as one would do to ward off the evil eye. Guiltily, he turned back to his work and quickened the pace.

"You do good work, Reb Chayim." Moishe examined his newly-repaired outer wall. "God willing, this will be the last time?"

"God willing, you'll pay me," said Chayim, but not very loudly. Still, Moishe must have heard something, for the man sighed deeply, pulled his coat tight around his chest.

"Oy, but these new taxes," said Moishe. "If anyone could make the *tsuris* even worse, it's the Czar. He's doubled the size of the army now, to fight those … those … things. Not that the army lifts a finger when the Jews get attacked, of course. And yet we're the ones whose taxes have been doubled. I swear, I'm barely making enough from my weaving to keep my own family fed."

Anger moved Chayim to hammer harder, but he kept his back stooped, his knees bent. The words hung there, like tools on his belt, but he could not seem to find the right size or shape to select. He knew Chava would be furious when he came home unpaid yet again. But if he came home, at least, that would be a victory, such was the state of things these days.

Chayim kept a careful eye on the drooping sun, and hurried home in time to meet his family. Chava and the children had packed up the Shabbat meal in near-silence. Chayim held his hands over his children's heads in the weekly blessing.

May God bless you and guard you.
May God make His face shine on you and show favor to you.
May God lift up His face on you and grant you peace.

Chava stared impatiently at him the whole time. She was holding a bag full of every knife the family owned.

"Hurry, hurry!" Gitl urged her younger siblings as each of the children picked up a plank of wood. "Once the sun goes down it's Shabbat," she said in a tiny pedant's tone, "and there's no lifting."

The family poured out into the street to meet all their fellows, the 306 remaining Jews of Tautskielvska as they marched in their silent progression up the hill to the synagogue. All hands were full. The women carried food, blankets, empty chamber pots. The poor men carried axes or makeshift pikes, while the rich carried sabers or even the occasional rifle. The Czar had long ago banned Jews from purchasing firearms, but Jews had always been a resourceful people and had their ways.

Rabbi Landsman stood at the gates and ushered them all in, his arms spread wide. The Rabbi was not a large man, yet Chayim always felt small in his presence. It was the set of Landsman's chin, the blaze in his eyes, the way his long white beard seemed to become one with the evening mist.

Landsman spoke no words, merely inclined his head, communicating silently with the congregation. One by one, each man deposited his weapons behind the pews of the synagogue, neatly arranged and stacked.

Soon the giant gates were closed and locked, the doors barred. As the local carpenter, Chayim, who nailed the bar shut, had the honor of performing the last act of work before the Holy Day of Rest began.

With the echo of the blow still ringing, Rabbi Landsman began the service. Chayim stole a glance at his wife and daughters before they disappeared behind the *mehitzah* that separated the sexes, then took his seat with the men and began to pray. As one, they chanted the psalms in call and response with the rabbi.

Throughout all the years of his life, Landsman had somehow retained a young man's voice. Oh, that voice! Chayim imagined that this must have been the voice Moses had heard speaking to him from the burning bush.

"Lecha dodi likrat kallah, pnei Shabbat nekabelah!" Let us welcome the Sabbath as we would a bride.

The first blow shook the synagogue doors, rattling them on their newly-repaired hinges. Behind the curtain, on the women's side, someone screamed.

Landsman glared sternly at the restless men before him and kept chanting. "Blessed are You, God, who has granted your people Israel this day of rest."

The men forced their eyes back down to the prayer books in their hands, even as the sounds of fists against the walls began to fall like rain.

It was bearable, thought Chayim, so long as the service went on.

"Aleinu le'shabeiach la'adon hakol, lateit gedulah leyotzeir bereshit. She'lo asanu k'goyei ha'aratzot, v'lo samanu k'mish'p'chot ha'adamah!" It is our duty to praise the Master of all, to acclaim the greatness of the One who forms all creation. For God did not make us like the nations of other lands, and did not make us the same as other families of the Earth.

The men rocked back and forth, shouted the words to drown out the moaning and pounding from outside. These were the words Jews had spoken for centuries—familiar despite how alien Hebrew could seem compared to the motherly familiarity of daily Yiddish. Chayim, like all the other men, had spoken them every Shabbat since his thirteenth birthday.

"God did not place us in the same situations as others, and our destiny is not the same as anyone else's. And we bend our knees, and bow down, and give thanks before the Ruler, the Ruler of Rulers, the Holy One, Blessed is God."

The door shook mightily, straining the bars Chayim had nailed across it, but the work of his hands held.

"Adonai is our God, there is none else. Our God is truth, and nothing else compares … therefore we put our hope in You, Adonai our God, to soon see the glory of Your strength, to remove all idols from the Earth, and to completely cut off all false gods; to repair the world."

Once the final psalms were sung, once the voices died down, the pounding and scraping outside seemed deafening. Some of the younger men, as usual, looked longingly at the stacked weapons by the pews, but by now Rabbi Landsman didn't even need to put a restraining arm on them. No work could be done on the Sabbath.

The stewards were starting up a *Beit Midrash* to discuss today's Torah passage, but all Chayim could focus on was Chava. He watched her as she tried to encircle all four children in her arms, shushing them and telling them stories. It would once again be a long, long Shabbat, a whole night and day of listening to the frustrated screeching outside, of watching the planks of the walls shake and rattle and wondering if one would break.

Meals were eaten halfheartedly, and even the gossip was spoken in muted tones. Rabbi Landsman had given up his personal study, the only other room in the synagogue, to house the chamber pots, which by sunrise were already filled and stinking. They could not be emptied, though, until the sunset came again. Until then, it remained Shabbat, and no Jew could do any work—that was the Law of Moses, handed down for millennia. Even when a thunderous bang announced the forced entry of a bloody hand, half rotted to the bone, sticking through the wall, the rabbi merely ushered the congregation back, out of its mad grasping range. The rest of the wall held, and so long as it did (and it would—Chayim had done quality work), the Jews were commanded to rest.

Chayim laughed bitterly to himself at the thought of that.

The morning Torah service proceeded, and Chayim made only a token effort at listening to this week's recitation. He counted the minutes, as he knew every other man among them was doing too, until sunset brought *havdalah*, when the rabbi passed around the spice box, lit the candle and dunked it in wine, announcing the end of the Sabbath and a return to the work week.

"Amen," said Rabbi Landsman. Then he gave a heavy nod.

As one, the men leapt to the back of the room and seized their weapons. The women and children were ushered to the Torah Ark. With the most precious things in their community thus all secured in one place, the men of Tautskielvska spread out. A few of the youngest, boldest ones took point. They tore off the nails on the restraining boards.

At once, the doors burst open, and the dead charged in.

That they looked like men and women no longer bothered Chayim, not after seeing what they could do—had done—to his townsmen. They were *golems*, human-shaped things that wore flesh (although barely) but had no soul. Blood poured from their mouths, like animals freshly slaughtered by the *shoichet*, and their teeth gnashed wildly, seeking the flesh of the living.

The living did not give in so easily. The men howled curses as they swung their weapons. Axes severed limbs and heads, pikes speared through suppurating flesh, guns reported with smoky bangs.

Daniel the candle-maker, wrestling with one of the monsters, paused in his struggles as the light of recognition dawned in his eyes.

"Esther?" he said softly, staring into the wild-eyed face of a thing that only looked like a young woman.

It was the last word he would utter, as the she-beast drove her jaws into his neck, tearing out gobbets of his flesh. Chayim charged over, shattering her head with a club, but it was too late. No doctor could save Daniel now, even if the Czar had allowed Jews to leave the shtetl to seek one out.

The melee lasted nearly half an hour. By the end, the synagogue floor was littered with limbs and corpses. Along with Daniel, two other men, one barely old enough to be a bar mitzvah, had died. But the women and children were safe, and Rabbi Landsman held the Torah scrolls high above the river of blood that now ran between the pews.

The rabbi's face contorted as he surveyed the scene, this perversion of the sanctity of the synagogue. His black eyes shone as if they were lit coals. Almost hidden beneath the mass of hair in his beard, his mouth trembled.

The rabbi opened his lips wide. "*Am Yisrael Chai!*" he shouted. Life to the people of Israel!

The congregation wearily returned the chant. There was little celebratory fever in Chayim, only a sense of release and exhaustion. *Now* was when they needed *Shabbat*, a day of rest. But this sunset marked a new day, and there was work to be done—more today than usual.

The rabbi handed the Torah to an attendant, then motioned for a shovel. It was all the signal the congregation needed.

The bodies needed burying, and before that, sorting. Every severed arm or leg, from the freshly slain and from the rotting golems, needed to be located, organized, matched up. They had all of them, victim and monster alike, once been human beings, and Jewish law demanded the intact burial of human beings, had set it, in fact, as the highest priority of the day.

It was terrible work. Chayim kept from vomiting, but others were not so hardy. He took no pleasure in watching Moishe tremble and shake as he hauled a detached pair of legs. What did money owed matter at a time like this?

Terrible work indeed, but they did it. Such was the lot of a Jew. The *mitzvot,* the commandments, were not options, as the rabbi was always so quick to remind.

Chayim had grown very accustomed to making coffins these days, had learned how to make stronger wooden dowels and fasteners since, again according to Jewish Law, nails were forbidden. Now more than ever before, coffins needed to stay closed.

It was nearly dawn when, aching from fatigue, Chayim returned to his family and began his morning prayers. Once again, the words, "Blessed are You, God, who gives life to the dead," came only with supreme difficulty. He wondered if, in the secrecy of their own homes, anyone was actually omitting it.

3.

The officer of the Czar's police was trying to look proud and haughty atop his horse, but his green coat was stained filthy with dirt and blood, his medals and epaulets dull and hanging off-kilter. Still, he held his saber high and spoke in imperious tones to the assembled Jews, in Russian, not Yiddish.

"Listen up, you filthy Christ-killers! By order of his Majesty the Czar, all subjects of the Empire are hereby required to unearth every gravesite within your town and set fire to the bodies there interred."

A storm of murmurs ran through the crowd. A few of the young men surged forward, but thought better of it when the policeman's other hand fell to the pistol at his side.

"Although you Jews may be too stupid to understand, the greatest minds of the universities in Moscow have determined that these creatures who are plaguing the Motherland will keep reviving unless their bodies are fully consumed and made ash. You have one day in which to accomplish this task, or the army will do it for you—and we won't stop with the graveyards, either."

With that he snickered, kicked his horse savagely, and rode off out of the shtetl, beyond the Pale where Jews could not venture.

Immediately after he faded from sight, the Jews of Tautskielvska began to shout.

"The army," said Ezra the fish peddler. "A fart on the Czar's army! Maybe if they stopped hassling us and fought the *golems* more, we'd be safer."

"A plague on the Czar," said Shprintze the butcher's wife. "May the golems eat his balls."

"I wouldn't wish such indigestion even on the golems," said her sister, Chana, the spinster.

"This isn't a joking matter!" cried Yankel, the richest man in town. He was still wearing his Shabbat finest, despite the fresh bloodstains, because he felt it made him look more important.

"This isn't a joking matter at all. Already, I hear that the gentiles throughout the land are blaming the Jews for this plague of monsters. If it isn't the army, it'll be the peasants."

"They blame the Jews for everything," said his younger brother, Faivel, who couldn't let himself be upstaged. "For bad weather, for when they're too drunk to *shtup* their wives."

"So we'd best not give them another excuse," said Yankel. "We have to comply. We will go to the graveyards, and we will take torches, and we will—"

"We will do nothing of the sort."

All eyes turned. The voice came from Rabbi Landsman. The crowd parted to admit him as he walked slowly up to Yankel. Even though Yankel was standing on a box, as Yankel tended to do an awful lot, the rabbi somehow seemed to overshadow the rich man.

"You know God's law. From dust we came, and to dust we return. We do

OTHER COVENANTS

not burn the dead."

"Yes, yes of course," said Yankel, "but Rabbi, surely present circumstances—"

"Are irrelevant," said Landsman. "There is no clause in the Torah or Jewish law that says we are exempt from burial duties should the dead rise again."

"But the Czar—"

"Our allegiance is to the Almighty, not the Czar. That is all."

"But—"

"That. Is. All."

A heavy silence reigned, and Yankel, after some useless blubbering, descended from atop the box and melted back into the crowd. Whispers rippled throughout the crowd, but none dared raise a voice against the rabbi.

Chayim's eyes found Chava and his children, saw their pale faces. As much as Chava's barbs annoyed him, it hurt him like a knife to see her so fragile right now, clutching at her hair with one hand, and at his son Motel with the other. He wondered how many more nights like the last one his family could endure.

The rabbi was turning to go back to the synagogue. Chayim felt his heart pounding like a hammer in his chest. But he had faced the living dead last night, and if he could show bravery before them, could he not, this once, speak his mind, demand what was his?

"Rabbi," he said, his voice half a cough.

Nevertheless, Landsman turned.

"Rabbi," Chayim began again. "Rabbi, please. If it could save our town … whether from the golems themselves, or just from the Czar … can't we make an exception?"

Landsman stared at him, eyes narrowing. Was it shock? Disbelief? Anger? Chayim had never been as good at measuring men's emotions as he was at measuring the dimensions of a house.

"We honor and respect the dead in this town," said the rabbi. "A body is not a shell. It is a part of who we are. What more proof do you need, than the fact that God, for whatever mysterious purposes, has brought these golems into our midst? We must follow the Laws."

"But *we* are not golems," said Chayim. "God gave us minds, and wills. We can choose."

The crowd had split in two like the Red Sea of old, creating an avenue in the center in which only Landsman and Chayim stood. The carpenter felt a cold sweat break out on his forehead as Landsman drew nearer.

"You are wrong," said the Rabbi. "Your thinking is upside-down! What separates us from those monsters is that we have our Laws. We have our self-control. If we burn our brothers and sisters, why not cast all our laws aside? Why not eat pork?"

Chayim found his hands becoming fists as he remembered the screams of the women, the death rattle of Daniel the candle maker.

"What does it matter if we eat pork, in a time like this?" Chayim cried.

Landsman trembled as he shot his finger out, his voice like thunder. "Now is precisely the time when it matters! What kind of Jews would we be if we only followed the Law in times of ease?"

Every man and woman shifted uncomfortably. None, not even the eldest, could recall a time when the rabbi had spoken to one of them like this. Indeed, even Landsman seemed somewhat surprised, and managed to rein in his tone.

"You are a fine carpenter, Reb Chayim, but do not be so arrogant as to think you can rebuild God's plan for us. The Czar will do as he will, but we will burn no bodies. Now go back to your duties. Are there not fences and doors to be mended?"

The rabbi turned and withdrew. In his wake, the crowd began to break up into its component parts. The excitement was over. There was bread to be baked, milk to be delivered, money to be loaned and loans to be collected. Chayim soon found himself standing very much alone.

4.

"So just like that, you let him go?"

"Let him go?" Chayim rubbed his temples. "Damn you, woman, your nagging alone should be enough to send all the golems fleeing back to Hell."

The carpenter fell, exhausted, onto the tattered chair in the corner of their kitchen. His wife and daughters were cleaning the dishes from supper and hanging the washing out to dry. Motel was playing with a small wooden horse Chayim had built for him, making it gallop up and down his arms and legs.

"This is just like you," Chava said, wringing out a dishrag as if strangling it. "You brood and even explode, but in the end, never claim your due."

"My due? Chava, this was the rabbi."

"So? He's not God."

"He's suffered more than any of us. Even in these times."

Chayim didn't need to say another word. There was not a Jew in the entire Pale of Settlement who had not heard the story, how the drunken soldiers had stormed Landsman's wedding so many years ago, what they did to his new bride right before his eyes and the eyes of the whole synagogue. How she took her life in shame a week later.

"Maybe he has," Chava said. "But that doesn't make him flawless."

"What do you want from me? That I should go take a torch to the grave-yard myself?"

"You heard Reb Yankel. Better you do it than the gentiles. They won't stop with the corpses."

"If Reb Yankel cares so much, then let him do it. Or hire men to. God knows he has enough money."

"It's not about money," said Chava, "it's about courage. And not even so much of that."

"Easy for you to say. What does a woman know of courage?"

Chava threw back her head and laughed. "Give birth four times, *schmendrick*, and then talk to me of courage."

"Besides," she said, drawing closer, "women speak to one another. Half the wives I talked to tonight say their husbands agreed with what you said. They think Landsman's in the wrong."

"Oho? Then why didn't they say it out loud?"

"Because men are like geese! They sit there quacking until a brave one finally goes out into the pond."

"Goes out, and gets eaten by a wolf."

"Rabbi Landsman is not a wolf."

"He doesn't need to be a wolf. He only needs to be right! And what if he *is* right? He's the rabbi. Who am I to disobey the laws set down by Moses?"

"Oh, you men and your laws! Can you eat your laws? No? That's why you need women, to cook. Can you live in your laws? No, that's why you need Chayim the carpenter, to build you a house. And just maybe you need Chayim the carpenter to take the first step and save us all."

"My grandfather was a rabbi—"

"Your grandfather is dead! God grant that we not come face to face with him tonight, but if we do, I would hope you'll stick a shovel in his head before he harmed a hair on Gitl's!"

Chayim staggered as if he had received a blow. Chava turned her eyes downward, perhaps realizing she had crossed some line.

It was too late. Chayim shook with rage-born palsy. He raised his hand as if to strike her, then pushed past his wife into the chilly night air.

He breathed heavily, watching his breath cloud out before him in the dim light of the setting sun. It was time for his evening prayers.

Lord, he stared up into the blood red sky, *what am I to do?*

God, as always, did not speak back to him. If He did, though, Chayim used to imagine His voice would sound like Rabbi Landsman's. But tonight, Chayim wondered if God would sound like his grandfather. When Chayim had been not much older than Motel was now, his grandfather first told him the story of when Abraham, father of them all, was asked to sacrifice his son Isaac up on the mountain. Abraham did not question.

His grandfather's voice echoed in his head, and this time it told him another story. When God told Abraham His plans to destroy Sodom and Gomorrah, Abraham had questioned. He had bargained for the lives of the people there if he could find but ten righteous men.

Chava peeked out from the doorway. Chayim turned and regarded his wife with tired eyes. "I see. You want me to be Abraham."

"No," she said with unexpected gentleness. She stepped out into the evening, stood up on her tiptoes, and kissed him on the forehead. "I want you to be Chayim. That's all I've ever wanted."

That night, Chayim found himself stumbling once again as he concluded his prayers. This time, he left out that final sentence. He would no longer praise God for resurrecting the dead. He had decided that, perhaps, God had different plans for them ... and possibly for Chayim, too.

5.

Chayim was halfway to the graveyard, torch in one hand and axe in the other, when the golems set upon him. There were half a dozen of them, racing towards him from all sides in that shuffling run of theirs. Their legs bent all the wrong way, as if they were beams trying to support too heavy a roof.

With a swing of the axe, Chayim felled one, then slammed the butt of the torch into the stomach of another. The pole sunk in with a sickening slurp and remained wedged.

Chayim let go of it and charged forward, knocking into the mass of them. He was not a small man, and the force of his charge hurled them to the ground. As he tried to rise, their limbs seized him, their skin as cold as a Russian winter.

From his belt he pulled his hammer, and began pounding with all his strength, shattering wrists, fingers, knuckles. Screaming in rage, he brought down the heavy metal weight on foreheads, jaws, clavicles. Blood spattered his face until he could see nothing else.

At last he arose, the golems twitching at his feet. The hammer in his hand was bent out of shape, half dislodged from the wooden base. He stared at it sadly. Samson had used the jawbone of an ass to save the Jews from the Philistines. This hammer, sadly, was not so epic a weapon. Sighing at the thought of the impossible cost of buying another, he let it drop to the ground, pulled the torch free of its fleshy prison. The fire had gone out, but he re-lit it and marched onward.

The cemetery lay just downhill from the synagogue. Where gentiles would line their graves with ostentatious crosses and headstones, Jews arranged simple slabs in rows, adorned only by small stones left as tokens by passersby. Chayim knew the graveyard well. Tevye the undertaker had been one of the first victims of the golems' fury, and as a result, his role had been distributed to all of the men in town.

Just this evening, Chayim had been present here when Rabbi Landsman said *kaddish* over the fallen dead from last night's battle at the synagogue. For a moment, in the moonlight, he thought he was back at the service, for there the rabbi stood at the graveyard gates, along with the four stewards.

"Good evening, Reb Chayim," said Landsman. His voice was dry and devoid of good will.

"Good evening, Rabbi," said Chayim. He realized he must have been a ghastly sight, all covered in blood and innards. The torch sat incriminatingly in his grip. There was no point in making excuses.

Neither was there a point in the rabbi stating the obvious. It was one thing to prevail against mindless, ambulatory corpses. It was another entirely to fight past five healthy, living, thinking men, even if taking up arms against a rabbi wasn't practically unthinkable.

The spirit that had so recently filled Chayim began to seep out his nostrils, steaming up the cold night air, deflating him.

Damn Chava, Chayim thought, *this is all her fault. She bewitched me into thinking I was doing God's work. Ha! What a waste of energy. And I will still have to get up in the morning and go to work, this time without my hammer.*

"Is there something you wish to say, Chayim?"

Chayim had nothing left now. Only the truth. "I fear for my children, Rabbi."

"As do I," said Landsman.

"I don't want them to die."

"I don't want their spirits to die. Life is not life without our principles."

Landsman indicated the sleeping town with his hand. "How do you think we have survived, when in every age the powerful have sought our death? Pharaoh? Haman? Antiochus? They all said to us, change your ways, or perish, and we held to our ways, and that is why we survived.

"Look around you, Reb Chayim. Look at the squalor that is Tautskielvska. Look at how we are taxed, how we are abused by the Czar. He can take from us anything he wants. Anything!"

The rabbi's voice quavered slightly as he bent forward, his voice no less powerful for its whispered volume.

Chayim nodded, remembering just what the *goyim* had taken from the rabbi. He tried, and failed, to keep the images from his mind, of what it would have been like if it had been Chava. Or, God forbid, Gitl.

"I am sorry for what they took from you," said Chayim. "On a day that should have been so joyful, no less. God dealt you a cruel hand back then."

"No!" said Landsman. "God did nothing but demand what He always demands of us."

The rabbi drew even closer. Chayim could smell the oaky scent of tea on his breath. "Do you want to ask me, perhaps? If the rumors they whisper about it are true? Well, it is true, I did not bury her. That is what the Law instructs us, when a Jew takes her own life. I did not tear my clothes, or doff my shoes. Year after year passes, and I do not light a candle for her *yartzheit*. Do you think I do not want to, Reb Chayim? Do you not think I do not deem my beloved Shevaleh worthy of more than a single recitation of the *kaddish* the day of her death?"

The rabbi's eyes wrinkled as he spoke, going through all the motions of weeping without releasing any tears.

"How could I do otherwise? How could I, when the local governor—may his name be obliterated!—came to pursue what he called justice? How he made his apology? He shoved a bag full of greasy kopeks into my hands, and made a lewd joke!"

Landsman took a moment to recover his composure. Then he pulled back, rejoined the stewards who had until now been keeping a respectful distance, trying to look everywhere but at the two other men.

"They can have anything," said the rabbi, "*anything*, from us. Except our dignity. Except our way of life. They can kill us, but they cannot take who we are away from us, not unless we serve it up to them on a silver platter. Would you have us do that, now? What if we did? How would *our* lives become anything more than a living death?"

Chayim opened his mouth helplessly. He was no Rambam or Hillel, no scholar of the Torah. He was not his grandfather.

"I am just a simple carpenter," said Chayim. "I do not know what makes a good man. I only know what makes a good house. A good house needs a foundation, and walls, and supporting beams and pillars."

"Our laws are those pillars," said Landsman, bringing his hands together as if to draw closure to the lesson. "Remove them, and our house falls."

Now Chayim felt the anger well up within him once more. The rabbi might know the Torah inside, outside, and upside down. The rabbi might know suffering even beyond the lot of most Jews. But Chayim knew carpentry.

"No," he said. "Remove *all* of the pillars, and the house falls. But remove just one, and it will remain."

Before Landsman could reply, words spilled out of Chayim's mouth. "I have heard that in the cities, Rabbi, there are Jews that do not wear hats or even skullcaps. Are they men whose lives have no worth? What if some day there are Jews who speak no Hebrew, who eat of pork, who dwell with gentiles? Will they be no more than living corpses? Will they not be worthy of life?

"We will have no way of even knowing the answer to those questions, Rabbi, if you do not let me burn these bodies. Either the gentiles will kill us, or the golems will, and either way, it is certain that the only future Jews will be dead Jews."

Landsman closed his eyes, gave a sad and heavy sigh. He motioned to the stewards, who began to advance on Chayim. The carpenter stood his ground, awaiting the inevitable.

"Stay right there," came a voice from behind them. It was Moishe, the shawl-weaver. In his hand he carried a lit torch.

Behind him stood Yankel the rich man and Faivel his brother, and behind them Ezra the fish-peddler, also with firebrands. Behind them stood Sarah the widow of Daniel the candle-maker, hand in hand with Chava, the wife of Chayim. Still more followed in their wake—dozens more men and women, shovels at the ready.

The stewards looked helplessly from the crowd to the rabbi, but Landsman had already turned his back on the scene. He clasped his hands to his chest and began praying quietly, refusing to watch as the mob began to dig and set fire to what lay inside.

He felt the heat at his back, heard the shouts and screams as some of the graves opened wide to reveal angry golems eager to strike. There was a great clattering of metal and rending of flesh, and the occasional gunshot. Soon the roar of the flames drowned it all out, all except the thoughts of God in his mind.

When the sounds of battle finally faded to the sounds of ragged cheers, Rabbi Landsman turned around. He saw the sooty faces of the Jews of Tautskielvska, their clothes torn and bloodied, framed by a wall of fire that smelled more ghastly than anything he had ever breathed in his life. Woe to the Jews, he thought, that they had lived to see such a day, when they would choke on the odor of hundreds of their fellows' bodies ablaze.

Chayim held his own shirt to his nose as he used his other hand to draw Chava close to him. She covered her face to hide her tears.

But Chayim could not close his eyes, could not wrench his gaze from the rabbi's mournful, stricken face. There was no pride in Chayim's heart, no sense of triumph.

It was like this, weary, sickened, and battle-shocked, that the Jews of Tautskielvska marched slowly forth to meet the oncoming storm of hoofbeats. Two dozen riders in uniform assembled at the edge of the shtetl, struggling to control their mounts as the horses reared at the sight and smell of the fires. Behind them marched a mob of gentile peasants, hoes and pitchforks at the ready.

Since by now everyone seemed to expect it, Chayim detached himself from the crowd and stepped forward to meet the small army.

"We've done as you asked," he said bitterly. "Our graves are alight. You need fear no monsters from Tautskielvska."

"Really?" asked one of the gentiles. The darkness and the shadows cast by the flames made it impossible to make out any individual faces. "It looks to me like there are still monsters aplenty here."

"You Jews brought this curse upon us," said another voice. "You're in league with these demons."

"That's ridiculous!" Chayim began. "Don't you have any idea what we've been through—"

"Our village was ravaged," a gruff Russian voice cried out.

"My wife was eaten alive!"

"My children were trampled!"

"All your fault!"

"Dirty Christ-killers!"

The accusations flew all at once, and Chayim clutched at the axe in his hand, now blunted beyond any good use. His words began to fail him, as they always had before.

"Enough!"

Only one voice could have possibly out-shouted that mob. Everyone, Jew and gentile alike, turned to face Rabbi Landsman, who stood alone, framed by the fires.

"You are right," he said. "I accept responsibility for this awful plague. It was the work of Jews, yes, but only one Jew. Only a Jew with the knowledge of magic that a rabbi possesses could have summoned such creatures."

"What?" Moishe gasped.

"The rabbi's gone insane!" said Yankel.

"You have to stop him!" Chava tugged at Chayim's sleeve. "You can't let him do this."

But Chayim shook her off. He may have been a simple man, but he knew exactly what the rabbi was doing.

"I summoned the monsters myself," said Landsman, "with a special mystical prayer, and now I turn myself in to face the Czar's justice."

With that, he held his open palms high in the air and marched into the waiting mob. They reached for him, a thousand clawing hands like those of the golems, but the mounted soldiers beat them back with batons. They took the rabbi into their circle, clasped him in irons.

"You, Jews," said the lead soldier as he turned his horse to go. "As punishment for your rabbi's crimes, Tautskielvska's homes must be empty by week's end."

"But ... but where will we go?" asked Gimpel the *schnorrer*.

"To Hell, for all I care," said the soldier. Then he turned to the mob behind him. "Come on now, you lot," he said. "Get a move on. We have our man. I don't want to stay around in this stench any longer."

He fired his rifle into the air twice, and the gentiles slowly began to withdraw.

Chayim craned his neck, jumped, and tried to see Landsman's form in the receding mob, but there was no sign of him.

The Jews of Tautskielvska were left standing, aimless.

Yankel the once-rich man raised his hands helplessly. *"Vey iz mir,* that we were born, to see such times."

"A week," cried Ezra the once-fish-peddler. "How can we possibly pack up our lives in a week?"

"We'll have less than that," said Chayim. His voice had returned to strength at last, and he knew now that, as a blessing or a curse, it would remain that way for the rest of his days. "The gentiles will learn the rabbi was lying soon enough. The golems will keep coming, after all, for as long as God wills it. When the peasants realize this, they will return, and no words or gunshots will rout them. We will need to be gone from this place, every man woman and child, by tomorrow night."

Groans and sighs from all around.

"Do it!" Chayim bellowed. "We have no other choice. We do not have the luxury of self-pity."

"Our poor Rabbi Landsman," said Moishe the once-shawlmaker. "How I pity him now, more than ever."

"How I envy him," said Chayim. "I envy him, because Rabbi Landsman is going straight to Heaven. As for us, who but God can tell?"

Miryam the Prophetess

James Goldberg

At age six, Miryam is in charge
of the baby
every time
the overseers come.

Behind the hut three families of Levites share
there's a ditch she and Aaron used to dare each other
to jump over—before the order that brought
her jumping days to a close. Now she lowers
herself down between its muddy sides and tries
to keep the little one still, and still, until
they can rise.

Once, two overseers
passed right over—
she held the baby's warm body close,
let him suck helplessly against her arm
to keep him from crying,
while she shared her silent terror
with her people's half-forgotten
God.

Once, the baby did cry.
And Miryam, trembling, heard her mother
in the distance beg the Egyptians
to let her husband leave his work
and go hunt the birds she heard calling
from the marshes by the riverside.
Though they believed her,
she couldn't stop shaking that night.

After three months, Miryam's mother
says she's had enough. Miryam watches
as she makes a little ship
for the child she'd never named,
and sends him out on the Nile.
It's a loss as, maybe, she'd always
expected. But one Miryam can't accept.

So Miryam follows the river's course,
peeks out between the reeds to watch
when the ark floats close to some
of the royal house's serving women.
"Look," one of them says, when she sees
the child inside. "This must be one of the Hebrews' children."
But Pharaoh's daughter has no compassion:
Miryam watches
and watches
and watches
while they hold the baby underwater
till it drowns.

It feels like a lifetime later
when she sweeps into Pharaoh's court
and calls down plagues on his house
and all his people.
And each time he tells her to stop,
she has no compassion.
Ten. Twenty.
A hundred, then a thousand plagues—
until the bleeding Nile turns the ocean red
and even the pyramids are beaten down
to dust.

These Rebellious Hussies

Rivqa Rafael

Worse'n solitary, the mindless work, the awful food of this prison in all but name, there's the Shabbat services. We's herded into the factory chapel, most unwilling of flocks, the matron begging us—aye, begging—to keep quiet. Not a chance, Mrs. Hutchinson.

She's always gabbing about how the chapel was inspired by the Great Synagogue of London. Not as though a Limerick wench like me would know, but I'd wager the pews *there* don't give your arse splinters. But no, she means the arched doorways and windows. Who fecking cares? The pews is set in a U-shape like every synagogue I've ever been dragged into. The ark's empty but for a few dusty prayerbooks; Torah scrolls ain't for the likes of us convict women. Not that I blames them, dunno what I'd do with a fancy scroll, given the chance.

Rabbi Daniel drones on and on from the central podium, like always. De-corrrrr-um. Charm is false and beauty is vain, fear Yahweh and be thankful for Yeshua, who died for our sins, but somehow we're still all sinners, and blah blah blah. Modesty. That's our cue—me and me girls stomp our feet, tattooing a drumroll onto the wooden floor. Criminals we might be, all but sold into slavery, but we can still have our fun—we just has to make it.

He tries again. Sniggering, we stomp again. He tries once more before he pushes on but there's that word again like clockwork, they never shut up about it, and this time we lift our pew—they wasn't nailed down, cheap fools—and *slam* it down. Over my shoulder I see Mr. Hutchinson's starting towards us, his face scrunched up all angry. This ain't the first time I've embarrassed our poor wee Factory superintendent and it sure won't be the last.

"Oi, ya want us modest, how's about some underclothes?" I yell, time almost up, and jump onto the pew, facing Mr. Hutchinson. So caught up in proving we're not given any, I is, I forget to check on me girls. They've piked, the scabs, and I'm on me own, baring my arse to Rabbi Daniel. Feck. Mr. Hutchinson is striding over with a guard and I look over my shoulder to see the Rabbi's expression while I still can.

But I never catch it. Because that's the first time I see you. You's surrounded by your own girls in a back pew, head tilted, eyebrows arched over dark gray eyes, and you's all I can think of when they drag me through the Factory yard to the solitary cells. The memory of those eyes warms my body, enough to keep the cold of the cell from creeping in. Worth it, every second.

✡

You curtsy to me when we finally come face to face in the Crime Class yard, a fresh 'C' stitched to my dress and petticoat—not for the first time, mark my words. "If it ain't the Irish mischief maker," you say. "Been hearing about you, Ellen Scott." I thrill to learn that you know my name. Suddenly I feel important. Notorious.

"You're not so bad yourself, Cath Owens, so's I hear," I push the words out smooth even though my heart's rattling in my chest. Casual like, as though your reputation for meanness and drunkenness ain't double mine of disobedience and idleness.

"Oh I'm bad." You grin and puff a ring of smoke in my direction. "You should stay away if you want out of here."

I wave a hand. "All the fun's in here. Out there it's just pompous twats what want you to slave for 'em."

Those gray eyes turn sharp, looking me over. To my surprise, you run a calloused hand over your amulets. Star, cross and hamsa; they're all finer than we convicts should be able to own. I'm as well versed as you are in the ways of obtaining such things, it's the contemplation that throws me. I like a sparkle much as the next wench but they don't guide me, well, not like *that*, anyway.

"Yeshua telling you what to do?" I can't resist the snipe. And anyway, I ain't scared of you. Or so I tells myself.

"His mum, more like." You snort at my blank expression. "What's this? I gots to tell an Irish girl about Asherah, the holy Shekhinah, queen of the universe, mother of us all? Thought your people understood *her*. The world really is upside-down here."

"Ben Diemen's Land, asshole of the Earth, land of opportunity."

Instead of the laugh I'm expecting, you click your tongue at me. "Asherah's power is strong here, don't you forget it. Look at all these women, together in one place. The good ones, doing their washing, the bad ones, playing their pranks, don't matter. There's more of us in here." Your eyes shine and for the first time I am a wee bit scared, wondering what I'm getting myself into, but there's this pull that makes me take a step forward and swallow the dryness in my mouth.

"Show me." It's the filthiest thing I've ever said, leaving behind any encouragement I've whispered to a lover in the dead of night, in alleys and ship bellies and hammocks here in the factory.

And you hear it in my voice and smile and that's it, I'm in, yours, lost.

✡

I'm in Crime Class for two months after that one and we make the most of it. That's two months of being stuck here with no chance of being sent out as a servant for a settler, and not even a chance of getting close enough to the gate to bribe our way out of an evening. The walls is thickest and highest around Crime Class, o'course. But we've both buttons aplenty to trade for grog and tobacco, and we're neither of us too shy to offer a wench a good time in exchange for something she's brought from outside.

Somehow, every prank is more fun together. We sing the rudest songs we know with the girls, get up a theater, all those things we've done since the sea voyage over, but I'd never have thought to taunt the Hutchinsons with it if we hadn't been plotting, like we do. We get the other girls up at midnight, the whole Crime Class, and settle in to sing raucously. We can be loud as thunder when we puts in the effort. It only takes a few minutes for the Hutchinsons' cottage to light up. Grinning, I imagine their grumpy faces as they lights their lamps. Their door slams.

I count down for the girls and by the time the matron has reached the top of the stairs, in her dressing gown and flanked by guards, we're back in our beds, candles out, giggling silently.

"Brilliant, Ellen," you say, making me tingle all over. "Again?"

And once we're done for the night, it's just us, pressed together in a hammock we ain't supposed to be sharing, but our official bedfellows know better'n to challenge us on that. Hands exploring each other, your skin on mine, and if I have to bare my arse a thousand times to keep things like this, I will.

✡

Knowing us, though, it ain't always light-hearted like that. I'm still not sure about all the Asherah stuff but the way you touch me, it's easier to believe you, and I can't argue with how it drives you.

"It ain't enough to profit here, we gots to do things for the women. Even the dullards, yeah?" You take a drag from your pipe while you wait for me to answer.

We's sitting arm in arm in the yard, trying to catch a bit of sun. It's rare that it reaches around Har Wellington, which covers our western aspect like a sleeping beast. "Bread riot?" I ask finally. Truth is, I ain't sure what you're getting at, but you've got that light in your eyes like you does when you're feeling holy.

"Was thinking of the guards. The Hutchinsons is a pair of prigs, but he's never laid a hand on any of us. The guards, though... some of them's decent, some of them not. The ones that ain't need some sense beaten into them."

You and I, we hear every whisper of gossip, sooner or later. We're the best folk to do this. I nod. "I'm down. Be fun, anyway."

Cupping my chin, you draw my face up so I'm looking into those shining peepers of yours. "Be a way to serve Asherah, and that'll bring her power to you."

"How'd she come to mean so much to you, love? All's I remember growing up is the synagogue being boring as feck, and they hardly even mentioned Asherah."

"Lucky, I suppose, having the right people teaching me. Our gang had a lady rabbi, y'know, to do our funerals and that."

"A *lady* rabbi? That ain't allowed!"

"Well, she was thought to be a boy, at first. Even so. Stubbornest wench I ever met. And the smartest. She knew... everything. All the laws. Secret stories the men don't tell you 'cause they want to keep you in place. Course, a proper synagogue would never hire her. She... lit a fire in me."

"I see that." I drag my hand up your side, subtle like, until you gasp.

"We all need a mother, she used to say. And who better than 'a woman clothed with the sun, and the moon under her feet, and upon her head a crown of twelve stars'?"

"What's that even mean?"

"That's Revelation. It's about Yosef's dream—his father and mother and the twelve tribes." You sketch them out in the air. "But she's the mother of all of 'em, see? She's Yeshua's mother, but also more; she was there long before Yahweh thought of having a son. The mother of all mothers, all women, all Israel, all people."

For a time I'm quiet, puffing on my pipe and leaning against you. I still don't know, but you make it sound glorious. And smacking lecherous guards around can't be a bad thing. "Dunno as I'll ever be like you," I say. "But I'm in."

✡

We hold court, hearing from every woman willing to speak to us until we have a picture of which guards is doing their jobs like good lads and which is cruel, even to the good girls, and which abuses their powers in the worst possible way. We know many stories already, but some are surprises, and getting all organized somehow makes it clear as day, how bad it is. Most of the babies in the nursery are fathered by lecherous settlers, nigh but impossible for us to punish from here, but plenty are got from guards taking advantage.

So we get started, acting out, sowing some fear in 'em first. You cackle in delight every time I jump a guard. "Stronger than you look, you bit of a thing," you say admiringly. "We can *do* this." You're not bad yourself, stockier and with a mean punch in you before you even get a knife out, and I'm sure to tell you so. After a few days we overhear muttering about what's got into us, and why *them* when we haven't laid a finger on some. And the shy girls see we mean business, and that's when the darkest truths come out.

Rabbi Daniel. The worst of the lot. I can scarce believe it and ain't surprised, all at once. We never knew, you and I, being as he targeted the quiet ones. The ones he was sure wouldn't snitch when he called them in for Bible study as an excuse. They say his wife's barren and he'll stop at nothing to spread his seed far and wide. That he checks every girl's file first to make sure she hasn't left a husband back home. Probably thinks he's right with Yahweh and Yeshua like that too, like his sin only matters if it's against a man.

You grip my hand so tight your knuckle turns white when you hear that perversion and you don't let go until the youngster stammering all this runs, sobbing with relief when we say we'll take care of it.

OTHER COVENANTS

Pipe dangling from your mouth, your feelings is well hidden when you ask, "What d'you wanna do to him?"

I clench my fists as we plan our line of attack. "Feck knows. Castrate him, if I could, so's he can't force himself on anyone ever again. If wishes were horses, aye."

"Asherah knows he'd deserve it." You cackle smoke all over the place. When you've caught your breath, you add, "I could do it, if I had enough rum in me."

"Love, no. They'd hang you, I reckons. He's the feckin' *rabbi*."

You lean back against my arm. "You might be right. Asherah's protection only goes so far." You shift a bit in place and I wait for you to come to a decision, knowing without looking you've curled the fingers of your free hand about your amulets.

Casual like, you draw a bone knife from your boot. Not much bigger than a letter opener, it's wicked sharp. "A warning, only, on the thigh—the *gid hanasheh*. He'll know what it means, he's a holy man." You snort, making it very clear that you don't consider him holy, not with what he's done.

"No rum, then?"

"No rum." You stand up.

"What, *now*?"

"And why not? Scared, love?"

"No."

"Good, 'cause I need you to distract Hutchinson."

The two of them's walking the yard together. Apart from our mob, the girls is bent over sewing or washing or weaving fishing nets. Everyone's on best behaviour with his worshipfulness here.

"Scott, Owens, to your washtubs," Hutchinson says wearily.

"I's a question for you," I say. "What's your mother think of them ears?"

"I beg your par—" he's interrupted by a scream from Rabbi Daniel. So that's what they means by blood-curdling; I always wondered, but I only has time to think of that later. Right now I's too busy staring at how you've cut through Daniel's trousers on the side of his right thigh; blood seeps out, plastering the black fabric to his leg. My heart hammers even though I'm just watching.

"What is the meaning of this?" Hutchinson grabs me and ties my wrists while guards tackle you and the Rabbi screams bloody murder. The rope digs into my skin and I can smell the blood even from here.

"I didn't do nothing! Feckin' hell, I was right here!"

"Solitary for both of them, and the iron collar for Owens."

You stand there and let them take you, your eyes shining, quoting Scripture or something else in Hebrew while the Rabbi stares at you, his face like ash.

✡

They let me go after a couple of days but they keep you in solitary for days, then weeks, and then they's decided. They're sending you away from Cascades, up to the new factory at George Town.

"Chin up," you say. "Time to expand, is all. I'll write you. May Asherah turn her face on you, my love."

I don't tell you I can't write back.

After they've dragged you off I seduce a doe-eyed new wench and nail her in the water closet but she ain't you, and there's still a hole in my heart. So I get up a riot and it's glorious, Cath, I wish you could have seen it. We turn our washtubs over and shout for bread while the water streams downhill but my heart's shouting for you. There's nothing like that feeling of a man looking at you with fear in his eyes, 'specially when he's supposed to be the one in charge, but damn if it don't taste better with you at my side. When Mr. Hutchinson tries to ring a bell to settle us down and I grab it and smash a guard's head with it's for you, it's all for you. Feck, I miss you.

✡

The next time I'm assigned out as a servant I skip out on my first night and make my way to the pub. There's no shortage of men, some hard and fine and some mank as, but all willing to buy me ale. Before I know it I'm smashed enough to clamber, unsteady on me feet, onto a table. I bust out a terrible version of a jig, flipping my skirt higher than you's supposed to. There's a freeman in the crowd I've always liked the look of but never had a chance to talk to. Yosef Hughes, his name is, and he's one of the finest specimens here, skin burned deep brown by the harsh sun of Ben Diemen's Land and eyes to match, dark and soulful, and his name is like a sign from Asherah that makes him stand out in the crowd, your voice whispering in my head.

Yosef cheers me on, sleeves slipping up to reveal his tattoo of a mermaid smoking a pipe. Later he says it reminds him of me, and even though the ink was etched in years before, I'm flattered enough to let him walk me home, which we both know means root in the alley, but it's nice to be asked, not grabbed at. Well, asked *first*. Pushed up against the wall of some poor sod's house, he does plenty of very agreeable grabbing. But afterwards, the memory of you slaps me in the face; not that you'd begrudge me my jollies, I knows that, but it hurts that I didn't think of you for a time.

He sees my face. "Thought you enjoyed yourself."

"Ain't that, on Asherah's name I did—" and I mean it "—s'just... nothing feels right without Cath, you know?"

Yosef tucks a lock of hair behind my ear. "Only natural to miss your girl."

"You don't care?" I arch an eyebrow at him.

"Left someone special back in the mother country too. I'll never see him again." He smiles back sadly, and I nestle into his arms. After a moment he says, "Get yourself free, why don't ya, Ellen? We could—"

I shove him, aghast. "Don't you even!"

To my surprise, Yosef laughs. "Yeah, that was stupid, even from me. She'll be back, don't you worry love." He almost whispers that last word, and somehow that of all things is what makes me blush.

"You think so?"

"George Town Factory's new, but already overcrowded. Did you hear about the women who died on the way there?" He pauses until I nod gravely. "They're nervous. She'll walk all over 'em. Give her time to be awful enough and they'll flick her back."

"And how'd you know so much about female factories, Mr. Hughes?"

He shrugs. "Settlers talk. Some's very concerned about what goes on behind those gates. Always worth listening to the rumbles."

"Didn't know they cared 'cept for how we work for 'em."

"That's part of it. 'What punishment will be sufficient for these rebellious hussies, seeing, that, by their misconduct, many families are inconvenienced, for the want of servants?'" He affects a posh accent for that bit while I snigger. "That was in the papers."

It's hard to get my words out, I'm laughing so hard. "No! What a bunch of prigs. Twats!"

"Yes, really! But some is truly concerned too, 'bout the babies dying and all that."

The laugh's knocked out of me. "Big of 'em."

Yosef wraps an arm around me. "Not big enough, I know. Might be nothing comes of it."

"S'good to know, regardless. My snitches never said. Maybe they don't read the paper like you. Ain't you all respectable and such. Not worried I'll ruin your marriage prospects?"

"Not especially."

I grin again. I like this one.

He takes my hand. "It's late. What'll we do to get you back to Cascades, hm?"

"We's probably done enough, but more noise never hurts."

"Well then. May I see you home, miss?"

We run through Hobart Town, whooping, and my heart hurts a wee bit less.

✡

It takes you more'n a month to get back, and in the meantime there's a letter. Hiding in the water closet, I read it with my finger under the writing, mouthing the words, searing them onto my heart even though they're tame and friendly. Nothing to be ashamed of, I know, but somehow I don't like the girls seeing me that way. When I'm done I fold the paper small and tuck it into my amulet. At night, I sneak out and ask Yosef to write a reply for me. He doesn't laugh, like I'd feared, just smiles like it's me doing him the favor and not the other way round. I talk out what news feels safe to put into writing.

"The girls and I is carrying on your—no, *our*—work, and maybe you heard already that the Rabbi was murdered. Don't worry, I'm in the clear, but they's all shaken." I pause to admire Yosef's clever hand at work. "I pray—" Yosef asks if I do really, and I has to stop myself from elbowing his ribs and spoiling my letter—"I pray this is a sign that your return is not far off. I … no, best not … With fond regards, Ellen."

Yosef looks up at me. "That's it?"

"S'pose. I dunno, is that enough of a letter? I never wrote one before."

He blows on the paper to dry the ink. "I'd be glad to receive it if I were her."

"Such a gentleman."

"It's for a good cause. I hope." He winks and folds the letter neatly.

"Asherah's tits … you could just ask, you great lummox."

✡

And sure enough, with the Rabbi out of the picture they deem it safe to send you back here, for all that Hutchinson gnashes his teeth about it. The compliments about his 'expertise' don't mean much in the face of the reality of you, so it ain't a bit surprising he's plotting to get you out almost as soon as you're in. Still, I wasn't expecting it to happen like this.

"The clerk says they's going to move you again. You ain't even done nothing, not much of nothing anyway," I hiss over your washtub, which you're ignoring, o'course. "They *know*."

"What do they know, bab?"

I crook my fingers lewdly.

"Can't be," you say. "They don't even think it's possible for women to love like that. It ain't even in the Torah!" You cackle, lungs rattling, and you should know, you've read it.

"They's must've got educated, cause he was pretty sure."

"Who told?"

"Dunno. I couldn't get it out of that arse of a clerk."

Your eyes narrow and my heart quails. "Maybe you should try harder."

At the lunch hour I go back to his office and ask again, whispering my offer into his ear and sinking to my knees when he nods, slack at the jaw.

✡

"Eliza Churchill. That bitch, that fucking cunt," you spit. "Here's what we do…"

The plan goes smooth as butter at first. We're both assigned out, as though they're still hoping we'll turn docile by magic and they won't have to deal with our unnatural behaviour at all. After a couple of days on the job—Asherah's tits, it's tedious work, being a servant, I have to keep myself reined in so tight, knowing it'll be worth it. To keep the ribald songs in my head and off my tongue, I hum *Eishet Hayil* to myself endlessly. You say it's a metaphor for wisdom and maybe you're right, I wouldn't know. It lulls my master (for now) into trusting me, as much any free settler can trust a convict wench anyway.

But then, at long last, we meet. And oh, I want to throw myself into your arms and kiss you so hard it hurts but I can't, not yet, your new master is there—making sure you don't buy drink, you say. And you do have that twitchy dry look about you. Still, we set off for the house Eliza's stationed at and ask to see her.

The look on her face. Her voice quavers. "Wh-why are you here?"

"You know why, you two-faced louse." I step forward and pull her bonnet off so I can grip her hair, forcing her to look you in the eye.

She's already snivelling when you push your face up to hers. "We want to hear your side of the story."

It's a trap, but she's too much of a twit to realize. She babbles about the gatekeeper and fencing stolen goods and testifying before the magistrate and you wait, holding in your rage until she finally admits that they asked about unnatural connections. "They asked, they already suspected, I didn't do nothing," she whines. She puts her face in her hands and gleaming on her right index finger is a gold ring.

Your face is so red and angry, even my belly flops once or twice. Out for a couple of days, you'd have dried up enough to be grumpy even without a traitor in our midst. Before you can respond, I grab her hand. "Nice sparkle," I say, glaring at you over Eliza's shoulder. "Does we owe you *mazal tov*?"

Despite the bind she's in, she smiles. "Thank you, I—"

I tighten my grip and twist. "Ratted out your sisters for the *indulgence* to marry," I use the official term with as much scorn loaded in as I can muster.

"I only wanted—" she starts.

"It's not too late," you say. "Tell 'em you made it all up."

"Oh, I couldn't, I'd lose my pardon, I'd—" As she blubs, my eyes meet yours and we know she's right, for all her foolishness, she ain't gonna do this for us.

"You'll lose something," you say. I frees my hand just in time as yours brushes over it, not gentle at all, to grip hers much tighter'n I did. You squeeze tight and I take the cue, wrenching the gold ring from her finger. She makes a desperate grab for it but I'm too fast, course I am, and in seconds it's in my pocket and she's kneeling on the floor, sobbing and we're running, hand in hand, giving your master the slip and breaking into an empty house and finally you're in my arms.

✡

Freedom don't last, o'course, never does, but it don't usually end with the constable pulling you off me, mouth agape. I push my skirts down as best I can, and my mind, ever the trickster, reminds me of the Rabbi's voice droning "modesty" endlessly. It don't stop me from throwing myself at the copper, nails ready and aiming for his eyes. But he's got friends with him, and before long we're both in irons and walked back to the Factory, musket muzzles pressing at our backs.

Hutchinson put me in solitary, and the separation from you hurts more than the iron collar what stabs my neck every time I move. When the girls come to see me and bring some food, it takes the bravest one to tell me: "They took Cath up to Launceston, like they was planning. I'm so sorry, Ellen. They've come down hard on everyone, can't even get up a good riot."

"They'll get one soon enough," I growl, pushing away the bowl of food they've brung. Ain't hungry.

✡

That should've been the end of the story, and it would've been if I didn't have a plan, and the mettle to go through with it. It'll be tricksier than you getting back from George Town, but I know I can do it. I bide my time, only partly by choice. Ten days of hell in the collar. Another month in solitary. Asherah knows what I'd do without the girls sneaking over, telling me stories to keep my wits about me. And yes, eventually I eat again, no need to fret.

And then, patience. Back to the grind, trading in buttons and mutton, pearls and girls. It'd be fine if you wasn't still gnawing at my heart. But I gotta let the time pass or it won't work.

There's a rhythm to it, see? Usually I ain't so cautious, it happens natural like. You has your fun, you's punished, course you's going to wait a bit before you has more fun.

But now, when it feels right in my gut, I gets to work. I start small, pulling Mrs. Hutchinson's bonnet off, scratching at the guards' faces when they come along to drag me from one place to another.

"At this rate, you'll never be pardoned, Scott," Mr. Hutchinson says as I'm dragged to solitary again. Only two guards. They haven't tied my wrists—sloppy.

"And who says I want to be?" I bend over and twist my shoulder, so one guard crashes into the other. Standing free, I leap onto the superintendent's back, wrapping my arms around his neck. Tight. He wheezes and struggles, but I'm gripping him with my legs. I only have a few seconds before the guards pull me off him, but it's enough. The guards have me pinned tightly and this time they cuff me. For a minute no one talks and the only sound is Mr. Hutchinson coughing.

When he speaks, it's like half his voice is gone and all that's left is sandpaper. I got him good. "Put the collar on her. And for Yahweh's sake don't be gentle."

✡

"We must keep you and your wife safe, of course. We can send her to Launceston." It's the only option, which is what I'm counting on. George

Town Factory's closed after one too many scandals of capsized boats and drowned convict women. They's building a new one at Ross, so they tells me, but it ain't ready yet.

"She should be in *gaol*," Mr. Hutchinson spits. "In irons, if not at the gallows. She tried to kill me! She's worse than the men, sir!"

"I'm sure," the magistrate raises an eyebrow, "at least as wicked as the young man we hanged for eating his fellow absconders."

I bite my lip; I'd always thought that one was a tall tale. My hands is folded neatly in my lap. It's hard to look bad enough to be sent to the factory of my choice, but not bad enough to be locked up with the male convicts.

Hutchinson slumps back into his seat.

"In any case," the magistrate continues, "I've been advised that no provisions can be made to detain women in the gaol. It's simply too impractical and too expensive."

It takes an effort not to smile to myself. "Not Launceston, Sir, please, I'll be good, I—"

"Scott," the magistrate says, "don't waste your breath."

I shut up. I can smile later. Grin, celebrate, cartwheel.

✡

It's a long journey by cart to Launceston, with guards who've been instructed not to fraternize with me. Time enough to think over everything. I got no regrets, even though part of me wonders if I'll ever see Yosef again. I can't help but fret about how they're treating you, whether they'll try to keep us separate, as though they could ever. Asherah knows I'm ready to do whatever it takes so we can be together. And somehow I can't shake the feeling that I'm drawing her power across this whole blasted island, like these thoughts of you is the breath of some wind of change. Catherine, my love, I'm coming for you.

Ka-Ka-Ka

C. L. McDaniel

Sammy snuck a glance over his shoulder. *Keep calm*, he told himself. *Breathe.*

He sipped from his takeaway coffee. The cafe was four blocks behind him. Should he retrace his steps? Continue ahead?

Move slow. Move smooth. He fought to keep the cup from shaking. The city streets were not safe for "his kind." Ever.

Sammy peeked again. His pursuer had also stopped. The man's distinctive blue hat and jacket stuck out against the gray storefronts.

No question. Sammy had become an "object of interest."

He took out his smartphone and pressed the luminous record button. Thank God for ZiVo, the app every Jew owned—and used.

Phone pressed to his ear, Sammy feigned conversation.

"This is Samuel Schwarz. I am walking up *Hauptstrasse* towards *Potsdamer Platz*. I have done nothing wrong, violated no laws. And yet the police pursue me. How sad that a Jew cannot stroll along a Berlin street and enjoy his morning coffee."

His lips framed each word precisely. The video of his speech and actions would upload automatically to his website, a public record the police could not erase.

Erase. The term made him shudder.

Oh, to be a black man living in Chicago, or Charlotte—or Houston! You had to give the Americans credit. They freely acknowledged the horrors of their history: the degradations of slavery, the abortive attempt at world domination, the abominations of the Culling Camps.

Today, every American schoolchild learned of these genocidal atrocities, and how such savagery must be prevented in the future, whatever the cost. Today, the small but influential African-American community was protected, nurtured, treated with respect.

But in the Unified States of Germany? If you were Jewish, you were "lazy," "inferior," "drug-addicted." You "lived in filth" and "leeched off the State." According to the right-wing television pundits, your entire race was nothing more than a bunch of criminals and welfare queens. "The white German's burden," as the hosts on *Fuchs und Freunde* liked to say.

A broad crosswalk bisected the street up ahead. Sammy had almost reached the curb when, to his dismay, the light changed. The red silhouette of a man with his arms extended warned pedestrians to stop and wait.

The officer following Sammy slowed his pace, but closed the distance between them. A bead of sweat slid from behind Sammy's ear and trickled along his jawline.

From his youth, he had been warned to be wary, to avoid situations such as this. He was barely ten when his father sat him down for "the Talk." It was how you knew you were on the verge of manhood in the Jewish community.

"Son," his father had begun. "The *Polizei* are not your friends. Stay away from them. Never ask them for help."

As if Sammy didn't know that already. Dodging cops was the first thing toddlers learned as they played in the ghetto alleyways.

No one had to tell you. You saw it with your own eyes. How the *Bullen* cruised Jewish neighborhoods, meting out "justice" with their nightsticks, frisking young Jewish men for no reason, calling them "half-dicks" and "hook noses" and "penny chasers."

You swallowed their insults when you wanted to howl at the injustice. But you had to stay silent.

"Do not raise your voice to them," his father had cautioned. "Stay polite. Say 'Yes, sir' and 'No, sir.' And whatever happens, never lose your temper. That's what they expect, the angry Jew, always violent, more animal than human."

The walk light changed to green, and Sammy ambled into the crosswalk. *No rushing. Do not call attention to yourself.* More of his father's teaching, internalized, transformed into a reflex.

Sammy proceeded across the intersection at a sedate pace. As he reached the far curb, the light turned red. The policeman ignored it and dashed across the street. A Jew would be arrested for such a violation. But not a cop.

Especially this kind of cop.

The officer locked eyes with Sammy. Bright blue eyes, to go with short blond hair and a chiseled Aryan torso.

Rivulets of sweat cascaded down Sammy's neck as he turned away and kept walking. Should he duck down a side street or remain where there'd be more witnesses? *Stick with the crowds,* he decided. The last thing he wanted was to get boxed in an alley. Then the cop could do whatever he pleased. The cell cam might ensure his attacker got punished, but Sammy would still be maimed or dead. He'd rather avoid both outcomes.

Sammy ran through his father's list of instructions.

If a Bulle *stops you, do whatever he says.*

Allow him to arrest you.

Remember his name and badge number.

When you are given your phone call, call home.

Avoid eye contact.

Ask for permission to move your hands.

Keep your answers simple and stay silent when you can.

Do not give him an excuse to kill you.

Sammy fixed his eyes on the sidewalk and shuffled on. *Right foot. Left foot. Keep moving.*

The *Polizist* closed in on his prey. The merry tune he whistled pierced Sammy's eardrums. "*Oh, I wish I was in the land of Wotan.*"

One of *their* songs, a tune for the initiated! The police had "true believers" scattered through their ranks. They'd meet outside the cities, on farms, in barns or fields. If you asked where they were going, they'd say, "To gossip with the cows. A *Kuh Klatch*, nothing more."

The ruse hid their true purpose—deciding who needed "special discipline." "Uppity" Jews disappeared like smoke on the wind. Relatives would say the victims had "gone to Poland," but everyone knew. Somewhere a body moldered under the ground. Fish feasted on an unholy meal. A cement slab sported an organic core.

It's going to happen, Sammy realized with a shock. In the next few minutes he could die, for the crime of walking while Jewish. He lengthened his stride, but did not run.

Friedrich Grau ran. They arrested him for "suspicious activities" and threw him in the back of a police van. When the van arrived at the station, Grau was dead. No charges were filed.

And Grau was not alone. The roster of the fallen scrolled through Sammy's mind.

Twelve-year-old Taber Ries, shot while playing with a water gun. No charges.
Arik Garfinkel, choked to death for selling black market cigarettes. No charges.
Rudolph Bremel, shot for reaching into his coat for his heart medicine. No charges.
Michael Bruck grabbed his waistband.
Josiah Becker wore a hoodie.
Oscar Radzik broke up a fight.
Shot.
Shot.
Shot.
Dead.
Dead.
Dead.
No charges.
No charges.
No charges.

"Halt!" a harsh voice called.

Sammy ceased all forward motion. He held his hands high and slowly began to pivot.

A shoulder dug into his back, slamming his body against the nearest wall. The impact jarred the phone from his fingers. It tumbled to the ground below.

"I said, 'Don't move.'"

The shoulder thrust forward, compressing Sammy's cheek against the bricks, chafing his skin. Blood seeped from tiny pricks.

To Sammy's horror, the cop leaned in close and cawed in his ear. Three tiny syllables, strung together like the call of a crow.

"*Ka-Ka-Ka.*"

K.K.K. For their slogan. *Kuh Klatsch Kann.*

Face wedged tight against the building, Sammy struggled to mutter three words of his own. "J-Jewish Lives Matter."

"What did you say?"

"I said, 'Jewish Lives Matter.'"

"Why would you say that?"

"Smile."

The pressure eased, enough for Sammy to glance down at his phone. The officer followed his gaze.

The device lay face up on the pavement, undamaged, still recording. The ZiVo app's iconic eye winked again and again and again.

The man's jaw clenched and unclenched. He stepped back and pretended to take a close look at Sammy. Out came his own phone. His thumb scrolled through several pictures.

"Excuse me," he said at last. "There has been a mistake. A man matching your description robbed a shop several blocks from here. About your height and also with a brown coat. The shopkeeper said he had a knife."

"That was why you handled me so roughly?"

"Standard procedure. For your safety and that of your fellow citizens. I'm sure you understand."

Sammy understood.

The cop's mouth drooped into a half-sneer.

"Have a nice day, *Mein Herr.*" He touched his hat and sauntered away, as if nothing unusual had happened.

In truth, nothing had.

Sammy picked up his phone and plodded down the street, cheek bleeding, head aching.

Today he had survived. Tomorrow he might not be so lucky.

Strength of My Salvation

Bogi Takács

Jakab

It was much, much too cold to be outside. Jakab's soft deerskin boots crunched on clumps of snow in the shadow of the castle walls. He sighed and leaned against a boulder, pulled his trumpet out from his sack.

"If they want me to play on the royal wedding, they might as well let me practice indoors," he grumbled to no one in particular, and a startled bird took flight, black against the snowclouds looming overhead. Jakab wondered briefly if he would damage his trumpet, playing outdoors, but this only made him feel defiant. They threw him out in the first place! He rubbed his gloved fingers at the mouthpiece in a futile attempt to warm it up, then he raised the trumpet to his mouth.

Footsteps, rushing. He quickly threw the trumpet in the sack and hoisted it on his shoulder, wondering whether to flee. He was on the wrong side of the walls, and many Magyar youths liked to aim rocks at Jews' heads.

"You! Hey, you!" A girl was running toward him, waving with both hands—she appeared Jewish, judging from her clothing. Jakab leaned against the boulder and tried to look self-assured, beyond his teenage years.

The girl came to a halt next to him, her face red with the exertion in the cold. She was entirely unfamiliar, though it was hard to tell, swaddled up as she was in coats and scarves.

"Are you Jakab Mendel?" she huffed.

"My father." He grimaced. They were always looking for his father, the prefect. Never for him. Why didn't his father ever use his middle name?

"*Younger* Jakab Mendel, then," the girl grinned at him.

"Oh?" He pushed himself away from the boulder. He wanted to appear suave, but he only felt clumsy. He wasn't used to talking to girls. "That would be me," he said after some hesitation.

He expected the girl would admonish him for being late for dinner, for the evening prayer, for who knows what; most likely, she was an emissary sent from the well-staffed kitchens of the family palace. Instead, she said, "I've been looking for you all over the place! I know you have a sword. Can you help me?"

He almost slipped on the snow as he tried to shift his weight away from her. "Of course I have a sword," he said, louder than he would have liked. "I am the son of the Jewish prefect!"

"Do you have it with you?" She glanced at the sack.

"No, that's my trumpet," he said and tried to turn so that it would be behind his back, away from her view.

"I need to see your sword!"

He frowned. "Who are you, anyway?" He thought even a kitchen servant would treat him with more courtesy.

"I'm Jáhel and I need your sword," she repeated, hands on hips.

"To cut Sisera's head off?"

She sighed. "Do all of you make the same joke?"

"Can you tell me who you are and why you need my sword all of a sudden?"

"I'm Jáhel the eldest daughter of Mojzes the synagogue keeper. And I need your sword because it might be the key to the biggest mystery in all of Buda Castle."

Jáhel

It was easy to convince him, and he did not even laugh at her or make a grab for her scarf. She should've just begun with the highest ranking lout, she told herself as the two of them trundled uphill along the winding path to the castle gates. She had little time before the men would be back for their evening prayer. But he kept on nagging!

"I show you the chest, and then you'll see," she said, her breath making tiny snowclouds in the air. "It has the same inscription as your sword."

"Wait, how do you know what inscription there is on my sword?"

Why did he need such a detailed explanation for everything? "All of them look the same, they are silver replicas of your father's golden sword," she said.

"Is this about my father again?"

"No, this is about you, because none of the other louts set to march with a sword on the royal wedding would deign to lend theirs to me!" Her steps increasingly turned into stomps. She felt like the Behemoth of old, trampling through the Near Eastern wastes. Instead, she was making her way through dirt, dried grass and the occasional clump of snow in the Kingdom of Hungary. She felt she had all the reasons in the world to be annoyed.

At least the lout had fallen silent. She had a bit of time to think, after the desperate rush around the castle environs, but she kept on getting distracted. Her cheap winter boots had soaked through, and she was beginning to grow genuinely afraid for her toes. At least her scarves kept her warm, but this was because individually, they would have offered little protection against the cold, so she'd wrapped herself in as many as she could. She risked a lot—but she had seen the glimmer of sanctity, and felt moved to act.

Everything was in such uproar. The court was getting ready for the royal wedding with the looming threat of an Ottoman invasion. Were the southern borders secure? Rumors about King Mátyás' new bride swirled with ever greater ferocity—those who had met Beatrix described her as cold and cruel, but the King genuinely seemed to dote on her. Yet, word was that Beatrix had strangled her Italian lover, to hide the evidence she would not marry King Mátyás unsullied. Would she use her influence with the King against the Jews? The men at synagogue had kept on interrupting their studying to discuss the situation, while she was growing frustrated, eavesdropping from the attic.

She was not interested in politics—she was interested in Torah and learning. But what she'd discovered in the attic prompted her to make her move immediately instead of waiting for a less uproarious time. Hadn't the great Rabbi Hillel said, "If not now, when?"

Jakab

His head was spinning. He must've seen her before, bossing the children of the well-off families around in the synagogue. He certainly recognized the temperament. He figured if he just went along with her, she would eventually leave him alone. And besides, this sounded interesting—a box found in the vast attic of the synagogue, well-hidden and only dislodged during the ongoing repairs...

He hurried up the stairs to his room, grabbed his sword hanging in its scabbard from a peg, removed the trumpet from his sack, and wrapped the sword in the coarse fabric. He brushed off a house-servant and ran back out, only afterward realizing that he did not even notice which servant it had been. He thought he should keep track of the household staff, lest someone like Jáhel daughter of Mojzes avoid his notice. He did not very much like being ordered around, and he could not quite understand what was going on.

She opened the synagogue and the two of them crept in. There was no one around, and the crumbs on the kiddush table looked thoroughly dry. They sneaked up to the attic, where holes in the roof amply proved the need for renovation.

Jáhel dragged a large, dusty chest out from a corner. "There is a slot on the side, near the bottom," she said. "I'm sure that's where one needs to insert the sword."

"This is a sword, not a key," he said, but he opened his sack and pulled his sword out of its scabbard regardless. The inscription glinted on a ray of light from the westering sun. It had divine names and psalm quotes: "Strength of my salvation" alongside a blessing of the Name.

The blade slid all the way into the chest, and something clicked.

Jáhel

"I knew it!" She tried to pry open the lid of the chest, latches rusted shut. Her heart strained against her chest and she felt like she was about to burst. "I'm sure it can be opened now! Did you hear it unlock?"

Jakab also sought a grip, but then he took a step back and stared at his hands. "Wait—what am I even doing?"

He glanced up and the expression on his face changed—he looked as if he was about to be run over by a galloping horse. "I ... I ..."

"What's going on?" Jáhel whispered. Not this, not now, when the box was almost open, the secret revealed—

"I'm ruining my gloves, Mother will be upset," Jakab muttered, then shook his head, as if to clear it. "What have you done to me?"

Jakab

He was stunned, his thoughts running to and fro like wild rabbits. He had seen something like this before. One of the elderly Torah scholars by the name of Izsák the Scribe had asked him to help carry a heavy bundle of manuscripts from the synagogue to his residence in the outer city. The elderly man took a wrong corner, deep in a recitation of psalms or some such—and instead of the house where he rented a room, they found themselves face to face with a gang of Magyar peasant youths.

Jakab had braced himself for an upcoming confrontation, his thoughts going incongruously to whether it would be sacrilegious to drop sacred texts into the mud. Izsák the Scribe simply motioned him to stand back, stared the gang leader in the eye and ordered him to move aside in such a stentorian Biblical voice that even the crows circling overhead squawked in fear.

They reached their destination unharmed, and from that moment on, Jakab Mendel was certain that Izsák the Scribe was a master of the Name, able to call on divine power to do his bidding.

But Jáhel was the daughter of a simple synagogue keeper, and judging from her messy blonde hair peeking out from underneath her scarves, at least someone in her family had been from the green plains of Ukraine instead of the sandy hills of the Near East.

Jakab took off his gloves and shoved them into his pouch. "You forced me to come here, ensorceled me to do this nonsensical task. I shall not—"

He noticed the tears gathering in her eye and stopped.

"I did not," she protested. "I did not, I—did I?"

Jáhel

She knew she was aware of things others weren't. That's how she had found the chest, how she'd noticed the barely legible inscription, how she could read it, letter by faded letter. In her mind's eye, it glowed with the power of the sacred.

And she very, very much wanted to open the chest. Who knew what it hid?

And he had been her last chance, after all the other sons of rich families had ridiculed her, called her names, called her a bastard. Her only chance.

"D-do you think I forced you?" she whispered. Her legs gave way and her bottom hit the floorboards with a loud poof.

"Is someone up there?" a man yelled from downstairs.

"Living G-d!" Jakab muttered. They froze as they heard steps coming up the creaking stairs.

They both knew that if someone found them hiding in the attic, together, the least plausible explanation would be that they had been about to open a treasure chest. They were young, but they were already the age when a man should not seclude himself with a woman who was not his wife.

Jakab leaned forward and whispered in her ear with great urgency. "Can you do it again?"

"Do what?" she whispered back.

"Force him, like you forced me!"

"I have no idea how I did it! If it was even me!" She thought, *Sometimes young people make rash decisions that seem nonsensical later. Isn't that what Mother always says?*

Yet she gritted her teeth and crouched down behind the chest. Reached out and however improper, dragged Jakab by his coat next to herself.

Then she wished, with all the fear rising in her like a giant column of heat, for them to be invisible.

Jakab

He could hardly believe his eyes, but the man had gazed right at them and the chest, shrugged and went back downstairs. Jakab's skin prickled.

Once he heard the front door close, he leaned to Jáhel. "That was amazing! You should study the mysteries!"

Jáhel spread her hands. "You think they would *teach* me the mysteries? Why do you think I have been up here?"

Why indeed, he thought. Was she trying to get into trouble?

She yanked at his coat again—the second time it was less startling—and pointed to a corner, at a tarpaulin. He stepped over to it and gingerly lifted it, only to reveal a codex of some sort, filled with dense Hebrew handwriting. He paged through it, mouthing the words of the headings. *The Book of Formation... The Book of Brightness... The Book of Raziel the Angel...* He looked up. "Where did you get this?"

"Izsák the Scribe has been studying it," she said. "But he spends winters with his relatives in Provence."

"Did he leave it behind?" This was increasingly hard to believe. Surely she had not stolen this priceless object?

She shrugged. "He is growing forgetful, I think. I didn't steal it if that's what you're assuming."

Jakab looked away, caught out.

"So are we opening the chest or are we not?" she demanded.

Jáhel

The chest held a bundle of plain white cloth, and inside the bundle, a manuscript. Jakab looked disappointed, but Jáhel leaned forward eagerly.

"This looks very... old," Jakab said.

"Exactly as old as it needs to be," Jáhel nodded. She would not lose an ounce of her enthusiasm just because this rich youngster couldn't see the importance of Torah learning.

"Can you read it?" Jakab asked. "It looks like an awful scribble."

"What do you think I've been doing when I wasn't cooking eggs for Father?" She began to recite—slower and more unsteadily than she would have liked, but clearly he had nowhere near as much practice as she had. He had been groomed for governance, not study. She felt self-satisfied for a moment, then reminded herself it was immodest to gloat. She leaned closer to the text. "Wind blows through the... er... plains of... Pannonia. Byzantium trembles and gives... uh, birth. Uh, to a... sword." She was embarrassed.

"No, go on, this makes sense. It refers to the Turkish empire, and that they are gearing up for an invasion." Jakab crouched next to her, his interest finally awakened.

"I have... preserved these secrets, so that the Jews of Buda can be... preserved. If you are reading this, know that it is a time of... danger, and because of this danger, I am... willing to... forego my oath." She looked up. "Jakab, when do you think this was written?"

"No idea," he shrugged. "It looks very old. Decades, at least. Maybe a hundred years. The Turkish empire is *always* gearing up for an invasion. Just read!"

"Fine, fine." She cleared her throat. "These passages give the key, to a... to a great secret, hidden in the Book of Formation and first... revealed to, Mojzes the Priest, in the holy city of Jerusalem, during the time of the First Temple." She frowned. "This makes no sense. Mojzes is a strange name for a priest, why not Áron or something? And if he lived in the time of the First Temple, he wouldn't have called it the *First* Temple, he would've just called it the Temple."

Jakab pointed at the text. "I don't think this was written by that Mojzes. It was written by someone else, who is going to, what was it? Forego his oath. To tell us the secret, I think."

"We will see," Jáhel said. "Let me concentrate." She was brimming with the glow of discovery.

Jakab

That night, Jakab could not sleep. He wandered the ramparts of the castle, spooking night watchmen who yelled at him to return indoors. He couldn't rest. Passages resounded in his skull, declaimed in Jáhel's sharp voice.

The following principle demonstrates a way to speed an object to great speed, to pierce armor and destroy fortifications. The next principle demonstrates a way to increase the effectiveness of divine names. Thereafter...

He had to tell his father about this. He in turn had to tell King Mátyás about this. The king was eager to strike against the Turks, even preemptively, and this manuscript could both turn the tide of war, and curry more favor for the Jews. But the manuscript also had a caveat, and this instilled fear in Jakab's heart more than the abstract principles that Jáhel could only hope to understand.

Beware the new queen, she is a murderer.

Jakab had learned to be wary of Gentile royalty, and up until this point, King Mátyás had been relatively friendly to Jews. In many other royal courts around Europe, Jakab could not have expected to own a horse, let alone carry a sword. Would this bloodthirsty queen-to-be import a hatred of Jews, too?

Jakab's fingers clutched the trumpet. The wedding celebrations were drawing closer and closer. The only thing that could save them was divine judgment.

But maybe together with Jáhel, they could find a way to invoke divine judgment themselves...

Jáhel

Instead of sleeping that night, Jáhel sneaked out to a storage chamber and drew lines and letters on the floor tiles with a piece of charcoal. She worked hard and with great determination, and by the time the roosters began to crow and dawn was at hand, she was able to accelerate a bean along a line.

The principles were solid. Hebrew letters that oppose and thus repulse each other, and paths laid out for the object to be moved. She realized as she was looking blearily at the sunset that if she could get this far, she could certainly build a larger one that could shoot cannonballs at unimaginable velocity. The information in the text was correct and clear. There were very few physical components that would not have scaled up well.

Jakab found her after she had dragged herself back into the chamber, sat in a corner to mull this over. She'd nodded off and had to rub her face vigorously.

"It works," she murmured to Jakab. "We need to tell your father."

Jakab furrowed his brow. "He doesn't talk much to me. He is a very busy man."

"He will listen if you show him this," Jáhel muttered, and scampered around on all fours to get her Kabbalistic cannon in motion.

Jakab

He was always nervous around his father. Jakab Mendel the Elder, for all intents and purposes *the* Jakab Mendel, was a grim, hard man who bore the weight of an entire Jewish community on his shoulders. The last time Jakab could remember his father being enthusiastic about him was when he read his bar mitzvah portion without a single error, and that had been years ago.

The prefect did not bring anyone with himself; he understood the need for secrecy.

"Should we show this to the king?" he murmured, brushing his beard with his palm as he carefully stepped around the tracks on the floor. Jáhel drew back from his path.

Jakab wasn't sure his father wanted an answer. "Father? If I may?" Jakab Mendel senior nodded, so he continued. "The new queen, um, the queen-to-be, I don't know if she can be trusted. With all the rumors... Who knows if she would sway the king's head, and turn him against us? They are Christians, they might easily say this is the work of the Devil."

"I'm not sure if the king himself can be trusted, either." Another sweep of the palm. "He has been remarkably friendly to us Jews so far, but this might upset the balance of power. He wants us as his subordinates. That's my task to enforce." He sighed, deeply, from his belly. "In either case, he does dote on the queen. Her word might be of great importance in this matter, and he is enlightened enough to consult her."

"If I may?" Jáhel perked up. She didn't wait for the prefect to nod, and spoke rapidly. Jakab felt slightly embarrassed. "If we use the principles in this text, we can also perform something like the Christians do, like a witch test, except it would actually work."

Witch tests don't work? Jakab did not dare interrupt the tide of words. Jáhel went on: "We could use the principles of attraction and repulsion laid out in the manuscript and determine if she is attracted to sanctity or repulsed by it! We would just need to get an object to her, which we can do at the wedding, when we present the gifts, and it would work out really—"

"You want to get an object to the queen," the prefect mused. "After the dance with the Torah scroll, we intend to present her with the scroll to kiss. The master of ceremonies thought that would be appropriate..."

Jakab took a deep breath, gathering his courage. "But what if they realize what we're doing, and then even the King turns on us, accusing us of sorcery?"

"We can do this surreptitiously. I can prepare the scroll," Jáhel said. "It will be easy. I will just sew some letters into the covering, and the crowns on top can be used to channel the divine influx..."

Jakab thought this sounded vaguely sacrilegious, or even secular. But they needed to act fast, for the Turkish armies were restless in the Balkans.

His father sighed. "I wish we had Rabbi Izsák to consult..."

Jakab felt the cold of the storage chamber begin to seep through his bones. While people praised his father as proactive in the service of his community, and ready for confrontations with Gentiles, he knew just how frequently his father had backed down. Jakab Mendel the Elder picked his battles carefully—and the fact that he was willing to take action this time meant the threat had to be severe indeed...

Jáhel

She rode with her father Mojzes, which was wonderful because he was eager to see as much of the wedding ceremonies as he could, even when he rode to places where he did not quite belong. No one quite dared to order him back—he looked for all the world like the biblical prophet, his beard gone prematurely gray and flowing freely over his chest. He did not braid or twist it up—he was conscious of the effect it had on Gentiles, and over the dinner table he often joked about it with his family.

Jáhel could see everything in view. The Jews rode first, a march of brown steeds decorated with white and brown ostrich feathers and all manner of finery. The young horsemen wore thick brown clothing against the weather, decorated with silver, and a matching, wide silver belt for their swords. Jáhel strained to see Jakab, who was riding almost at front, right behind his father leading the march. She had seen them pass by, the elder Jakab Mendel in a sharp-pointed helmet padded with heavy velvet, showing his high rank as the prefect of all Hungarian Jewry.

There was some consternation up ahead. Apparently, the march had ridden out before the king had a chance to join it. Royal guards on horseback urged back the crowd. Jáhel gasped as he saw King Mátyás ride past, with Prince Kristóf. She only saw them for an instant, but the king looked tired, his face worry-worn. Jáhel wondered if the defense situation in the south had taken a turn for the worse.

Order restored itself after the king had passed, but this split the front of the march with the young horsemen and the two Jakab Mendels from the rest. Jáhel nudged her father until they were next to two Jewish horsemen, stolid middle-aged folk carrying a richly embroidered wedding chuppah—not for the royal couple, who were Christian, but to protect the Torah scroll from the elements. Mojzes unmounted from the horse and he was handed the scroll to carry, as an honor to him due to his faithful work as the synagogue keeper. Jáhel pulled on the reins and settled in behind the chuppah with the horse. She wanted to stay out of sight—she had no particular honor to be present for, and her task was clandestine in the extreme.

She maneuvered until she was mostly hidden behind another horseman carrying a large flag embroidered with the Hebrew words *Shema Yisrael*, and decorated with shields of David and pentagrams of a protective nature. She thought this might protect her, in a very physical sense. She had no idea what would happen once the queen came in contact with the Torah scroll. How violently would she be repulsed? She had explained everything to her father and he had agreed to the risks, but she couldn't help but feel scared for him.

Jakab

He straightened himself in the saddle, took a deep breath, and started blowing his trumpet. He had worked the melodies to perfection, after his family'd finally given in to his arguments that practicing outdoors might ruin his instrument. The songs were familiar to him, their words praising kinghood and dominion. *David, the king of Israel, lives and endures. The L-rd is king, the L-rd has reigned, the L-rd shall reign forever and ever.*

He had opted for the simpler tunes in consultation with the master of ceremonies—these had seemed catchier and easier to please the Gentile Magyars, even though Jakab felt they gave the ceremonies an air of slightly childish celebration. He remembered that he'd last played some of these tunes at his little nephew Efráim's third birthday. He was glad for the choice, because it was hard enough to play music while on horseback and out in the cold, though the throngs had warmed up the air somewhat, and he was less worried about ruining the trumpet.

The king and queen arrived as he was midway through the last tune of the first set. He finished it off with a flourish and remained silent while his father offered the formal greetings of the Jewish community to the royal couple. His words were liberally borrowed from the Bible, as it was customary; Jakab wondered if the Magyar nobles understood the references. He personally thought the speech was glorious, befitting the royal pair.

Jakab noticed with some alarm that Queen Beatrix kept on frowning. What displeased her so? Did she have something against Jews? The speech was short and snappy, and the rich Jewish traders joined in with the common folk. The elders were waiting under another large tent to keep the wind from chapping their faces, while younger people thronged on the outskirts of the crowd because they tolerated the cold better. Jakab played again, with relish tinged with apprehension. As the dancers swirled and the horses neighed, he could not help looking for Jáhel and her father. He did spot the Torah scroll, moving slowly forward through the masses of people, but where was his friend and co-conspirator?

The young people made rings around the Torah, danced and sang. *There is no one like our G-d, there is no one like our L-rd, there is no one like our King, there is no one like our Savior.* Would they be saved from calamity?

The rings slowly opened up.

Jáhel

Her gut felt hard and cold. As the dancers opened a path to the royal couple, she drew a bit closer to better observe the queen's reaction.

King Mátyás smiled affably, even if his smile was somewhat exhausted. He offered his royal greetings in the customary plural, and criers passed his words to the crowds in the back—the Magyar citizens of Buda and all the other marchers were further back still, waiting for their turn.

The King nodded to the Queen, and both of them stepped forward to the chuppah. Jáhel watched in terror as her father presented the queen with the Torah scroll. The queen smiled, then gasped and drew back as if burned. The King looked at her in consternation, then stepped back himself, a carefully fixed neutral expression on his face. "We appreciate being presented with the Ten Commandments," he said. A voice snickered in the back—the King apparently did not quite know what a Torah scroll was, but who would dare explain it to him?

This was as clear a *No* as they were going to receive from the Heavens. Jáhel patted her horse's neck with a trembling hand, and tried to remain as quiet and still as possible amid the jubilations. Her thoughts galloped ahead feverishly. They could not reveal the secrets to the King. She needed to find another use for the divine power to save them, and she needed to do it fast. Who knew when the Ottoman armies would begin to advance again?

Jakab

He rode up to her in the crowd. "Did you see it?" he asked.

Jáhel stared up at him with wide, shocked eyes. "She would not kiss the scroll. She would not even touch it. It burned her," she muttered.

"That's what I thought, but you were closer," he said. "What now?"

"We were given this power to preserve us from the Turkish invasion," she said, "and that's exactly what we're going to do, with the aid of the Heavens." She shook her head. "But I have absolutely no idea how!"

"Let's just celebrate for now," Jakab offered, though he himself had little desire to rejoice. "We can't eat their food, but my father had organized a feast. He brought, he brought..." Jáhel was staring at him speechless, which demonstrated the gravity of the situation. He continued: "He brought two whole adult deer, two young does, eight peacocks whole..."

Jáhel finally showed a reaction. She grimaced. "So much effort to slaughter deer properly! And are peacocks even kosher?"

Jakab shrugged. "The Jews of Italy eat them, so that should be good enough for us. Let's go, at least we can take a look, fill our bellies and save our worries for tomorrow."

Jáhel did not seem convinced, but she fell into pace after his horse.

Jáhel

Inside the palace, the courtyards were in turmoil. Having stabled their horses, the two of them ventured ahead. Jáhel tried in vain to figure out what was going on, then she finally resorted to grabbing the cloak of a young servant boy. She was getting used to this. "What's going on?"

"The Queen, Her Majesty, has ordered that only the closest circles of the royal pair be seated with them. Everyone needs to be reseated, they are emptying out three large halls across from here, carrying over the food... Excuse me, I must go," he hurried away.

Jakab was grinning at her. "We can sneak in. With all the seating confusion, no one will notice us."

"But—" This seemed like the last thing she wanted to do. Was he trying to show off? Demonstrate his manly bravery? But she was indeed hungry, after such a long time out in the cold on horseback. "Fine," she grunted at him. "What do we say if they ask who we are?"

"Well, I am the son of the prefect." He puffed out his chest. He was definitely showing off.

"Sure, but have you been invited?"

"No, but *prefect* sounds like a high rank." He slammed a hand on his hip, jangling the sword they'd used to open the chest. "And we are dressed in our finery."

"But what should I say?"

"You are, uh..." *Please do not say I am your fiancée,* Jáhel thought at him, but tried not to push with the divine power. She simply hoped. "...You are visiting from the Polish court," he said.

She grinned with great relief. "Finally my light hair will be good for something," she said.

"Let's go! Maybe we can even sneak into places that are usually not open."

She cheered up a bit. Maybe they could find out something, a weakness of the Queen perhaps, or something else that would tell them how to make use of the great secret. And their stomachs needed to be filled, too.

"But wait," she said. "If we go get the kosher meat, then we'll be seated with Jews. And they will surely realize we don't belong."

"We can get the kosher meat, and say we are taking it to the synagogue. And then just sneak to another table where they don't know us, sit down and eat."

That sounds all too easy, Jáhel thought, but she was committed to the adventure.

Jakab

He licked grease off his fingers. The food was delicious, fit for the royal table—if not the King's table per se. "This went very smoothly," he said to Jáhel. "Are you sure you did not do anything to them?"

"I would not, Heaven forbid!" Jáhel shook her head and chuckled, probably suppressing a burp. They were both full to bursting. She smiled. "They will need to roll us out of here."

"And now for the evening's entertainments," a young herald yelled above their heads. Everyone quietened down. Jakab grimaced. What now? How would they be able to leave unnoticed? If he needed to summon his father's authority, surely there would be repercussions from him afterward.

"A visit to the royal wine cellars, with a special treat to accompany the tasting!" the herald declaimed.

"We are full! We cannot move!" an elderly man with an already wine-soaked voice shouted back.

The herald did not miss a beat. "Come, come, young sirs and ladies," he grabbed both Jakab and Jáhel's hands. "Save the honor of the elder generation!"

Jáhel looked at Jakab in fright. "B-but, do you have kosher wine?" she blurted out.

"We have the finest kosher wines from the meadows and hills of Lombardy," the herald yelled, dragging them away from the table. His face was familiar to Jakab—and most of the young Magyar men that he knew, he knew from street altercations. Someone behind them said, "Shouldn't those two have been seated with the Jews?" But then all voices faded into the din of the celebration, only to let up once they reached the entrance of the cellars.

Jakab took a deep breath. If there was a time to be a hero, it was surely now. "If you want to kill us, you'll have to go through me first," he said.

"What?" The herald blanched. "This was an earnest offer! And you are much better company than those grandfathers back there."

They stared at each other in silence for a moment, then Jáhel broke out in laughter. "Did you bring us here because you needed an excuse to get drunk?"

The herald bowed his head apologetically, but Jakab could see he was grinning.

Jakab did not want to drink to excess, but this was a great improvement over the fistfight he had already been imagining in his head—or being tossed down the cellar steps, insensate, to his death. "Onward!" he waved in the direction of the cellar. He felt like they could use a moment of respite.

Jáhel

She only took little sips for form's sake—she wanted to keep a clear head. As Jakab and the young Magyar herald were filling their crude mugs to the brim, chuckling to each other and laughing, she wandered around. She would not get another look at the palace cellars anytime soon, and she was curious about everything. She was also growing uncomfortable with the other two's eagerness to sample all varieties of wine, regardless of their kosher status. They seemed to be getting on very well.

Behind a row of large barrels, she spotted a nook, left in darkness by the torchlight. She put down her still mostly full mug and squiggled through to the nook, scraping her festive clothing and dusting her palms. Cold air was coming out from the nook. Some kind of secret passage? She got back out from behind the barrels and returned with a torch in hand, gingerly balancing it, hoping it wouldn't be blown out by the moving air or her haphazard motions in the narrow space. She muttered a few words of a protective psalm and ventured inside. She wished she had Jakab's sword at hand.

She could see clumps hanging, moving slowly in the draft. Hams? No, they were too light for that. Bundles of herbs, she realized after a few moments of her trying to make sense of what she saw. They smelled of at least five different fragrances, and she was growing woozy. She went ahead, but jumped and startled when she heard some sort of grinding noise from further ahead, as if someone was rolling a large boulder. The wind was disturbed. Was someone closing the path on the other side? She was suddenly terrified of being locked in. She stumbled—she managed to hold on to her torch, but she'd sprained her ankle, and the air was filling with the smell of burnt hair. The torch must have caught at it, ever so slightly, but enough to cause such a discomfiting smell. She patted at her head with one hand and held out her other arm with the torch, her entire body shaking. She walked backward, finally gathering the courage to turn around. Light peeked out from the entrance, back where she'd come from, and relief rushed through her. She wheezed loudly and almost dropped the torch again as she stepped out of the passage.

She returned to the two boys and resisted the now-familiar urge to yank at the herald's colorful garb. "Hey, you," she said, "What's your name?"

"Misi, at your service," he offered an exaggerated bow, and grinned at her as he straightened up. She couldn't help thinking he looked a bit like a squirrel.

"Misi, can you tell me what's in that cranny over there?" She pointed toward the barrels.

"Oh, that's just one of the tunnels. The castle hill is full of them," Misi shrugged. "I think Uncle Józsi is drying herbs in that one or something. They're long and straight and just go like *whoosh!*" He made a sweeping gesture with his arm, losing some of the wine from his mug in the process. "All the way across the hill. At least these ones. Some of the others are more twisty-turny, and you can get lost in them."

Jáhel nodded, but her thoughts were already elsewhere. *Long and straight and go like whoosh.* She could have many uses for a tunnel like that. She looked at Jakab. "Look, I really appreciated the food and the drink, but I think we might need to go."

He looked at her in puzzlement, then understanding seemed to dawn in his slightly clouded eyes. They said goodbye to Misi, and promised him they'd put in a good word for him and his service, then they rushed up the stairs—Jáhel as if she'd been chased by wolves, Jakab lagging slightly behind.

Jakab

They went back to the synagogue attic, their now-customary hideout. Jáhel paced anxiously, disturbing the dust. "I know exactly what we're going to do," she declared. Jakab wasn't quite clear on the details, so he just nodded and murmured something for her to go on.

"If we can accelerate a cannonball along a path, we can surely accelerate a small wheelbarrow." Her eyes were glistening in the semi-darkness. "If we set it up in a tunnel, we might be able to evacuate everyone from the castle hill area when the Turks come to attack. This way we can use the secret knowledge to save everyone!"

He scratched his head. "But there are no tunnels underneath our buildings."

"We can just dig one. It can start right under the synagogue. Eventually we might even be able to connect it to one of the tunnels that already exist."

He looked at her incredulously. "How will we be able to hide that from the Magyars? We can dig at night? For months? Years?"

"I never said it wouldn't be a sacrifice," she furrowed her brow. "The *text* didn't say it wouldn't be a sacrifice."

He spread his hands. "Look, it was hard enough on us to just get this far. When did you last have a good night's sleep?"

"You're just bitter you have to replace your cushy Torah study with hard labor," she snapped. "Have you ever scrubbed a pot in your entire life?"

He had to admit he hadn't.

"Look, you do know the story of Choni HaMe'agel?" she asked. "From the Talmud?"

He shrugged again. How did she know all this? Was she going to lecture *him* on Torah study? She must have spent a lot of time spying on the men from the attic.

She started to tell the story. "Choni HaMe'agel was wandering and thinking about the Psalm, 'When G-d returned the captives of Tzion, we were like dreamers'. Do you know that one?"

"Yeah, sure," he nodded, embarrassed. "From the Pesach Haggadah?"

"That's the one. So, the captivity lasted seventy years, but can one dream for seventy years? Choni HaMe'agel was thinking about this as he came upon an elderly man planting a tree. He was surprised and asked, why are you planting this tree? Doesn't it take very long to bear fruit? Then the elderly man said, it takes seventy years."

Jakab felt contrarian. "What kind of tree takes so long to bear fruit?"

Jáhel shrugged. "A walnut tree, I think."

"But are there even walnut trees in the Promised Land?"

"I don't know, some kind of tree, okay?" She resumed her pacing. "So it takes seventy years. Why do you plant this tree if you can't benefit from it yourself? And the man responded, When I came to this world, I found trees like this in it, so just as the people who came before me planted these trees for my sake, so shall I plant this tree for the sake of the people who will come after me. Then Choni HaMe'agel lay down to sleep, and he slept for seventy years... and when he woke up, he found the tree full-grown and a young man picking its fruit."

"Nuts are not a fruit."

"Are you listening? These are words of Torah!"

Jakab thought these were her own words, more likely, but he was engrossed. She had an animated way of telling tales. He mumbled an apology.

"So he found this tree," she went on, "and asked the young man who he was—and he was the grandson of the older man he'd spoken to. From this we learn, well, what do we learn from this?" She outright glared at him.

He backed down. "Fine, fine, I see your point. Even if we don't benefit from this tunnel, our children or grandchildren might benefit from it."

"Just like that," Jáhel nodded, evidently pleased. She came to a standstill in front of Jakab, grinning. "And we'll be able to use the divine names for preserving lives, not for taking them. Let the Magyars and the Turks fight amongst each other. We shall endure."

"Like David, King of Israel," he added.

She looked relieved. "Amen and amen," she said. "Let's go tell your father."

Jáhel

She would dig—her father would dig—her sisters and brothers would dig. And Jakab would dig, his face smeared with rich black Magyar soil, his hands wrapped in rags but still blistered from the shovel handle. She would lay out metal, direct craftsmen who'd been sworn to silence with a halakhically-binding oath. She would place letters and adjust them, she would fine-tune paths and connections. She would work, as best she could, and she would have Rabbi Izsák advise her—Rabbi Izsák, who had left his treasured manuscript behind on purpose, the only man in the synagogue who'd noticed her attempts to learn Torah.

And by the time Queen Beatrix died in disgrace in a Neapolitan palace, the tunnels were well ready; and before Prefect Jakab Mendel the Younger also passed on, in the circle of his family, he conveyed the knowledge to his children. Thus it happened that when the Magyar kingdom sunk into bitter civil war and the Turkish armies took the castle of Buda, many of the Jews simply vanished. The Christians spread rumors that the Turkish soldiers had massacred them, while the Turkish generals had ordered them brought to Constantinople; but the truth was that thousands of Jews had never arrived in the heart of the Turkish empire, nor were they buried in the Jewish cemetery of the castle hill. And if you were ever to notice familiar faces in far-off cities, the people would hurry away from you in silence, keeping the secret of the tunnels that had caved in behind them.

The Golem (1933)

Gwynne Garfinkle

Karloff lumbers through Karl Freund's
dream-like film, innocence and brutality
warring within his massive frame
until a little girl plucks the amulet
from his chest and he falls

Leslie Howard plays the rabbi's son
professor returned home from the big city
to shoulder his late father's task
reawakening the golem
to protect his people

Howard is clean-shaven
elegant as ever in his smart suits
the ultimate English gentleman
but openly acknowledging his Jewishness
which some considered career suicide

"But why?" I asked my screenwriter dad
after I watched the film on TV
one Saturday afternoon
three decades after the Nazis
shot down Howard's plane

"Those were different times," Dad said
and told me how, in the 1940s
Harvard reneged on his scholarship
(they'd already filled their Jewish
quota for the year)

Howard scoffed at the repercussions
of making *The Golem*
so what if he was no longer a matinee idol
it meant years of character parts
none of the romantic milquetoasts he loathed

by the time Franchot Tone got the part

of Ashley Wilkes in Hitler's favorite movie
Howard had gone home to England
where he'd make anti-fascist films
until his death

in 1975, my parents took me to see
the new Mel Brooks comedy, *High and Loew*
with Gene Wilder as the rabbi's harried son
and Peter Boyle as the golem
it was my gateway to classic horror

A 1933 film of *The Golem*, directed by Karl Freund and starring Boris Karloff, was proposed but never made. Freund had been cinematographer of *Der Golem* (1920). Leslie Howard disliked playing Ashley Wilkes and called *Gone With the Wind* (1939) "a terrible lot of nonsense." His plane was shot down over the Bay of Biscay in 1943.

The Face That Launched a Thousand Ships

Milton Verskin

When Spinoza heard that a crazed mob had just murdered Prime Minister De Witt and his brother, his peace of mind was shattered, and he lost all sense of reason. The news was horrifying. The mob dragged the brothers to a scaffold with such violence that they were mutilated and dead when they got there. They nevertheless strung up the bodies upside down, as in a butcher shop, and ripped them to pieces. Spinoza leapt up from his desk and, without thinking, shouted that he would rush out immediately and denounce the mob, show them exactly what they were—filth, scum, the ultimate in barbarity. And then, losing his mind completely, he added that, in order to drive his point thoroughly home, he would hammer a placard to the scaffold, written in the clearest Latin, saying exactly what he thought of them in two simple words, "*Ultimi Barbarorum.*" Fortunately, his landlord, Hendrik Van der Spijk, dragged him, shouting and kicking, back to his room, and locked the door.

When Van der Spijk eventually unlocked the door, Spinoza admitted that he had behaved like an idiot and apologized. However, although he seemed to be his old calm self again, inwardly he was in turmoil. If this could happen here in The Hague, there was no place in the world where it could not happen. Passion trumps reason, and his whole philosophy might be wrong.

Other thoughts came into his mind, as they nearly always did when he was distressed. Most prominent was what happened to his little Misha, the puppy his father gave him when he turned four. He loved his little Misha, a terrier with soft white and tan fur. One day when he was out with his father, a dishevelled hobo wanted to pet his dog. Misha barked; the hobo got angry, lifted his cane and beat him repeatedly with all his strength. By the time Spinoza's father managed to pull the hobo away, Misha was lying on the pavement, whimpering, with many bones broken, and within an hour he was dead. Spinoza wept.

"I love my little Misha. My little Misha. I love …"

His father picked him up and stroked his head.

"We'll buy you another little puppy and you'll love him too."

"No, he won't be beautiful like… "

"Yes he will, and you'll love him very much, just like Misha."

"He won't be beautiful like Misha. I've never had a dog like Misha."

He refused, adamantly, to have another dog.

"Because," he said, "the man might come again."

All through his life, images of that scene kept coming back to him no matter how hard he tried to stamp them out, and with those images came the terrible fear that if he were ever to allow himself to love anything so much, he might suffer that same loss again.

It was while Spinoza was in this frame of mind that Van der Spijk introduced him to Eshkeh, the shoemaker's wife. They were Litvaks, originally from Krasivaya, a shtetl in Liteh, near Minsk. Spinoza's imagination was inflamed. Her eyes, her hair, the changing expressions on her face as she responded to the conversation, he had never seen anyone so unutterably beautiful. And the warmth and cadences of her voice. He knew that he was making an idiot of himself; passion again trumped reason. But he also felt, with blind certainty, that for her, too, this was love at first sight. He made himself get up and leave the room, and for a long time after that he struggled with his emotions. He had to think rationally. His was the life of the mind, the effort to reach a clear understanding of God, to love God, the only possible object of love which would last forever and never change. Was all that to be trumped by adulterous imaginings?

Then circumstances changed. Coming home one evening from a Talmud class, Eshkeh's husband was run over by a runaway carriage. It was a quick but very painful and frightening death. Spinoza was stunned. Yet more non-rational violence. Everything flowed from God, he knew that; it flowed inevitably, and wisdom lay in understanding and acceptance. Nevertheless, wisdom was hard to grasp when every day, the irrational seemed to triumph.

Since the marriage had been without love, Eshkeh's mourning did no more than fulfill the requirements of ritual and decorum. Immediately after the funeral, Spinoza paid her the customary comforting-the-mourner visit. She was surprised to see him, but was obviously pleased. Reason told him to stay away after that, but passion prevailed. He visited her the next day and every day after that, and their conversation flowed. She told him about her family in Krasivaya, her parents, her sisters, her cousins, and her aunts—lots of funny stories. She was an excellent raconteur, and in return he provided her with a careful outline of some of his beliefs. God or Nature, *Deus sive Natura*, these are interchangeable terms, different terms for the same thing. Everything flows inevitably from God or, in other words, from Nature. The only things we can change are our thoughts, and we are truly happy only to the extent that our reasonable thoughts control our passions.

When a letter arrived from her mother, she told him the news.

"My sister has a new baby, a little boy. They named him Shlaymeh—Shlay-meleh—after our grandfather, my father's father."

"And his sister, the little girl? How has she responded to the new arrival?"

"Aydeleh's three. She says that she's not little, she's *Big*. When they told her that a new little brother had arrived in the house, she was pleased. Then she went quietly to my mother and asked 'Gran'ma, is a brother a boy or a girl?'"

Spinoza felt a rush of affection for that little girl, and also for Eshkeh.

When the thirty-day mourning period ended, he said, "God takes no pleasure in our discomfort. On the contrary, the greater our joy, the more we join in his nature. Let us be wise, then, and refresh ourselves with pleasant food and drink, with perfumes, with the soft beauty of growing plants, and beautiful, joyful music, all, of course, in moderation."

He was translating from his book, from Latin into an attempt at conversational Dutch, and he knew that he was being a bit ridiculous. She tried not to laugh, but he could see the corners of her mouth twitching. What would she have said about the placard he very nearly hammered onto the De Witts' scaffold?

"I'm quite an eccentric old fellow..." he said, and she interrupted with an emphatic "You're not old."

He was forty, but feeling curiously young.

They made simple meals together. Every now and then he would bring wine. He had a long-stem clay pipe and used a carefully-chosen tobacco. After their meals they'd sketch portraits of people they knew or she'd take out her lute and they'd sing to her improvised accompaniments—Italian and French songs and some John Dowland, all in Dutch translation. She taught him some Yiddish folk songs, but his accent was funny.

These were all moderate pleasures, in line with the moderation he had worked so hard to achieve. But there was no moderation. His imagination was afire. Her stories and songs, the play of light on the contours of her hair, her face and all its changing expressions, crowded his mind and filled his whole being with massive upsurges of joy. But then, very quickly, the inexorable laws of human nature took effect and he found himself in the grip of painful emotions. Eshkeh. Whatever in his life flowed from God flowed first through her. What if she were to die, or go away, or reject him, or if it should turn out that her charm camouflaged a vicious shrew? It was exactly as his writings would have predicted, love, hope, fear, anxiety, the one giving rise to the other. His life was out of control.

And a new emotion which he never knew existed took hold of him, an overflowing of he knew not what, and an ineffable tenderness. The Stoics were wrong, of course, when they said that a rational man can completely overcome his passions. But had not his book demonstrated that their unruliness must subside when, under the impact of rational thought, they are seen from the perspective of eternity?

Then came a dramatic change. He arrived one morning at his usual time and she said, "Another letter came today from my mother and I've got another Aydeleh story."

"Tell me."

"She's still small for her age. She was walking past the schoolhouse with my mother, holding hands, and suddenly she broke loose and ran ahead, and a whole troop of older children came running out straight towards her. My mother panicked. She was sure they'd knock her down. But you know what? The children saw her and stopped straight away and they were all saying 'What a cute little girl.' One said it and then another, 'What a cute little girl.' Aydeleh looked up at them—you can imagine her serious little face—and she said, 'I'm *Big*.'"

Spinoza watched the play of emotions on Eshkeh's face as she told her story—love and amusement, also yearning and a deep sadness—Krasivaya was so far away—and he was suddenly overcome with that overflow of emotion which he could not define. His words came spontaneously, no thought, no planning; he heard them almost as if he were listening to someone else.

"I love you."

She half smiled but said nothing.

"I love you very much."

She remained silent. How was he to deal with this silence?

"With all my heart," he said, "and with all my soul and with all my might. Deuteronomy, chapter six, verse five."

Her expression changed slightly, a three-quarters smile, perhaps acknowledging his joke. Was she formulating a tactful rejection?

"To make myself clear," he said, "by *love*, I mean a joy concomitant to the idea of an external cause, you being the external cause. My book, Part Three, Definition of the Emotions number 6."

"I love you too," she said, and they both laughed.

A Jewish marriage was irrelevant to Spinoza but vital to Eshkeh. So the question then arose, what about the *herem*, the ban of excommunication imposed on him by the Portuguese Sephardic synagogue in Amsterdam? The ban stated that, on account of the terrible heresies he practiced and taught, and other unspecified enormities he had committed, he was to be forever cut off from the people of Israel, from all the tribes of Israel, and no one was permitted to communicate with him in any way, or read anything he had written. Therefore, was there a rabbi anywhere in the world who would solemnize their marriage?

The answer turned out to be yes. They approached Reb Maysheh Rivken, a Litvak, originally from Minsk, who ministered to the few Ashkenazi Jews living in the villages and farmsteads around The Hague. When Spinoza mentioned his excommunication, Reb Maysheh interrupted him.

"The famous *herem*," he said. "Portuguese Sephardim—those goings-on sixteen years ago—tell me, when do you want to get married?"

Nine months later, Eshkeh gave birth to a little boy, Miguel, named after Spinoza's father. Their days were filled with a mixture of joy and anxiety, fully in accordance with the applicable propositions of his book, but it was joy that predominated.

Another letter arrived from Krasivaya, and Eshkeh read it aloud. Little Aydeleh was growing up. She could do somersaults and was trying to walk on her hands. She loved going on outings, the weekly market, the synagogue, her grandfather's workshop, the river bank.

"Gran'ma, I want to explore. Gran'ma, can we go today and explore? But I *want* to explore."

It would be so wonderful if the two of them, Aydeleh and Miguel, could be friends. Eshkeh's face expressed a mixture of pleasure and intense sadness. She was amused by her mother's stories, and at the same time she was overcome by a painful longing to see her again. A new thought came to him. They should move to Krasivaya. Her face would light up, that sudden smile, a thousand expressions would flit across her face, joy, love, gratitude, exuberance, a long, sustained tenderness. But he had to stop himself. He had to think it through before speaking to her. It was sheer passion which gave rise to this idea. Was it at all rational?

So he went for a long walk and thought about it in the light of reason. For Eshkeh, a lonely foreigner far from nearly all the people she cared for, The Hague was a place of much sadness, sapping her energy and zest for life. A move to Krasivaya would certainly bring joy into her life and therefore into his as well. And their little boy, Miguel, named after Spinoza's father, how he would benefit! The outlook was good. All his previous moves had worked out well for him—from Amsterdam to Rijnsburg, from Rijnsburg to Voorburg, from Voorburg to The Hague—therefore, why not from The Hague to Krasivaya? His life there, of course, would, in many ways, take a turn for the worse. Trapped in that small, closed, unsophisticated Litvak shtetl, twelve thousand miles away, far from his friends and the international scientific community, he would be going to synagogue every day and writing his philosophy in secret. But that was a small matter compared to the benefits. Reason, therefore, endorsed the decision which passion had dictated.

But there was yet more of the irrational holding him in its grip. Perhaps his real motivation was quite different. Theatre in the Hague, plays, opera and music, were not enough to ease his arduous intellectual journey and the huge self-control it required. As with his new little niece, perhaps he needed to satisfy his restlessness and "explore." What if that were true? What if all these seemingly rational thoughts of his were no more than a cover for a shallow, crass restlessness? If so, if that were really the case, then—so what! The decision came suddenly, imposing itself on him from outside, beyond his power to control. He would rush back to her and he would say "Eshkeh, Eshkeh, let's move to Krasivaya, we can move tomorrow." And her response—her face would say it all.

They arrived in Krasivaya a few days before Passover. Eshkeh's family welcomed them with all the warmth they had expected, hot meals, delicacies, hugs, stories and a constant stream of visitors. Aydeleh, after several minutes of reticence, climbed up into his arms and from there up onto his shoulders. Her father—his father-in-law—met with a few friends every Monday and Thursday evening to study Talmud. They had attended yeshivas together in their youth and were advanced students. They were meeting that night. Would Spinoza like to join them? Spinoza was exhausted from the trip but eager to go. So he went, and they liked the different and creative ways in which he approached his studies. They were a happy group of men, successful and contented in their careers, respected and influential in the *shtetl*, lovers of both Talmud and good tobacco. It was fun to be with them.

He soon became their informal leader. His reputation spread. Borruch

Shpinozer, *der Naier Rambam,* the new Maimonides. Scholars travelled from all over Liteh to hear his lectures, not only on Talmud, but also on biblical interpretation and philosophy, and, within a fairly short time, the group burgeoned forth into the highly influential Krasivaya Seminary Theologico-Politicus.

Counterpointed against these happy events was the frightening news that kept coming from all around them. Hungarian rebels took some time off from their rebellion to murder most of the Jews in Uhersky Brod. The Jewish quarters in Worms and Prague were destroyed. Mobs attacked Jews in Vilna, Cracow, Posen, Brest-Litovsk, and more. For Spinoza, these stories triggered thoughts about the murderous mob ripping apart the bodies of the De Witt brothers—the triumph of the irrational. If that could happen in The Hague, it could happen anywhere, especially in this primitive place where the Khmelnitsky massacres and the brutish triumphs of the Muscovite army were still within living memory.

Eshkeh spoke with intense urgency.

"We must get out of here."

Did she want to move back to The Hague?

"We must get out of here, you, me, the children, the whole family."

But how?

"And the whole of Krasivaya. We must all get out."

She had a plan. They had to persuade all the Jews of Krasivaya to move to America, immediately; they had to persuade all the Jews, wherever they were.

"You must talk to them. Talk, Borruch, they will listen to you."

This was a different Eshkeh, a different face. How could she speak this way when the wild mindlessness of the false messiah Shabbetai Tzvi was not only within living memory, but still hugely influential?

"I am not Shabbetai Tzvi," he said.

"Of course you're not Shabbetai Tzvi, and that is exactly why it has to be you who must talk to them."

"How does that qualify me to talk to six hundred thousand Jews and … "

"Borruch, please. Hear me. You're a philosopher. You don't need Shabbetai's *kabbalah* to convince them how quickly we must escape. Talk to them, Borruch!"

He struck an oratorical pose. "My friends! My dear friends! Lend me your ears. I will call the ships of Tarshish to bring you from afar, for the Lord your God has glorified you. Isaiah, chapter sixty, verse nine."

"Borruch, please. We can joke later."

"Alright. We can joke later. But if we find that we are not welcome in your promised land, what will we have? Shabbetai Tzvi and Borruch Shpinozer—the famous Failed Messiah and the almost as famous Failed Philosopher."

"But if we don't sail? What if we don't sail quickly enough? In your heart, Borruch, you know exactly what will happen. Hear me, Borruch, you must, *must* talk to them."

The intensity of her face. Her eyes. The drawn muscles around her mouth.

She was right. In his heart he did know it. But this was mere passion, the intensely irrational was dominating his mind, aggravated again by that restless stirring within him—from Amsterdam to Rijnsburg, from Rijnsburg to Voorburg, from Voorburg to The Hague, from the Hague to Krasivaya—and now, excitingly, from Krasivaya to New York.

"We'll talk about it," he said.

They talked, but not in the way he had envisaged. She had a clear plan. New York would be good for the Jews. The Dutch had been there, and now the English, not the Dutch of the Netherlands nor the English of England, but a new breed, with different ideas and different values. There was a risk. Of course there was, there's always risk; we have so little knowledge, and who can know the future?

"We can sail and find we-don't-know-what," she said. "Of course that's true. Borruch, let me talk your language. Hear me. What are the probabilities? Rationally. What are the probabilities?"

Spinoza kept thinking. The issues were becoming clear. Her idea about Americans being a new breed was wrong. Human nature is human nature. But it was nevertheless true that a different kind of society was indeed growing in America, and the outlook for the foreseeable future seemed good. Reason, therefore, was leaning in favor of her emotional outburst, no one could ask for more, and suddenly, there was a happy stirring of emotion rising within him. Life was good. Like little Aydeleh, he wanted to "explore."

The rest is well-known. Spinoza spoke first to the men at the Seminary and then at the synagogue. Eshkeh became the face of the whole project. She joined Spinoza and his Seminary friends in arduous trips across Liteh, from *shtetl* to *shtetl* and city to city. Wherever Litvaks congregated, there they went. One day, perhaps, they would travel to Jews beyond Litvak country. To begin with, she addressed only women's meetings, but then she addressed everyone. She spoke quietly and with carefully controlled emotion. People leaned forward in their seats to listen.

"My dear friends. We are living in a land of cruelty and unrest. All around us there are brutish people doing brutish things—to us and to our brothers and sisters. In the past, here in this land, and now, in lands very close to us. I feel the terrors of this land. Even when there is silence today, I know that tomorrow there will be terror. And after tomorrow, and again after that. There will be fire—*in feier un flam hot men uns gebrent*—in fire and flame they have burnt us. My friends, we must run, far away, we must run, quickly, before it is too late. We have always cried. They burnt us and we cried. Where could we run to? But there is a land that people do run to and have peace. That land is the new land of America. I see it in my mind, a land far away from the brutishness which thrives around us. *Goyim* who have been tortured by other *goyim* find ships, and sail to live there in peace. We also, my friends, we also can live there in peace, we and our children and our children's children. But we must go quickly—quickly before it is too late. Hear me, my friends, my dear, dear friends, the fires are burning. There are ships and more ships, we must sail over the sea to find peace, to a land where we and our children and our children's children can live and not die. Hear me my friends!"

And they heard her. Committees were formed to raise money for the move. Wagons had to be hired, and ships. There was opposition to the project, particularly from some of the rabbis who saw this as no better than the Shabbetai Tzvi debacle. Nevertheless, within less than a year, hundreds of ships were sailing back and forth over the Atlantic. Hardly a Litvak was left behind.

The new Krasivaya Seminary Theologico-Politicus was reopened in a modest house on the southern tip of Manhattan and now, after several moves, it stands on West 89th Street. It's a simple, spacious building, with quiet study rooms and a large library. The Krasivaya synagogue next door, with its inscription, *Deus sive Natura*, in simple Hebrew lettering, is a well-known landmark. The Shpinozerers, as the Litvaks came to be called, became a major force in the professional, scientific and cultural life of the city. Jonas Salk, Albert Einstein, Leonard Bernstein, Aaron Copland and, of course, Marie Curie—after her conversion to Judaism—were some famous Shpinozerers.

When Eshkeh died on her fiftieth birthday, Spinoza's followers marvelled at how he conducted himself. He was, they said, the truest possible exemplar of his philosophy, calmly accepting her death as having flowed, like all else, inevitably from God. His inner thoughts, however, and likewise his philosophy, were more complex than any of his followers knew. Right until the end of his life, he suffered vicious nightmares featuring the mob that attacked the De Witt brothers and the hobo who beat little Misha to death. The more he loved his wife and son, the more obsessed he became with fears that they might soon be injured or die. And when she died, the loss was unbearable. When alone in his bedroom, he would often find himself overcome with weeping. Eshkeh's voice echoed constantly in his memory—the songs she used to sing, and the songs they used to sing together. Her face dominated his imagination. His emotions, stronger than ever, continued overflowing towards her—and also to his son Miguel, who was named after his father.

He should have known that exactly this would happen. His own writings were clear. When you love God, you love what can never change. When you love a human being, your love is tainted by uncertainty and anxiety, a poison shattering your peace of mind and obstructing your love for God. *But is that correct?* He had to think about it. What about his love for Eshkeh and for his son Miguel, who was named after his father? Wasn't all that love in fact the divine pathway to his love for God, the intensity of which went way beyond anything he had previously contemplated? If that were so, how could it fit into the careful schemata of his writings? Hints pointing to his answer appear in his last work, the *Ego Tuque*, published in English as *I and Thou*, and the scholarly literature on this subject is still growing.

At his request, lovingly accepted by all his followers, Vermeer's famous portrait of Eshkeh contemplatively reading a book hangs in the synagogue where the Torah scrolls are kept, inside the *orren kaydesh*—the face that launched a thousand ships, and so very much more.

PEDANTIC NOTES

The Real and the Alternate History:

1. Spinoza was born in Amsterdam in 1632. He moved from Amsterdam to Rijnsburg, then to Voorburg, then to The Hague where he died in 1677. His contemporaries saw him as particularly charming and even-tempered. He was an ascetic but allowed himself moderate pleasures including music, art, social intercourse and perhaps also theatre. He sketched good portraits, but none survive. He never married.

2. The *herem* (writ of excommunication) was imposed on him in 1656.

3. Shabbetai Tzvi (1626-1676), was a kabbalist and false messiah whose influence remained strong even after his expedition to Palestine failed.

4. In the alternate history, Spinoza, alas, misquotes Isaiah.

Kaddish for Stalin

Allan Dyen-Shapiro

Every year since 1946, when David's dad was six years old, he had commemorated the death of his hero, Joseph Stalin. At eighty-five, Dad wasn't going to break his tradition.

"But Stalin wasn't a Jew." David sweated in the poorly air-conditioned building, so he loosened his necktie. For balance, he grasped the gate to the spartan room where his father sat on a wooden chair. The place reeked of ammonia floor cleaner.

"You think I don't know this?" Dad hacked into a handkerchief and wiped his brow with the sleeve of his work shirt. When Dad recovered, he glared at David, made a clucking sound, and rolled his eyes. "Doesn't matter. Get me a damn *Yahrzeit* candle."

The man hadn't mellowed with age. "It's against the rules."

The excuse elicited a stern expression. "You're the big *macher*. Go talk to your friend, the manager of this establishment. He was willing to spy on me for you."

Not exactly. But Dad was correct—Moshe would give permission. David wouldn't ask. It would delay getting Dad home to his comfortable sofa and his blood pressure medication.

"You return after five years away, you ask what you can do for me, and I tell you. Such a wealthy capitalist with all his Chinese banker friends, and he can't buy his father a candle?"

David's head throbbed. He tasted bile. "No, Dad."

Dad shrugged his shoulders, frowned, and thrust his chin forward in defiance.

Did David even have to explain? "It's a fire hazard. You're in an enclosed space. The guards won't let you light a candle in your jail cell."

✡

The previous day, David had arrived by train in Birobidzhan, capital of the Jewish Autonomous Oblast, after catching the morning's flight from Beijing into Khabarovsk. He had grown up here, so it made sense that he, rather than his partners Mengyao or Xiaojian, attend the opening of their first restaurant in Siberia. Besides, neither of his partners spoke Yiddish.

As he disembarked from the train, David's cell phone rang. The name listed on the caller ID brought a smile: David's boyhood friend Moshe Feinberg. But the Chief of Police wasn't calling him to be sociable.

"David, there's been vandalism at your greenhouses. The chillers for buildings two and five were smashed. All of the plants died."

"Crap," David said. "You think it's one of the workers?" He'd been so beneficent, steering the jobs to displaced farmers, and this was how they repaid him?

"Not sure. There's been talk of unionization. You brought big changes—they've only known collectives. Some are complaining about the wages."

Ingrates. They would rather be unemployed?

The monsoons hadn't come for four years. The absence of rain hadn't dictated David's business plan for the region—they had invested in greenhouses because of the freezing winters—but it meant no local farmer could supply his restaurant. The cost of flying produce from Beijing would eliminate profits.

After seating himself on a bench opposite the ticket counter, David pulled a tablet computer from his satchel. From the company's homepage, he navigated to the greenhouse management software and found rooms dedicated to scallions, garlic, green beans, chili peppers, and cabbage. Greenhouse five backed up greenhouse two; none of the other seven grew any of these crops.

The saboteur knew what he was doing. Lack of these five ingredients made virtually every dish in the chain's Szechuan-Korean fusion menu impossible. "Any suspects?"

"The attack was at night when nobody was around, so no witnesses."

And had there been some, the anti-capitalist agitators would have pressured them to keep mum. "So what will you do to catch the criminals?"

Moshe's voice rose in pitch. "Well, we are stretched a bit thin—"

"We'll pay for it." No need to beat around the bush. If the depressed economy in Siberia meant it took additional expenditure to open the restaurant, so be it.

Birobidzhan's refusal to accept the Chinese model—communist in name; capitalist in practice—complicated economic recovery. David and his partners came, bringing jobs, and the locals turned up their noses. Stubbornly, the region clung to its communal farms and light industrial collectives established in the time of Joseph Stalin and favored by Stalin's protégé Andrei Zhdanov, who had assumed leadership following Stalin's untimely death from a stroke. David's homeland—indeed, the entire Soviet Union—would at least have de-Stalinized had either Khrushchev or Malenkov won out in their power struggle with Zhdanov. Instead, both died from unnatural causes, and Zhdanov ruled into his eighties. Only recently had the leadership in the Jewish Autonomous Oblast decided to pursue yuan over rubles, extending tax credits to capture investment from Beijing and Harbin-based businesses like David's.

Moshe agreed to muster the necessary manpower for a patrol.

That evening, Moshe picked David up from his hotel and drove him out to Valdgeym, formerly the location of the region's oldest collective farm. After years of drought and pest-related crop failure, the venture had dissolved, leaving the farmers penniless. David's company had leased the land from the state-run holding enterprise for forfeited property.

They left the car on the side of the road and trudged over the hill leading to the site. Moshe pulled a spray bottle from a pouch clipped to his belt and pushed it into David's hands. "The mosquitoes will love the smell of your fancy hotel soap."

"Already put insect repellant on." His friend thought David wouldn't remember? Back in high school, they had walked home together many times after attending an evening play at the Kaganovich Theatre or a concert at the community center. While boys in China might have dabbed on a bit of cologne, the cloying smell of DEET had been the perfume of kids from Birobidzhan. Sure, the insects hadn't been as prevalent since the drought, but with global warming, some of them now carried West Nile Virus.

"Keep the bottle. You'll need more soon."

Moshe had tried to dissuade him from accompanying the patrol, but David needed to see that his money was well spent. Someone who had taken such care in selecting the most damaging targets did so to send a message. This person would show up that evening to see the dead plants, confirming receipt of the "communiqué." Only with the man paying the bills present would the watch for the saboteur last until morning.

"The boss goes out with the beat cops?" David asked.

"I'm only here to escort our 'foreign' guest. The mayor insisted." The gravel road crunched under their work boots. "From now on, no talking. Our trap won't work if the criminal hears us kibitzing." Moshe pointed at a tree. The men approached and hid in its shadow. From this vantage point, they could see the chillers and the access route for the entire complex. Moshe had said five other officers would walk the perimeter of the facility.

For four hours, nothing moved. The wind rustled, the cooling system motors hummed, and mosquitoes buzzed. David's back ached. His eyelids grew heavy.

A blast from Moshe's radio jolted David out of semi-slumber. "Got him," a staticky voice said. "Snooping around. Shining a flashlight through a window."

"You're sure it's the sledgehammer guy?" Moshe paused, awaiting a response.

"The shoe prints matched those from yesterday. And he confessed. We're bringing him in."

"Excellent. Thanks." Moshe clipped the radio to his belt and stood. "I'm calling it a night. Let me drive you back to your hotel. I'll get the report from the arresting officer tomorrow. Swing by after nine, and I'll fill you in on the details."

In the morning, David wolfed down the hotel breakfast—pickled herring, chopped liver on toasted rye bread, strong coffee—and walked the fifteen minutes to the police station. He could have asked the desk clerk to summon a cab, but after five years, he wanted to see the statue of Tevye, the fictional milkman, in the town center. He hadn't read Sholom Aleichem since high school, but the public art, a gift from the Chinese government, had always brought a sense of home.

Much had changed since David's youth. Far more cars whizzed along the downtown streets. Growth meant potential customers to eat at his restaurant, so David welcomed it. Birobidzhan had grown from a hardscrabble village of wooden buildings in Stalin's time to the sleepy hamlet of David's boyhood in the 1970s to a bustling regional capital, crowded with concrete block architecture. The town remained proletarian while revering its heritage as the centre for Yiddish cultural autonomy and socialism envisioned in the Stalin-endorsed propaganda that had first drawn Jews in the 1930s. By 2025, half a million, mostly workers and farmers, struggled, like Tevye, to eke out a living in this mountainous enclave with its rocky soil and terrible climate.

So why did they stay? David strolled right by the answers: the signs—for a barber, a butcher, a bagel shop—all written in Yiddish. Conversation in the patio of the coffee shop he passed—four old men debated the merits of the new stage adaptation of a novel by Bergelson, the Yiddish writer for whom David was named. The smells—the aroma of fresh challah wafted from a bakery, and that of pungent vinegar, from the barrels of a pickle stand. Aside from a few ultra-Orthodox neighborhoods in Brooklyn and Tel Aviv, in the rest of the world, Yiddish language and culture had withered away. David's crazy father would add that socialism had died in Israel and had never lived in America, and capitalism was antithetical to Jewish values. *Bah.*

Stalin had established the Jewish Autonomous Oblast on the Chinese border not because he loved Yiddish culture but to settle the hinterland. When Sino-Soviet tensions ramped up in the late 1940s, Zhdanov lavished incentives on Moscow Jews willing to move there, and the population surged. Now, in an irony Sholom Aleichem would have appreciated, the town had developed a taste for Asian food. Or so David and his business partners hoped.

Upon reaching the brick building with a sign proclaiming it the headquarters of the Directorate for Internal Affairs, David climbed the stairs and let himself in through the glass doors. When told to state his business by the guard, he dropped Moshe's name and, after a pat down, was shepherded to Moshe's office.

Without getting up from his desk, Moshe raised his eyebrows and shook his head.

"What?" David asked.

"Your *meshuggeneh* father." Rather than explain, Moshe led David in silence down to the holding cells. After an hour of accusations and recriminations, David acquiesced to his father's request and left for the grocery store to buy a *Yahrzeit* candle.

✡

"Here you go. And I also bought a book of matches." The ibuprofen David had taken had yet to kick in. His head throbbed. But if it meant appeasing Dad, he had been willing to suffer the glares of shoppers and clerks he'd encountered. With the number of homeless people sleeping in the town square, some resentment of anyone wearing an expensive suit was inevitable.

Dad placed the candle in a corner of the cell, against the wall, and struck a match. "So, Mister Rootless Cosmopolitan, you want to say Kaddish with me?"

Unbelievable. David crossed his arms and paced outside Dad's cell. "You're using an antisemite's favorite slur and praying over him? You, the one who taught me religion was the opiate of the masses?"

"*Feh!*" Dad pulled a chair up to the bars. "The purges of '36 only went after bourgeois elements. Stalin founded our homeland so Jews would have a place of their own. So they wouldn't flock to decadent capitals like Paris or London or New York. Even he didn't anticipate the lure of China for Jewish boys. I'm surprised you can still speak Yiddish. By the way, how's your *faygele* boyfriend?"

"Husband. We got married four years ago in Harbin, right after China legalized gay marriage. It was the closest big city to his parents' farm." David hadn't seen the point in inviting a father who disdained him to the wedding.

"*Oy-yoy-yoy!*" Dad shook his head, tugged on his ear. "His folks okay with a mixed marriage?"

They hadn't objected to David's Jewish ancestry. However, Confucian notions of a filial duty to contribute children that persisted in the countryside of Heilongjiang Province left them sad. They had the class not to mention it, but David knew. His father wouldn't have been so polite. It was a bit ridiculous. Marrying at age fifty, even had he been straight and attracted to a Jewish woman, he might not have fathered children. "They were happy their son was marrying someone who had grown up on a collective farm. You'd approve of their politics."

Dad offered a tight-lipped smile. "Can I borrow your cell phone? The storm troopers have taken mine."

Rather than argue about the pejorative, David handed it over. "Who do you want to call?" He grasped one of the metal bars with each hand and leaned against the gate.

Not looking up, Dad tapped on the touchscreen. "Downloading the Find-a-Minyan app. I need eight more men to say Kaddish. Nine, if you can't remember the words."

This was too much. "Really, Dad?"

"Some of us honor our heritage. Your homeland is more than just a business opportunity."

It wouldn't even be much of a business opportunity if David couldn't keep his father from destroying the greenhouses. With how frail Dad appeared, it surprised David that the eighty-five-year-old could even lift a sledgehammer, although the night in jail could account for his haggard appearance. Better to play along. "Fine. I'll be part of your minyan."

The cell phone beeped. "We have ten. *Yisgadal v'yiskadash …* "

When finished with the prayer, both men stared at the candle as it burned, inhaling the sweet scent of melting wax. Dad broke the silence. "So, you remember the Kaddish. If only you had remembered to be a socialist, you wouldn't be bringing your Chinese money home to build greenhouses. Your capitalist friends have ruined Jewish agriculture. We can't compete."

"Capitalism? Not the drought? The problem here is climate change." His father understood agricultural science. Why would Dad side with Luddites and take up a sledgehammer?

Agriculture and food products had dominated the Oblast's economy from the get-go. The homeless David had seen had probably been farmers. Their lives had been torn apart, and damaged men lash out. Perhaps, one of them put Dad up to this. It was ironic that, even here, they would scapegoat the Jewish businessman. But his own son's greenhouses? What message did Dad think his actions sent?

"I've been wondering about one thing. Maybe you can enlighten me. You dedicated half of your space to growing potatoes. I don't know what this *fakakta* fusion cuisine is, but Szechuan food uses potatoes. So does Korean food. Not that many potatoes. You're not opening a McDonalds, although I imagine you considered becoming Birobidzhan's burger and French fry king. *Nu*? What gives?"

How to answer? The issue was tricky. Lacking a better idea, David opted for the truth. "Hand me the cell phone."

When Dad complied, David brought up his company website, navigated through several hyperlinks, and touched a button on the browser to call the plug-in for Mandarin-to-Yiddish translation. "A side venture." He returned the device to his father. "What do you see?"

Not what he was expecting, apparently. His brow furrowed, and his hands shook. "Why did you put your mother's picture on a Chinese website?"

"I used her recipe."

"For Chinese food?"

"For latkes." David remained silent, shifting his weight back and forth between his legs, while his father perused the site.

When Dad returned his gaze to David, he raised his eyebrows. "Your hoity-toity clientele go for Jewish peasant food?"

"No. It's a separate enterprise. Food trucks at construction sites and factories. The Chinese workers love it. We call them Jewish pancakes."

Dad chortled until it segued into a hacking cough. After recovering, he pointed a finger at David. "So you *have* come home to sell greasy, fried potatoes in the *shtetl*, after all. It's not Chanukah. You think anyone will buy them?"

Did he detect a grudging pride in his father's voice? "This Jewish boy is doing pretty well selling stir fry to the Chinese," David said.

Dad nodded, returned his gaze to the phone. His lips turned up in a half-smile. "What's this link to? The green button that says stories."

"Try it." The lawyers had fretted over copyright, but in the end, David had overcome their objections. David's chest tightened. He held his breath.

Dad's eyes grew wide. His hands gripped the phone so tightly the muscles in his arms tremored.

"You did the translations yourself?"

Once Dad made eye contact, David nodded, stood up straight. "I kept the mimeographs you'd given me when I was a kid. I scanned them before I translated them. I can send you the files if you like. We printed a few hundred words of each on the back of paper we used to wrap the latkes. The customers were reading them, emailing our office, and begging for the endings. So I put them on the website."

Dad had embodied Birobidzhan's Stalinist ideal: a worker who toiled in the fields and returned home to write fiction, in Yiddish, by candlelight. David had rejected this identity, so no matter what he achieved, Dad had treated him like a failure. But David had never lost respect for his father's accomplishments.

Dad rose, paced the cell, stared at the flickering flame. "So workers are eating your mother's food and reading my stories?"

"Yes, Dad." With both hands, David grasped the bars and leaned forward, his face half-inside the cell. His heart pounded.

A grin spread across Dad's visage. "If I let you spring me from this place, can you take me to your restaurant? I haven't had your mother's latkes since she passed twenty years ago. You think your cooks can make them for me?"

It was David's turn to smile. "I gave them the day off. But I can whip you up a batch."

"I'd like that." Dad's hands grasped one of David's. The old man shed a tear. As did David.

The candle continued to burn.

Shtetl Days

Harry Turtledove

Jakub Shlayfer opened the door and walked outside to go to work. Before he could shut it again, his wife called after him: *"Alevai* it should be a good day! We really need the *gelt!"*

"Alevai, Bertha. *Omayn,"* Jakub agreed. The door was already shut by then, but what difference did that make? It wasn't as if he didn't know they were poor. His lean frame, the rough edge on the brim of his broad, black hat, his threadbare, long black coat, and the many patches on his boot soles all told the same story.

But then, how many Jews in Wawolnice weren't poor? The only one Jakub could think of was Shmuel Grynszpan, the undertaker. *His* business was as solid and certain as the laws of God. Everybody else's? Groszy and zlotych always came in too slowly and went out too fast.

He stumped down the unpaved street, skirting puddles. Not all the boot patches were everything they might have been. He didn't want to get his feet wet. He could have complained to Mottel Cohen, but what was the use? Mottel did what Mottel could do. And it wasn't as if Wawolnice had—or needed—two cobblers. It you listened to Mottel's kvetching, the village didn't need one cobbler often enough.

The watery spring morning promised more than the day was likely to deliver. The sun was out, but clouds to the west warned it was liable to rain some more. Well, it wouldn't snow again till fall. That was something. Jakub skidded on mud and almost fell. It might be something, but it wasn't enough.

Two-story houses with steep, wood-shingled roofs crowded the street from both sides and caused it to it twist here and turn there. They made it hard for the sun to get down to the street and dry up the mud. More Jews came out of the houses to go to their jobs. The men dressed pretty much like Jakub. Some of the younger ones wore cloth caps instead of broad-brimmed hats. Chasidim, by contrast, had fancy *shtreimels*, with the brims made from mink.

A leaning fence made Jakub go out toward the middle of the narrow street. Most of the graying planks went up and down. For eight or ten feet, though, boards running from side to side patched a break. They were as ugly as the patches on his boots. A hooded crow perched on the fence jeered at Jakub.

He had to push in tight to the fence because an old couple from the country were pushing a handcart toward him, and making heavy going of it. The crow flew away. Wicker baskets in the handcart were piled high with their fiery horseradish, milder red radishes, onions, leeks, and kale.

"Maybe you'll see my wife today, Moishe," Jakub called.

"Here's hoping," the old man said. His white beard spilled in waves halfway down his chest. He wore a brimless fur cap that looked something like an upside-down chamber pot.

OTHER COVENANTS

Chamber pots.... The air was thick with them. Shmuel Grynszpan had piped water in his house, as his wife never tired of boasting. Not many other Jews—and precious few Poles—in Wawolnice did. They said—whoever *they* were—you stopped noticing how a village stank once you'd lived in it for a little while. As he often did, Jakub wished *they* knew what they were talking about.

Signs above the tavern, the dry-goods store, the tailor's shop, Jakub's own sorry little business, and the handful of others Wawolnice boasted were in both Polish and Yiddish. Two different alphabets running two different ways... If that didn't say everything that needed saying about how Jews and Poles got along—or didn't get along—Jakub couldn't imagine what would.

He used a fat iron key to open the lock to his front door. The hinges creaked when he pulled it toward him. *Have to oil that,* he thought. Somewhere in his shop, he had a copper oilcan. If he could find it, if he remembered to look for it.... If he didn't, neither the world nor even the door was likely to come to an end.

He was a grinder. Anything that was dull, he could sharpen: knives, scissors, straight razors (for the Poles—almost all the Jewish men wore beards), plowshares, harvester blades. He was a locksmith. He repaired clocks—and anything else with complicated gearing. He made umbrellas out of wire and scrap cloth, and fixed the ones he'd made before. He sold patent medicines, and brewed them up from this and that in the dark, musty back room. He would turn his hand to almost anything that might make a zloty.

Lots of things might make a zloty. Hardly anything, outside of Grynszpan's business, reliably did. Wawolnice wasn't big enough to need a full-time grinder or locksmith or repairman or umbrella maker or medicine mixer. Even doing all of them at once, Jakub didn't bring home enough to keep Bertha happy.

Of course, he could have brought home more than the undertaker made and still not kept his wife happy. Some people weren't happy unless they were unhappy. There was a paradox worthy of the Talmud—unless you knew Bertha.

Across the way, the little boys in Alter Kaczyne's *kheder* began chanting the *alef-bays*. While Alter worked with them, their older brothers and cousins would wrestle with Hebrew vocabulary and grammar on their own. Or maybe the *melamed's* father would lend a hand. Chaim Kaczyne coughed all the time and didn't move around very well any more, but his wits were still clear.

Jakub went to work on a clock a Polish woman had brought in. His hands were quick and clever. Scars seamed them; you couldn't be a grinder without things slipping once in a while. And dirt and grease had permanent homes under his nails and in the creases on top of his fingers. But hands were to work with, and work with them he did.

"Here we are," he muttered: a broken tooth on one of the gears. He rummaged through a couple of drawers to see if he had one that matched. And sure enough! The replacement went into the clock. He didn't throw out the damaged one. He rarely threw anything out. He'd braze on a new tooth and use the gear in some less demanding place.

The woman came in not long after he finished the clock. She wore her blond hair in a short bob; her skirt rose halfway to her knees. You'd never catch a Jewish woman in Wawolnice in anything so scandalously short. She nodded to find the clock ticking again. They haggled a little over the price. Jakub had warned her it would go up if he had to put in a new gear. She didn't want to remember. She was shaking her head when she smacked coins down on the counter and walked out.

He eyed—not to put too fine a point on it, he leered at—her shapely calves as her legs twinkled away. He was a man, after all. He was drawn to smooth flesh the way a butterfly was drawn to flowers. No wonder the women of his folk covered themselves from head to foot. No wonder Jewish wives wore *sheitels* and head scarves. They didn't want to put themselves on display like that. But the Poles were different. The Poles didn't care.

So what? The Poles were *goyim*.

He sharpened one of his own knives, a tiny, precise blade. He often did that when he had nothing else going on. He owned far and away the sharpest knives in the village. He would have been happier if they were duller, so long as it was because he stayed too busy to work on them.

A kid carrying a basket of bagels stuck his head in the door. Jakub spent a few groszy to buy one. The boy hurried away, short pants showing off his skinny legs. He didn't have a police license to peddle, so he was always on the dodge.

"*Barukh atah Adonai, elohaynu melekh ha-olam, ha-motzi lekhem min ha-aretz*," Jakub murmured. *Blessed art Thou, O Lord our God, King of the Universe, Who makest bread to come forth from the earth*. Only after the prayer did he eat the bagel.

Yiddish. Polish. Hebrew. Aramaic. He had them all. No one who knew Yiddish didn't also know German. A man who spoke Polish could, at need, make a stab at Czech or Ruthenian or Russian. All the *Yehudim* in Wawolnice were scholars, even if they didn't always think of themselves so.

Back to sharpening his own knives. It had the feel of another slow day. Few days here were anything else. The ones that were, commonly weren't good days.

After a while, the front door creaked open again. Jakub jumped to his feet in surprise and respect. "Reb Eliezer!" he exclaimed. "What can I do for you today?" Rabbis, after all, had knives and scissors that needed sharpening just like other men's.

But Eliezer said, "We were talking about serpents the other day." He had a long, pale, somber face, with rusty curls sticking out from under his hat brim, a wispy copper beard streaked with gray, and cat-green eyes.

"Oh, yes. Of course." Jakub nodded. They *had* been speaking of serpents, and all sorts of other Talmudic *pilpul*, in the village's *bet ha-midrash* attached to the little *shul*. The smell of the books in the tall case there, the aging leather of their bindings, the paper on which they were printed, even the dust that shrouded the seldom-used volumes, was part and parcel of life in Wawolnice.

So . . . No business—no money-making business—now. Bertha would not

OTHER COVENANTS

be pleased to see this. She would loudly not be pleased to see it, as a matter of fact. But she would also be secretly proud because the rabbi chose her husband, a grinder of no particular prominence, with whom to split doctrinal hairs.

"Obviously," Reb Eliezer said in portentous tones, "the serpent is unclean for Jews to eat or to handle after it is dead. It falls under the ban of Leviticus 11:29, 11:30, and 11:42."

"Well, that may be so, but I'm not so sure," Jakub answered, pausing to light a stubby, twisted cigar. He offered one to Reb Eliezer, who accepted with a murmur of thanks. After blowing out harsh smoke, the grinder went on, "I don't think those verses are talking about serpents at all."

Eliezer's gingery eyebrows leaped. "How can you say such a thing?" he demanded, wagging a forefinger under Jakub's beaky nose. "Verse 42 says, 'Whatsoever goeth upon the belly, and whatsoever goeth upon all four, or whatsoever hath more feet among all creeping things that creep upon the earth, them ye shall not eat; for they are an abomination.'" Like Jakub, he could go from Yiddish to Biblical Hebrew while hardly seeming to notice he was switching languages.

Jakub shrugged a stolid shrug. "I don't hear anything there that talks about serpents. Things that go on all fours, things with lots of legs. I don't want to eat a what-do-you-call-it—a centipede, I mean. Who would? Even a *goy* wouldn't want to eat a centipede . . . I don't think." He shrugged again, as if to say no Jew counted on anything that had to do with *goyim*.

"'Whatsoever goeth upon the belly . . . among all the creeping things that creep upon the earth,'" Reb Eliezer repeated. "And this same phrase also appears in the twenty-ninth verse, which says, 'These also shall be unclean unto you among the creeping things that creep upon the earth; —'"

"' —the weasel, and the mouse, and the tortoise after his kind.'" Jakub took up the quotation, and went on into the next verse: "'And the ferret, and the chameleon, and the lizard, and the snail, and the mole.' I don't see a word in there about serpents." He blew out another stream of smoke, not quite at the rabbi.

Eliezer affected not to notice. "Since when is a serpent not a creeping thing that goeth upon its belly? Will you tell me it doesn't?"

"It doesn't *now*," Jakub admitted.

"It did maybe yesterday?" Eliezer suggested sarcastically.

"Not yesterday. Not the day before yesterday, either," Jakub said. "But when the Lord, blessed be His name, made the serpent, He made it to speak and to walk on its hind legs like a man. What else does that? Maybe He made it in His own image."

"But God told the serpent, 'Thou art cursed above all cattle, and above every beast in the field: upon thy belly shalt thou go, and dust shalt thou eat all the days of thy life.'"

"So He changed it a little. So what?" Jakub said. Reb Eliezer's eyebrow jumped again at *a little*, but he held his peace. The grinder went on, "Besides, the serpent is to blame for mankind's fall. Shouldn't we pay him back by cooking him in a stew?"

"Maybe we should, maybe we shouldn't. But that argument isn't Scriptural," the rabbi said stiffly.

"Well, what if it isn't? How about this . . . ?" Jakub went off on another tangent from the Torah.

They fenced with ideas and quotations through another cigar apiece. At last, Reb Eliezer threw his pale hands in the air and exclaimed, "In spite of the plain words of Leviticus, you come up with a hundred reasons why the accursed serpent ought to be as kosher as a cow!"

"Oh, not a hundred reasons. Maybe a dozen." Jakub was a precise man, as befitted a trade where a slip could cost a finger. But he also had his own kind of pride: "Give me enough time, and I suppose I could come up with a hundred."

A sort of a smile lifted one corner of Reb Eliezer's mouth. "Then perhaps now you begin to see why Rabbi Jokhanan of Palestine, of blessed memory, said hundreds of years ago that no man who could not do what you are doing had the skill he needed to open a capital case."

As it so often did, seemingly preposterous Talmudic *pilpul* came back to the way Jews were supposed to live their lives. "I should hope so," Jakub answered. "You have to begin a capital case with the reasons for acquitting whoever is on trial. If you can't find those reasons, someone else had better handle the case."

"I agree with you." The rabbi wagged his forefinger at Jakub once more. "You won't hear me tell you that very often."

"*Gevalt!* I should hope not!" Jakub said in mock horror.

Reb Eliezer's eyes twinkled. "And so I had better go," he continued, as if the grinder hadn't spoken. "The Lord bless you and keep you."

"And you, Reb," Jakub replied. Eliezer dipped his head. He walked out of the shop and down the street. A man came in wanting liniment for a horse. Jakub compounded some. It made his business smell of camphor and turpentine the rest of the day. It also put a couple of more zlotych in his pocket. Bertha would be . . . less displeased.

Shadows stretched across Wawolnice. Light began leaking out of the sky. The rain had held off, anyhow. People headed home from their work. Jakub was rarely one of the first to call it a day. Before long, though, the light coming in through the dusty front windows got too dim to use. Time to quit, all right.

He closed up and locked the door. He'd done some tinkering with the lock. He didn't think anybody not a locksmith could quietly pick it. Enough brute force, on the other hand . . . Jews in Poland understood all they needed to about brute force, and about who had enough of it. Jakub Shlayfer's mobile mouth twisted. Polish Jews didn't, never had, and never would.

He walked home through the gathering gloom. "Stinking Yid!" The *shrei* in Polish pursued him. His shoulders wanted to sag under its weight, and the weight of a million more like it. He didn't, he wouldn't, let them. If the *mamzrim* saw they'd hurt you, they won. As long as a rock didn't follow, he

OTHER COVENANTS

was all right. And if one did, he could duck or dodge. He hoped.

No rocks tonight. Candles and kerosene lamps sent dim but warm glows out into the darkness. If you looked at the papers, electricity would come to the village soon. Then again, if you looked at the papers and believed everything you read in them, you were too dumb to live.

Bertha met him at the door. *Sheitel*, headscarf over it, long black dress . . . She still looked good to him. She greeted him with, "So what were you and Reb Eliezer going on about today?"

"Serpents," Jakub answered.

"*Pilpul.*" His wife's sigh said she'd hoped for better, even if she hadn't expected it. "I don't suppose he had any paying business."

"*He* didn't, no," the grinder admitted. "But Barlicki's wife came in for her clock. I had to swap out a gear, so I charged her more. I told her before that I would, but she still didn't like it."

"And God forbid you should make Barlicki's wife unhappy." Bertha knew he thought the Polish woman was pretty, then. How long would she go on giving him a hard time about that? The next couple of days ought to be interesting. Not necessarily enjoyable, but interesting.

He did what he could to show Bertha he appreciated her. Nostrils twitching, he said, "What smells so good?"

"Soup with chicken feet," she replied, sounding slightly softened. "Cabbage, carrots, onions, mangel-wurzel . . ."

Mangel-wurzel was what you used when you couldn't afford turnips. Chicken feet were what you put in soup when you wanted it to taste like meat but you couldn't afford much of the genuine article. You could gnaw on them, worrying off a little skin or some of the tendons that would have led to the drumsticks. You wouldn't rise up from the table happy, but you might rise up happier.

He stepped past her and into the small, crowded front room, with its rammed-earth floor and battered, shabby furniture. The little brass *mezuzah* still hung on the doorframe outside. He rarely gave it a conscious thought. Most of the time he only noticed it when it wasn't there, so to speak. Stealing *mezuzahs* was one way Polish kids found to aggravate their Jewish neighbors. Not only that, but they might get a couple of groszy for the brass.

Bertha closed the front door behind him and let the bar fall into its bracket. The sound of the stout plank thudding into place seemed very final, as if it put a full stop to the day. And so—again, in a manner of speaking—it did.

✡

Jakub walked over to the closet door. That the cramped space had room for a closet seemed something not far from miraculous. He wasn't inclined to complain, though. Oh, no—on the contrary. Neither was Bertha, who came up smiling to stand beside him as he opened the door.

Then they walked into the closet. They could do that now. The day was over. Jakub shoved coats and dresses out of the way. They smelled of wool and old sweat. Bertha flicked a switch as she closed the closet door. A ceiling light came on.

"Thanks, sweetie," Jakub said. "That helps."

In back of the clothes stood another door, this one painted battleship gray. In German, large, neatly stenciled black letters on the hidden doorway warned AUTHORIZED PERSONNEL ONLY. Being an authorized person, Jakub hit the numbers that opened that door. It showed a concrete stairway leading down. The walls to the descending corridor were also pale gray. Blue-tinged light from fluorescent tubes in ceiling fixtures streamed into the closet.

Jakub started down the stairs. Bertha was an authorized person, too. She followed him, pausing only to close the hidden door behind them. A click announced it had locked automatically, as it was designed to do. The grinder and his wife left Wawolnice behind.

Men and women in grimy Jewish costumes and about an equal number dressed as Poles from the time between the War of Humiliation and the triumphant War of Retribution ambled along an underground hallway. They chatted and chattered and laughed, as people who've worked together for a long time will at the end of a day.

Arrows on the walls guided them toward their next destination. Explaining the arrows were large words beside them: TO THE SHOWERS. The explanation was about as necessary as a second head, but Germans had a habit of overdesigning things.

Veit Harlan shook himself like a dog that had just scrambled out of a muddy creek. That was how he felt, too. Like any actor worth his salt, he immersed himself in the roles he played. When the curtain came down on another day, he always needed a little while to remember he wasn't Jakub Shlayfer, a hungry Jew in a Polish village that had vanished from the map more than a hundred years ago.

He wasn't the only one, either. He would have been amazed if he had been. People heading for the showers to clean up after their latest shift in Wawolnice went right on throwing around the front vowels and extra-harsh gutturals of Yiddish. Only little by little did they start using honest German again.

When they did. The fellow who played Reb Eliezer—his real name was Ferdinand Marian—and a pimply *yeshiva-bukher* (well, the pimply performer impersonating a young *yeshiva-bukher*) went right on with whatever disputation Eliezer had found after leaving Jakub's shop. They went right on throwing Hebrew and Aramaic around, too. And the reb and the kid with zits both kept up a virtuoso display of finger-wagging.

"They'd better watch that," Veit murmured to the woman who had been Bertha a moment before.

"I know." She nodded. She was really Kristina Söderbaum. They were married to each other out in the *Reich* as well as in the village. The people who ran Wawolnice used real couples whenever they could. They claimed it made the performances more convincing. If that meant Veit got to work alongside his wife, he wouldn't complain.

The guy who played Alter the *melamed* caught up to Veit and Kristi from behind. In the wider world, he was Wolf Albach-Retty. "Hey, Veit. Did you see the gal who flashed her tits at me this morning?" he exclaimed.

"No! I wish I would have," Harlan answered. His wife planted an elbow in his ribs. Ignoring her, he went on, "When did that happen?"

"It was early—not long after the village opened up," Wolf said.

"Too bad. I was working on that clock for a lot of the morning. I guess I didn't pick the right time to look up."

"A bunch of the kids did. Boy, they paid even less attention to me than usual after that," Albach-Retty said. Veit laughed. The *melamed* rolled his eyes. "It's funny for you. It's funny for the damn broad, too. But I'm the guy who had to deal with it. When I was *potching* the little bastards, I was *potching* 'em good." He mimed swatting a backside.

"Nothing they haven't got from you before," Veit said, which was also true. Everything the villagers did in Wawolnice was real. They pretended the curious people who came to gawk at them weren't there. But how were you supposed to pretend a nice set of tits wasn't there (and Veit would have bet it was a nice set—otherwise the woman wouldn't have shown them off)?

"Worse than usual, I tell you." Wolf leaned toward self-pity.

"You'll live. So will they," Veit said. "If they don't like it, let 'em file a complaint with the SPCA." Kristi giggled, which was what he'd hoped for. After a moment, Wolf Albach-Retty laughed, too. That was a bonus.

The corridor to the showers split, one arrow marked MEN, the other WOMEN. Veit stripped off the heavy, baggy, dark, sweaty outfit of a Wawolnice Jew with a sigh of relief. He chucked it into a cubbyhole and scratched. The village wasn't a hundred percent realistic. They did spray it to keep down the bugs. You weren't supposed to pick up fleas or lice or bedbugs, even if you were portraying a lousy, flea-bitten kike.

Theory was wonderful. Veit had found himself buggy as new software more than once coming off a shift. So had Kristi. So had just about all the other performers. It was a hazard of the trade, like a director who happened to be an oaf.

He didn't discover any uninvited guests tonight. Hot water and strong soap wiped away the stinks from Wawolnice. He took showering with a bunch of other men completely for granted. He'd started as a *Pimpf* in the *Hitler Jugend*, he'd kept it up through the Labor Service and his two-year hitch in the *Wehrmacht*, and now he was doing it some more. So what? Skin was skin, and he didn't get a charge out of guys.

Reb Eliezer and the *yeshiva-bukher* were still arguing about the Talmud in the shower. They were both circumcised. Quite a few of the men playing Jews were. Prizing realism as it did, the Reenactors' Guild gave you a raise if you were willing to have the operation. Veit kept all his original equipment. He didn't need the cash that badly, and Kristina liked him fine the way he was.

He grabbed a cotton towel, dried himself off, and tossed the towel into a very full bin. A bath attendant in coveralls—a scared, scrawny Slavic *Untermensch* from beyond the Urals—wheeled the bin away and brought out an empty one. Veit noticed him hardly more than he did the tourists who came to stare at Wawolnice and see what Eastern Europe had been like before the *Grossdeutsches Reich* cleaned things up.

You were trained not to notice tourists. You were trained to pretend they weren't there, and not to react when they did stuff (though Veit had never had anybody flash tits at him). It was different with the bath attendant. Did you notice a stool if you didn't intend to sit down on it? More like that.

Veit spun the combination dial on his locker. He put on his own clothes: khaki cotton slacks, a pale green polo shirt, and a darker green cardigan sweater. Synthetic socks and track shoes finished the outfit. It was much lighter, much softer, and much more comfortable than his performing costume.

He had to twiddle his thumbs for a couple of minutes before Kristi came down the corridor from her side of the changing area. Women always took longer getting ready. Being only a man, he had no idea why. But he would have bet the ancient Greeks told the same jokes about it as modern Aryans did.

She was worth the wait. Her knee-length light blue skirt showed off her legs. Veit wasn't the least bit sorry the *Reich* still frowned on pants for women. Her top clung to her in a way that would have made the real Jews on whom those of Wawolnice were based *plotz*. And the *sheitel* she had on now was attractively styled and an almost perfect match for the mane of wavy, honey-blond hair she'd sacrificed to take the role of Bertha Shlayfer.

"Let's go home," she said, and yawned. She shook her head. "Sorry. It's been a long day."

"For me, too," Veit agreed. "And it doesn't get any easier."

"It never gets any easier," Kristi said.

"I know, but that isn't what I meant. Didn't you see the schedule? They've got a pogrom listed for week after next."

"*Oy!*" Kristi burst out. Once you got used to Yiddish, plain German could seem flavorless beside it. And Veit felt like going *Oy!* himself. Pogroms were a pain, even if the tourists got off on them. Sure, the powers that be brought in drugged convicts for the people playing Poles to stomp and burn, but re-enactors playing Jews always ended up getting hurt, too. Accidents happened. And, when you were living your role, sometimes you just got carried away and didn't care who stood in front of you when you threw a rock or swung a club.

"Nothing we can do about it but put on a good show." He pointed down the corridor toward the employee parking lot. "Come on. Like you said, let's go home."

The corridor spat performers out right next to the gift shop. Another sign reading AUTHORIZED PERSONNEL ONLY and a prominently displayed surveillance camera discouraged anyone else from moving against the stream. A ragged apple orchard screened the gift shop and the parking lot off from Wawolnice proper. That was good, as far as Veit was concerned. The gift shop was about paperbacks of *The Protocols of the Elders of Zion* and plastic Jew noses and rubber Jew lips. Once upon a time, no doubt, the village had been about the same kinds of things. It wasn't any more, or it wasn't exactly and wasn't all the time. As things have a way of doing, Wawolnice had taken on a life of its own.

Veit opened the passenger-side door for his wife. Kristi murmured a word of thanks as she slid into the Audi. He went around and got in himself. The electric motor silently came to life. The car didn't have the range of a gas auto, but more charging stations went up every day. Though petroleum might be running low, plenty of nuclear power plants off in the East made sure the *Reich* had plenty of electricity. If they belched radioactive waste into the environment every once in a while, well, that was the local Ivans' worry.

He drove out of the lot, up the ramp, and onto the *Autobahn*, heading east toward their flat in Lublin. A garish, brilliantly lit billboard appeared in his rearview mirror. The big letters were backwards, but he knew what they said: COME SEE THE JEW VILLAGE! ADMISSION ONLY 15 REICHS-MARKS! The sinister, hook-nosed figure in black on the billboard was straight out of a cartoon. It only faintly resembled the hardworking reenactors who populated Wawolnice.

"I hate that stupid sign," Veit said, as he did at least twice a week. "Makes us look like a bunch of jerks."

"It's like a book cover," Kristina answered, as she did whenever he pissed and moaned about the billboard. "It draws people in. Then they can see what we're really about."

"It draws assholes in," Veit said morosely. "They hold their noses at the smells and they laugh at our clothes and they show off their titties and think it's funny."

"You weren't complaining when Wolf told you about that," his wife pointed out. "Except that you didn't see it, I mean."

"Yeah, well..." He took one hand off the wheel for a moment to make a vague gesture of appeasement.

Lublin was about half an hour away at the *Autobahn*'s *Mach schnell!* speeds. It was clean and bright and orderly, like any town in the *Grossdeutsches Reich* these days. It had belonged to Poland, of course, before the War of Retribution. It had been a provincial capital, in fact. But that was a long time ago now. These days, Poles were almost as much an anachronism as Jews. The Germans had reshaped Lublin in their own image. They looked around and saw that it was good.

"Want to stop somewhere for dinner?" Veit asked as he pulled off the highway and drove into the city.

"Not really. I am tired," Kristi said. "We've got leftovers back at the flat.

If that's all right with you."

"Whatever you want," he said.

They could have afforded a bigger apartment, but what would the point have been? They poured most of their time and most of their energy into the village. If you weren't going to do that, you didn't belong at Wawolnice. They used the flat as a place to relax and to sleep. How fancy did you need to be for that?

Kristina warmed up some rolls in the oven. A few minutes later, she put sweet-and-sour cabbage stuffed with veal sausage and rice into the microwave. Veit's contribution to supper was pouring out two tumblers of Greek white wine. "Oh, thank you," his wife said. "I could use one tonight."

"Me, too." Veit went on in Hebrew: *"Barukh atah Adonai, elohaynu melekh ha-olam, borei p'ri ha-gafen." Blessed art Thou, O Lord our God, King of the universe, who bringest forth the fruit of the vine.*

"Practice," Kristi said as they clinked the big, heavy glasses.

"Aber natürlich," Veit agreed. "If you don't use a language, you'll lose it." He assumed the flat had microphones. He'd never heard of one that didn't. How much attention the *Sicherheitsdienst* paid…. well, who could guess? Then again, who wanted to find out the hard way? If you started praying in the dead language of a proscribed *Volk*, better to let any possible SD ear know you had a reason.

The microwave buzzed. Kristina took out the glass tray, then retrieved the rolls. Veit poured more wine. His wife put food on the table. He blessed the bread and the main course, as he had the wine. They ate. He made his portion disappear amazingly fast.

"Do you want more?" Kristi asked. "There is some."

He thought about it, then shook his head. "No, that's all right. But I was hungry."

She was doing the dishes when the phone rang. Veit picked it up. *"Bitte?"* He listened for a little while, then said, "Hang on a second." Putting his palm on the mouthpiece, he spoke over the rush of water in the sink: "It's your kid sister. She wants to know if we feel like going out and having a few drinks."

She raised an eyebrow as she turned off the faucet. He shrugged back. She reached for the phone. He handed it to her. "Ilse?" she said. "Listen, thanks for asking, but I think we'll pass…. Yes, I know we said that the last time, too, but we're really beat tonight. And there's a pogrom coming up soon, and we'll have to get ready for that. They're always *meshuggeh*…. It means crazy, is what it means, and they are…. Yes, next time for sure. So long." She hung up.

"So what will we do?" Veit asked.

"I'm going to finish the dishes," his wife said virtuously. "Then? I don't know. TV, maybe. And some more wine."

"Sounds exciting." Veit picked up the corkscrew. They'd just about killed this bottle. He'd have to summon reinforcements.

They plopped down on the sofa. TV was TV, which is to say, dull. The comedies were stupid. When a story about a cat up a tree led the news, you knew there was no news. The local footballers were down 3-1 with twenty minutes to play.

And so it wasn't at all by accident that Veit's hand happened to fall on Kristina's knee. She made as if to swat him, but her eyes sparkled. Instead of pulling away, he slid the hand up under her skirt. She swung toward him. "Who says it won't be exciting tonight?" she asked.

✡

Getting ready for the pogrom kept everyone hopping. The reenactors who played Wawolnice's Jews and Poles had to go on doing everything they normally did. You couldn't disappoint the paying customers, and the routine of village life had an attraction of its own once you got used to it. And they had to ready the place so it would go through chaos and come out the other side with as little damage as possible.

A couple of buildings would burn down. They'd get rebuilt later, during nights. Along with everyone else, Veit and Kristi made sure the hidden sprinkler systems in the houses and shops nearby were in good working order, and that anything sprinklers might damage was replaced by a waterproof substitute.

Veit also moved the Torah from the Ark in the *shul*. A blank substitute scroll would burn, along with a couple of drugged and conditioned convicts who would try to rescue it. The Poles would make a bonfire of the books in the *bet ha-midrash*—only not out of the real books, only of convincing fakes.

People slept in their village living quarters, or on cots in the underground changing areas. Hardly anyone had time to go home. They wore their costumes all the time, even though the laundry did tend to them more often than would have been strictly authentic.

Eyeing a bandage on his finger—a knife he was sharpening had got him, a hazard of his village trade—Veit Harlan grumbled, "I'm Jakub a lot more than I'm me these days."

"You aren't the only one," Kristina said. His wife was also eligible for a wound badge. She'd grated her knuckle along with some potatoes that went into a *kugel*.

"We'll get to relax a little after the pogrom," Veit said. "And it'll bring in the crowds. Somebody told me he heard a tourist say they were advertising it on the radio."

"'Come see the Jews get what's coming to them—again!'" Kristi did a fine impersonation of an excitable radio announcer. It would have been a fine impersonation, anyhow, if not for the irony that dripped from her voice.

"Hey," Veit said—half sympathy, half warning.

"I know," she answered. Her tone *had* been too raw. "I'm just tired."

"Oh, sure. Me, too. Everybody is," Veit said. "Well, day after tomorrow and then it's over—till the next time."

"Till the next time," Kristi said.

"Yeah. Till then," Veit echoed. That wasn't exactly agreement. Then again, it wasn't exactly disagreement. Wawolnice moved in strange and mysterious way. The *Reich* Commissariat for the Strengthening of the German Populace knew in broad outline what it wanted to have happen in the village. After all, National Socialism had been closely studying the Jewish enemy since long before the War of Retribution. Without such study, the Commissariat would never have been able to re-create such a precise copy of a *shtetl*. Details were up to the reenactors, though. They didn't have scripts. They improvised every day.

The pogrom broke out in the market square. That made sense. A Polish woman screeched that a Jew selling old clothes—old clothes specially manufactured for the village and lovingly aged—was cheating her. Rocks started flying. Jews started running. Whooping, drunken Poles overturned carts, spilling clothes and vegetables and rags and leather goods and what-have-you on the muddy ground. Others swooped down to steal what they could.

When the *melamed* and the boys from the *kheder* fled, Veit figured Jakub had better get out, too. A rock crashing through his shop's front window reinforced the message. This part of Wawolnice wasn't supposed to burn. All those elaborate fire-squelching systems should make sure of that. But anything you could make, you could also screw up. And so he scuttled out the front door, one hand clapped to his black hat so he shouldn't, God forbid, go bareheaded even for an instant.

Schoolchildren, plump burghers on holiday, and tourists from places like Japan and Brazil photographed the insanity. You had to go on pretending they weren't there. A pack of Poles were stomping a man in Jewish costume to death. One of the convict's hands opened and closed convulsively as they did him in. He bleated out the last words that had been imposed on him: "*Sh'ma, Yisroayl, Adonai elohaynu, Adonai ekhod!*" *Hear, O Israel, the Lord our God, the Lord is one!*

Another performer playing a Pole swung a plank at Veit. Had that connected, he never would have had a chance to gabble out his last prayer. But the reenactor missed—on purpose, Veit devoutly hoped. Still holding on to his hat, he ran down the street.

"Stinking Yid!" the performer roared in Polish. Veit just ran faster. Jews didn't fight back, after all. Then he ran into bad luck—or rather, it ran into him. A flying rock caught him in the ribs.

"Oof!" he said, and then, "*Vey iz mir!*" When he breathed, he breathed knives. Something in there was broken. He had to keep running. If the Poles caught him, they wouldn't beat him to death, but they'd beat him up. They couldn't do anything else—realism came first. Oh, they might pull punches and go easy on kicks where they could, but they'd still hurt him. Hell, they'd already hurt him, even without meaning to.

Or they might not pull anything. Just as the reenactors in Jewish roles took pride in playing them to the hilt, so did the people playing Poles. If they were supposed to thump on Jews, they might go ahead and thump on any old

Jew they could grab, and then have a drink or three to celebrate afterwards.

A woman screamed. The shriek sounded alarmingly sincere, even by Wawol-nice standards. Veit hoped things weren't getting out of hand there. The less the senior inspectors from Lublin or even Berlin interfered with the way the village ran, the better for everybody here. "Jews" and "Poles" both took that as an article of faith.

Veit ducked into one of the buildings where Jews lived in one another's laps. As long as nobody could see him from outside... A woman in there gaped at him. "What are you doing here?" she asked—still in Yiddish, still in character.

"I got hurt. They banged on my teakettle once too often," he answered, also sticking to his role. He grabbed at his side. Would he have to start coughing up blood to convince people? He was afraid he might be able to do it.

What kind of horrible grimace stretched across his face? Or had he gone as pale as that village miracle, a clean shirt? The woman didn't argue with him any more (for a Wawolnice Jew, that came perilously close to falling out of one's part). She threw open her closet door. "Go on. Disappear, already."

"God bless you and keep you. I wish my ribs would disappear." He ducked inside. She closed the outer door after him. He fumbled till he found the light switch. Then he went to the inner door, identical to the one in his own crowded home. He was an authorized person, all right. On the far side of that door lay the modern underpinnings to the early twentieth-century Polish village.

Now he didn't have to run for his life. Slowly and painfully, he walked down the concrete stairs and along a passageway to the first-aid center. He had to wait to be seen. He wasn't the only villager who'd got hurt. Sure as hell, pogroms were always a mess.

A medical tech prodded his ribcage. "*Gevalt!*" Veit exclaimed.

"You don't have to go on making like a Jew down here," the tech said condescendingly. Veit hurt too much to argue with him. The neatly uniformed Aryan felt him some more and listened to his chest with a stethoscope, then delivered his verdict: "You've got a busted slat or two, all right. Doesn't seem to be any lung damage, though. I'll give you some pain pills. Even with 'em, you'll be sore as hell on and off the next six weeks."

"Aren't you even going to bandage me up?" Veit asked.

"Nope. We don't do that any more, not in ordinary cases. The lung heals better unconstricted. Step off to one side now for your pills and your paperwork."

"Right," Veit said tightly. The tech might as well have been an auto mechanic. Now that he'd checked Veit's struts and figured out what his trouble was, he moved on to the next dented chassis. And Veit moved on to pharmacy and bureaucracy.

A woman who would have been attractive if she hadn't seemed so bored handed him a plastic vial full of fat green pills. He gulped one down, dry, then started signing the papers she shoved at him. That got a rise out of her: she went from bored to irked in one fell swoop. "What are those chicken scratches?" she demanded.

"Huh?" He looked down at the forms and saw he'd been scribbling *Jakub Shlayfer* in backwards-running Yiddish script on each signature line. He couldn't even blame the dope; it hadn't kicked in yet. Maybe pain would do for an excuse. Or maybe least said, soonest mended. He muttered "Sorry" and started substituting the name he'd been born with.

"That's more like it." The woman sniffed loudly. "Some of you people don't know the difference between who you are and who you play any more."

"You've got to be kidding." Veit wrote his own name once again. "Nobody wants to break *my* ribs on account of who I am. That only happens when I put on this stuff." His wave encompassed his *shtetl* finery.

"Remember that, then. Better to be Aryan. Easier, too."

Veit didn't feel like arguing. He did feel woozy—the pain pill started hitting hard and fast. "Easier is right," he said, and turned to leave the infirmary. The broken rib stabbed him again. He let out a hiss any snake, *treyf* or kosher, would have been proud of. The medical tech had been right, dammit. Even with a pill, he was sore as hell.

✡

"We have to be *meshuggeh* to keep doing this," Kristina said as she piloted their car back toward Lublin at the end of the day.

"Right now, I won't argue with you." Veit wasn't inclined to argue about anything, not right now. Changing into ordinary German clothes had hurt more than he'd believed anything could. The prescription said *Take one tablet at a time every four to six hours, as needed for pain.* One tablet was sending a boy to do a man's job, and a half-witted boy at that. He'd taken two. He still hurt—and now he had the brains of a half-witted boy himself. No wonder his wife sat behind the Audi's wheel.

She flashed her lights at some *Dummkopf* puttering along on the *Autobahn* at eighty kilometers an hour. The jerk did eventually move over and let her by. Veit was too stoned for even that to annoy him, which meant he was very stoned indeed.

Kristi sighed as she zoomed past the old, flatulent VW. "But we'll be back at the same old stand tomorrow," she said, daring him to deny it.

"What would you rather do instead?" he asked. She sent him a reproachful side glance instead of an answer. Wawolnice offered more chances for honest performing than almost anywhere else in the *Reich*. Television was pap. The movies, too. The stage was mostly pap: pap and revivals.

Besides, they'd been at the village for so long now, most of the people they'd worked with anywhere else had forgotten they existed. Wawolnice was a world unto itself. Most of the kids in the *kheder* really were the children of performers who played Jews in the village. Were they getting in on the ground floor, or were they trapped? How much of a difference was there?

Veit didn't feel too bad as long as he held still. With the pills in him, he felt pretty damn good, as a matter of fact. Whenever he moved or coughed, though, all the pain pills in the world couldn't hope to block the message his ribs sent. He dreaded sneezing. That would probably feel as if he were being torn in two—which might not be so far wrong.

Moving slowly and carefully, he made it up to the apartment with his wife. He started to flop down onto the sofa in front of the TV, but thought better of it in the nick of time. Lowering himself slowly and gently was a much better plan. Then he found a football match. Watching other people run and jump and kick seemed smarter than trying to do any of that himself.

"Want a drink?" Kristi asked.

One of the warning labels on the pill bottle cautioned against driving or running machinery while taking the drugs, and advised that alcohol could make things worse. "Oh, Lord, yes!" Veit exclaimed.

She brought him a glass of slivovitz. She had one for herself, too. He recited the blessing over fruit. He wasn't too drug-addled to remember it. The plum brandy went down in a stream of sweet fire. "Anesthetic," Kristi said.

"Well, sure," Veit agreed. He made a point of getting good and anesthetized, too.

No matter how anesthetized he was, though, he couldn't lie on his stomach. It hurt too much. He didn't like going to bed on his back, but he didn't have much choice. Kristi turned out the light, then cautiously straddled him. Thanks to the stupid pain pills, that was no damn good, either. No matter how dopey he was, he took a long, long time to fall asleep.

✡

They went back to Wawolnice the next morning. Cleanup crews had labored through the night. If you didn't live there, you wouldn't have known a pogrom had raged the day before. Just as well, too, because no pogrom was laid on for today. You couldn't run them too often. No matter how exciting they were, they were too wearing on everybody—although the Ministry of Justice never ran short on prisoners to be disposed of in interesting ways.

Putting on his ordinary clothes at the apartment had made Veit flinch. He'd swallowed a pain pill beforehand, but just the same… And changing into his Jew's outfit under Wawolnice hurt even more. No wonder: the left side of his ribcage was all over black-and-blue.

"That looks nasty," Reb Eliezer said sympathetically, pointing. "Are you coming to *shul* this morning?"

"*Fraygst nokh?*" Veit replied in Jakub's Yiddish. *Do you need to ask?* "Today I would even if it weren't my turn to help make the *minyan*."

A couple of *yeshiva-bykher* were already poring over the Talmud when he got to the cramped little synagogue. The real books were back in place, then. The men who made up the ten required for services ranged in age from a couple just past their *bar-mitzvahs* to the *melamed*'s thin, white-bearded father. If the old man's cough was only a performer's art, he deserved an award for it.

They all put on their *tefillin*, wrapping the straps of one on their left arms and wearing the other so the enclosed text from the Torah was between their eyes. Phylacteries was the secular name for *tefillin*. It had to do with the idea of guarding. Veit's aching ribs said he hadn't been guarded any too well the day before. Wrapped in his *tallis*, he stood there and went through the morning service's prayers with the rest of the men.

And he had a prayer of his own to add: the *Birkhas ha-gomel*, said after surviving danger. *"Barukh atah Adonai, eloheinu melekh ha-olam, ha-gomel lahayavim tovos she-g'malani kol tov."* Blessed art Thou, O lord, our God, king of the universe, Who bestowest good things on the unworthy, and hast bestowed upon me every goodness.

"*Omayn*," the rest of the *minyan* chorused. Their following response meant *May He Who has bestowed upon you every goodness continue to bestow every goodness upon you. Selah.*

At the end of the services, the *melamed's* father poured out little shots of *shnaps* for everybody. He smacked his lips as he downed his. So did Veit. The two kids choked and coughed getting their shots down. Their elders smiled tolerantly. It wouldn't be long before the youngsters knocked back whiskey as easily and with as much enjoyment as everyone else.

One by one, the men went off to their work on the village. Reb Eliezer set a hand on Veit's arm as he was about to leave the *shul*. "I'm glad you remembered the *birkhas ha-gomel*," the rabbi said quietly.

Veit raised an eyebrow. "What's not to remember? Only someone who isn't *frum* would forget such a thing. And, thank God, all the Jews in Wawolnice *are* pious." He stayed in character no matter how much it hurt. Right this minute, thanks to his ribs, it hurt quite a bit.

Eliezer's cat-green stare bored into him. To whom did the rabbi report? What did he say when he did? A Jew in a Polish village wouldn't have needed to worry about such things. A performer who was a Jew in a Polish village during working hours? You never could tell what somebody like that needed to worry about.

"Thank God," Reb Eliezer said now. He patted Veit on the back: gently, so as not to afflict him with any new pain. Then he walked over to the two men studying the Talmud and sat down next to one of them.

Part of Veit wanted to join the disputation, too. But the services were over. He had work waiting at the shop: not so much work as his wife would have liked, but work nonetheless. Eliezer did look up and nod to him as he slipped out of the *shul*. Then the rabbi went back to the other world, the higher world, of the Law and the two millennia of commentary on it and argument about it.

The day was dark, cloudy, gloomy. A horse-drawn wagon brought barrels of beer to the tavern. A skinny dog gnawed at something in the gutter. A Jewish woman in *sheitel* and headscarf nodded to Veit. He nodded back and slowly walked to his shop. He couldn't walk any other way, not today and not for a while.

A tall, plump, ruddy man in *Lederhosen* snapped his picture. As usual, Veit pretended the tourist didn't exist. When you thought about it, this was a strange business. Because it was, Veit did his best *not* to think about it most of the time.

Every now and then, though, you couldn't help wondering. During and after its victories in the War of Retribution, the *Reich* did just what the first *Führer* promised he would do: it wiped Jewry off the face of the earth. And, ever since destroying Jewry (no, even while getting on with the job), the Aryan victors studied and examined their victims in as much detail as the dead Jews had studied and examined Torah and Talmud. The Germans hadn't had two thousand years to split hairs about their researches, but they'd had more than a hundred now. Plenty of time for a whole bunch of *pilpul* to build up. And it had. It had.

Without that concentrated, minute study, a place like Wawolnice wouldn't just have been impossible. It would have been unimaginable. But the authorities wanted the world to see what a horrible thing it was that they'd disposed of. And so twenty-first-century Aryans lived the life of early twentieth-century Jews and Poles for the edification of … fat tourists in *Lederhosen*.

Repairmen had installed a new front window at the shop. Remarkably, they'd also sprayed it, or painted it, or whatever the hell they'd done, with enough dust and grime and general *shmutz* to make it look as if it had been there the past twenty years, and gone unwashed in all that time. Wawolnice was tended with, well, Germanic thoroughness. A clean window would have looked out of place, and so in went a dirty one.

As Veit opened up, the voices of the children chanting their lessons floated through the morning air. He'd been an adult when he came to the village. Would the boys grow up to become the next generation's tavern-keeper and rabbi and ragpicker … and maybe grinder and jack-of-all-trades? He wouldn't have been a bit surprised. The *Reich* built things to last. Chances were Wawolnice would still be here to instruct the curious about downfallen Judaism a generation from now, a century from now, five hundred years from now …

You learned in school that Hitler had said he intended his *Reich* to last for a thousand years. You also learned that the first *Führer* commonly meant what he said. But then, you had to be pretty stupid to need to learn that in school. Hitler's works were still all around, just as Augustus Caesar's must have been throughout the Roman Empire in the second century A.D.

Something on the floor sparkled. Veit bent and picked up a tiny shard of glass the cleaners had missed. He was almost relieved to chuck it into his battered tin wastebasket. Except for the lancinating pain in his side, it was almost the only physical sign he could find that the pogrom really had happened.

He settled onto his stool, shifting once or twice to find the position where his ribs hurt least. The chanted lessons came through the closed door, but only faintly. The kid who went around with the basket of bagels—no *kheder* for him, even though it was cheap—came by. Veit bought one. The kid scurried away. Veit smiled as he bit into the chewy roll. Damned if he didn't feel more at home in Yiddish than in ordinary German these days.

In came Itzhik the *shokhet*. "How's the world treating you these days?" Veit asked. Yes, this rasping, guttural jargon seemed natural in his mouth. And why not—*fur vos nit?*—when he used it so much?

"As well as it is, Jakub, thank the Lord," the ritual slaughterer answered. He often visited the grinder's shop. His knives had to be sharp. Any visible nick on the edge, and the animals he killed were *treyf.* He had to slay at a single stroke, too. All in all, what he did was as merciful as killing could be, just as Torah and Talmud prescribed. He went on, "And you? And your wife?"

"Bertha's fine. My ribs … could be better. They'll get that way—eventually," Veit said. "*Nu*, what have you got for me today?"

Itzhik carried his short knife, the one he used for despatching chickens and the occasional duck, wrapped in a cloth. "This needs to be perfect," he said. "Can't have the ladies running to Reb Eliezer with their dead birds, complaining I didn't kill them properly."

"That wouldn't be good," Veit agreed. He inspected the blade. The edge seemed fine to him. He said so.

"Well, sharpen it some more anyway," Itzhik answered.

Veit might have known he would say that. Veit, in fact, had known Itzhik would say that; he would have bet money on it. "You're a scrupulous man," he remarked as he set to work.

The *shokhet* shrugged. "If, *eppes*, you aren't scrupulous doing what I do, better you should do something else."

Which was also true of a lot of other things. After watching sparks fly from the steel blade, Veit carefully inspected the edge. The last thing he wanted was to put in a tiny nick that hadn't been there before. At length, he handed back the slaughtering knife. But, as he did, he said, "You'll want to check it for yourself."

"Oh, sure." Itzhik carried it over to the window—the window that might have stood there forgotten since the beginning of time but was in fact brand new. He held the knife in the best light he could find and bent close to examine the edge. He took longer looking it over than Veit had. When the verdict came, it was a reluctant nod, but a nod it was. "You haven't got a *shayla* on your *puppik*, anyway," he admitted.

"Thank you so much," Veit said with a snort. A *shayla* was a marks of disease that left meat unfit for consumption by Jews. His *puppik*—his gizzard—probably had a bruise on it right this minute, but no *shaylas*.

"So what do I owe you?" Itzhik asked.

"A zloty will do," Veit said. The *shokhet* set the coin on the counter. After one more nod, he walked out into the street.

Those chickens will never know what hit them, Veit thought, not without pride. The knife had been sharp when Itzhik handed it to him, and sharper after he got through with it. No one would be able to say its work went against Jewish rules for slaughtering.

Jewish rules held sway here, in Wawolnice's Jewish quarter. Out in the wider world, things were different. The *Reich* let the performers playing Poles here execute—no, encouraged them to execute—those convicts dressed as *shtetl* Jews by stoning them and beating them to death. Assume the convicts (or some of them, anyhow) deserved to die for their crimes. Did they deserve to die like that?

As Veit's recent argument with Reb Eliezer here in the shop showed, Jewish practice leaned over backward to keep from putting people to death, even when the letter of the law said they had it coming. He'd learned in his own Talmudic studies that an ancient Sanhedrin that executed even one man in seventy years went down in history as a bloody Sanhedrin.

Again, the modern world was a little different. Yes, just a little. The *Reich* believed in *Schrechlichkeit*—frightfulness—as a legal principle. If you scared the living shit out of somebody, maybe he wouldn't do what he would have done otherwise. And so the *Reich* didn't just do frightful things to people it caught and condemned. It bragged that it did such things to them.

Along with the quiz shows and football matches and historical melodramas and shows full of singers and dancers that littered the TV landscape, there were always televised hangings of partisans from Siberia or Canada or Peru. Sometimes, for variety's sake, the TV would show a Slav who'd presumed to sleep with his German mistress getting his head chopped off. Sometimes she would go to the block right after him, or even at his side.

All those executions, all those contorted faces and twisting bodies, all those fountains of blood, had been a normal part of the TV landscape for longer than Veit had been alive. He'd watched a few. Hell, everybody'd watched a few. He didn't turn them on because they turned him on, the way some people did. He'd always figured that put him on the right side of the fence.

Maybe it did—no, of course it did—when you looked at things from the *Reich's* perspective. Which he did, and which everyone did, because, in the world as it was, what other perspective could there be? None, none whatsoever, not in the world as it was.

But Wawolnice wasn't part of the world as it was. Wawolnice was an artificial piece of the world as it had been before National Socialist Germany went and set it to rights. Performing here as a Jew, living here as a Jew, gave Veit an angle from which to view the wider world he could have got nowhere else.

And if the wider world turned out to be an uglier place than he'd imagined, than he could have imagined, before he came to Wawolnice, what did that say?

He'd been wrestling with the question ever since it first occurred to him. He was ashamed to remember how long that had taken. He wasn't the only one, either. To some of the reenactors who portrayed Jews, it was just another gig. They'd put it on their résumés and then go off and do something else, maybe on the legitimate stage, maybe not. Down in Romania, there was a

Gypsy encampment that reproduced another way of life the National Socialist victory had eliminated.

For others here, things were different. You had to be careful what you said and where you said it, but that was true all over the *Reich*, which amounted to all over the world. Adding another layer of caution to the everyday one you grew up with probably—no, certainly—wouldn't hurt.

✡

No sooner had that thought crossed his mind than the shop door swung open. In strode … not another village Jew, not a village Pole with something to fix that he trusted to Jakub's clever hands rather than to one of his countrymen, not even a tourist curious about what the inside of one of these hole-in-the-wall shops looked like. No. In came a man wearing the uniform of an SS *Hauptsturmführer*: the equivalent of a *Wehrmacht* captain.

Veit blinked, not sure what he was supposed to do. The Wawolnice in which he lived and worked—in which he performed—lay buried in a past before the War of Retribution. A Wawolnice Jew seeing an SS *Hauptsturmführer* would not automatically be reduced to the blind panic that uniform induced in Jews during the war and for as long afterwards as there were still Jews. A modern Aryan still might be reduced to that kind of panic, though, or to something not far from it.

If a modern Aryan was reduced to that kind of panic, he would be smart to try not to show it. Veit let the *Hauptsturmführer* take the lead. The officer wasted no time doing so, barking, "You are the performer Veit Harlan, otherwise called Jakub Shlayfer the Jew?"

"That's right. What's this all about?" Veit answered in Yiddish.

The SS man's mouth twisted, as if at a bad smell. "Speak proper German, not this barbarous, disgusting dialect."

"Please excuse me, sir, but our instructions are to stay in character at all times when in public in the village," Veit said meekly, but still in the *mamaloshen*. He'd thought Yiddish was a barbarous dialect when he started learning it, too. The more natural it became, the less sure of that he got. You could say things in German you couldn't begin to in Yiddish. But the reverse, he'd been surprised to discover, also held true. Yiddish might be a jaunty beggar of a language, but a language it was.

All of which cut no ice with the *Hauptsturmführer*. He laid a sheet of paper on the counter. "Here is a directive from your project leader, releasing you from those instructions so you may be properly questioned."

Veit picked up the paper and read it. It was what the SS man said it was. "*Zu befehl, Herr Hauptsturmführer!*" he said, clicking his heels.

"That's more like it," the SS officer said smugly. Veit counted himself lucky that the fellow didn't notice obedience laid on with a trowel.

Making sure to treat his vowels the way an ordinary German would—in this shop, remembering wasn't easy; Veit felt as if he were using a foreign language, not his own—the reenactor said, "Sir, you still haven't told me what this is about."

"I would have, if you hadn't wasted my time." Nothing was going to be— nothing could possibly be—the *Hauptsturmführer*'s fault. He leaned toward Veit. No doubt he intended to intimidate, and he succeeded. "So tell me, Jew, what your rabbi meant by congratulating you on your prayer this morning."

He couldn't have practiced that sneer on authentic Jews. Authentic Jews were gone: gone from Germany, gone from Eastern Europe, gone from France and England, gone from North America, gone from Argentina, gone from Palestine, gone from South Africa, gone even from Shanghai and Harbin. Gone. *Spurlos verschwunden*—vanished without a trace. Off the map, literally and metaphorically. But he must have seen a lot of movies and TV shows and plays (Jews made favorite enemies, of course), because he had it down pat.

First things first, then. Veit pulled his wallet from an inside pocket on his coat and took out his identity card. He thrust it at the SS man. "*Herr Hauptsturmführer*, I am not a Jew. This proves my Aryan blood. I am a performer, paid to portray a Jew."

Grudgingly, the officer inspected the card. Grudgingly, he handed it back. "All right. You are not a Jew," he said, more grudgingly yet. "Answer my questions anyhow."

"You would do better asking him." Veit pressed his tiny advantage.

"Don't worry. Someone else is taking care of that." The officer stuck out his chin, which wasn't so strong as he might have wished. "Meanwhile, I'm asking you."

"All right. You have to understand, I'm only guessing, though. I think he meant I played my role well. I got hurt when the village staged a pogrom yesterday—a broken rib."

"Yes, I've seen the medical report," the SS man said impatiently. "Go on."

"A real Jew, a pious Jew, would have given the prayer of thanksgiving for coming through danger at the next *minyan* he was part of. I play a pious Jew, so I did what a pious Jew would do. The actor who plays the rabbi"—Veit came down hard on that—"must have thought it was a nice touch, and he was kind enough to tell me so. Please excuse me, but you're wasting your time trying to make anything more out of it."

"Time spent protecting the *Reich*'s security is never wasted." The *Hauptsturmführer* might have been quoting the Torah. He certainly was quoting his own Holy Writ. He stabbed a forefinger at Veit. "Besides, look at the village. This is a new day. The pogrom never happened."

"*Herr Hauptsturmführer*, they've fixed up the village overnight. My ribs still hurt," Veit said reasonably. He reached into a coat pocket again. This time, he took out the plastic vial of pain pills. He displayed them in the palm of his hand.

The SS man snatched them away and examined the label. "Oh, yeah. This shit. They gave me some of this after they yanked my wisdom teeth. I was flying, man." As if embarrassed that the human being under the uniform had peeped out for a moment, he slammed the vial down on the counter.

Veit tucked the pills away. He tried to take advantage of the officer's slip, if that was what it was: "So you see how it goes, sir. I was just playing my role, just doing my job. If I have to act like a dirty Jew, I should act like the best dirty Jew I can, shouldn't I?"

"Dirty is right." The *Hauptsturmführer* jerked a thumb at the window behind him. "When's the last time somebody washed that?"

"I don't know, sir," Veit answered, which might have been technically true. He wasn't flying—his latest pill was wearing off—but he knew he might burst into hysterical laughter if he told the SS man that window had gone into place during the night to replace one smashed in the pogrom.

"Disgusting. And to think those pigdogs actually got off on living like this." The SS man shook his head in disbelief. "Fucking disgusting. So you remember you're playing a fucking part, you hear?"

"I always remember," Veit said, and that was nothing but the truth.

"You'd better." The *Hauptsturmführer* lumbered out of the shop. He slammed the door behind him. For a moment, Veit feared the glaziers would have another window to replace, but the pane held.

He wasn't due for the next pill for another hour, but he took one anyhow, and washed it down with a slug of plum brandy from a small bottle he kept in a drawer on his side of the counter. The warnings on the vial might say you shouldn't do that, but the warnings on the vial hadn't been written with visits from SS men in mind.

He wondered how Reb Eliezer's interrogation had gone. As they'd needed to, they'd picked a clever fellow to play the village rabbi. But the SS specialized in scaring you so much, you forgot you had any brains. And if they were questioning Eliezer, maybe he didn't report to anybody after all. Maybe. All Eliezer had to do was stick to the truth here and everything would be fine … Veit hoped.

He also wondered if the rabbi would come over here to talk about what had happened. There, Veit hoped not. The *Hauptsturmführer* had proved that the *shul* was thoroughly bugged. No great surprise, that, but now it was confirmed. And if they'd just grilled one Jakub Shlayfer, grinder, the walls to his shop were bound to have ears, too. Would Reb Eliezer be clever enough to realize as much?

Eliezer must have been, because he didn't show up. Before long, the potent pill and the slivovitz made Veit not care so much. He got less work done than he might have. On the other hand, they didn't haul him off to a *Vernichtungslager*, either, so he couldn't count the day a dead loss.

✡

OTHER COVENANTS

"I'm tired," Kristi said as they walked across the parking lot to their car.

"Me, too." Veit moved carefully, like an old man. The rib still bit him every few steps.

"Want me to drive again, then?" his wife asked. She'd thrown out a hint, but he'd tossed it right back.

"Please, if you don't mind too much."

"It's all right," she said.

Veit translated that as *I mind, but not too much.* He waited till they were pulling onto the *Autobahn* before saying, "Let's stop somewhere in Lublin for supper."

"I've got those chicken legs defrosting at home," Kristi said doubtfully.

"Chuck 'em in the fridge when we get back," Veit said. "We'll have 'em tomorrow."

"Suits me." She sounded happy. "I didn't feel much like cooking tonight anyway."

"I could tell." That was one reason Veit had suggested eating out. It wasn't the only one. He hadn't told her anything about what had happened during the day. You had to assume the SS could hear anything that went on in Wawolnice. You also had to figure they could bug an Audi. But you had to hope they couldn't keep tabs on everything that went on in every eatery in Lublin.

"That looks like a good place," he said, pointing, as they went through town.

"But—" she began. He held a vertical finger in front of his lips, as if to say, *Yes, something is up.* No dope, Kristi got it right away. "Well, we'll give it a try, then," she said, and eased the car into a tight parking space at least as smoothly as Veit could have done it.

When they walked into the Boar's Head, the maître d' blinked at Veit's flowing beard. They weren't the style in the real world. But Veit talked like a rational fellow, and slipped him ten Reichsmarks besides. No zlotych here. They were village play money. Poland's currency was as dead as the country. The Reichsmark ruled the world no less than the *Reich* did. And ten of them were plenty to secure a good table.

Veit and Kristi ordered beer. The place was lively and noisy. People chattered. A band oompahed in the background. It was still early, but couples already spun on the dance floor. After the *seidels* came, Veit talked about the *Hauptsturmführer*'s visit in a low voice.

Her eyes widened in sympathy—and in alarm. "But that's so stupid!" she burst out.

"Tell me about it," Veit said. "I think I finally got through to him that it was all part of a day's work. I sure hope I did."

"*Alevai omayn!*" Kristi said. That was a slip of sorts, because it wasn't German, but you had to believe you could get away with a couple of words every now and then if you were in a safe place or a public place: often one and the same. And the Yiddish phrase meant exactly what Veit was thinking.

"Are you ready to order yet?" The waitress was young and cute and perky.

And she was well trained. Veit's whiskers didn't faze her one bit.

"I sure am." He pointed to the menu. "I want the ham steak, with the red-cabbage sauerkraut and the creamed potatoes."

"Yes, sir." She wrote it down. "And you, ma'am?"

"How is the clam-and-crayfish stew?" Kristi asked.

"Oh, it's very good!" The waitress beamed. "Everybody likes it. Last week, someone who used to live in Lublin drove down from Warsaw just to have some."

"Well, I'll try it, then."

When the food came, they stopped talking and attended to it. Once his plate was bare —which didn't take long—Veit blotted his lips on his napkin and said, "I haven't had ham that good in quite a while." He hadn't eaten any ham in quite a while, but he didn't mention that.

"The girl was right about the stew, too," his wife said. "I don't know that I'd come all the way from Warsaw to order it, but it's delicious."

Busboys whisked away the dirty dishes. The waitress brought the check. Veit gave her his charge card. She took it away to print out the bill. He scrawled his signature on the restaurant copy and put the customer copy and the card back in his wallet.

He and Kristi walked out to the car. On the way, she remarked, "Protective coloration." Probably no microphones out here—and if there were, a phrase like that could mean almost anything.

"*Jawohl*," Veit agreed in no-doubt-about-it German. Now they'd put a couple of aggressively *treyf* meals in the computerized data system. Let some SS data analyst poring over their records go and call them Jews—or even think of them as Jews—after that!

Again, Veit got in on the passenger side. "You just want me to keep chauffeuring you around," Kristi teased.

"I want my ribs to shut up and leave me alone," Veit answered. "And if you do the same, I won't complain about that, either." She stuck out her tongue at him while she started the Audi. They were both laughing as she pulled out into traffic and headed home.

✡

As the medical technician had warned, getting over a broken rib took about six weeks. The tech hadn't warned it would seem like forever. He also hadn't warned what would happen if you caught a cold before the rib finished knitting. Veit did. It was easy to do in a place like Wawolnice, where a stream of strangers brought their germs with them. Sure as hell, he thought he was ripping himself to pieces every time he sneezed.

But that too passed. At the time, Veit thought it passed like a kidney stone, but even Kristina was tired of his kvetching by then, so he did his best to keep his big mouth shut. It wasn't as if he had nothing to be happy about.

The SS didn't call on him any more, for instance. He and his wife went back to the Boar's Head again. One *treyf* dinner after an interrogation might let analysts draw conclusions they wouldn't draw from more than one. And the food there *was* good.

He was pretty much his old self again by the time summer passed into fall and the High Holy Days —forgotten by everyone in the world save a few dedicated scholars . . . and the villagers and tourists at Wawolnice —came round again. He prayed in the *shul* on Rosh Hashanah, wishing everyone *L'shanah tovah* —a Happy New Year. That that New Year's Day was celebrated only in the village didn't bother him or any of the other performers playing Jews. It was the New Year for them, and they made the most of it with honey cakes and raisins and sweet kugels and other such poor people's treats.

A week and a half later came Yom Kippur, the Day of Atonement, the most solemn day of the Jewish calendar. By that extinct usage, the daylong fast began the night before at sundown. Veit and his wife were driving home from Wawolnice when the sun went down behind them. He sat behind the wheel; he'd been doing most of the driving again for some time.

When they got to their flat, Kristi turned on the oven. She left it on for forty-five minutes. Then she turned it off again. She and Veit sat at the table and talked as they would have over supper, but there was no food on the plates. After a while, Kristi washed them anyhow. Neither a mic nor utility data would show anything out of the ordinary.

How close to the ancient laws did you have to stick? In this day and age, how close to the ancient laws could you possibly stick? How careful did you have to be to make sure the authorities didn't notice you were sticking to those laws? Veit and Kristi had played games with the oven and the dishwashing water before. In light of the call the SS *Hauptsturmführer* had paid on Veit earlier in the year (last year now, by Jewish reckoning), you couldn't be too careful—and you couldn't stick too close to the old laws.

So you did what you could, and you didn't worry about what you couldn't help. That seemed to fit in with the way things in Wawolnice generally worked.

At *shul* the next morning, Kristi sat with the women while Veit took his place among the men. How many of the assembled reenactors were fasting except when public performance of these rituals required it? Veit didn't know; it wasn't a safe question, and wouldn't have been good manners even if it were. But he was as sure as made no difference that Kristi and he weren't the only ones.

After the service ended, he asked his village friends and neighbors to forgive him for whatever he'd done to offend them over the past year. You had to apologize sincerely, not just go through the motions. And you were supposed to accept such apologies with equal sincerity. His fellow villagers were saying they were sorry to him and to one another, too.

Such self-abasement was altogether alien to the spirit of the *Reich*. Good National Socialists never dreamt they could do anything regrettable. Übermenschen, after all, didn't look back—or need to.

And yet, the heartfelt apologies of an earlier Yom Kippur were some of the first things that had made Veit wonder whether what people here in Wawolnice had wasn't a better way to live than much of what went on in the wider world. He'd come here glad to have steady work. He hadn't bargained for anything more. He hadn't bargained for it, but he'd found it.

You needed to ignore the funny clothes. You needed to forget about the dirt and the crowding and the poverty. Those were all incidentals. When it came to living with other people, when it came to finding an anchor for your own life ... He nodded once, to himself. This was better. Even if you couldn't talk about it much, maybe especially because you couldn't, this was better. It had taken a while for Veit to realize it, but he liked the way he lived in the village when he was Jakub Shlayfer better than he liked how he lived away from it when he was only himself.

✡

People who worked together naturally got together when they weren't working, too. Not even the ever-wary SS could make too much of that. There was always the risk that some of the people you hung with reported to the blackshirts, but everyone in the *Reich* ran that risk. You took the precautions you thought you needed and you got on with your life.

One weekend not long after the high Holy Days, Wawolnice closed down for maintenance more thorough than repair crews could manage overnight or behind the scenes. Autumn was on the way. By the calendar, autumn had arrived. But it wasn't pouring or freezing or otherwise nasty, though no doubt it would be before long. A bunch of the reenactors who played Jews seized the moment for a Sunday picnic outside of Lublin.

The grass on the meadow was still green: proof it hadn't started freezing yet. Women packed baskets groaning with food. Men tended to other essentials: beer, slivovitz, *shnaps*, and the like.

One of Kristi's cousins was just back from a hunting trip to the Carpathians. Her contribution to the spread was a saddle of venison. Her cousin was no *shokhet*, of course, but some things were too good to pass up. So she reasoned, anyhow, and Veit didn't try to argue with her.

"Let's see anybody match this," she declared.

"Not likely." Veit had splurged on a couple of liters of fancy vodka, stuff so smooth you'd hardly notice you weren't drinking water ... till you fell over.

He waited for clouds to roll in and rain to spoil things, but it didn't happen. A little dawn mist had cleared out by midmorning, when the performers started gathering. It wasn't a hot day, but it wasn't bad. If shadows stretched farther across the grass than they would have during high summer, well, it wasn't high summer anymore.

Kids scampered here, there, and everywhere, squealing in German and

Yiddish. Not all of them really noticed any difference between the two languages except in the way they were written. Lots of reenactors exclaimed over the venison. Kristi beamed with pride as Reb Eliezer said "I didn't expect that" and patted his belly in anticipation. If he wasn't going to get fussy about dietary rules today ...

They might have been any picnicking group, but for one detail. A car going down the narrow road stopped. The driver rolled down his window and called, "Hey, what's with all the face fuzz?" He rubbed his own smooth chin and laughed.

"We're the Greater Lublin Beard-Growers' Fraternity," Eliezer answered with a perfectly straight face.

All of a sudden, the Aryan in the VW wasn't laughing any more. The official-sounding title impressed him; official-sounding titles had a way of doing that in the *Reich*. "*Ach, so.* The Beard-Growers' Fraternity," he echoed. "That's splendid!" He put the car in gear and drove away, satisfied.

"Things would be easier if we *were* the Greater Lublin Beard-Growers' Fraternity," Veit remarked.

"Some ways," Reb Eliezer said with a sweet, sad smile. "Not others, perhaps."

Alter the *melamed*—otherwise Wolf Albach-Retty—said, "There really are clubs for men who grow fancy whiskers. They have contests. Sometimes the winners get their pictures in the papers."

"Our whiskers are just incidental." Veit stroked his beard. "We raise *tsuris* instead."

Wolf hoisted an eyebrow. Yes, he made a good *melamed*. Yes, he was as much a believer as anyone here except Reb Eliezer. (Like Paul on the road to Damascus—well, maybe not *just* like that—some years before Eliezer had been the first to see how a role could take on an inner reality the Nazi functionaries who'd brought Wawolnice into being had never imagined.) All that said, everyone here except Wolf himself knew he was a ham.

If the SS swooped down on this gathering, what would they find? A bunch of men with beards, along with wives, girlfriends, children, and a few dogs running around barking and generally making idiots of themselves. A hell of a lot of food. No ham, no pig's trotters, no pickled eels, no crayfish or mussels. No meat cooked in cream sauce or anything like that. Even more dishes than you'd normally need for all the chow.

Plenty to hang everybody here, in other words, or to earn people a bullet in the back of the neck. Suspicious security personnel could make all the case they needed from what was and what wasn't at the picnic. And if they weren't suspicious, why would they raid?

Someone here might also be wearing a microphone or carrying a concealed video camera. Being a Jew hadn't stopped Judas from betraying Jesus. Even the so-called German Christians, whose worship rendered more unto the *Reich* than unto God, learned about Judas.

But what could you do? You had to take some chances or you couldn't live. Well, you could, but you'd have to stay by yourself in your flat and never come out. Some days, that looked pretty good to Veit. Some days, but not today.

Reb Eliezer did what he could to cover himself. He waved his hands in the air to draw people's notice. Then he said, "It's good we could all get together today." He was speaking Yiddish; he said *haynt* for *today*, not the German *heute*. He went on, "We need to stay in our roles as much as we can. We live them as much as we can. So if we do some things our friends and neighbors outside Wawolnice might find odd, it's only so we keep them in mind even when we aren't up in front of strangers."

Several men and women nodded. Kids and dogs, predictably, paid no attention. What Eliezer said might save the reenactors' bacon (*Not that we've got any bacon here, either,* Veit thought) if the SS was keeping an eye on things without worrying too much. If the blackshirts were looking for sedition, they'd know bullshit when they heard it.

"All right, then." Eliezer went on to pronounce a *brokhe*, a blessing, that no one—not even the most vicious SS officer, a Rottweiler in human shape—could have found fault with: "Let's eat!"

Women with meat dishes had gathered here, those with dairy dishes over there, and those with *parve* food—vegetable dishes that could be eaten with either—at a spot in between them. Veit took some sour tomatoes and some cold noodles and some green beans in a sauce made with olive oil and garlic (not exactly a specialty of Polish Jews in the old days, but tasty even so), and then headed over to get some of the venison on which his wife had worked so hard. Kristi would let him hear about it if he didn't take a slice.

He had to wait his turn, though. By the time he got over to her, a line had already formed. She beamed with pride as she carved and served. Only somebody else's roast grouse gave her any competition for pride of place. Veit managed to snag a drumstick from one of the birds, too. He sat down on the grass and started filling his face ... after the appropriate blessings, of course.

After a while, Reb Eliezer came over and squatted beside him. Eliezer seemed a man in perpetual motion. He'd already talked with half the people at the picnic, and he'd get to the rest before it finished. "Having a good time?" he asked.

Veit grinned and waved at his plate. "I'd have to be dead not to. I don't know how I'm going to fit into my clothes."

"That's a good time," Eliezer said, nodding. "I wonder what the Poles are doing with their holiday."

He meant the Aryans playing Poles in Wawolnice, of course. The real Poles, those who were left alive, worked in mines and on farms and in brothels and other places where bodies mattered more than brains. Veit stayed in character to answer, "They should grow like onions: with their heads in the ground."

Eliezer smiled that sad smile of his. "And they call us filthy kikes and Christ-killers and have extra fun when there's a pogrom on the schedule."

OTHER COVENANTS

Veit rubbed his ribcage. Eliezer nodded again. "Yes, like that."

"Still twinges once in a while," Veit said.

"Hating Jews is easy," Eliezer said, and it was Veit's turn to nod. The other man went on, "Hating anybody who isn't just like you is easy. Look how you sounded about them. Look how the Propaganda Ministry sounds all the time."

"Hey!" Veit said. "That's not fair."

"Well, maybe yes, maybe no," Reb Eliezer allowed. "But the way it looks to me is, if we're going to live like *Yehudim*, like the *Yehudim* that used to be, like proper *Yehudim*, sooner or later we'll have to do it all the time."

"What?" Now Veit was genuinely alarmed. "We won't last twenty minutes if we do, and you know it."

"I didn't mean that. Using *tefillin*? Putting on the *tallis*? No, it wouldn't work." Eliezer smiled once more, but then quickly sobered. "I meant that we need to live, to think, to feel the way we do while we're in Wawolnice when we're out in the big world, too. We need to be witnesses to what the *Reich* is doing. Somebody has to, and who better than us?" That smile flashed across his face again, if only for a moment. "Do you know what *martyr* means in ancient Greek? It means *witness*, that's what."

Veit had sometimes wondered if the rabbi was the SS plant in the village. He'd decided it didn't matter. If Eliezer was, he could destroy them all any time he chose. But now Veit found himself able to ask a question that would have been bad manners inside Wawolnice: "What did you do before you came to the village that taught you ancient Greek?" As far as he knew, Eliezer— Ferdinand Marian—hadn't been an actor. Veit had never seen him on stage or in a TV show or film.

"Me?" The older man quirked an eyebrow. "I thought everyone had heard about me. No? ... I guess not. I was a German Christian minister."

"Oh," Veit said. It didn't quite come out *Oy!*, but it might as well have. He managed something a little better on his next try: "Well, no wonder you learned Greek, then."

"No wonder at all. And Hebrew, and Aramaic. I was well trained for the part, all right. I just didn't know ahead of time that I would like it better than what had been my real life."

"I don't think any of us figured on that," Veit said slowly.

"I don't, either," Reb Eliezer replied. "But if that doesn't tell you things aren't the way they ought to be out here, what would?" His two-armed wave encompassed *out here*: the world beyond Wawolnice, the world-bestriding *Reich*.

"What do we do?" Veit shook his head; that was the wrong question. Again, another try: "What *can* we do?"

Eliezer set a hand on his shoulder. "The best we can, Jakub. Always, the best we can." He ambled off to talk to somebody else.

Someone had brought along a soccer ball. In spite of full bellies, a pickup game started. It would have caused heart failure in World Cup circles. The pitch was bumpy and unmown. Only sweaters thrown down on the ground marked the corners and the goal mouths. Touchlines and bylines were as much a matter of argument as anything in the Talmud.

Nobody cared. People ran and yelled and knocked one another ass over teakettle. Some of the fouls would have got professionals sent off. The players just laughed about them. Plenty of liquid restoratives were at hand by the edge of the pitch. When the match ended, both sides loudly proclaimed victory.

By then, the sun was sliding down the sky toward the horizon. Clouds had started building up. With regret, everyone decided it was time to go home. Leftovers and dirty china and silverware went into ice chests and baskets. Nobody seemed to worry about supper at all.

Veit caught up with Reb Eliezer. "Thanks for not calling Kristina's venison *treyf*," he said quietly.

Eliezer spread his hands. "It wasn't that kind of gathering, or I didn't think it was. I didn't say anything about the grouse, either. Like I told you before, you do what you can do. Anyone who felt differently didn't have to eat it. No finger-pointing. No fits. Just—no game."

"Makes sense." Veit hesitated, then blurted the question that had been on his mind most of the day: "What do you suppose the old-time Jews, the real Jews, would have made of us?"

"I often wonder about that," Eliezer said, which surprised Veit not at all. The older man went on, "You remember what Rabbi Hillel told the *goy* who stood on one foot and asked him to define Jewish doctrine before the other foot came down?"

"Oh, sure," Veit answered; that was a bit of Talmudic *pilpul* everybody—well, everybody in Wawolnice who cared about the Talmud—knew. "He said that you shouldn't do to other people whatever was offensive to you. As far as he was concerned, the rest was just commentary."

"The Talmud says that *goy* ended up converting, too," Eliezer added. Veit nodded; he also remembered that. Eliezer said, "Well, if the *Reich* had followed Hillel's teaching, there would still be real Jews, and they wouldn't have needed to invent us. Since they did … We're doing as well as we can on the main thing—we're human beings, after all—and maybe not too bad on the commentary. Or do you think I'm wrong?"

"No. That's about how I had it pegged, too." Veit turned away, then stopped short. "I'll see you tomorrow in Wawolnice."

"Tomorrow in Wawolnice," Eliezer said. "Next year in Jerusalem."

"*Alevai omayn*," Veit answered, and was astonished by how much he meant it.

✡

They wouldn't have needed to invent us. For some reason, that fragment of a sentence stuck in Veit's mind. He knew Voltaire's *If God did not exist, it would be necessary to invent him.* Before coming to Wawolnice, he'd been in a couple of plays involving the Frenchman. Frederick the Great had been one of Hitler's heroes, which had made the Prussian king's friends and associates glow by reflected light in the eyes of German dramatists ever since.

If a whole *Volk* had nobody who could look at them from the outside, would they have to find—or make—someone? There, Veit wasn't so sure. Like any actor's, his mind was a jackdaw's nest of other men's words. He knew the story about the dying bandit chief and the priest who urged him to forgive his enemies. *Father, I have none*, the old ruffian wheezed. *I've killed them all.*

Here stood the *Reich*, triumphant. Its retribution had spread across the globe. It hadn't quite killed all its enemies. No: it had enslaved some of them instead. But no one cared what a slave thought. No one even cared if a slave thought, so long as he didn't think of trouble.

Here stood Wawolnice. It had come into being as a monument to the *Reich*'s pride. *Look at what we did. Look at what we had to get rid of*, it had declared, reproducing with typical, fanatical attention to detail what once had been. And such attention to detail had, all unintended, more or less brought back into being what had been destroyed. It was almost Hegelian.

After talking with Kristina, Veit decided to have the little operation that would mark him as one of the men who truly belonged in Wawolnice. He got it done the evening before the village shut down for another maintenance day. "You should be able to go back to work day after tomorrow," the doctor told him. "You'll be sore, but it won't be anything the pills can't handle."

"Yes, I know about those." Of itself, Veit's hand made that rib-feeling gesture.

"All right, then." The other man uncapped a syringe. "This is the local anesthetic. You may not want to watch while I give it to you."

"You bet I don't." Veit looked up at the acoustic tiles on the treatment room's ceiling. The shot didn't hurt much—less than he'd expected. Still, it wasn't something you wanted to think about; no, indeed.

Chuckling, the doctor said, "Since you're playing one of those miserable, money-grubbing kikes, of course you'll be happy about the raise you're getting for going all out."

"As long as my eel still goes up after this, that's the only raise I care about right now," Veit answered. The doctor laughed again and went to work.

Bandaging up afterwards took longer than the actual procedure. As Veit was carefully pulling up his pants, the doctor said, "Take your first pill in about an hour. That way, it'll be working when the local wears off."

"That would be good," Veit agreed. He got one more laugh from the man in the white coat. No doubt everything seemed funnier when you were on the other end of the scalpel.

He didn't have Kristi drive home; he did it himself, with his legs splayed wide. He couldn't feel anything—the anesthetic was still going strong—but he did even so. He dutifully swallowed the pill at the appointed time. Things started hurting anyway: hurting like hell, not to put too fine a point on it. Veit gulped another pill. It was too soon after the first, but he did it all the same.

Two pain pills were better than one, but not enough. He still hurt. The pills did make his head feel like a balloon attached to his body on a long string. What happened from his neck down was still there, but only distantly connected to the part of him that noticed.

He ate whatever Kristi put on the table. Afterwards, he remembered eating, but not what he'd eaten.

He wandered out into the front room and sat down in front of the TV. He might do that any evening to unwind from a long day of being a Jew, but this felt different. The screen in front of him swallowed all of his consciousness that didn't sting.

Which was odd, because the channel he'd chosen more or less at random was showing a string of ancient movies: movies from before the War of Retribution, movies in black and white. Normally, Veit had no patience for that. He lived in a black-and-white world in Wawolnice. When he watched the television, he wanted something brighter, something more interesting.

Tonight, though, with the two pain pills pumping through him, he just didn't care. The TV was on. He'd watch it. He didn't have to think while he stared at the pictures. Something called *Bringing up Baby* was running. It was funny even though it was dubbed. It was funny even though he was drugged.

When it ended and commercials came on, they seemed jarringly out of place. They were gaudy. They were noisy. Veit couldn't wait for them to end and the next old film to start.

It finally did. *Frankenstein* was about as far from *Bringing up Baby* as you could get and still be called a movie. Some of the antique special effects seemed unintentionally comic to a modern man, even if the modern man was doped to the eyebrows. But Veit ended up impressed in spite of himself. As with the comedy, no wonder people still showed this one more than a hundred years after it was made.

He took one more green pill after the movie and staggered off to bed. He slept like a log, assuming logs take care to sleep on their backs.

When he woke up the next morning, he wasn't as sore as he'd thought he would be. And he'd rolled over onto his side during the night and hadn't perished, or even screamed. He did take another pill, but he didn't break any Olympic sprint records running to the kitchen to get it.

"You poor thing," Kristi said. "Your poor thing."

"I'll live." Veit decided he might even mean it. Once he soaked up some coffee and then some breakfast—and once that pill kicked in—he might even want to mean it.

Caffeine, food, and opiate did indeed work wonders. His wife nodded approvingly. "You don't have that glazed look you did last night."

"Who, me?" Veit hadn't been sure he could manage indignation, but he did.

Not that it helped. "Yes, you," Kristi retorted. "You don't sit there gaping at the TV for three hours straight with drool running down your chin when you're in your right mind."

"But it was good." No sooner had Veit said it than he wondered whether he would have thought so if he hadn't been zonked. Kristina's raised eyebrow announced louder than words that she wondered exactly the same thing.

Maybe he wouldn't have enjoyed the silliness in *Bringing up Baby* so much if he'd been fully in the boring old Aristotelian world. But *Frankenstein* wasn't silly—not even slightly. Taking pieces from the dead, putting them together, and reanimating them … No, nothing even the least bit silly about that.

As a matter of fact … His jaw dropped. "*Der Herr Gott im Himmel,*" he whispered, and then, "*Vey iz mir!*"

"What is it?" Kristi asked.

"Wawolnice," Veit said.

"Well, what about it?" his wife said.

But he shook his head. "You weren't watching the movie last night." He didn't know what she had been doing. Anything that hadn't been right in front of him or right next to him simply wasn't there. She'd stuck her head into the front room once or twice—probably to make sure he could sit up straight—but she hadn't watched.

And you needed to have. Because what was Wawolnice but a Frankenstein village of Jews? It wasn't meant to have come to life on its own, but it had, it had. So far, the outsiders hadn't noticed. No mob of peasants with torches and pitchforks had swarmed in to destroy it—only performers playing Poles, who were every bit as artificial.

How long could they go on? Could they possibly spread? Reb Eliezer thought so. Veit wasn't nearly as sure. But Eliezer might be right. He might.

One more time, *alevai omayn.*

Afterword

Those minutes in the car together, parked in the driveway after grocery shopping in a snowstorm, are a blur lost to this timeline. What I do remember is that my co-editor Mark Shainblum and I wanted to wait for the snowfall to cease being horizontal. Canadians that we are, hope springs eternal. While waiting, one of us—and to this day, neither of us recalls who—came up with the idea for a Jewish alternate history anthology, and the other replied "I know what the title would be: *Other Covenants*!"

A household move, a baby, and a few years later, we attended a science fiction convention where the late, great Tor Books Senior Editor David G. Hartwell was in attendance. He knew Mark well, and was kind enough to treat me like an old friend, even though we had just met for the first time in the green room. A real *mensch* and a gentleman if I've ever met one. At some point, he asked us about projects, and we pitched *Other Covenants*. He loved it immediately, adding that if we could interest a group of established authors in being part of the project, he might be willing to take it on.

I'd like to say that the rest was history, but what happened at that point was life. And *Other Covenants* was put on the back burner, with the hope that we would be able to return to it one day.

In 2017, we found a publisher, and opened to submissions. Unfortunately, that publishing relationship was ill-fated, and *Other Covenants* was left homeless in late 2019, only a few months before the beginning of the COVID-19 pandemic, and the unexpected illness and death of my mother. At that point, everything simply … stopped—for my family, and for the world.

Truth be told, at that point, Mark and I thought the project was finished. And once our contributors ended their contracts, we knew that there was a real risk that they would choose not to stay with the project.

Oh, we of little faith.

During those two years in the wilderness, before our new publisher, Larry Yudelson of Ben Yehuda Press, stepped in and picked up the anthology, all thirty of the project's contributors were free to choose. And yet, they stayed. This, despite no guarantee that the book would ever materialize. Most continued to check in once in a while to poke us and ask how *Other Covenants* was doing, as if it were an old friend. That it wasn't doing much didn't seem to discourage anyone, to our relief.

This is the part where symbolism is going to be applied with a trowel. You know, covenant, *brit*—commitment. It's difficult to escape the biblical dovetailing here. I mean, really. The only thing missing is a *mohel* and a glass of schnapps to dull the pain. (Just a little off the top, please!)

Because I sense a *shiur* coming on, I'll keep the analogy—and my analysis—brief. But what is a covenant anyway?

Known as a *brit* in Hebrew, a covenant is a relational I-thou type of agreement, similar to an oath, between two parties, with reciprocal responsibilities based on shared purpose and commitment. In the Hebrew Bible, the *Tanakh*, there are many examples. There is the Noahic covenant between God and humanity in Genesis 9, where God promises never again to destroy the world by flood, with humanity taking on obligations as well. In Genesis 12-17, the covenant between God and Abraham is forged, in which the patriarch is promised abundant descendants, with circumcision being a covenant-marker, and absence of this mark on the flesh representing breach and a cutting off of a person's line. And finally, there is the covenant at Mount Sinai/Horeb, in Exodus 19-24 and Deuteronomy, where God promises to make the Israelites "a kingdom of priests and a holy nation" if they observe the *mitzvot*, the commandments (Exodus 19:6). This covenant called for absolute loyalty and mutual responsibilities.

Essentially, a covenant was an agreement in which words were meant to be backed up with your feet. And if the actions didn't match those words, this was viewed as a breach of contract, with the inevitable consequences to history.

The authors featured in this anthology honored the spirit of covenant in a way that went above and beyond the call of duty. In fact, for several years, they were no longer obligated to stay with the project at all. We really can't thank them enough for their commitment and care.

As for the history of Judaism, and what could have been, as I've told my university students *ad nauseam*, I wear two hats. One is the rabbi's confessional hat—the one I wear as an insider in the Jewish community. The one that tells me that the historicity of the Exodus and Hannah's desperate prayer for a child in 1 Samuel 1:9-28 don't matter as much as what these narratives about freedom and human longing do to our *kishkes*.

The other is the scholar's hat—the one that informs me that the Noah story was almost certainly influenced by the Mesopotamian flood stories. That, but for politics and demographics, the winning Judaism could have been *Enochic* Judaism, not Mosaic Judaism. That there may be timelines where Karaite Judaism came to dominate the rabbinic model. Or perhaps, other covenants made between human and God, human and human. What promises might Jewish groups and individuals have made on timelines different from our own? What covenants could have been, if *only*?

Yet, as I've worked with Mark to edit this anthology, I've found myself wearing a third hat. That of the mystic focused on *tikkun olam*—world-mending. The one that I wear when I want to believe that Anne Frank was never a victim of the Nazis, like the Anne of Matthew Kressel's story in these pages. When I envision a Judaism where the philosopher Spinoza was not only *married*, but happily, and moved to the United States, as he does in the tale by Milton Verskin. When I entertain imaginings about women in the Hebrew Bible and the great, national leaders they could have been.

Perhaps there are alternate timelines on which this anthology was published elsewhere, and ones where it wasn't published at all. But then there is this one, where it was published by Ben Yehuda Press—the best publisher for this book, at this time. Everything happens in its season, after all. Book publishing is no different.

This book in particular calls for a blessing, I think.

Baruch ata Adonai, Eloheinu Melech haolam, shehechiyanu, v'kiy'manu, v'higianu lazman hazeh.

Blessed are You, Adonai our God, Sovereign of the cosmos, who has kept us alive, sustained us, and brought us to this season.

Because, all things considered—and to paraphrase Kurt Vonnegut, of blessed memory—if this timeline isn't nice, I don't know what is.

Andrea D. Lobel
Ottawa, Ontario, Canada
September, 2022

Special Thanks

To the following who supported this book's Kickstarter campaign:

Aaron Feldman ✡ Aaron Krevans ✡ Abuelite Héctor ✡ Adam L Slotnick ✡ Adrienne Seel ✡ Alan Rosenthal ✡ Alex B Mezhvinsky ✡ Alex Neumann ✡ Alis Franklin ✡ Allan Weiss ✡ Amanda Day ✡ Amy Heller ✡ Andrea Tatjana ✡ Andrew Broadston ✡ Andrew Hatchell ✡ Anna Venishnick Shomsky ✡ Anonymous ✡ Anonymous ✡ Anthony R. Cardno ✡ Asher Winfield ✡ Auberne' Fox-Hughes ✡ Azariah Betzalel ✡ Benjamin Newman ✡ Benjamin Resnick ✡ Brendan Myers ✡ Brian Rohr ✡ Caleb Bilenkin ✡ Caleb Slama ✡ Carla Sulzbach ✡ Carolyn Penney ✡ Cathy Green ✡ Chelle Parker ✡ Cliff Winnig ✡ Constance ✡ Courtney Vincent ✡ Daniel Zigman ✡ Dave Pherigo ✡ David Burszan ✡ David M. Rheingold ✡ David Weiss ✡ David Zvi Kalman ✡ DBS ✡ Debra Lieven ✡ Dr. Takácsné Éva ✡ Ea ✡ Eldan Goldenberg ✡ Eliot Mohrmann ✡ Eliza Blair ✡ Elizabeth R. McClellan ✡ Em Broude ✡ Emet Keshet ✡ Emily Pinkwas ✡ Erik DuBois ✡ Esther Em Kamm ✡ Esther Switzenbaum McGriff ✡ Ethan Jucovy ✡ Gabor Por ✡ Gene Melzack ✡ Gene Young and Katherine Alexander ✡ Gerard Peter Coen ✡ Gilad Meron ✡ Hadar Aviram ✡ Henry in Ottawa ✡ Howard Blakeslee ✡ J. Florence Martin ✡ Jacob "Crazy J" Goldman ✡ Jacob Goldstein ✡ Jacob Newman ✡ Jacob Zieper ✡ Jake Krakovsky ✡ James Egan ✡ Jennifer S. Brown ✡ Jenny Wilde ✡ Jeremy Brett ✡ Jeremy Duncan ✡ Jes Anna Dolan-Wolfe ✡ Jesse Casanova ✡ Jessica Kirzane ✡ John & Solomon Costello ✡ John Baltisberger ✡ John Dupuis ✡ Jonathan Lebowitz ✡ Jordan King-Lacroix ✡ Judd Karlman ✡ Julie Phillips ✡ Kathryn Schild ✡ Kenneth Schneyer ✡ Kerry aka Trouble ✡ Ketzirah Lesser ✡ Laila Goldberg ✡ Larry Lennhoff ✡ Lauren Linsalata ✡ Lawrence M. Schoen ✡ Leigh Dragoon ✡ Lilitu Babalon ✡ M. G. Doherty ✡ M.M. Scaison ✡ MacLaren North ✡ Maeve Haldane ✡ Malkah Rivkah Yugend ✡ Marlaina Cockcroft ✡ Matthew Bess ✡ Matthew Gauvain ✡ Maya Rachel Klein ✡ Melissa Leilani Larson ✡ Merav Hoffman ✡ Michael A. Burstein ✡ Michael Fessler ✡ Michael Haynes ✡ Michael Kahan ✡ Michael Zions ✡ Michaela R. Lubbers ✡ Mindie Simmons ✡ Miriam Krause ✡ Moskowitz with Rabbits ✡ Moti Rieber ✡ n/a ✡ Naomi S ✡ no thank you ✡ no thanks ✡ Parker D Hicks ✡ Parker Whiteway ✡ Patti Haskell ✡ Phoebe Heller Doros ✡ Quinn McCulley ✡ Rabbi Erik Uriarte ✡ Rabbi Joel N. Abraham ✡ Rabbi Joshua Fixler ✡ Rabbi Oren Z. Steinitz ✡ Rabbit Stoddard ✡ Rachel Kahn-Troster ✡ Rachel Silber ✡ Rebecca Miller ✡ Reid Krell ✡ Richard D Dworsky ✡ Ross Gianfortune ✡ Rotem Raviv ✡ Roy Fisher ✡ Ruthanna Emrys ✡ Ryn Silverstein ✡ Ryndie Azevedo ✡ S.L. Kay/Koba! ✡ Saffie Kaplan ✡ Sam Roberts ✡ Sam Rutzick ✡ Samara Metzler ✡ Sara Norris ✡ Sarah bat Chaya HaLevi ✡ Sarah Pinsker ✡ Sarah Sammis ✡ Sarena Ulibarri ✡ Shana Jean Hausman ✡ Shoshana (JewishMemesOnly)

✡ Shulamith Berger ✡ Spider Betzalel Perry ✡ Stephanie Lucas ✡ Stephen D. Rynerson ✡ Steven J. Weinberger ✡ Stu Barrow ✡ Stuart Chaplin ✡ Tasha Turner ✡ Terry Federko ✡ Tess Nolan ✡ the Verskin family ✡ Tim Bernard & Ashira Konigsburg ✡ Tom ✡ Tracy O'Brien ✡ Tzipora Talia ✡ Viveka Nylund ✡ VK ✡ Warren Wacholder ✡ Zak Kramer ✡ Zoe Kaplan

**And super special thanks to
two people whose extraordinary support
for this book merits immortalization:**

Alex B. Mezhvinsky, aka Ezra Ben Leib
   (See "Rise and Walk the Land" on page 240)

David M. Rheingold
   (See "Kaddish for Stalin" on page 299)

About the Authors

Esther Alter is a short fiction writer, game designer, and software engineer. Her work has been published in khōréō and *Baffling Magazine*. Her other projects can be found at subalterngames.com. Follow her on Twitter @subalterngames.

Rabbi Patrick Beaulier is founder and Executive Director of the PunkTorah network of Jewish educational programs, including Darshan Yeshiva, an online Jewish conversion program. In 2020, Patrick co-launched Pluralistic Rabbinical Seminary, focusing on incubating innovative Jewish projects around the world. Patrick also serves as spiritual leader for Kehillah, Richmond, VA's independent Jewish community.

Isak Bloom is a gay, Mad, and disabled post-Soviet Jew; formerly disconnected, he's currently in the middle of formalizing his halakhic status. He was born in the Urals, grew up in Dublin, and after a sojourn in Germany, came to reside in Edinburgh.

Eric Choi is a writer, editor, and aerospace engineer in Toronto. He has twice won the Prix Aurora Award for his story "Crimson Sky" and the Chinese-themed speculative fiction anthology *The Dragon and the Stars* (DAW) co-edited with Derwin Mak. With Ben Bova, he co-edited the hard SF anthology *Carbide Tipped Pens* (Tor). His first short fiction collection *Just Like Being There* (Springer) was released in 2022.

Jack Dann is a multi-award winning author who has written or edited over eighty books, including the international bestseller *The Memory Cathedral, The Rebel, The Silent*, and *The Man Who Melted*. His latest novel is *Shadows in the Stone* (IFWG Publishing). His latest collection is a Centipede Press *Masters of Science Fiction* volume. He lives in Australia on a farm overlooking the sea. You can visit his website at jackdann.com.

Allan Dyen-Shapiro is a Ph.D. biochemist currently working as an educator in Southwest Florida. He has sold stories to venues including *Flash Fiction Online* and *The Grantville Gazette*. He also co-edited an anthology of SFF set in the Middle East. His blog and links to his stories are at allandyenshapiro.com. Follow him on Twitter (@Allan_author_SF); friend him on Facebook (allandyenshapiro.author).

Hunter C. Eden is a Denver-based essayist, critic, and dark fantasy writer whose work has appeared in *Weird Tales, City Slab, Ravenous Monster Horror Webzine*, and *Tablet Magazine*. His novella *The Path of Jackals*, a dark, Cairo-based mystery introducing Sephardi war-correspondent-turned-private-detective (and possible vessel for the Egyptian gods) Fennec Suleiman, appeared in Volume I of P.I. Tales's ongoing Double Feature imprint.

Gwynne Garfinkle is the author of a novel, *Can't Find My Way Home* (2022), and a collection of short fiction and poetry, *People Change* (2018), both published by Aqueduct Press. Her work has appeared in such publications as *Fantasy, Escape Pod, Strange Horizons, Uncanny, Apex, Mermaids Monthly*, and *Not One of Us*.

James Goldberg's family is Jewish on one side, Sikh on the other, and Mormon in the middle. He is the author of four poetry collections: *Let Me Drown with Moses, Phoenix Song, Song of Names*, and *A Book of Lamentations*. By day, he works at the History Department for the Church of Jesus Christ of Latter-day Saints.

Elana Gomel is an academic and an award-winning writer. She is the author of six academic books and numerous articles on subjects such as narrative theory, science fiction, and serial killers. Her latest project is the *Palgrave Reader of International Fantasy*. She has published more than a hundred fantasy and science fiction stories, several novellas, and five novels. She is a member of HWA and can be found at citiesoflightanddarkness.com and on social media.

Matthew Kressel is a three-time Nebula Award, a World Fantasy Award, and a Eugie Award finalist. He has published dozens of short stories in online and print magazines and anthologies, and his work has appeared in multiple "Year's Best" anthologies. His Jewish-themed fantasy novel *King of Shards* was hailed as "Majestic" by NPR Books. Find him online at @mattkressel and matthewkressel.net.

Claude Lalumière (claudepages.info) is the author of more than 100 stories. His books include *Objects of Worship* (2009) and *Venera Dreams: A Weird Entertainment*, which was a selection of the Great Books Marquee at Word on the Street Toronto 2017. His work is translated into nine languages. Originally from Montreal, he now lives in Ottawa.

D.K. Latta's published stories are mainly in the field of SF/F but also include everything from Sherlock Holmes pastiches, to horror, to superheroes (including novels featuring Captain Canuck, Silver Streak, and the Lev Gleason-era Daredevil) as well as pop culture essays. Born in Canada, he was reared in a haunted house and nurtured on a wildly unbalanced diet of old pulps, comic books, and speculative fiction.

Seymour Mayne is the author, editor, or translator of more than seventy books. His latest collections include *Cusp: Word Sonnets* (Ronald P. Frye & Co., 2014), the personal anthology, *In Your Words: Translations from the Yiddish and the Hebrew* (Ronald P. Frye & Co., 2017), and *Le chant de Moïse* (Mémoire d'encrier, 2018), a bilingual English-French selection of biblical poems. His most recent is a book-length offering of new work, *Perfume: Poems and Word Sonnets* (Ronald P. Frye & Co., 2020). He is Professor Emeritus at the University of Ottawa.

C.L. McDaniel is a theater and psychology teacher living in Berlin, Germany. He co-starred in the film *Weather House* (2017) and his original theatre piece "Voices through the Wall" was featured on the BBC World radio program *The Strand*. His professional publications include "And Flights of Skuhwiggle" on the *Cast of Wonders* podcast, 2018, and "Wet Work," published in Flame Tree's *Urban Crime* anthology, 2019.

Jack Nicholls bounces between living as a British writer in Australia and an Australian writer in Britain. In both places, Jack can be found writing everything from children's books to cultural essays, but they always come back to science fiction as the best reflection for fractured times. You can find links to Jack's speculative fiction and their irregular newsletter 'Letters from Jack' at www.jacknicholls.net.

David Nurenberg, Ph.D. is a professor of education with many academic publications, including *What Does Injustice Have to do With Me?*, a book about teaching social justice in affluent schools. He has contributed to various roleplaying sourcebooks, and wrote *Silent Knife,* a novel in White Wolf's *Vampire: The Requiem* series. David denies any connection to the secret Jewish Space Laser Corps (but then, of course he would, wouldn't he?) Visit him at doctornurenberg.com or at his podcast, ed-infinitum.com.

Dr. Gillian Polack is an award-winning Jewish-Australian speculative fiction writer and an Ambassador for Australia Reads. Her most recent novel is *The Green Children Help Out*. In 2020 she received the A. Bertram Chandler Award for lifetime achievement in science fiction. She is an ethnohistorian with a special interest in how story transmits medieval and modern culture. Her most recent non-fiction book is *Story Matrices: Cultural Encoding and Cultural Baggage in the Worlds of Science Fiction and Fantasy.*

You are what you write, which is why most of **Rivqa Rafael's** fiction is about queer and/or Jewish women. Find her award-winning and shortlisted stories in *Strange Fire* (Ben Yehuda Press), *Strange Horizons, Escape Pod,* and elsewhere. Rivqa lives in Sydney, where she studies psychology, and dabbles in kitchen alchemy. She can be found online at rivqa.net.

Jessica Reisman grew up on the east coast of the U.S., was a teenager on the west coast, and now lives in Austin, Texas. She's been a writer, animal lover, devoted reader, and movie aficionado since she was small. She's had two novels published and her first collection of stories, *The Arcana of Maps*, came out in 2019. Visit storyrain.com for more.

Benjamin Rosenbaum's stories have been nominated for the Hugo, Nebula, BSFA, Sturgeon, and World Fantasy Awards, and translated into 25 languages. His first novel, *The Unraveling*, a neogendered far-future coming-of-age tale, is available now from Erewhon Books. He lives near Basel, Switzerland. Learn more at benjaminrosenbaum.com.

Alex Shvartsman is a writer, translator, and anthologist from Brooklyn, NY. He's the author of *The Middling Affliction* (2022) and *Eridani's Crown* (2019) fantasy novels. Over 120 of his short stories have appeared in *Analog, Nature, Strange Horizons*, and many other venues. His website is alexshvartsman.com.

Robert Silverberg has been a professional science-fiction writer since 1955, and has written hundreds of short stories and novels. He is a many-times winner of the Hugo and Nebula awards and in 2004 was named a Grand Master by the Science Fiction Writers of America. Among his best known books are *Nightwings, Dying Inside*, and *Lord Valentine's Castle*.

Max Sparber is an author from Minneapolis. His speculative fiction has appeared in *The Best of Strange Horizons: Year One* and *People of the Book: A Decade of Jewish Science Fiction and Fantasy*. He has had stories anthologized in *Fangs and Broken Bones, Strangely Funny, Sanctuary, Black Buttons* Vol. 3, *Ye Olde Magik Shoppe*, and *Under the Full Moon's Light*, Orson Scott Card's *Intergalactic Medicine Show*, and *Trembling With Fear*.

Bogi Takács is a Hungarian Jewish agender trans person (e/em/eir/emself or they pronouns) and an immigrant to the US. E is a winner of the Lambda award for editing *Transcendent 2: The Year's Best Transgender Speculative Fiction*, and a finalist for the Hugo and Locus awards. Bogi's debut short story collection *The Trans Space Octopus Congregation* was published by Lethe in 2019. You can find Bogi talking about books at bogireadstheworld.com, and on various social media as bogiperson.

Lavie Tidhar is author of *Osama, The Violent Century, A Man Lies Dreaming, Central Station, Unholy Land, By Force Alone, The Hood* and *The Escapement*. His latest novels are *Maror* and *Neom*. His awards include the World Fantasy and British Fantasy Awards, the John W. Campbell Award, the Neukom Prize and the Jerwood Prize, and he has been shortlisted for the Clarke Award and the Philip K. Dick Award.

Harry Turtledove writes fantasy, alternate history, other science fiction, and, when he can get away with it, historical fiction. He is an escaped Byzantine historian, having been corrupted at an early age by L. Sprague de Camp's *Lest Darkness Fall*. Telling lies for a living beats the hell out of honest work. Turtledove is married to fellow writer Laura Frankos. They have three daughters, two granddaughters, and three overprivileged cats.

Milton Verskin is a retired lawyer whose interests include reading (novels, history, philosophy and whatever else catches his fancy), playing piano (almost exclusively baroque), and writing (working on a novel and has another two awaiting revision). He is also active in Torah-reading and leading the odd service at shul, bicycle-riding, playing ping-pong with his wife, enjoying their five grandchildren, and meeting friends for tea, coffee, conversation and walks.

Allan Weiss is a Toronto fiction writer and Professor of English and Humanities at York University. He is the author of three story cycles: *Living Room* (2001), *Making the Rounds* (2016), and most recently *Telescope* (2019). Other works, both realist and fantastic, have appeared in *Wascana Review*, *On Spec*, and the *Tesseracts* anthologies, among others. His scholarly works include *The Routledge Introduction to Canadian Fantastic Fiction* (2021), and he is the Chair of the Academic Conference on Canadian Science Fiction and Fantasy.

Jane Yolen has well over 400 books published. Among her latest are two volumes of adult poetry—*The Black Dog Poems*, written with Peter Tacy, and *Kaddish: Before the Holocaust and After*, which won the 2022 Sophie Brodie Medal for the year's best book of Jewish content. Her latest fantasy novel is *Arch Of Bone*. Her work has won many awards, including two Nebulas, several World Fantasy Awards, and the Skylark Award. Six colleges have given her honorary doctorates.

ʳ the Editors

ᵣea **D. Lobel** is an ordained rabbi with a Ph.D. in Religion. A lecturer at Carleton University and an academic librarian, she also serves as a rabbinic mentor at Darshan Yeshiva, and sits on the Board of ALEPH Canada, which works to foster Jewish Renewal. An award-winning writer and editor, Andrea also has an academic research habit spanning the history of religion and science, magic, mathematics, cultural astronomy, space exploration, and artificial intelligence, as well as religious authority. You can find her at andrealobel.com and on Twitter at @AD_Lobel.

Mark Shainblum is an award-winning writer and editor of science fiction and comics. He co-edited two previous anthologies, *Arrowdreams: An Anthology of Alternate Canadas* (Nuage, 1998) and *Superhero Universe: Tesseracts Nineteen* (Edge, 2015). In comics, he co-created *Northguard* and *Angloman* with Gabriel Morrissette, and also wrote *Captain Canuck*, Michael Moorcock's *Corum*, and *Auric*. Mark is a recipient of the Aurora Award for Canadian science fiction, and was inducted into the Canadian Comic Book Creator Hall of Fame in 2016. Mark is active on Facebook, and his website is www.shainblum.com.

Copyright and Permissions

Also available from Ben Yehuda Press

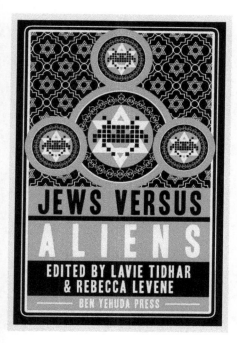
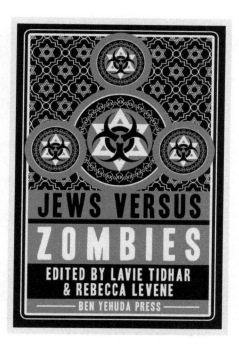